MIDNIGHTS

A. CHARLES DRAGON

So sinks the mind in deep despair
And sight grows dim; when storms of life
Inflate the weight of earthly care,
The mind forgets its inward light
And turns in trust to the dark without.
This was the man who once was free
To climb the sky with zeal devout
To contemplate the crimson sun,
The frozen fairness of the moon —
Astronomer once used in joy
To comprehend and to commune
With planets on their wandering ways.
This man, this man sought out the source
Of storms that roar and rouse the seas;
The spirit that rotates the world,
The cause that translocates the sun
From shining East to watery West;
He sought the reason why spring hours
Are mild with flowers manifest,
And who enriched with swelling grapes
Ripe autumn at the full of year.
Now see that mind that searched and made
All Nature's hidden secrets clear
Lie prostrate prisoner of night.
His neck bends low in shackles thrust,
And he is forced beneath the weight
To contemplate the lowly dust.

Boethius

1990

There was a draft. Ronny Ormsby felt the hair on his arms waver on end after each dense, frigid gust howled down the block. The face reflected by the windowpane stared past him while the back of his hand searched for the gap through which invasive tendrils of icy air probed his girlfriend's living room. Another long, slow wave rumbled down the street outside. It thundered past the window, rattling it as cold jets hissed around the sill's edges. The ceiling light behind Ronny dimmed. His reflection faded. He watched his hand travel down his side—its hunt for the draft's source answered, if not necessarily satisfied—and reach into his back pocket. Ronny's hands returned with a bent cigarette and a lighter. He puffed. The blazing cherry in the window smoldered, then disappeared behind a cloud. Tobacco smoke spilled across the window. When it parted, the view returned.

The world was more than a month into the new year, but nothing about it felt new. A new college. A new girl. A new decade. The rest of the world, in apparent resignation, contented itself to meekly weather the storm until signs of spring emerged. In the meantime, bricks and pavement continued to erupt with blisters. Wrought iron bars fortified first and second stories, then a third for good measure. The slow frost gnawed wider the cracks of distressed homes where paternal television sets quizzed weary mothers' knowledge of the whereabouts of their children as a nightly public service. It struck Ronny that if it was ten o'clock and someone did not know where their children were—if they survived long after sunset in the bitter, barren world beyond their parents' supervision—wherever they may wander, they might not care to be found.

The sun would eventually reappear for another seasonally abbreviated arc and the city's foot traffic would find itself funneled once more through haphazard troughs of frozen snow. Municipal machinery, deployed on overtime during twilight hours, churned stained slush and loose refuse together into towering aggregate sentinels—cold, unsteady pillars teetering on the brink where the sidewalk loomed over the gutter. They slouched atop the same places they had been thrust, propped upright to come level with the indifferent eyes of hurried passersby. These things took care of themselves and given time each mess would collapse in on itself into lesser pieces for the sewer grates at the bottom of brackish pools to sluggishly ingest. Coming up short for a consecutive appearance, the sun would begin to sag again and signal to those with the means to seek shelter. The rest remained exposed, patient if nothing else, as they awaited vernal promises yet delivered.

More tobacco smoke filled Ronny's nose. Notes of clove accompanied the billowing fumes, though they had not risen from his own cigarette. The tape deck clicked shut behind him and the stereo's speakers hissed in anticipation. Depeche Mode. A restless grumble escaped Ronny's mouth.

The windowpane creaked against the shifting pressure without and a chill crept from Ronny's shoulders down to his forearms. The sensation faded and he continued to stare through the naked, curtainless living room window at the scene framed within it. Rows of two-story duplexes lined either side of the block. Webs of ice spread across the windshields of the empty, darkened cars parked on either side of the road. Another car made a repeat pass down the block, appearing to Ronny in search of some rare spot of its own to be left for the night. It paused by a potential gap next to a hydrant and, after some thorough and pained deliberation, sped away abruptly in frustration. The sudden chirp of the vehicle's tires made Ronny blink. His focus relaxed and pulled back to the flickering spots of light multiplying around his reflection. Alice's friends scurried from one end of the room to the other. One-by-one, candle wicks awoke and danced in the room mirrored behind him as final preparations were made. Another chill forced his eyelids to clamp down. When he flicked them open, he found his perspective shifted. Ronny saw his reflection differently. His silhouette centered in the window's frame. The outside world stared in.

"Ronny," Alice whispered. "Is everything alright?"

He turned, cupping an empty palm beneath the extensive and neglected ash clung to what remained of his cigarette. The living room swung back into view, and he sank into the cushions of Alice's well-relaxed couch. His hand extended toward the ash tray balanced atop one of its drooping arms.

"Yeah. All good."

Alice replied with a courteous, if skeptical, nod. She returned her attention to the business of her chattering roommates. The cassette tape and the conversations continued to unwind, though Ronny found himself adrift beyond either and anchored to none. He chose to narrow in on the music. If it was not what he would have called his cup of tea, he was never much of a tea drinker all the same. In eighteen years, Ronny never *got* music. The sound system in Alice's apartment was buttressed on either side by the sort of music library that would cause any packrat to swell with pride. Overburdened shelves sagged beneath rows of vinyl record sleeves and a henge of clear cassette cases which promised to topple if anyone unintentionally extracted a load-bearing tape. For his own part, Ronny never amassed anything which could reasonably be deemed a formal or even intentional collection of music. What few cassettes could be found in his car were hand-me-downs—mix tapes from friends who held out hope they might yet turn him onto something or gifts from desperate relatives reluctantly indebted to Columbia House. The last time he summoned the initiative to enter a record store and carry out anything for himself had been in High School. *Joshua Tree,* he remembered. In three years, he pressed play on it as many times. The tape never left his car after he purchased it, for no reason other than that it could never have found its way into Mother's home.

Popular music is the Devil's forked tongue, she would faithfully remind him.

Ronny left it there: clutched tightly within his car's tape deck and deliberately free of Nance Ormsby's knowledge. The tones presently spilling into the living room were much more mechanical and far harsher than U2. Ronny watched the pair of spools spin. Magnetic tape wound its way from one to the other through the stereo's clear, front-loading deck. If he was a fan of any music at all, he was certainly no fan of Depeche Mode—though it was certainly a relief to Ronny that Alice had not made the selection. If that were the case, he was certain they would all be listening to New Kids by now. It had not taken him long to swipe Alice's copy of *Hangin' Tough* after the first time she forced the entirety of its A- and B-sides past his eardrums. The tape remained hidden, though Z100 remained committed to spinning its titular single no fewer than three times an hour, every hour.

"Tony's almost ready," Alice announced, her attention returning to Ronny. "Cheryl and Holly haven't been able to shut up about these new books he dug up from the school's archives. You'd think they actually believe something might happen this time."

Ronny fought to stop his expression souring. When he was reasonably confident that he had failed, he permitted himself to turn it toward Tony. Alice's singular male roommate was the oldest among her group of friends. Based on what Ronny saw—the way Tony dressed and the way he spoke—he assured himself the junior-year student posed no romantic threat to his relationship with Alice. Tony sat in the center of the living room floor with his legs crossed beneath him. The long, exaggerated sleeves of his shirt swung as his wrists flicked impatiently at the stack of papers resting in his lap. A good number of the candles now blazing in the room formed recognizable patterns across the floor, the foremost of which encircled the night's self-designated master of ceremonies. Ronny did not feel the chills anymore as his eyes traced circles and crisscrossing geometry between the strategically placed flames. The skin around his neck chafed at his shirt's collar.

"Haven't we sat through all this Ouija shit before," Ronny grumbled. "The seances, the mirror tricks. Now you want to try and burn down your apartment with more of this… voodoo or whatever?"

"Oh, come on," Alice teased. "You know it's all fun and games. You don't have to take it too seriously."

"*I* don't have to take it too seriously? What about *them?*"

Ronny gestured the center of the room and Alice's eyes followed. Cheryl and Holly hurried from place to place, filling any unoccupied, relatively flat space in the room with what appeared to Ronny to be surplus Halloween decorations. Images of saints and spirits and Catholic sacraments shined from the local bodega's finest selection of prayer candles. Tapestries and other interestingly patterned sheets were thumb-tacked to walls, hung from archways, and draped over the banister separating the apartment's living room from the stairs which led down to the first-floor entryway. In several places, delicate piles of ash were already beginning to build up on the bases of incense holders. At the center of it all, Tony held a purple, silk cloth in one hand and an ornate silver bowl in the other. His black-painted fingertips guided the handkerchief in circles around the inside of the bowl, while his mouth spoke silent words to none of the room's physical occupants. When his cleansing ritual appeared complete, Tony set the freshly polished silver vessel down on the floor in front of him. He picked up a pair of velvety looking pouches at his side and loosened their drawstrings. From the first he poured a stream of powder into the gleaming bowl. While the residual dust continued to settle, he drew from the second pouch a malicious looking knife. He gently placed it down to cross from rim to rim atop the bowl. The dagger's tip pointed toward Tony. The sight summoned Nance Ormsby into Ronny's thoughts. His imagination seated her at his right side on the couch. She would not have cared for the rock and roll music. She would have cared a great deal less for Tony's ritual—though she would not have found the intersection of the two a surprise in the slightest degree.

"Yeah," Alice slowly agreed. "They get pretty into this stuff. They're enthusiastic, that's all. Y'know… just a little intense. But in a *fun way.*"

Alice could not complete her sentence with a straight face. The smile that twitched across her lips made Ronny start to laugh, but his voice quickly cracked and a cough stung his throat. The air around him bulged with the heavy fumes burning from dozens of candle wicks, incense sticks, and exotically flavored cigarettes. His eyes stung and a pocket of warm, damp air began to expand beneath his wool sweater vest.

Ronny slid his shoes off. He drew his knees up onto the cushions and leaned his shoulder onto the couch's arm. The ashtray still rested there, suggestively. Ronny reached for the pack in his back pocket. His hand stopped short, then bolted back to his mouth as the air tweaked his throat again. He suppressed the cough and wheezed into his palm. Tears filled his eyes as he bounced upright. He turned and saw the window behind him once more. With everything in the room blazing away as it was, it would be impossible for him to lift it even a crack without an arctic gust howling into the room and pitching a tornado of ash. Ronny twisted away from the window and decided to take a break from smoking instead.

Beyond the ash tray, piled onto the floor past the arm of the couch, was a stack of books topped by a vibrant, undulating lava lamp. Many of the books looked old. Their spines were too worn to make out any lettering by candlelight alone, burning plentifully as it was. There was only one book, resting conspicuously near the middle of the pile, which appeared printed in the nearest half of the twentieth century: *Advanced Dungeons & Dragons Handbook, 2nd Edition.*

Nance, a fervent Presbyterian with Scottish and Dutch roots burrowed deeper than any Stuyvesant or Roosevelt, would have been thoroughly apoplectic. The venerable images of Catholic saints and modern music were dangerously indulgent, but the demonic sorcery and devil worship which roll-playing games represented to Nance Ormsby stooped to another ring of hell altogether. Ronny might as well have extended an invitation to Satan himself to join their dinner table if he ever entertained a fantasy game thereupon. For the duration of his time under her roof, his mother envisioned their home besieged by the ceaseless spiritual assault of a world driven mad by heavy metal music and Saturday morning cartoons. She felt the Devil's presence everywhere, from her children's school curricula to grocery store bar codes. That had not deterred Ronny flicking through the pages of D&D players' manuals at the homes of his more liberated middle- and high-school colleagues. He had never seen such artwork before—monsters and demons and weapons and... *babes.* The images came flooding back into his mind as his hands reached out toward the stack of books. A yellow blob of wax wriggled and sighed in the hot, red water of the lava lamp as Ronny braced it with one hand. His other hand slid the book sideways, careful not to disrupt the rest of the stack. It was partly due to the drab nature of the other books and the dull light around him that Ronny did not notice the deck of cards also resting atop the stack until it tilted and began to cascade onto the carpet.

Alice and the rest of her friends had settled down and were arranging themselves on the floor around Tony. None noticed the cards now splayed around Ronny. Ronny realized he may as well have been altogether absent, as Tony began to speak seemingly exclusively to those assembled in his more-immediate vicinity.

"I don't need any of you telling Dr. Lewis or anyone else at the history department about this," Tony warned. "Dr. Lewis knows that I've been transcribing all of his oldest books for him."

He lifted the top page of his stack of papers. The accordioning pages of unseparated, tractor-fed printer paper stretched upward, then settled back down.

"But this stuff, what I'm transferring onto the school's computer system, is only a small part of everything I've found in the back of the archives."

"I read it on one of the library's computers," Cheryl said. "Wild stuff. Real dark."

"Not as dark as the source material," Tony added.

His hands reached behind him and returned with a flimsy, disintegrating leather portfolio full of yellowed paper.

"This is the original copy. Nearly four hundred years old and written by hand not far from where we now sit."

"Was any of it true? The guy went nuts and dropped off the face of the earth?"

"I don't know if *'nuts'* is the right word. If there's a fine line between crazy and genius, this is some kind of testament. The author claims to have been possessed. Under the command of some other power, he went and reproduced an entire book of witchcraft and spells from memory onto these pages. *Then* he dropped off the face of the earth."

"So, either he's absolutely insane," Alice said, "or he tapped into something."

"Which is why I figured it would be better to test it out before I just threw the last chapter onto the school's BBS and ended up the same way."

Ronny prayed Alice had not seen how dramatically his eyes rolled as Tony spoke. Quite the opposite, she appeared utterly transfixed as either of her friends. His own attention could not be kept on Tony's nonsense if his life depended on it. Instead, it returned to the mess of cards. Despite Ronny's rather sheltered upbringing, he recognized immediately that this was no deck of fifty-two.   The tarot cards featured fantastical scenes, not too dissimilar to the affected ancientness of the artwork in the *Dungeons & Dragons* rule book. The backs of the cards were printed with leafy, interwoven ribbons of gold and brown vines. A few were flipped upright, and their faces stared back at Ronny. He reached out for the nearest card and spun it around to orient it toward him.

The Fool.

A carefree young man with a bindle-stick in one hand and a flower in the other strolled toward a precipice. Two more nearby cards were also face up. Ronny gathered them closer.

The Tower.

A bolt of lightning lanced the roof of a drab, ancient structure. Flames belched from its windows and defenestrated a pair of unfortunate souls tumbling through stormy skies.

The only other card to land upright featured no printed title. Ronny patted the sides of the reconstituted deck together and pulled it up to him. A man lay face down on the ground with ten long blades buried in his back. Ronald sniffed and found his sinuses growing tighter as he sucked air into his nose.

"If he's right," Tony continued, "All I have to do is douse this dagger in these ashes just as I'm done reciting these lines."

Tony gripped the dagger in both hands and dangled it over the silver bowl. The powder within had been chalky and white when he first poured. It glowed softly now, yellow to nearly green around the bowl's polished edges. A small trail of smoke wafted up toward the blade. Ronny had been distracted. He did not remember hearing a lighter. Nance reappeared in his mind again. As Ronny grew older, he increasingly disregarded his mother's puritanical rhetoric as excessive and even ignorant—more the product of popular hysteria than a true commitment to spirituality. He watched the hungry fumes twist and rise until they teased the dagger. In that moment, more than any in the past, it struck Ronny that Mother had not necessarily been wrong.

"O, thou weary," Tony bellowed.

Ronny had never heard Tony's voice rise much higher than a whisper. Now the meek, slender man reached deep.

"Watch the horizon fall under the tide,
Turned upon Fortune's wheel by wheels within wheels."

Dull embers ringed the room. They gnawed at the candles and incense, and wove bands of carbon and perfumed smoke into the thickening air. The residue clung to Ronny's throat and the heat began to stifle his chest. Reddening eyes turned back to the window and the dark, cool world waiting outside. Ronny's palm found the windowpane. Fog rimmed his fingers as the cold glass seeped into his skin.

> *"Cast down with goode times, whence horrors bide,*
> *That power's twisting faces ye gazed, now unseals."*

The stifling heat drained from Ronny's hand, though the air trapped beneath his sweater continued to draw new sweat. He could see Alice. Her reflection shined through the foggy glass in the crook between his thumb and index finger. When they were alone, he could not imagine feeling closer to her. At other times, such as the one in which Ronny found himself at that moment where their relationship was exposed to the company Alice kept and the experiences to which she was increasingly drawn, he felt the gulf of differences open between them. Alice's acquaintanceship with her roommates dated back no further than the start of the current semester. When she agreed to split the rent on an apartment in Bensonhurst with them a few weeks later, Ronny had been more than skeptical. They were all students together and all freshmen at KIT—save Tony, a couple years their senior. The university's Gravesend campus was only a few stops away on the N-line. The location itself was completely sound. It was the people within who gave Ronny pause.

> *"Fairest darkness itself, wrapped*
> *and swaddled within stolen light—*
> *Bleak stars borne heavy crowns*
> *nearer to Heavens without suns,*
> *And bearing Eternity's other vestiges*
> *and insatiable appetite.*
> *'Twas thy fate to reign o'er shackles*
> *and the shackles' to be undone."*

K-Tech had not been Ronny's first choice, nor had it been second or third. For the average Hackley alumnus, invoking names like Brown or Cornell, accompanied by the cutest shrug and sigh, served primarily as safety schools. Accepting anything else—anything *less*—could only mean some WASP's son had shit the bed. Thusly, in his own time at Hackley, Ronald Orsmby, Jr. registered somewhere below the average of his classmates. He excelled preeminently, he realized, in one particular area: when it came to well and truly shitting one's bed, Ronny found his place cemented for all eternity. Ronny's stint in prep school did not turn out as either of his parents planned. To say that Ronald, Sr. had been *displeased* to discover his brand new 500SL—a custom order fresh from the factory—borrowed without permission and shortly thereafter extricated from the school's lap pool was a major understatement. Nor would it have been accurate to say he expressed an abundance of pride when he discovered it was his platinum AmEx, similarly borrowed, which filled the trunk of said vehicle as well as Ronny and his friends with whiskey. In the aftermath, Nance would have scoffed when it came to pass that only the Kingsboro Institute of Technology in Gravesend, Brooklyn replied with anything other than a *'but we must regretfully inform you that we cannot at this time'*—would have scoffed at the singular exception to near-universal rejection—had Mother's seething shame diminished near enough to grace verbal communication or existential acknowledgment upon her son.

> *"From that ancient Ocean's floor,*
> *grown higher is that murk upon whiche slouches,*
> *Groaning stone halls which echo*
> *fanatical rhapsodies in unmeasured time.*
> *His sleeping Infernal Pantheon's Kingdom*
> *of grotesque, wicked Houses,*
> *Towering ever o'er pitch-black fields*
> *of the gathering, rotten, fetid slime."*

Ronny's eyelids slammed shut. He knew exactly how bloodshot they must have looked by how dry and scratchy they felt as tears flooded back over them. Clammy hands fussed at the buttons on his shirt. The materials embedded into his neck loosened, though Ronny still felt excessively hot.

Though Ronny and Alice never met until a week after each relocated to Brooklyn, they both spent the first eighteen years of their lives no more than a dozen or so miles apart on opposite ends of Westchester County. Alice came from a comfortably working-to-middle-class family, nominally if not observantly Jewish. They seemed happy. Warm. Happier and warmer than the one into which Ronny found himself borne. He felt guilty when the subject of his difficult relationship with his parents came up, though he found rare gratitude for the tendency with which his upbringing impressed upon him to never speak of such. His own lapses with Mother and Ronald, Sr. were partly due to him being at once pridefully stubborn and a reliable fuck-up. Alice, on the other hand, had been permanently deprived of her own father. Ronny never met Larry Weber and never would. The county surveyor took his own life, without warning, when Alice was still in kindergarten.

How could Ronny possibly complain about his own home life—about the parents he never saw because the visits made him feel uncomfortable and bored—after Alice told him that the last time she heard her father's voice was when he abruptly excused himself from the dinner table to *'lay down for a bit?'* She told Ronny she had not cried. She had been too young to understood why, a few minutes after her father disappeared upstairs, the air shook and made her ears pop. Most five-year-olds have the good fortune to be unable to contextualize the shattering report of a .44 caliber revolver. Years later, while sorting through his boxed belongings, Alice found the letters—warnings left behind for her mother to find. Unspecified mistakes. Vague threats.

"Rumble call of terrible, gilded machinery
spun to snarl and bend—
Ezekial's revelation shrouded 'neath veil violent
and obscured vision of sooth,
Of manie great wheels within wheels,
grinding a continuum of eyes without end,
In their endless vigil for innocence
spilt by the hands of hopeless youthe."

Ronny felt the cold air bridging the gap between the window and his nose. Pair after pair of twin light beams glided down the block in intermittent waves. It was late, Ronny reckoned. Open spots would prove by the hour fewer and farther between. His thumb and index finger rubbed the opposite wrist, peeling his watch band from where it imprinted into swollen skin. Nearly midnight, the tight wristwatch agreed. A giggle squirmed out from between the stanzas rolling off Tony's tongue.

"Shh," Alice whispered. "Come on, Holly—don't interrupt."

Alice did her best to maintain order. Tony continued. The cracks were there, though. Ronny wagered if it were not the silly, archaic nonsense once more filling the stuffy air, it would be the awkward tension which broke the dam completely. Despite Alice's insistence, there was a nervous laugh and a smile within her own voice. She appeared interested, though Ronny suspected she might also be interested in aiding the ritual to play out toward a quicker conclusion.

Ronny wiped his sleeve across his forehead. He felt his pulse shiver with every frigid gust rattling the ill-sealed window. Howling currents billowed down the block, blustering over meandering traffic and stirring the naked tree branches. They teased the glass with urgent promises of relief from the bloated, ashy air attacking Ronny's nostrils. Sopping, heavy wool sleeves could not stop sweat building with every wave of heat which rolled from his chest out toward his limbs. It soaked into his clothes. Polycotton turned to bindings at his joints and kept even more warmth trapped within.

"Praise is sung to dark King Belial,
and until His Crown dismiss,
Hundred and one hundred more
at end of blade, to beat of drum.
Our bloodshed calls thee,
who shine darkly in that bleak abyss,
Dance yon feet and flourish knives
to hurry His Great, Dread Maelstrom."

Light flashed in Ronny's eyes. His focus fixed on the idling headlights on the street below. The hydrant disappeared as the car came to a stop. A desperate move, he thought, and risky too. In all his time in Southern Brooklyn, Ronny never observed an especially heavy police presence. The sight of a patrol car parked in front of someone's house or circling the block more than once was cause to summon every gossip in the neighborhood. The only reliable way to make them appear, no matter the hour, was to leave one's car unattended anywhere near a hydrant or *No Standing* zone any longer than a mere second—the highest crime in the eyes of *New York's Finest* assigned to serve their Sixty Fourth Precinct.

Another wave of heat. When the warmth found no escape at the ends of Ronny's limbs, it rolled back inward and pressed up into his skull. His vision flashed black. When the heat and the darkness racking his vision faded, Ronny felt the window against his forehead, cold and dancing as the currents battered it. The car was still there, blocking the hydrant. Someone had extinguished its headlights.

"What? I'm trying."

"Shh," Alice repeated.

The metal tab at the top of the windowpane sparked with the release of static energy. Ronny's fingers twisted it toward him. A dog barked.

"There are truths which bring men comfort,
and truths which rend soul from mind.
Planes of ashen cities top the rising depths
to where the lost are drawn,
Where dreams fill opened eyes
when no escape their souls can find."

Layers of lead paint and grime and mildew cemented the window's wooden frame to the sill's tracks. Ronny's arm shuddered.

"Awakened, walking, dreaming—
it tears away thy temper
and raises the Kingdom 'neath the Midnight Dawn."

There was a loud crack and a burst of air. Ronny rose from the couch as his arms followed the window up along its track. A whirlwind of ash and heat brushed over Ronny's damp forehead. He watched his reflected silhouette strobe as dozens of flames flickered behind him. The silver bowl tumbled and clattered. Twisting tongues of chartreuse embers sparkled and curled upward until they broke against the ceiling. Tarot cards sprayed into the air for a second time and a chorus of gasps and laughter erupted. Ronny's chest bulged and fresh, cold air filled his lungs. A hand darted past his shoulder, slammed down on top of the window, and shoved it back down to crash against the sill.

"Just what in the hell do you think you're doing?"

In the months since being introduced to Alice's roommates, Ronny barely heard Tony speak much louder than a murmur. He was raving now, more desperate and frustrated than even the confident projections which had most recently seized his voice.

"Sorry," Ronny replied, surprised and still exhausted from the overwhelming heat. "It felt like I was gonna die."

Ronny's muscles slowly returned to his conscious control. He shrank down and turned to face the room once more. Most of the candles had been extinguished by the sudden gust and left the room much dimmer. Several had toppled. Cheryl was already on her feet, turning some upright and reigniting others. Specks of dust and ash, liberated from their piles beneath burning incense sticks, drifted lazily back down to coat the room in a dingy, even layer of soot. Holly was rolling on the floor. The infectious giggles consumed her, pitching her into a full-on laughing fit until she abruptly sprang from the carpet. She collapsed against the living room's stereo. Alice also watched her, then turned toward Ronny. She made a show of a deliberate, heavy sigh, then smiled sympathetically.

There was still undeniably hostile energy near the edge of Ronny's periphery. While normalcy gradually returned to the rest of the room, one figure refused to burdge. Tony had yet to release his grip on the window. His mouth sputtered. Every muscle in his body vibrated, unable to recompose themselves.

"Like I said, man," Ronny wheezed over a nervous laugh, "I'm sorry."

The stereo clicked and whirred. Holly had inserted a new tape and pressed play. Tony's shoulders drooped, defeated as New Edition landed the final blow. The words he struggled to form melted before they could escape his mouth and formed little more than a frustrated hiss. He spun on his heel and stomped back to the center of the room. In a flurry of action, his hands gathered up the dagger, the leather binder, and the stack of printer paper. He yanked at the upturned silver bowl and yelped. The ornamental blade shined as it spun in the air. Its blade dug into the floor as the bowl and the rest of his hastily huddled supplies landed to either side. Tony pulled his burnt fingertips up to his mouth and cursed in between soothing, cooling blows. Ronny felt bad, but absurdity still hung in the atmosphere between specks of drifting ash. He elected to keep his mouth shut rather than risking further injury to the ego of his girlfriend's strange roommate. The couch cushion next to him sank and suddenly Alice was resting against his arm.

"Y'know," she whispered. "You shouldn't've done that."

"Babe, I *said* I was *sorry*..."

"I'm sure you are. But what I mean is, now he's only gonna lord it over us—taunting us that we'll never really know how real the whole thing could've been. He'll be back at it, soon enough."

Ronny did his best to keep from laughing too loudly. He turned his attention to the rattling noise that crept up the stairs from the apartment's ground floor entrance. It was not the first time he remembered Alice's downstairs neighbors returning home drunk and unaware of which door belonged to them. There was a jiggling sound. Ronny listened and visualized the frustrated drunk struggling to force their own key into someone else's deadbolt. The door groaned as someone pressed their weight against it. Ronny raised his index finger in the air and glanced at Alice to see if she had also heard the struggle.

"Listen," he said with a grin. "Hear that?"

Alice's head turned toward the stairs, but shuddered as another, louder thud landed against the distant front door.

"Who is that?"

"I dunno, did you invite Steve?"

Ronny watched Cheryl and Holly exchange looks of mutual confusion. He saw them jump and shriek when the final blow thundered up the stairs. The blast faded with a dry, splintering crack. Ronald's feet swung out from beneath him and braced him upright on the couch. One hand grabbed Alice's shoulder while the other searched the vicinity for something blunt to be weaponized. Only the ash moved, still settling lazily, while the room waited. The lull was cut short when the commotion at the bottom of the stairs resumed. Metal scratched and pried at fractured wood. A fist or an elbow knocked away splintered debris. Warped hinges groaned, then cracked away from the frame completely. Through the opened doorway, somewhere in the world beyond, Ronny heard the dog barking again.

Feet trampled over the dismantled remains of the apartment's entrance strewn about the base of the stairs. A second pair followed them. They climbed slowly, steadily, heavily over each step. Ronny shuddered when the woman's head rose over the banister. He realized he was no longer breathing. Her solitary, impassive expression hovered amidst the candlelight and the ashen haze. The woman's hair was light blonde and thin, parted down the middle and hanging straight over the sides of a small round face from which two frigid blue eyes pierced outward. Metal rings and studs arced over pale skin. Another shadow materialized behind her, broader and more masculine. The man towering over her shoulder wore a similarly inscrutable mood on his gaunt, wide face, though noticeably less stern and impassive, if slightly amused. Wide, brown waves with auburn crests were greased backward from his pronounced widow's peak to the back of his head. It was difficult to estimate their age, Ronny realized. The light, limited as it was, reached them differently. Time meant something else in the liminal spaces they filled as they drew nearer the center of the room. The man spoke.

"Buncha' clowns."

Ronny's grip on Alice tightened. In the corner, by the stereo, Cheryl and Holly pressed themselves flat against the wall as if they hoped to melt through it entirely. Tony shrank closer to the floor amidst the disarray of computer printouts and their ancient source material in its shabby, worn binder. While Ronny urged his mind to restart, Tony's voice cracked first.

"What d'you want?"

The woman's eyes glided downward. As her glare levelled with him, Tony flinched.

"Y-yeah," Alice forced through her constricted throat. "We're just a bunch of broke college kids. We haven't got anything worth getting hurt over."

"Oh dear," the woman purred, a grin crawling up the side of her mouth. "Youse've got no idea."

The man moved and the shadows receded from him at a leisurely pace. A pair of black biker boots carried him along an animated stroll as he traced the edges of the room. One leather glove rose and travelled along his side, gently drifting over a line of books resting atop a long shelf.

"Looks like there's plenty'a good shit to me," he said.

The man's hand became less gentle. With every step, books tumbled down behind him. When he reached the end, he paused to look thoughtfully at a Magic 8-Ball serving as a book end. He wound his open palm behind him. Cheryl and Holly let out another shriek as his hand flew forward and smacked the fortune-telling toy. It bolted through the air until it crashed against the wall between the two girls. With a loud crack, the 8-Ball burst open. Its plastic shell tumbled into a pool of black fluid on the hardwood floor. Ronny tried to jump up from his seat, but his muscles were too numb. He felt disoriented. The world seemed dimmer.

"You got one very important thing," the woman continued. "Something that wasn't meant for you. Wasn't meant for every other *little puke* to throw up on their library computer, neither. For that, somebody's gotta pay."

Adrenaline coursed through Ronny's head, though his body still refused to respond. His neck was frozen, though his eyes continued to swivel wildly about the room. They wanted desperately to reorient him. They scouted the walls, but all they brought him were multiplying shadows. Light withered and the room was left to hang weightless in expanding gloom.

"Made this all easy 'nuff for us, though. Signed your stupid name to every computer entry."

A dwindling candlewick caught Ronny's attention. Its flame shrank until it disappeared. A thread of smoke escaped and stretched thin as it rose into the air.

"Pieces of the past come floatin' back up to the surface every day. Some stuff stays hidden longer than others. Some stuff is forgotten by accident, some by design. But most times, nobody gets to choose what comes an' what goes."

The woman moved. Due to the dwindling light, Ronny could not say with any certainty if it was her feet that carried her or she floated on her own over the growing mess. Her hand plucked the dagger from where it stood, blade exhumed from the nick it made in the hardwood floor.

"People forget real easy," she continued, admiring the knife as it turned in her hand. "It's what keeps 'em safe. Mostly, it's what keeps 'em sane. The downside is, eventually they forget too much for their own good. They become blind to what's beneath 'em— what's right under their noses. They forget to be afraid. Safety is an illusion, but the carelessness it comes with is very real."

The endless void surrounding them grew at once woefully vast and horribly intimate. In every corner of Ronny's vision, candles suffocated, flames snuffed one-by-one and bringing the darkness closer.

"Our bloodshed flows for thee," the woman recited, *"who shine darkly in that bleak abyss.* D'you know what that means?"

"I-I mean, I'm just…," Tony whispered. "I'm a student of history, is all."

"That's real convenient," she replied. "I can think of a few things that ain't gonna be 'round no more."

There was movement. A dozen flames fluttered at once. Holly bolted away from the wall. The rubber sole of her shoe squeaked as it skidded across the puddle liberated from the 8-Ball. Her knee dug into the floor and her hands planted in front of her. When Holly craned her head upright, she found herself level with the barrel of the black handgun protruding from the man's right hand.

"Awakened, walking, dreaming…"

Ronny shivered beneath the cold, damp wool of his sweater. He felt his heart pound in every part of his body. His ears suddenly felt like they had been stuffed with cotton balls, but he heard the woman continue to echo Tony's lines. Though she had not moved, her words grew distant. Only Alice's fingers, gripped ever tighter within his hand, kept him tethered to reality. Ronny watched the final wick sputter and turn to smoke. Alice's fingernails dug into his skin.

"It tears away thy temper and raises the Kingdom 'neath the Midnight Dawn."

Inscription upon the Veterans' Memorial in Lady Moody Triangle, Gravesend, Brooklyn; Dedicated Sunday, October 4, 1987:

GRAVESEND WAS FOUNDED IN 1643
BY LADY DEBORAH MOODY
WHO NAMED THIS COMMUNITY
AFTER HER HOME TOWN GRAVESEND,
ENGLAND. FOUNDED ON THE PRECEPTS
OF
RELIGIOUS FREEDOM, GRAVESEND,
WHICH MEANS
AT THE END OF THE GROVE,
DERIVES ITS NAME FROM
TWO SAXON WORDS
"GRAFES ENDE"

Gefluister over Bokkenrijders en de Wind; *"Whispers of Buckriders and the Wind"*
Translated from original Dutch, author unknown, early 17th Century:

Howls the wind o'er heath and hill,
As occurred then and does so still.
Past fertile field and dry-stone wall,
Beyond where eyes of Limburg fall.
'Neath the looming shade of the woods,
Slithers a column of black hoods.

Shouldering yields freed from farmer after farmer,
Spared of guilt o'er what took bloody hands to garner.
A den of thieves and rogues too robust to keep codes,
Thus begat highwaymen grown too fat for the roads.
Bled to the last of the locals, the stale brigands did turn,
To the fire and bore mind, heart, and soul eager to burn:

"For our desires, for your charm,
We swear this oath, we raise an arm.
Lift us nearer your peerless might,
And in your honor rule the night.
No longer our fathers' wayward ones,
We are the Devil's favorite sons!"

Darkness smothered the roaring flame in the pit.
Nerves shied as woodland fell 'neath perverse quiet.
A cry rose, though soft, and made some men retreat,
While others crowed at the common, bestial bleat.
When four cloven hooves came followed by eight score,
Those who balked or laughed did refrain furthermore.

Trot to full gallop, mounted brutes,
Rumbling forest to its roots.
At woods' edge, they kicked up no dust,
Hindlegs bucked and to sky were thrust.
Moon eclipsed by twin curling horns,
And forty thieves on rams, airborne.

To all corners of the Netherlands their storm spread,
Where disbelief faded to be replaced by dread.
Mounted and boundless, from raids no province was spared,
Plunder was found wherever the Buckriders dared.
There and back on the wind, they were fleeting as ghosts,
But for their echoing, indomitable boasts:

"Across houses, across gardens,
Across stakes, our wicked bargain.
Over the Rhine, into Cologne,
We cry our vow, be it well known:
To take, to hew, with reach unbound,
Swill madness like wine 'til drunk, drowned."

And so, where the bandits' shadows fell, plates did grow empty.
Stolen fruits and missed meals rought lean times from those of plenty.
Steeple bells on Sunday morn' tolled a tale of rage and blame,
As eyes climbed goodly pulpits who knew ever evil's Earthly name.
When church doors parted, His righteous flock hurried to the square,
To pitch a bonfire, blind the night, and scorch all they could snare.

T'was the first Buckrider who fell,
To warn his dark brothers, he yelled:
"To the shadows, devilish knaves,
Else they behold ye, quicker to graves."
His legion of comrades took flight,
To hide, wait, then resume the blight.

Yet the holy fire did not cool—
with such fervor could it ever?
With such favor, with such hunger,
who dares shame the Lord's endeavor,
Or engenders their voice in some place
before the mob to make case?
What few cried were jury-tried,
tied to stakes amidst fiery embrace.
One hundred more were consumed
before the coals permitted smolder,
While banished Buckriders watched and laughed,
less merely one, grown bolder.

Likewise, many congregations,
Found great glory and elation,
When from dripping hands blood was cleaned,
After cleansing many a fiend,
And bearing witness on neighbors,
Cast down for others' vile labors.

The heaths and hills still whisper of deadly designs,
As do the dry-stone walls which surround rows and lines,
Of unmarked tombstones given to the wrongly accused,
And laughter of thieves uninjured, rather amused.
The Devil's own still rule 'til sun's rise turns hooves fleet,
Black fleece in wind which echoes that wicked, choral bleat.

Part I:
Per the Patrol Guide

Sun. 02/11/1990, 0030 hrs.

One

"Those aces and eights,
may be a curse or a friend.
Don't raise the stakes,
if you're holding the dead man's hand,
ooon… Card Sharks!"

Card Sharks. Without turning her head, Lucy Madrigal knew that meant half past midnight. The rerunning game show's opening fanfare chimed from the wood-paneled television set in the corner of the basement cafeteria of the Elysian Fields Adult Rehabilitation Center dependably as any clock.

"And here's the host of Card Sharks: Jim Perry!"

Although it was the dead of night in a peripheral corner of the city which never slept, it was still early for Lucy. As her attention toward the television waned, there was little to indicate that the rest of her day promised much improvement. For a start, she was only one hour into an eight hour and thirty-five minute tour as a police officer in the Sixty Fourth Precinct of the New York City Police Department, which put her in less of a good mood with each appearance as such. Secondly, what she referred to as her *'morning'*—either through habit or sarcasm—was, if one felt inclined to engage semantics, the middle of the night. The so-called *midnights* shift to which she was assigned began after dusk. It continued, most demonstrably in the winter months, until the sun barely crept back over Brooklyn. As Lucy sat alone, she marked the passage of time by the UHF rotation of syndicated game shows on the rehabilitation center's aging television. *Password Plus, Card Sharks, Family Feud, Let's Make a Deal.* By the time *Press Your Luck* came on, the night was halfway through. Lucy was no fan of game shows in particular, but the chatter and music kept her from falling asleep on the job. After the first few weeks, she realized the overnight broadcast schedule burned into her brain and married with her sense of time. Now that she had passed nearly three months' worth of 'midnights' in the basement of the second largest halfway home in Brooklyn, she was unsure that she would ever be able to shake it.

It was not routine for a police officer to spend most of their tour of duty cooped up in an assisted living facility's cafeteria. In fact, per the Patrol Guide—the Department's voluminous manual of rules and procedures—*cooping* was a violation named in several sections of regulations and ripe for a plethora of very nasty disciplinary actions. Lucy's official assignment was read out to her at the beginning of every night just as it was printed each day on her platoon's roll call. On paper, she was assigned to a *'Special Post 99,'* a fixed foot post about a block away from the Fields; however, this post was not particularly routine either. Or productive. Lucy's eyes took a walk around the room. Christmas decorations covered the walls when she found herself reassigned to her special assignment the previous December. She continued to be deployed as such when the cardboard cutouts of Christmas trees and Santa Clauses were replaced with big red hearts and Cupids. Not without remorse, Lucy wondered what she would watch them pull out of storage for Easter.

Every day since her banishment commenced had followed the same routine: after roll call, a lonely walk from the Sixty Fourth Precinct to the B6 followed by a ride to her very own sidewalk footpost; a visual inspection of her domain for anything out of the ordinary—which there never was; wait a few minutes to make sure no one tried to pay her an early, unexpected visit; and finally, confident the coast was clear, down Lucy delved into the basement of the Fields to the tune of *Password Plus's* closing credits. The staff extended an invitation not long after they noticed the stationary and quite evidently bored cop moping by the corner of their building while her dwindling hopes for a reversal of misfortune melted. After Lucy found a quiet, secluded place in their basement cafeteria to warm up, they left her to herself. There were nights when everyone housed in the five floors overhead managed to stay at rest. On other nights, the rumbles would materialize in some distant corner. It might begin with a mournful plea, travelling along the walls and floorboards. If left unanswered, it typically ended with pounding feet and palms over a chorus of jeers and complaints from neighboring rooms and floors aroused by the struggle. Hands were too full upstairs to notice Lucy once she achieved invisibility underground.

She was grateful, nonetheless. Without shelter, the mercury hovered somewhere in the single digits. Windchill could bring the temperature to zero and below. Any souls who chose to wander through Bensonhurst and Bath Beach at this hour did so at the mercy of indifferent winds tearing away any shred of warmth such wanderers might struggle to hold.

Lucy did not view staying warm—staying *alive*—as a betrayal of her oath, although suffering was the point of her assignment. In the strictest official terms, she served as foot patrol, fixed to one very specific corner of one very specific intersection to ward off a pattern of auto break-ins which plagued the neighborhood. It was an official understatement as well, though the menace was real. While her tenure was not long, Lucy had long concluded that no wise person in any of the five boroughs could ever leave their car's tape deck plugged into the dashboard overnight. She never observed any inanimate object undergo metaphysical transformation, grow a pair of legs, and walk away, but she had returned to her car in the morning greeted by a broken window, toll change removed from the ashtray, and the vehicle's locked glovebox broken open and tossed. Thusly, her valuables followed her, even when parked less than a block from the Sixty Fourth Precinct's station house.

** Click * Click * Click**

The signal crackled out of Lucy's radio and interrupted her late-night daydream, unsettling as any to which the Fields was prone. To anyone else's ears, it was interference. An accidental, if brief, transmission. For Lucy, it was a lifeline. She gathered her radio off the tabletop and hooked it back onto her gun belt. Rows of tables parted near the broad entrance to the cafeteria's industrial freezer. The insulated metal door squealed and yawned just wide enough for her arm to reach within, lean around to the hook on the inside wall, and retrieve her uniform jacket. She zippered the crisp, chilly outerwear and climbed the stairs. Motionless streets and darkened windows greeted her outside the main entrance. Dry, winter wind hissed over every surface. Around the corner, on Bay Parkway, a few headlights grew and then faded in the distance. Lucy reentered the circle outlined in chalk on the sidewalk. Each minute that passed permitted the night air to nibble away the warmth she brought with her. Lucy was nonetheless grateful for the warning. Herman Melendez could be relied upon to click his radio transmitter three times whenever he was chauffeuring the midnight platoon commander over to her location. He was discreet too, for Lieutenant Cordell had yet to catch on. Her back twitched. The shivers were beginning. Melendez always gave her ample time to ready herself. The price for such wiggle room was excess exposure.

Lucy did not find herself in the lurch for long. As another shiver prompted her elbows to clench against her ribs, the distinct leer of a Crown Vic's headlights approached. The marked patrol car ambled up to the curb. Little escaped the vehicle's dark interior sealed behind the closed window, save for hints of a rigid disposition afflicting its front row passenger. The faint outline of Lieutenant Cordell's face, illuminated by the reddish glow of the car's dashboard, swiveled stiffly in her direction. Officer Melendez sat behind the steering wheel on the other side. He jerked the gear shifter into park and slumped in anticipation of the display proximity would once more make him a reluctant witness. Most of the precinct was ambivalent to Lucy's circumstances, but a few approached her sympathetically to offer their help. Not long after finding sanctuary within the Fields, she worked out an arrangement with Melendez. Cordell liked to dictate his routine *very clearly*. When the supervisor's appointed rounds came within five minutes of her post, Melendez keyed his radio three times. The nonverbal code was distinct and subtle enough not to penetrate the bubble of Cordell's obliviousness.

Lucy's flattened hand rose to her temple and rendered the raised car window a salute so rigid and textbook that it bordered on parody. The window remained rolled up while Cordell studied her with a motionless glare. If Lucy observed any singular strength in the midnights' senior-most supervisor, foremost was his imperviousness to irony. Exaggerated as her gesture might be, he lacked any capacity for the kind of reflexiveness which might decipher the act's insincerity. Fools were blind to everything exceeding the scope of that which they wished to see. Cruel people felt starved if they could not feel bigger. Experience demonstrated to Lucy that Lieutenant Cordell was a cruel fool. Experience also dictated she might be expected to maintain her salute for up to a minute before the lieutenant budged and returned the courtesy and release her. As another shiver racked her muscles, she wondered which tact would ultimately reap greater discomfort—to continue dispensing the disregarded sarcasm which unintentionally nourished his ego, or to slouch in earnest and arouse the reflexive wrath of injured pride. Finding neither the more appealing, Lucy chose to stop suppressing her shivers. Cold as the air was as it whipped around her, it was nowhere near as frigid as the look directed toward her from within the warm patrol car. Nearest to satisfaction as Cordell was capable, he cranked the window no lower than a few inches. His hand jerked away from his temple in a terse, impatient salute of his own.

"Approach," he croaked.

Withholding any extraneous verbal acknowledgement on her part, Lucy crossed the chalk outline. She bent down closer to the seated supervisor. Lieutenant Cordell's arm awkwardly bent over the top of the window. His hand latched onto the shield pinned to Lucy's jacket. The displeasure on his face curdled into something impossibly sourer.

"You better pray I never find you with that shield a single degree over freezin'," Cordell warned. "If I catch you coopin', you can bet I'll find a way to have that shield for good."

"Sorry to disappoint," Lucy replied under her breath.

"Lemme get your book."

Lucy pulled the rectangular, blue activity log from her jacket's inner pocket. She flipped it open to the latest page chronicling the current tour's notations, up to and including her arrival on post. Her *patrol* of the Field's basement remained omitted. Before she could pass the booklet voluntarily, the lieutenant snatched it from her hand and yanked it into the car.

"Don't think I'm gonna give you the chance to fix any last-minute shit in there."

The pages of the memo book flipped violently as Cordell turned through them. His eyes darted from side to side, skimming backwards through time for any errors or inconsistencies around which he might pitch his next fit. All he found was accumulated frustration, which he let vent through his mouth in a huff. The lieutenant reluctantly turned the pages back to the latest date and time. The tip of his pen struck paper and began to memorialize his own observations. Lucy could only brace herself, rigid against the cold, while she watched the lieutenant scribble line after line. Thoughts and criticisms flowed with furious, poetic passion. She glanced over at Melendez. Their eyes met. He offered a slight, sympathetic shrug as consolation. Gradually, Lieutenant Cordell's pen slowed. Intensity faded visibly and the emptiness of his mind emerged onto his face in a blank stare; however, the man's scorn remained unbound by the limits of his pen. His venom concentrated around a question.

"Officer Madrigal. Are you *remorseful* yet?"

It was an unexpected question and an even more unexpected display of spontaneity. He was trying to catch Lucy off guard, possibly antagonize her, and goad some careless remark. It was obvious that she was not thrilled with her circumstances. Any attempts to insert small talk withered in the face of greater hostility months before. Forced sincerity and respect were gone. Lucy pretended to freeze on a footpost, as was designed for her. Meanwhile, she consoled herself with eight hours' worth of fifteen-year-old game show reruns in the basement of a run-down rehab center. Remorse was no longer a factor. She resolved not to blow up in his face. Nor would she apologize or beg to make amends. Lucy opened her mouth and prayed that only the shortest, least satisfying of answers would come out. All three of their radios abruptly cut through the silence.

"Six Four Adam, Central," the voice on the other end yelled at the dispatcher. *"I'm gonna need a bus to my location forthwith… Oh, God, multiple buses to my location. Put a rush on 'em! I need additional—"*

Lucy recognized the voice. Sector Adam belonged to Officers Schilling and Antonio. From somewhere out of the otherwise dead air, Freddy Antonio screamed for the aid of ambulances. Owing to the subdued pace of her assignment, she was left with plenty of time and attention to eavesdrop on what everyone else was doing while they patrolled the Six Four. Lucy recalled, just after midnight, that the central dispatcher gave Freddy and his partner a fairly routine-sounding noise complaint—a neighbor calling about a college party that was getting out of control. Freddy sounded unimpressed when he acknowledged the assignment. Twenty-or-so minutes later and he sounded shaken. Cordell must have been thinking the same. His hand jolted down to his side and brought his radio up to his mouth.

"This is the Six Four patrol supervisor. Advise on the condition over there."

"Multiple DOAs, Lieu!" Freddy yelled back.

"Oh, what's this shit now?" Lieutenant Cordell begged of no one in particular.

When the universe returned no answer, he rubbed the bridge of his nose. His finger pressed the transmitter again.

"Central, redirect sectors Charlie and David to back Adam. Show me responding as well."

Lucy's coworkers cried for help. Abandoning her defenses, she stepped forward to get the lieutenant's attention.

"Lieu, let me jump in with you guys. I can help."

"Bullshit! I'm not about to let you tag along so you can hide in the back of my car to warm up. You think you're slick, but I've got your number. Nice try, little girl. You ain't goin' nowhere."

The lieutenant's voice screamed to a pitch, indignant in the face of the supposed audacity of Lucy's proposal.

"After I clean up this nonsense, I'll be back. We can have a little chat about insubordinate rookies who don't know how to properly address their superiors… *Catch!*"

With a flick of his wrist, Lucy's memo book spun out of the window. She watched it tumble through the air past her head and land in the dead center of the chalk confines marked on the sidewalk.

"Go!"

Cordell yelled at his driver and the Crown Vic's tires screeched. The light rack on the car's roof bloomed red and white as the car sped away. Lucy crossed back over the chalk line and bent down. One hand collected her memo book. The other gestured to the exhaust rising in Cordell's wake.

"'Properly address' this, asshole."

The plexiglass double-doors slid open. If they ever entertained such an effort, the Fields would never win recognition for being an attractive or state-of-the-art medical facility. Or the cleanest. Or the best smelling. But the warm air that hugged Lucy was as close to support as she figured herself likely to encounter before the night was complete. She passed the empty security desk and reached the stairs. Even the briefest absence from the subterranean dining and recreational area was enough of a sensory reset to shock the constitution upon return. Decades of flimsy struggles to curb dependencies upon harder substances with heavy tobacco use steeped the facility's halls and common areas in a glossy, yellow film. Amber-tinted paneling imprinted with a facsimile of natural woodgrain covered the first five feet of the walls. Mental anguish and psychotic episodes manifested by fist and foot-sized indentations made their particleboard reality more evident. Rising from the top of the wood panels up to the drop-ceiling, a wallpaper strawberry patch glistened beneath a nicotine dew. The lingering odor of stale smoke filled Lucy's nostrils as she sulked along a faded desire path ground into the blue and green plaid carpeting. Her senses would become numb, as they did on every return to her preferred table.

To Lucy's surprise, the room featured a new addition. Company made their way downstairs in her absence. The kitchen closed between seven in the evening until seven the following morning. Residents would lounge around, if they were physically capable, but most were ushered to their quarters by the facility's staff before Lucy ever arrived. When Lucy sat down, she noticed that one of the residents now took up his own post at another distant dining table. At least, she assumed he was another resident of the Fields. Even hunched over the table, his size was obvious. His long salt and pepper hair was gathered into a greasy ponytail, save for a few rebellious strands that drooped along the sides of his head. The remnants of a goatee were slowly being drowned by a rising mess of untrimmed whiskers on his cheeks and neck. Numerous tattoos, green and blue from age, covered his arms and neck. Some resembled Marine symbols and unit designations. Others implied outlaw biker codes. But it was the vacant, distant eyes that marked him. The overflowing ashtray and the rapid, mechanical tokes. Lucy leaned and looked down. No shoes, red anti-skid socks—the signature apparel in the Fields' perennial catalogue. Lucy tried to estimate how long she had been gone. She counted the butts poking up over the rim of the man's ashtray. At least a half pack had begun to form a heap.

The resident's eyes never returned from their thousand-mile focus to meet her own. She flipped her book open to see what Cordell had spent so much time, space, and ballpoint ink to cement among her other official department recordings:

0045: 2/11/90, Lt. Cordell visited Probationary Police Officer Madrigal. Officer was observed to continue to be unable to render sufficient courtesy toward her superiors. Officer's professional appearance inadequate. Officer was patiently and explicitly provided with instructions to improve insufficiencies. Any further refusal by Officer to adopt said instructions will be resolved with appropriate departmental discipline and serious consideration of probationary status. These and previous deficiencies will continue to be documented for reference.

Cordell was building a case against her. This came as no shock to Lucy. She had been set up for failure. Her memo book was full of similar notes and supporting evidence. Her initial reaction to these comments had been heartbreak. Time hardened her heart. Further consultations with her colleagues made it apparent that no one else's logs contained any sort of similar criticism, despite many other fellow officers' open and blatant disregard for protocols or professionalism. Officers who skipped their duties early or shirked uniform standards received no similar lectures or punishment. Lucy knew she was not like them. She had earned enhanced attention.

The game shows continued, and Lucy considered the past, before her current assignment. On her last day in the Police Academy, at the end of the previous July, they told her she would be going to the Six Four. Except for the occasional excursion to visit family in the borough, she grew up in Lynbrook, where most of her fellow Long Islanders did their best to pretend the two worlds did not share the same landmass. On day one, Lieutenant Cordell took Lucy on as a trainee and driver. It began earnestly enough and continued the next day. Every day afterward, he wanted her in his car. By December, the arrangement had grown uncomfortable. She told him as much in terms she felt indirect enough to mitigate the risk of offense—or retaliation. In a precinct with nearly one hundred uniformed patrolmen and seven female officers on its roster, she felt watched. Lucy overheard the jokes when they thought she was out of earshot, at least from those who cared to attempt discretion. She remembered the laughs. Speaking up for herself had not been made easy and the result was—

"Hey! 'Scuse me."

The raspy voice pulled Lucy away from difficult memories. She returned to a greater volume of electronic commotion. Panic erupted from her radio. She turned. Still seated, the big man loomed larger now that his eyes levelled with her.

"Your radio. Sounds like all Hell's breakin' loose out there."

Two

"This is Six Four David, Central. We're only a couple blocks out!"

"*10-4, David. Remember to signal 10-84 upon arrival. Arrive alive.*"

Tabitha Williams's radio squawked with feedback as the dispatcher acknowledged her transmission. Every other police radio tuned to the Sixty Fourth Precinct's frequency competed for the same, limited airtime. On any other night, the channel would have been dead. Rows of slumbering houses flashed red and white as they caught the glare of the lights spinning atop the marked '89 Caprice which Officer Williams shared with her partner, Jimmy Daley. She watched Jimmy manipulate the steering wheel with the casual nonchalance of a milk run, despite the labored roars of the car's engine.

"You sure this is the best way?"

"It *can* be," Jimmy replied, "so long as you approach one-ways with a very open mind. And a light touch."

A slight dip of Jimmy's hand turned the car's front end a block earlier than she expected. By the grace of the advanced hour and the mass of police vehicles already choking the middle the block, there was no oncoming traffic or rights of way with which to contend as they swerved onto 63rd Street.

"See, Tabby? Easy as pie."

The Caprice veered toward the side of the road and skidded to a stop within an inch of another patrol car's front bumper. The air forgotten inside Tabby's chest hissed past her teeth when she finally allowed it to vent. In nearly eight years working alongside Jimmy, she knew that she would find herself riding shotgun more often than not. And for however many more years she served, Jimmy would always hold twenty years over her. That kind of seniority carried a lot of entitlement, if not always the keenest wisdom. In many cases—most noticeably in Jimmy's—it also seldom correlated with proactivity. Mere seconds before their car was redlining its way across Bensonhurst, Jimmy had been resting his eyes. And snoring. Loudly enough, in fact, that it took Tabby's elbow several digs between his ribs before he too noticed Schilling and Antonio blowing up the airwaves.

"Six Four David, Central," Tabby sighed. "Show us 84."

The car swayed on its suspension. Jimmy rocked the vehicle once more and rode the momentum to come unstuck.

"What's the house number," he asked, "an' where the hell is everybody else?"

Despite the congestion, the other marked vehicles all appeared deserted.

"Twenty-three fifty-six," Tabby called back as she lifted herself up to the doorframe. "I think they said it was the second-floor apartment."

Red and white circles of light danced across red brick and vinyl siding. But for the idling, abandoned emergency vehicles, Tabby saw no other signs of life. Six Four patrol cars were left scattered around the block and congregated around no particularly obvious address. She squinted. The kaleidoscopic lights dazzled her eyes and obscured the numbers on the identical, semi-detached houses. That all the streetlamps and porch lights appeared to be suffering from power failure did little to assist the search. In fact, there appeared to be no functional light sources attached to anything other than the arriving vehicles. Tabby swiveled her Maglite into her palm and followed the beam from one house to the next. Door after door shined back ascending numbers.

There was no twenty-three fifty-six. Tabby's eyes and the spotlight counted the even side of the block to where their destination should have appeared. Instead of a door with the appropriate markings, her gaze stumbled across a fractured threshold and plummeted with the beam into darkness. Emptiness and lifelessness poured from the yawning doorway to siphon any lingering spirit from the barren night. Sudden flickering and erratic activity begged her attention upward. Evidence of a hasty search stumbled into view of a bare, second-story window. Tabby turned sideways. It was a tight squeeze to cross between the bumpers of the cars parked along the shoulder of the street and onto the sidewalk. She bounced from asphalt to cement and reached the house's stoop in two strides. Atop the narrow alcove were two companion doorways. The door to Tabby's left stood intact. Its neighbor no longer stood at all, dislocated with demonstrable violence to bare inner abyss. Brass hinges dangled on dislocated screws at the edge of the splintered frame. They shuddered and swayed. The house shook. Tabby raised her flashlight and leaned forward. A pair of feet rumbled down a flight of stairs on the other side of the crippled entrance. She reeled backward in an attempt shift her weight and make way. Lieutenant Cordell charged out of the darkness without pause. His expression soured when momentum brought him into a near-collision with Tabby. The lieutenant caught himself and stammered.

"Williams!"

"Lieu, what happened? Is everyone alr—"

Cordell was not listening. While he reasserted his balance, he looked straight through Tabby. Displeasure turned to contempt.

"And Daley," he grunted.

Jimmy moved at a pace which a generous observer might describe as steady and deliberate. It was his custom. Tabby started to repeat her question. She was interrupted before she could form a single word.

"*You two*," Cordell growled again. "You two are to stay outside. *Right here*. Don't pull any disappearin' acts."

"Lieu, we just—"

"And don't touch a *goddamned thing*, neither. Paramedics, crime scene, and the detective squad are all on their way. Nobody else is allowed inside—yourselves included."

The lieutenant did not wait for a reply. He stumbled down the stoop to the sidewalk and stormed past Jimmy.

"Just stand here and… Don't. Do. Anything. Jimmy, I can count on you for that much, right?"

"You got it, boss," Jimmy purred.

He raised his hand to flash an 'OK' as Cordell brushed past him. The lieutenant was moving too fast to notice his subordinate's digits retract and reconfigure into an extended middle finger. Suggestions of a decidedly intimate nature concerning the lieutenant and his own mother exited Jimmy's mouth on profane whispers. Cordell could not hear them over the volume of his own self-pity.

"How come this shit only happens when I'm covering patrol," he whined. "Melendez! Will you unlock the *goddamn* car, already?"

The stairs behind Tabby rumbled again. Herman Melendez popped his head out of the doorway. He gave her a nod and began to descend toward the street and the impatient, flustered supervisor he was tasked to drive.

"The fuck happened in there?" Tabby asked. "Are Schilling and Antonio okay?"

"Those two, sure. They'll be fine," Melendez replied, voice trailing as he poked his thumb over his shoulder. "But the bunch that lived *up there*…"

"Wait, what d'you mean?"

"What I mean is, Sector Adam might've rolled up a little late."

A chorus of sirens bellowed near the end of the block. Warm amber joined the revolving parade of colors strobing the neighborhood. Brake lights flared. A pair of ambulances slowed as they twisted into the already jumbled mess of emergency vehicles.

Melendez did not wait for any follow up questions. He continued toward the street and tossed the keys to Cordell. The lieutenant cursed when he missed the pitch. He cursed some more when the keys fumbled between his hands and into the door's lock. Cordell was too distracted to see Tabby follow his driver back into the street. When she caught up with Melendez, he was briefing the arrived paramedics.

"For fuck's sake, Herman, just tell me what we're dealin' with here."

"Well," he started, eyes darting between her and the house. "It's bad up there. *Real* bad."

Melendez was known for being affable. When a tense atmosphere needed defusing, he was quicker to jokes than temper. The uncharacteristic seriousness afflicting his face unnerved Tabby.

"There's kids up there. Not like children, I mean. College-aged kids. Five of 'em. Multiple gunshot wounds. Must've been a couple dozen rounds lit off. Four are goners. Schilling says the fifth's got a weak pulse—at least she did when he first got here."

"Shit. We got perp descriptions or anything?"

"Nah, whoever did the deed made sure their only witnesses didn't have too much to say. None of the lights work and we didn't see it at first, but they left a message of their own. In blood. Over every square inch of the living room walls."

A pair of doors labeled 'Gravesend' and 'General' popped open on the back of one of the ambulances. The team of paramedics wrestled a gurney onto the street. Wheels unfolded beneath and clattered onto the sidewalk.

"Not my first choice for healthcare," Melendez said dryly. "Somebody up there better be lookin' out if there's gonna be any witnesses left walkin' outta that little corner of Hell."

Tabby took point at the base of the stoop, not distant enough from Lieutenant Cordell's watchful, miserable eyes. The first ambulance crew to emerge from the house looked nearly disturbed as Melendez. When Schilling followed the paramedics and the stretcher, Tabby noticed his already fair complexion turned a shade paler. His arm was raised overhead while his hand cradled a clear, plastic sack. The I.V. line swayed and swiveled like a jump rope down to the passenger bouncing beneath the gurney's straps. Tabby could not see a face beneath the layers of bedsheets and medical blankets swaddling the patient from the bitter cold.

The victim was loaded into the ambulance and the paramedics jumped in behind to continue rendering whatever aid they could.

Schilling tossed the bag in his hand to one of them. His attention turned to the lieutenant's car. The officer sprinted over and rapped his knuckles against Cordell's window. Tabby bit the side of her cheek. If she had not, she would have burst laughing at the look on Cordell's face when he jumped and slammed his head against the interior of the car's roof.

"Do you have any idea just who the hell I'm on the phone with?"

"Uh—no, sir! Sorry, sir," Schilling apologized. "But the bus is rolling out with one of the victims. I'm gonna follow 'em to the E.R."

"What about the other victims? When are they gonna be removed to the hospital?"

Schilling's shoulders rose slightly and then quickly sank. Tabby heard the weight of his sigh from over twenty feet away.

"There's only gonna be the one goin' to Gravesend, Lieu. As far as the other four... they already called it. Time of death was midnight-thirty. Medical examiner's office is en-route."

"Shit," Cordell hissed. "More phone calls."

The naked, shivering tree branches dimmed as the ambulance and its wailing siren faded away. Save for the light of the full moon peering between the swishing limbs, Tabby became aware of just how dark the block was. Every streetlamp and house light on either side of her hung lifeless. Lights glowed faintly in the distance— maybe a hundred feet on her right, another hundred to the left. It struck her that whatever effected the outage, she stood near its focal point.

"Hey, Jimmy."

"Hmm?"

Jimmy sputtered and stirred within the house's alcove. But for the cigarette smoldering at the corner of his mouth, Tabby would have otherwise guessed she pulled him out of a nap. He shifted his weight from one foot to the other without removing his shoulder from the wall. Tabby watched loose stitches stretch away from where the distressed leather attached to the soles of his boots as they ground against the cement porch.

"Did'ya hear Central say anything about any power problems? Any ConEd jobs?"

"Me? I didn't hear *shit*."

"Sure," Tabby sighed. "Sounds about right."

Over her shoulder, blanketed within the shadows gathered at the top of the stoop, the cherry flared at the end of Jimmy's cigarette. The glow spread with every labored puff. Faint, orange lines climbed the sagging expanses of his cheeks.

"Officer Williams!"

Tabby jumped. A pair of car doors slammed shut by the street. She had not seen any new headlights approaching. As for the lack of engine noise, the wind must have washed away any such rumblings. However he managed to materialize without drawing her attention, Detective Sam Vernon strolled in Tabby's direction. Much to her regret, the lack of electric light did nothing to obscure her view of the smug grin beaming from the detective's face. She could see clearly through his casual gait to the barbs readying to be sprung.

"Sam," Tabby growled. "Pleasure."

"Pleasure's all mine, girly."

"'Bout time you crawled over here. Did you catch this one or are you just making an appearance and autographing the paperwork?"

The detective bristled. His partner, Ricky Delavan, hustled up onto the sidewalk.

"Y'know, this really brings back some memories, Tab," Vernon sneered. "But how's about you enlighten me an' Rick here about what this bunch'a crazy kids upstairs got up to while you and Bob's Big Boy were *allegedly* on patrol?"

"Nobody's filled you in yet? Or just disappointed you didn't get an invite?"

"If I wanted to catch lead poisoning at a house party, I'd crash one'a those gang-banger bashes up in Flatbush or Bed Stuy. Hell, that's probably where we'll collar the mope who robbed this joint."

"*Shit*, go tell Cordell we can shut this crime scene down. You've already got the whole case figured out."

"Doesn't take a Sherlock Holmes to figure out where all the bodies are pilin' up. It sure as hell ain't down here in Bensonhurst."

"Let me guess: bad things only happen in bad places around bad people, right? When bad things happen in *good places*, it must've been because those *bad people* couldn't keep it to themselves."

"There you go," Sam laughed, either oblivious or impervious to Tabby's sarcasm. "There might just be a detective's shield out there for you, after all!"

Tabby remembered when she sat next to Sam in the Police Academy. In nearly ten years, his logic was simple, predictable, and ignorant as ever. Thus far, her observations had done little to deprive him any promotions. Spinning red and white lights trace the contours of the gold shield clipped to the lapel of his wool coat. Several of the lower discs in Tabby's spine began to throb as memories of an old injury stirred. She felt her chest tighten, as it was prone to do whenever she caught sight of *her* shield strutting around on Sam's chest. When she could no longer ignore the ache in her teeth, she forced herself to relax her jaw. There was little her conscious mind could do to stop cursing herself for allowing her own work to pin the same detective's shield to a pretender.

The tension must have grown too great. Delavan broke the silence.

"Anyone make contact with the downstairs neighbors or the next door over? No way an entire street—let alone somebody sharing walls—coulda' slept through a mess like this."

"Doesn't look like anyone was home," Tabby sighed. "Might be outta town. Might still be out enjoyin' their Saturday night."

"If you hear anything—"

"*You'll* be the first to know, Ricky. Don't worry."

"'Preciate it, Tabby," Delavan replied. "*Loathe* as I am to pull Sam away, I'm freezin' my ass off."

"Yeah, it's been a real gasser," Vernon crowed. "But as my partner said, our *investigative acumens* are need elsewhere. Step aside… if you'd be so kind."

"Don't let me keep you. Follow the smoke trail up to Jimmy. An' try not to let what's left of the door hit you on the way in."

Vernon was on the move and pretended not to hear, but the way his smile melted betrayed his ears. When he reached the top of the stoop, he paused. Jimmy did not budge. The standoff was brief. It ended when the detective huffed, twisted sideways, and shuffled past the larger officer. There were some virtues Tabby wished to channel from her impassive partner. Jimmy never acknowledged Sam, physically or verbally. Over the course of a lifetime, he perfected an aloofness to certain types of people, which he assured Tabby was inclusive of—but not limited to—people who laughed at their own jokes, those who absentmindedly jangled the change in their pockets, and Jets fans. This earned Detective Vernon exactly three strikes in Jimmy's eyes and, therefore, near universal indifference but for the occasional glaring reminder that any attempts to breach such a harmonious state would be met with outright, aggressive contempt. Tabby struggled to achieve the same. She closed her eyes and urged the surplus pressure to drain. She immediately came up short. Vernon's sneer remained, floating in the darkness behind her eyelids.

Unexpected motion spared Tabby the detective's intrusive, lingering presence. Across the street, on the first floor of another house mirroring the appearance of the one she guarded, a pair of window curtains fluttered. Tabby squinted. There was a head behind them, and it stared back at her. A long nose brushed aside the sheer cloth and pressed closer to the window. The eyes were dark. A pair of alert ears swiveled. The German Shepherd tilted its head, then barked. For as long as they watched each other, Tabby never saw the dog's eyes blink. The playful yelp was meant for her.

Lieutenant Cordell sat with his elbows perched atop his knees and head buried in his hands. He might have been rocking himself back and forth. Whatever was being imparted to him on the other end of the car's hard-wired phone frustrated him to the point of absolute distraction. The dull throb rolling up and down Tabby's spine refused to subside. The bottoms of her feet, numb from the cold seeping up through her soles, begged to be stretched. She wondered if Cordell would even notice if she conducted her own canvass, head in the sand while he struggled to satisfy his own superiors. Tabby turned to search for her partner. There were only shadows behind her now. She saw no embers, no whisps of tobacco. Wherever Jimmy stood, he was either between smokes or had ashed-out as he slept standing up. Tabby was confident *Big Boy* could handle himself.

It felt good to feel the world moving beneath her feet once more. The house across the road and every other house stretching in either direction appeared members of the same generation. Red brick, semi-detached duplexes separated by narrow and often tenuously shared driveways. The same tracts of identical houses filled many of the broad gaps between the venerable, if sagging, Victorians of South Brooklyn. Her grandmother lived in an identical duplex, miles away in Canarsie. The crowded townhouses represented the final crops of ancestral fields and farms belonging to ancient families with names forgotten to all but subway stops and street signs. The rubble left by makeshift colonial shanties and the cinders of obsolete industries, enriched by fine, residual lead and arsenic particles, decomposed in backyards and drifted along with basement dust. Spring would come in a few months' time, impossible as the frozen wind stinging Tabby's face made such a forecast seem. As they had a year earlier, neighboring pensioners would break apart the topsoil and turn over the earth in perennial gardens with their spades and shovels. They would plant their tomatoes, peppers, and zucchini, and the plants would absorb the ashes of time to bear new fruit.

Tabby felt the dog's eyes follow her. When she placed her foot on the stoop's first step, the Shepherd bolted away and left the curtains billowing. It followed her to the front door at the top of the stairs and snorted at the other side of the mail slot. Tabby's knuckles connected with the door and a volley of howls and barks erupted on the other side. Hushing tones approached and the loud yelps melted into whines and worried grunts. After momentary appraisal through the door's peephole, Tabby heard a succession of cylinders turn to release deadbolts. With a slight shudder and crack, the door unsealed itself from the frame in which it rested. The figure of an older woman peered out through the narrow gap. One hand held the door open no wider than necessary to facilitate conversation; the other was preoccupied with the excitable dog who desperately wanted to slip through.

"Evening, ma'am," Tabby said. "It's late, I know. I'm real sorry if I woke you up. I saw your dog in the window and had a few ques—"

"Officer! Goodness gracious," the woman interrupted. "Thank you all for coming. Thank you, lord!"

Her voice oscillated between relief and terror. Tabby could sense that energy transferring to the animal behind her.

"No need to apologize, we were already wide awake after all that commotion across the way. I called as soon as I heard them fighting."

"Whatever it was that you heard, like I said, I was wondering if I could ask you some questions."

"Yes, yes. Step inside," she said as she pulled the door back. "And don't mind Molasses. She's loud and a little worked up, but she's just a big, sweet baby."

The woman stepped aside to invite Tabby in. Molasses, however, did not appear eager to make way for polite entry. The dog's nose sniffed and poked more franticly than ever. Tabby squeezed into the warmth of the first-floor apartment while Molasses squirmed and looped endlessly around her knees. The woman reached toward a small table near the entryway swelled and twisted the knob at the base of a kerosene lamp. The flame inside the glass lamp pulsed and the apartment's entryway brightened. Molasses continued to whimper and wiggle until, abruptly satisfied, she spun around disinterestedly and trotted off.

"Much appreciated. I promise I'll keep this short."

Tabby loosened the zipper on the front of her jacket and let the warmth flow in. Her hand pulled a bundle of scrap paper and a pen from an inside pocket.

"Can I get your name?"

"Lydia Dunwell," she replied. "I've lived here forty-two… no, forty-three years."

"What do you remember hearing right before you called?"

"Well, we had just gone to sleep. Molasses and I always go to bed around eleven. But the poor girl, she was so restless. As soon as I began to drift off, Molasses would stir. There were these kids outside—a pair of 'em—slammin' their car doors shut. I looked over at my alarm clock and saw that it was still a few minutes 'til midnight. Nothin' out of the ordinary there, though. Let me tell you, the way people on this street bang around at all hours! Nobody respects their neighbors anymore—"

"You heard car doors slam," Tabby interrupted. "Tell me what happened next."

"Well, maybe a minute or two later I'm tryin' to get back to sleep, but I heard something even louder. Sweetheart, I nearly fell outta my bed. It sounded like someone hit a tree with their car! After that, my poor Molasses was runnin' in circles, barkin' her head off. I haven't seen her possessed like that since the Fourth of July fireworks. Do you know how late these people stay up with those, those... *rockets* they tear up the sky with? I swear, you'd think the ceiling was gonna come crashin' down on top'a you!"

"Right, so the dog is barking. Does Molasses do anything else? Does she go to the front window at all?"

"Yes, I was just getting to that. So, I walk from my bedroom, which is in the back of the house and come out here to the living room..."

Mrs. Dunwell picked up the lamp by its handle. It dangled beneath her hand as she motioned through an archway toward the adjoining living room.

"I walked over to that window, right there. But all I saw was a parked car, blocking the johnny pump."

"Any idea what kind?"

"Oh, you know the type. Same as any other fire hydrant, I suppose."

"Uh, no... ma'am. The make of the *car*."

"I'm not sure, dear. It was dark, maybe gray. It had four doors. Beyond that I couldn't really say. My Anthony used to do all the driving. He's not with us anymore."

Lydia's eyes sank to the floor. She crossed herself with her right hand. Tabby's own eyes wandered reflexively, permitting the widow a moment of privacy. Much of the wallpaper lining Mrs. Dunwell's living room stood hidden behind a patchwork of framed, black-and-white photographs. Snapshots of younger Lydias, braced on either side by a young family, beamed a hundred times over. In all but a handful, a gentleman of a consistently similar age smiled next to her. In some he wore wide, pinstriped lapels and tab collars secured by narrow neckties—in others, the dress uniform of the Army Air Corps.

"But one thing I did notice," Lydia continued shakily, "was someone sittin' behind the steering wheel. Whatever happened after all the door slammin'—or that horrible crashing sound—there was someone sittin' in the car all the while, with the headlights dimmed. I figured they'd dropped a couple'a people off, but why wait there for so long afterwards? If you don't care about wakin' people up, why turn the lights off?"

"Do you remember what that person looked like? Was it a man or a woman? Young, old?"

"These college students treat that apartment like a flophouse. I'm certain they were young. The face looked round, soft—either a boy barely twenty or a girl no more than a few years older. They had long hair. Looked blonde, or half shade darker. Mousy. Back in my day I could tell you it was a woman I saw, but with the way kids grow out their hair, who knows?"

"Did you see anything else suspicious?"

"That house across the street, number twenty-three fifty-six. After I heard that crash and looked outside and saw the car, it looked like they left their front door wide open again. Like I said, with these kids it's always the same thing. Come fall, they'd throw parties late into the night. As if the noise wasn't bad enough with the door closed, they'd leave it hangin' open and we'd have to hear their music blastin', too. But I try to be patient, dear. I don't like to complain. Other than all that racket, I didn't want to get my blood pressure up. The noise wasn't *too* bad. Not yet, at least."

"What made you finally call 911?"

"Honey, the darndest things started happenin'. I heard the cuckoo clock in the kitchen chirpin' when it struck midnight. I gave up on trying to go back to sleep right away. Molasses had stopped barking, but I could tell she was still worked up, pacin' around and cryin' the way she does. I left the living room and went to look for my aspirins in the medicine cabinet. I didn't care if those kids were gettin' up to something in the middle of the night, just as long as I wasn't gonna catch a headache over it. But as I'm standin' in front of the bathroom sink and openin' the bottle, I noticed something. The light over the sink—it was gettin' dimmer."

"Yeah, looks like there's a power outage on your block."

"No dear," Lydia whispered. "That's what I thought at first, too. But like I said… darndest thing."

Mrs. Dunwell reached toward a light switch on the wall. She flipped it up, then down. She repeated the demonstration a few more times. Save for the fluttering light of the lantern, the darkness remained.

"Now… watch this."

Lydia followed the woman's lantern to an ancient space heater in the corner of the living room. She twisted one of its knobs with her free hand. A few seconds passed. Tabby heard a buzzing noise. A whiff of dry, electric warmth drifted up to her nose. Deep within the metal box, rows of jagged coils vibrated, dimly red at first and then bright orange behind the heater's mesh screen.

"It's not the power," Tabby mumbled.

"No. It's just the light bulbs. They all burned out. Once I left the sink, I saw 'em: one at a time, in every room. For some, it took a couple'a seconds. Others flickered and popped right away. They all just… died away. After maybe a minute or two, the whole house was dark."

"How…"

"At the time I still didn't realize it was just the lightbulbs. I figure they were bringin' in all kinds of fancy stereos, or hi-fis, or what-have-you's for their party, and suckin' up all the electricity. But that was the last straw—whatever was happening, when I picked up the phone, I heard the dial tone. The emergency line still answered."

"Did you hear anything else after that?"

"After I got off the phone with the dispatcher, I felt my way down to the basement where my Anthony always kept the storm lanterns. I must've been down there for a few minutes. It took me a bit before I was able to find the lamps and lug 'em back up here. As I was comin' back up the stairs, I heard the slammin' of the car doors again. Then tires tires screechin', like they were in a real hurry. When I reached the front window again, the pump was clear. All I saw was that same car racin' away."

"Did you see how many people were inside, or what they looked like?"

"I'm sorry dear, I don't know. They took off so fast they were already at the end of the block before I could look. Reckless. Drivin' that fast and still didn't have their headlights on. And I didn't see any lights on across the street or hear any music or noise anymore either, so I figured the party must've broken up once the power went out. A little bit later, a patrol car pulled up. Next thing I knew, half of the police department is in front of my house and you're knocking on my door."

Tabby's stomach refused to produce an appetite when Lydia Dunwell offered to open a tin of biscuits or brew her a cup of tea. The details swirled in her mind, sparse as they were. Whatever happened or however the woman recollected the events, Tabby found her lines of questioning exhausted. She found *herself* exhausted. There was nothing left but to thank Mrs. Dunwell for her time.

"Officer, you never told me what happened over there."

She had not. Tabby had seen nothing past the wreckage of the front door and the hurried evacuation by the paramedics. She knew of the signs of violence described by Melendez. She knew what Lydia recalled. Beyond that, she knew only that she had nothing of comfort to offer.

"I know I complained about the noise and the parties and everything before. It's just that I saw that ambulance rushin' someone away on a stretcher. What I mean is—are those kids okay? Is everything… *safe?*"

Based on their conversation and Tabby's knowledge of the neighborhood in general, the greatest threats to Lydia Dunwell's serenity up to this point were fireworks and raucous youth. Tabby did not know how she could tell someone who spent over forty years of her life on the same block that four-going-on-five of her neighbors had been murdered in a midnight home invasion by persons still unknown and very much at large—much less how she could ever dare to keep it a secret.

"It looks like things might've gotten a little out of control," Tabby admitted. "We're still piecing everything together. I'm real grateful you could talk with me and I'm sure it'll be a big help."

Tabby deflected with every step she took back toward Lydia's front door. When she walked out onto the cold stoop, a blue van pulled up in the middle of the street. Bright, sober letters announced the arrival of the *Office of the Medical Examiner*—the *Meat Wagon* as it was affectionately referred by those who shepherded the dead into its back doors.

"Officer Williams…"

Tabby sighed. She cursed the timing and turned back to Mrs. Dunwell.

"I know I might just sound like another local busybody. I try not to be a bother over every little thing. But I worry. It's just Molasses and me now, alone together. Has been ever since the last time I saw that van—since the last time I saw my Anthony. Please… tell me what happened tonight."

Shying away from the warmth of Lydia Dunwell's home, the frigid wind stung not nearly as sharp as the guilt in Tabby's chest.

"Lydia… Mrs. Dunwell," Tabby started. "I'm being honest when I say that I'm not too sure myself. I wish I could tell you what happened. What I *can* say is, I'm gonna do everything I can to find out. But for now, truthfully, I don't know much more than you."

"No, you don't," a nasally voice snarled behind her.

Tabby spun around. Sam Vernon leaned his right foot two steps up onto Mrs. Dunwell's stoop. He perched his arms on top of his raised knee. Lips curled over nicotine-stained teeth as he continued to speak.

"So, how's about you stick to what you *do* know and try not to spill the beans on an ongoing investigation."

Still mindful of the witness in their presence, Tabby fought the urge to profane loudly and liberally.

"You lose your better half?" she forced through clenched teeth.

"We're canvassing the neighborhood for witnesses. Because that's *our* job. Unlike yourself, *we* don't abandon our responsibilities to wander off and do whatever we want. So far, either nobody's home or nobody saw nothing. But plenty of people are askin' me questions about their lights like I'm from ConEd."

"This one heard a lot," Tabby said. "You should let Delavan know. He can bring her in for an interview in the daytime."

"Oh yeah? Well, I say there's no time like the present."

Detective Vernon bounced up the steps past Tabby. Wary and a little nonplussed, Lydia Dunwell watched the exchange from the other side of her doorway.

"Thanks for the tip, girly. Guess that makes *two* I owe you for, now."

"Look, I've already got notes—"

"Nah," Vernon sneered. "You're good. I'll take care of the interview, the *right* way. I've got a gift for gettin' what I need outta people. Just like you've got a gift for babysitting ol' Jimmy over there. On the *other* side of the street. Best if we both stick to what we're best at, know what I mean?"

"But—,"

"I said: *You're. Good.*"

Tabby's vision flashed red. Sam Vernon slid up to the doorway and gently guided Mrs. Dunwell back inside. Tabby flew back to the top of the landing only to meet the door as it closed firmly in her face. She stared at the faded paint and considered slamming her head against the door until it broke through. She sighed and turned around. Her next fantasy involved snapping the top from her pepper spray and tossing the leaking canister into Vernon's unmarked car. Each step to return her across the street demanded every ounce of self-control she could summon and produced more than a few creative designs on theoretical revenge. Otherwise, Tabby was left with the feeling that she witnessed history repeat. Vernon had not given credit where it was due before. She knew he never would.

Molasses started barking again. The dog snarled and yapped at another unexpected visitor in its home. Visions of the German Shepherd sinking its teeth into the detective's backside fueled the remainder of Tabby's return trip to the crime scene.

Lieutenant Cordell stuttered through his hastily scribbled notes while his shoulder cradled the car's built-in phone against his ear. Those few words which did escape the vehicle sounded profusely, pathetically apologetic. If the Inspector or Chief on the other end did not appreciate Cordell's very late call or quality of the details therein, they made sure to make him squirm for their own displeasure. Flashbulbs flared in the window over the duplex's alcove. Every camera flash painted a portrait of Medical Examiner's Office investigators and Crime Scene Unit technicians jockeying and bumbling against one another. Beneath the chaos, the shadows atop the stoop stirred naught but for one smoldering cigarette.

"Why d'you even try to keep polite with that prick?"

"You mean, *detective* prick," Tabby replied. "And if you could read my mind, *polite* wouldn't be the right word."

"Exactly the problem," Jimmy wheezed as he exhaled. "Speak your mind. I'd tell that shitheel off every chance I got if I'd been robbed like you was—not that anybody ever considered me too much'a the *detectin'* type."

"Damnit, what good would it do? The whole thing's rigged. I woulda' still missed out. Woulda' still got bounced to midnights. But if I hadn't—that asshole… *that* could've been me."

"Damn right, you coulda been that asshole. And now *that asshole's* livin' inside your head, rent-free."

"It wouldn't matter if I blew up in his face just now. He'd just get even more satisfaction out of it, and I'd still be stuck out here every night with…"

"With me? Pretty bad, I know."

"I'm sorry, Jimmy, but just… forget it."

Tabby's compounding regrets wafted through the air with the lingering tobacco smoke. One or both were causing the pressure in her head to build until a small mercy descended from the shadows behind Jimmy. A man in a baby blue jumpsuit with the seal of the Office of the Chief Medical Examiner cleared his throat. As he leaned out of the doorway, Tabby noticed the heavy, dark smears covering his clothes.

"Hey, could one'a youse give us a hand up here?"

Jimmy tucked his cigarette into the corner of his mouth. His palms clapped together as he brushed them against one another.

"Yeah, sure," he sighed. "Better prove myself useful."

Tabby could not force her eyes to meet with Jimmy's. When she looked back up at the doorway a moment later, he was gone.

What little warmth Tabby built up in Mrs. Dunwell's house fled quickly. The frost crept through the outer layers of her jacket and numbed the tips of her toes. She emptied her mind of imaginary arguments and apologies until only the inarticulate odor of shame remained. When the first stretcher made its descent, Tabby was unsure that the men from the morgue who were guiding it down the steps would be able to match its momentum. The first few mechanical *thunks* seemed cautious enough, but the reckless clattering which preceded the thick, black bag's emergence into the night narrowly avoided the gurney careening onto the sidewalk. Straining to bring the gurney to a halt before it teetered over the edge of the stoop, the men in jumpsuits exchanged nervous looks of relief and nodded at Tabby. The next two trips to the back of their van displayed more care until Tabby heard a new commotion above her.

"Aww, *shit!*"

The exclamation was followed by a loud *thud*. Without hesitation, Tabby turned to follow Jimmy's voice. She jumped over what remained of the door and its frame. Despite many trips by a multitude of municipal representatives and emergency personnel, debris still cluttered the landing. Tabby's feet flew over the obstructive mess. She did not expect her boots to land with a splash. Something cold and viscous pooled on the carpeting by the base of the stairs leading up to the apartment. It splashed up onto Tabby's pants and clung to the bottom of her sole as she dragged her foot onto the first step. Every tread she climbed was similarly saturated.

It was too dark. Tabby reached for her flashlight, pointed its lamp toward her feet, and clicked it on. Deep red streaks flooded the edges of her boots. She followed the beam of light up to the cuffs of her pants. Her navy-blue hems were stained black. Tabby looked up and watched a river of blood slowly drip down every step from the next floor. She continued to climb until the beam of her flashlight extended over the banister at the top of the stairs and the rest of the apartment came into view. She could hear noises sputtering uncontrollably from her mouth. Like the thoughts circling her head, they failed to reconstitute themselves into coherence. She searched for the source of the blood. Red trails ran down every wall from the bottoms of drying letters, twisting and swirling into interlocked circles and spiraling, endless sentences.

Rising depths… barren Elysia… infernal pantheon… King Belial.

The same phrases repeated over and over. Some were in English. Others resembled sounds and letters which Tabby might have otherwise successfully recognized if her panicked mind permitted thoughtful, measured reflection. Other sensations and other stimuli fought for her attention. A vile bouquet of odors attacked her nose. Iron and sulfur. Blood and stale gun smoke. Every surface wept humanity and agony. Tabby felt her knees wobble. Her stomach flipped.

"Ugh, *fuck*. Help me up!"

Jimmy's cry pulled Tabby back to earth. She scanned the bloodstained surreality until her flashlight reached the edge of the living room's sofa. Jimmy sprawled, legs drenched red, with one elbow up on the couch behind him. A stretcher had tipped and now pinned him to the ground. One of the Medical Examiner's investigators grappled with the upended body bag, but struggled to find footing on the slick, saturated floor.

"Musta' twisted my damn ankle liftin' this thing," Jimmy grunted.

The stairs bounced with every step Jimmy limped. Tabby considered it a miracle that, as they returned to the landing, the weight he rested against her shoulder had not caused them both to tumble down each bloody step.

"Oh, what the *fuck!*"

Despite the exceptional pains of Lieutenant Cordell's telephone conversation, the commotion within the crime scene finally diverted his attention. He greeted the two officers at the base of the stoop as they hobbled through the doorway.

"What did I explicitly tell the both of youse *not* to do?"

"Jimmy slipped while helping the M.E.'s," Tabby replied. "It's his ankle."

She lowered her shoulder and let Jimmy slide down onto the top step.

"'*Stay outside,*' I said. '*Just guard the entrance,*' I said. How could I have made it any clearer? You cooked up another cute scam for yourself this time, didn't you Daley? How many months are you gonna be out for this one?"

"I really think I need to see a doctor, boss," Daley said as he winced in pain.

"Fine. Whatever," Cordell sneered. "Williams! Call another bus for your partner. We sure got more than enough *dead weight* here tonight, don't we?"

Tabby grabbed her portable radio and hailed the dispatcher. She released the button and turned her hand over. Red smears dried in the creases of her skin. They continued down her sleeves, thicker and wetter until they coalesced at the bottoms of her pants. Red reflections of the moon shined up at her from the tips of her shoes. Another wave of bitter, frigid air rolled down the street and the blood soaking into the threads of her clothes grew colder. Tabby shivered.

Three

"It's about this guy. Not only is he fightin' the bad guys, but he's gotta fight the system, too."

He introduced himself to Lucy as Apollo.

"Or, at least, he's *tryina'* fight. He's got these bosses that don't understand the real sufferin' goin' down on the streets. Like, there's these real bad dudes takin' over the old neighborhood, but the higher ups just wanna sweep it all under the rug, y'know? All they care about is if people find out, like, *how bad* things've really gotten, all the politicians an' the newspapers are gonna have a field day! An' the hero, Armstrong Wolfe, that's the guy played by Bruce Phillip Marcus—y'know, Bruce Phillip Marcus from Sky Shark? Where he's flyin' that experimental helicopter? Looked nothin' like the Hueys they gave us back in '68, though—"

Apollo bore little resemblance to the other patients Lucy occasionally witnessed drifting around the Elysian Fields Adult Rehabilitation Center in the smaller hours. In what she estimated to be his early fifties, he was not only younger than most of his neighbors in the Fields, he displayed few of their common frailties. Other residents suffered from a combination of moderate-to-severe physical and mental impairments—their faces dyskinetic by cyclical institutionalization and antipsychotic chemistry, ceded to the idle gnashing of jaws and tongues. Apollo, on the other hand, seemed unusually vibrant and strong. His broad frame belonged to someone who dedicated no minor portion of their youth to strength training. Whatever slouch he might now affect in his posture was more likely meant to prevent his head grazing the basement's drooping ceiling. If his tattoos were any indication, he had been a veteran and an outlaw biker. At this moment, in this place, Apollo was a film critic. Without any prompt on Lucy's part, he recapitulated the plots of every movie he had seen over the past thirteen years with vacillating intensity for the better part of two hours without pausing for breath.

"In reality, the super-top-secret choppers are quieter, too. Like, silent. You can't hear 'em with your ears, but when the fillins' start rattlin' in your teeth—that's them, alright. I used to work with the feds on this stuff. They got these lasers built onto the noses of the helicopters. Them fuckers can shine right through the damn walls—don't even need to spy on youse through your windows or the telephone wire no more."

Lucy offered her host a polite nod before permitting her eyes to disengage his own. It had not taken too long for her to understand that Apollo did not expect any reply or approval from her. He was compelled to articulate every thought in his head, and he may have done just that whether she nor anyone else were present to receive them. While physically robust, any thought explored long enough brought Apollo to expose one or more deeply rooted veins of paranoia and delusion. He let his mouth dredge every corner of his mind and never failed to arrive at some dark manifestation or supreme presence. For all the logical inconsistencies—which Lucy quickly found any examination or correction of such to be counterproductive—a perfect explanation always materialized immediately. No doubt, no hesitation. Apollo was a train rolling along its tracks, unsteadily or precariously as some seemingly external temperament dictated. If Lucy thought herself any kind of conductor, once the controls failed to respond she became just another passenger.

"That's why I come down here at night, y'know? When they're buzzin' around, shootin' their lasers into peoples' dreams while they're sleepin'. That's their favorite time to look in on you. When your defenses are down an' your brains workin' overtime to see the real truth."

A hush fell over the radio about the same time Apollo began to speak his mind. Perhaps he missed the explosive, frenzied chatter. When the transmissions ebbed, Apollo filled the silence with his own imagined theatrics. Lucy did not mind. The only signs of activity coming through the radio were the arrival or departure of one specialty unit or another, or obligatory, curt inquiries from distant, high-ranking functionaries. For the past hour, even those brief, clipped comments disappeared. Lucy reached over the table. She picked up her radio and twisted the volume knob until it clicked off. She turned the dial back and watched the red light come back to life. A quick electronic beep confirmed that no blame lie with her battery. The airwaves had died on their own.

"I don't dream no more. But that's *my* choice! I come down here when I feel 'em comin' on—the dreams, I mean. They can look high and low, but they can't see me down here 'cuz these walls is solid! Don't build 'em like they used to... no, sir..."

Lucy never noticed Apollo in the basement before this night. At least, she could not *remember* seeing him before. She had yet to hear his thoughts trail off as they did now, faded to dissatisfied rattles rumbling from his throat and out through his nose along with two plumes of tobacco smoke. Lucy wondered how such a person could have escaped her attention, or how she could have evaded Apollo's generous and outspoken stream of consciousness. Mostly, she wondered what he found in his own mind that suddenly quieted him.

The television in the corner remained tuned to the same marathon of game show reruns. With late-night television programming came late-night television commercials, where local sponsors with local budgets could lure customers out of the local audience. The ending credits to an episode of *Truth or Consequences* scrolled off the top of the screen and faded to black. Two piercing blue eyes emerged from the darkness a half-second before a serene, angular face and a very loud sweater joined them. The man turned to the camera and smiled.

"Sometimes, life can be difficult. Sometimes, we cannot quite figure out what is holding us back. Hello, my name is Doctor Martin Glass. I have experienced a difficult life, too. I looked high and low for the answers to my prayers…"

Lucy shivered. She cast an involuntary glance toward the radiator pipe running along the cafeteria's baseboards. It was impossible to know, just by looking, if the building's boiler had lapsed, but Lucy could not help herself. What she did confirm was that Apollo's chair was empty. A wisp of smoke drifted toward the ceiling from a nearby, overflowing ashtray. The flip-top of his crushed cigarette pack lay open to demonstrate the depletion of its contents. She had not seen Apollo lift himself up from his table, nor had she heard him shuffle up the stairs and out of the room. After a careful scan, Lucy concluded that only she and Martin remained.

Doctor Glass wore a sweater which managed to feature each primary color in hazardously contradictory geometric patterns. Beneath this was a pale pink shirt buttoned up to his Adam's apple. The effect of the combination was less than flattering. Limited in fidelity as the local-access camera was, the colors bled into one another on the convex screen and strained the limits of the geriatric television's similarly limited cathode-ray picture tube. Before Lucy could decide if Doctor Glass's top button restricted the flow of blood to his brain, his image faded to a static shot of a cathedral while he continued to speak.

"Men of the cloth offered to trade tithes for salvation with one outstretched palm, while their other hand held their flock at a distance, lest they dare commune directly with the Creators."

The picture on the television shifted again, this time to a familiar room full of founding fathers.

"Men who proclaimed certain truths self-evident declared that all were endowed by the Creators with equal rights to life, liberty, and the pursuit

of happiness. Meanwhile, these enlightened patriots dressed their fellow men in the same chains and shackles as their livestock and auctioned them off to the highest bidder."

This image faded away. In its place appeared a triumphant-looking Lenin, gesturing out toward a crowd with his worker's cap in hand.

"Men of the people, eyes red with fury, came along and shouted that the masses are equal owners of the fruit of their labors—that they could emancipate themselves from need by seizing power and distributing it amongst themselves as equals."

Lenin's portrait faded. The face of Joseph Stalin filled the screen, a toothy smile beneath his broad moustache. This too gradually transitioned to footage of Berliners hammering away at graffitied concrete.

"Behind closed doors, beyond the eyes of the masses, they crowned themselves the new kings. Now we witness their own cyclical downfall."

The history lesson came to an end and the camera returned to Doctor Glass, seated in a scholarly looking office.

"I have heard many a word and many an idea during my search for the truth, my brothers and sisters. So many, that I grew weary. I laid my head down one evening, and I asked 'why can it be so hard to merely survive, let alone thrive, in a world pretty as a rose yet wicked as the thorns?' But the universe graced me with good fortune that night. In dreams, the universe speaks clearly, and the clarity which I received I have eternalized for you all in my book, Chthonics. *Allow my collected wisdom to guide you as you open your mind, bare your soul, and discover the true nature of your deepest desires without the burdens of shame or guilt. I welcome you to bring your questions, your fears, your dreams, and your loved ones down to our revolutionary therapy center, the Oneirological Process Mission. We have renovated the old Loew's Oriental Theater in Bensonhurst and rechristened it as a theater of dreams. Your dreams. My dreams. Our dreams. Do not spend another night in darkness, my brothers and sisters—call right now for a copy of* Chthonics *or pick one up in person today!"*

Darkness swallowed Doctor Glass's office—if it was in fact a real office and not the same set dressing shared by every attorney specializing in personal injury suits and workers' compensation claims. Doctor Glass faded into the shadows, only to be replaced by the opening theme to *Match Game.*

Another commercial, another re-run. Another stagnant night alone. Over the course of her exile, Lucy adapted to the routine of eavesdropping on the radio transmissions of cops who did not have to spend the entire night alone with the likes of Martin Glass or Gene Rayburn. Weeks turned into months and the time in the rearview mirror compressed. Lucy had yet to deal with any disruptions to the pattern. She looked at her radio. Tonight was different: dead air filled the wake left by the earlier surge of chaos. Time slowed to a crawl. Lucy leaned back on her chair's rear legs. Her fingers tapped an impatient rhythm on the tabletop. Even Apollo had better places to be.

Out of the corner of Lucy's eye, the red light on the corner of her radio blinked.

"Six Four lieutenant, on the air?"

Central sounded as if she had just been roused from her own dreams as she attempted to raise up Lieutenant Cordell. There was a pause. The dispatcher began to repeat her message at the same moment that Cordell chose to respond.

"On the air, Central... what is it?"

The lieutenant seemed no more interested in disguising his annoyance and exhaustion than Central did her own drowsy vocal cords.

"Be advised, a call for a family dispute in the Six Four is being code-changed to a 10-34 assault in progress. All of your sectors are still assigned to the job on 63rd Street or out at the hospital in regard. I'm gonna need to pull one of your units off and have them redirect—"

"No, Central! My units stay where they're at!"

"Lieutenant, I can't keep this 34 holding."

The dispatcher offered as patient a response as possible. What she received was more dead air. Lucy saw Cordell in her mind— hastily yanking out his copy of the platoon's roll call and racking his brain. He would pour over his units while letting off some choice expletives to vent his frustration at Central's persistence. Lucy followed along on her own mental copy of the night's roster. Indeed, all four patrol sectors were preoccupied with various aspects of the calamity on 63rd Street. All that was left was—

"Raise up Post 99, Central. You make sure they respond to this one."

Lucy felt her center of gravity shift. The chair's raised front legs drifted further from the floor on their own. Before she could topple backward, Lucy twisted forward and overcorrected. Instead of tumbling backwards, all four legs slammed back onto the cafeteria floor and catapulted her upright.

"Lieutenant, be advised I can't assign a solo post to an assault in progress—"

"Damnit, Central! Just assign the job like I told you!"

Cordell's eruption caught the dispatcher off guard. If she had any colorful response of her own, she made sure to air it before proceeding with her own transmission.

"Is there a Post 99 on the air in the Six Four?"

In nearly three months, Lucy's professional existence lie buried between the deepest lines of Leonard Cordell's personal shit list.

No one else acknowledged her in any official capacity. Necessity—more likely desperation—decreed otherwise. It was not difficult to believe the universe was petty and spiteful as the lieutenant. Or maybe nature could find vacuums and grossly idle police anything but abhorrent for only so long. Central posed a valid question. Lucy prayed that her prolonged non-existence had not robbed her a functional radio voice.

"Yes, Central. This is post—*special* post 99. On the air."

"*Please respond to a 10-34 assault in progress at 300 Bay 17th Street. Third-party caller states he hears a loud argument and the sound of glass breaking inside a first-floor apartment. Check and advise—*"

"*And don't think this changes your damn assignment,*" Cordell suddenly returned to the airwaves. "*If I catch you—*"

"—Special Post 99, read loud and clear."

Cordell was not finished. His shouts faded as Lucy twisted her volume knob low as it would go.

The frozen wind no longer tore at the barren world outside the Fields, yet the motionless air felt colder than Lucy remembered. She pulled her jacket's zipper high as it could go. Her fists balled tightly and dug deep into her pockets. Rigid elbows braced her sides and protected the precious little warmth she carried beneath layers of clothing. Lucy turned a corner and found Cropsey Avenue deserted as the mile she hobbled down Bay Parkway. Bay 17th Street lie not much further ahead and offered no new signs of life. When balmy, summertime Saturday evenings stretched into a Sunday mornings, the narrow, tree-lined blocks of numbered Bay Streets would never completely turn in for the night. Early suns would rise to find old men still perched over checkerboards, covered in the ashes of smoldering De Nobili and Parodi. Their wives slumped in lawn chairs around dwindling jugs of Carlo Rossi and gossiped while their Dixie cups left burgundy rings on the concrete. Entire living rooms rolled out onto the terraces, sidewalks, and intermittent strips of grass beneath canopies of linden and elm leaves. Briny air wafted off Gravesend Bay to deliver the relief which electric fans—or the lack thereof in many cases—could not.

February presented a different landscape. The dog days' gentle currents of natural air conditioning during remained frigid Atlantic squalls, accelerating down identical red brick canyons of low-rise, conjoined apartment buildings. The repetitious indentations of terraced courtyards passed by Lucy on both sides of the street as she sought out building number three hundred. Each courtyard featured two entryways positioned close to the inside corners. Lucy nearly reached the end of the block when she located her destination. If the building featured any signage identifying it as number three-hundred, she did not see it. Nor was it required—the commotion which she heard echoing down the block three buildings earlier reached its pitch and confirmed as much.

"Post 99, Central. You can show me 84 on Bay 17."

Lucy did not need to ask for an apartment number. Across the tenement's entire three-story façade, there was only one set of lights still beaming out into the night. Combined with shouts and curses loud enough to defy the shuttered windows, there was little doubt where the domestic battle was raging. But it was also memory that informed Lucy. Brief as her time in the neighborhood had been, she knew where she was the moment her feet crossed into the building's courtyard for not the first time. There were some addresses, she learned, which accounted for a much higher percentage of emergency calls than their neighbors. One particular apartment in this part of Bath Beach did its best to earn official attention on a biweekly basis. At the end of the previous fall, she helped shuffle a handcuffed man along the same sidewalk toward the back of a waiting patrol car. The man was unusually tall, but wiry and slender everywhere except his midsection, which distended into an obscene beer belly. His odd stature, when combined with his Coke-bottle eyeglasses and unusually high-pitched voice, could fill an unsuspecting adversary with false confidence.   Despite the restraints, he still proved difficult to shepherd for any fewer than four officers. Lieutenant Cordell teased her that she had met a local legend: Adam Valerie.

Slurring and cracking as it bellowed, Lucy was certain who the voice belonged to. Adam's words were nearly unintelligible at any level of intoxication. His intentions were clearer. She slipped past the building's front door—its latch conveniently vandalized and disabled—and jogged up a short set of stairs to the main hallway connecting all the first-floor apartments. She continued to follow the noise around a corner and to the end of the hall. Lucy stopped by the door marked *1A* and took a moment to appreciate the full weight of her tactical disadvantage before making any attempt to announce herself. She leaned in and listened. Something heavy crashed against the other side of the door. Lucy jumped backward and clenched her teeth as whatever it was—whatever it *had been*— shattered on the ground. Only a flimsy door separated her from chaos and violence. For the moment.

Adam had two sons. They were never directly implicated in any of the scams the Six Four's squad of detectives traced back to the Valerie home, but they could be relied upon to make any forays past the front door end in far more than a headache. For the moment, all Lucy could hear was Adam and his distinctive speech. More furniture began to tumble and she decided that she could not wait any longer to determine exactly who occupied the receiving end. Lucy reached out and gave the door three quick taps with her knuckles. The commotion on the other side ceased immediately. She paused again. Her call earned no direct acknowledgement, but it had attracted inquiry from a pair of feet crunching over domestic debris. The person in the apartment now regarded her through the peephole. Without giving them too long to consider, Lucy withdrew her nightstick and landed a few extra whacks against the door.

"Oh, whothefuck is it? Whada'youse want?"

The garbled voice gave Adam Valerie away. His shadow shifted by the base of the doorway as he struggled to angle his thick, prescription lenses against the peephole.

"Police," Lucy replied. "Just checkin' to see if everything's alright in there."

"Police? Nobody here called no *fuckin'* cops," he stammered back at her. "Charlie! Didya' call the cops over to my house, ya little chickenshit?"

"Sir, it's almost four in the morning. Half the block could hear you yelling. Hell, we could hear you from the car before we'd even turned down the block."

It was a calculated bluff. Lucy knew that a veteran of police interaction such as Adam Valerie would only give a young, female officer the time of day with extreme reluctance. If he knew she had come alone—on foot, no less—it could get ugly.

Indeed, the shadow at the bottom of the door disappeared. Debris scattered once more as Adam's feet shuffled away. If he peered through windows and saw that the coast was clear, he might bail into the night. Or he might see through her attempted deception and return with a bat. Lucy gripped her nightstick. The door swung open sooner than she expected.

"Lemme' the fuck outta this shithole!"

He was younger than Adam. Scrawnier, too. If he saw Lucy at all, he gave little indication as he turned on his heel and shouted back into the apartment.

"You didn't earn none'a this cash yourself anyways, ya' grimy old *fuck!*"

Not a single piece of furniture stood upright past the threshold. Lucy was doubtful much of it had been in order prior to more recent skirmishes, but the devastation was still impressive. It sounded as if a bull was running loose in the apartment. A familiar face rounded a corner in the narrow apartment and stampeded into the hallway. Lucy jumped again to avoid being crushed. Bespectacled and pot-bellied, Adam Valerie shook the floor as he emerged.

"You'dunno shit about what I do, boy! I'd beat your head in right here an' now if youse hadn't called the pigs like the ingrateful little shit you are!"

"Nobody called *nobody*."

A third voice stepped out from behind the senior Valerie. The man appeared to be in his mid-twenties with a head full of wacy, brown hair that came even with Adam's own thinning pate.

"We don't need no cops here, ma'am," he continued. "My brother 'n my dad just got into a little disagreement is all. Ain't that right, Charlie?"

"Oh fuck off, Dex," the younger Valerie son hissed. "I've had plenty'a your help tonight."

"Alright, enough," Lucy yelled. "It's way too late for all this noise. Either tell me what happened or go your separate ways."

"Officer," Charlie said as he turned to Lucy, "I can't be on the hook for takin' from someone what ain't rightfully his to begin wit', right? Ain't that the way the law works?"

Lucy reeled. A noxious wave of stale sweat and rotten gums washed over her face. Charlie was significantly shorter than either his older brother or father. He did not look much younger than Dexter, either. Lucy guessed that if he was not in his early twenties, he rapidly approached the end of some particularly rough teens. Patches of light blond fuzz sprung from his upper lip and chin, and failed to make connections at the sides of his mouth. The hair on his head hung in tangled strands down to his shoulders. It was the same light blond that he wore on his face, but darker overall beneath an unaddressed buildup of grease. A dark, red line ran along his forehead, then curved and dribbled down from temple to jaw. Lucy turned slightly and took a deep breath through her mouth, circumventing her sinuses altogether.

"You're bleeding. You wanna tell me about that gash on your head?"

"Fuck it, officer. Maybe I do."

Dexter leaned closer to his younger brother and whispered to him through clenched teeth.

"Charlie, man. I love you, but *shut the fuck up*."

"He can answer for himself," Lucy interrupted. "Everyone wants to talk but nobody wants to tell me what's going on that brought me here."

Charlie opened his mouth to respond. Lucy steeled herself at the sight. Proudly, she stopped herself flinching at the sight of long-neglected yellow teeth framed by brown gunk and sickly gumlines. She braced for another barrage of halitosis, but while Charlie's mouth hung open, no words came out. He looked back to his father and scowled. When his gaze reached his brother, his lips closed tight. A snort escaped Charlie's nose as he turned and stomped back toward the building's front entrance. A volley of fresh insults from Adam chased him through the doorway. Lucy followed him out into the courtyard.

"Kid, wait a second. I gotta call you a bus to look at that cut."

"I don't know if you heard, miss," Charlie called over his shoulder. "Like the old man said, we don't need no cops here."

"Hey," Adam shouted from the other side of the front door. "That little asshole just pinched fifty bucks offa' me, officer! Whaddabout me? What if I wanna press some fuckin' charges, already?"

"Okay," Lucy sighed. "So then tell me what happened and I'll take a report."

"What? *Fuck no!* I don't talk to no *goddamned* cops!"

Lucy wanted to scream. She wanted to yank Adam's face closer to her own and curse and shout until the world ended.

"I don't know that the hell was goin' on here earlier, but it's over now. This is done."

Shock blunted enough of Lucy's anger to release her eyes from the daggers they stared at Adam Valerie. She had not expected the backup she manufactured to dupe the Valeries to actually materialize. While Charlie continued to rush out of the courtyard and onto the sidewalk, another figure approached.

"And you, rookie. Do you know how to listen to your damn radio or does the academy just skip over that completely nowadays?"

She recognized Tabitha Williams from roll call, though she could not recall ever sharing a conversation with the other officer. Lucy looked down at her radio. The red light flared to indicate a transmission, but she heard nothing. She inspected the volume knob. It was still dialed to its lowest volume before turning the radio off entirely. She meant to mute the lieutenant—and blocked everyone else for that matter.

"Officer Williams. I was just… Cordell raised me up over the air and—"

"Yeah, I know. I heard. Next time, don't go in alone. Cordell's a horse's ass. Don't go gettin' yourself hurt on his behalf."

Shame flushed across Lucy's face. Whether it was due to rust or poor judgment, embarrassment gripped her throat.

"I know. I'm sorry, Officer Williams."

"Christ," she snorted, "Tabby's fine. Just tell me what you've gotten yourself into here."

"Shit, Officer—*Tabby*… I don't know. I've got a lot is all I know."

Tabby rolled her eyes. She raised her own radio to her mouth.

"This is Six Four David, Central. Show me 84 with Post 99. No further to this location."

After Tabby received Central's acknowledgement, she walked up to the building's front door and scanned the first-floor hallway. Neither Adam nor Dexter were anywhere to be found.

"It came over from a third party," Lucy continued. "They called and said someone was fighting. As soon as I got here I was promptly informed by both a bleeding man and his aggressor that the both of them *didn't need no cops*."

"Yeah, that sounds right. The Valerie Special. You'll get used to it."

"Sure, maybe if Cordell actually lets me go back on patrol at some point before he finds me an early retirement."

"Careful what you wish for. You've still got a couple decades of nonsense like this ahead of you. In the meantime, pullin' a steady paycheck to coop yourself up all night in the basement of some nut house ain't the end of the world, neither."

Lucy's face flushed again. Her eyes shot downward.

"You know about that too, huh?"

"This is midnights. If it weren't for gossip and gas station coffee we'd never make it to see the sun come back up."

Lucy felt the wind flee her lungs.

"Once it gets back to the lieutenant, that's it for me."

"No, no!" Tabby said. "I didn't mean it like that. Don't worry—Cordell's got his head stuck too far up his own ass to know what's goin' on half the time. And you can trust Melendez, too. He's a good guy for lookin' out for you."

That the conspiracy continued to unwind did little to bring Lucy comfort. She wondered if there was anyone in the Six Four who did not know the extent her little scheme. Even if Cordell was a joke to them, she felt like the punchline—and not for the first time. Lucy might have found temporary escape from the lieutenant's wrath, but the rest of her fellow officers had yet to forget that which aroused it in the first place.

"Come on, let's get outta here," Tabby said. "Looks like tonight, you're getting your wish. My partner slipped and broke his ass. That means you get to close out the tour with me."

"Really?" Lucy chirped.

"Yeah, really. Cordell wasn't thrilled about it, neither. He was even less thrilled when he realized who'd have to fill in. I would've been here sooner but I had to change into a clean uniform first. Let's wrap this up… whatever *this* is that you've got here."

The Valeries were long scattered since the first opportunity. Lucy last saw Charlie stomping away along the darkened sidewalk. His father and brother had seemingly withdrawn back into their apartment, until Lucy saw Dexter appear on the other side of the building's glass-paneled front door. He pushed the door open and followed in his brother's footsteps toward the same sidewalk. A black trash bag dangled from his hand.

"Ladies," he said with a wink.

Lucy took a step and began to stop him. She felt a hand on her shoulder.

"Listen," Tabby said. "Do you hear that?"

Lucy stopped. She listened. When she looked at the building's exterior, she found the Valeries' lights finally extinguished to match their neighbors'.

"Umm, no. I don't hear anything."

"Exactly. No victim, no perp. No crime or report, either. Everyone went their separate ways. Lesson one, rookie: voluntary compliance always beats doing things the hard way."

"The hard way?"

"You didn't look too eager to get between the big man and junior, yourself. One day you might have to, but it didn't go that way tonight. Now, come on. I'm freezing my ass off. That's lesson two: a good cop doesn't get cold."

"Huh. Is there a third one?"

"A good cop doesn't get wet. Or hungry. Neither, really."

Lucy followed Tabby to the street where her patrol car waited. Behind the marked Caprice, she saw Charlie. He glared over the steering wheel of a gray four door, five if the hatchback was counted. Dexter caught up with his brother, jumped into the passenger's seat, and tossed a bag into the back. Leaving not a moment to spare, the car's engine revved before the car door closed. The officers had yet to reach their own vehicle when the Valerie brothers disappeared at the end of the block and into the night. Lucy watched their taillights disappear and reached for the driver's side door handle.

"Ahem…"

Lucy heard someone clearing their throat. She realized that she and Tabby were both standing on the same side of the car.

"Sorry, kid. Your seat is on the other side."

Four

The gas pedal sputtered and quaked under Charlie's foot. His right hand cranked the shifter into third gear while his other foot ripped the clutch. No matter how artful his handling of the car, sickly noises chased the '77 Nova down Eighteenth Avenue. If it woke up the entire neighborhood, the racket never rose above the curses Charlie hurled at his father in his mind. He glanced to his right. The imaginary expletives found a new target in Dexter Valerie.

Charlie swiped at the sweat beading by the sides of his forehead. The evening left his mind anxious and his bloodstream short on scag as morning approached. His eyes twitched between the road and his brother.

Dexter. Confidant. Older. Taller. A drunk who still swore he was nigh upon a year clean. Even seated by his side, Charlie regretted that his eyes needed to angle upward just to connect a proper scowl. His fingers constricted around the steering wheel. No such anxieties were mirrored in Dexter's posture. Charlie's fingernails dug even deeper.

Charlie had planned to spend the evening as he spent any other—planted in front of the Saturday Late Movie. Dennis Weaver and his faceless foe inside the tanker truck were scheduled to engage in the greatest game of chicken ever immortalized in made-for-television cinema. Before the opening credits could roll, Dexter intervened with other plans. Charlie wished he never left the couch. He remembered sitting outside that house for what felt like hours. In the judgment of his wristwatch, Dexter and his girlfriend were gone fewer than fifteen minutes. When they returned from their visit—collecting something owed to a common acquaintance—they bore the stains of brutality. Clothes, faces, hands. After the streetlights died and the world went dark, even if he could not see it, Charlie could not deny the smell of blood. Dexter and Bethany carried it back into the car with them. They dropped her off and spent the better part of the following hour working like men possessed, scrubbing and scouring the car and then themselves. The old man did not notice—until Charlie lifted the bills from his unattended wallet. It came to blows and in the end, Charlie wore fresh blood. The cops saw. They had not cared. If anyone found a red smear on the inside of his car now, who else would care? Charlie knew the answer from experience. Nobody batted an eye at another roughed up lowlife.

Charlie's hand pulled away from the shifter and probed the pocket of his hooded sweatshirt. His fingers slipped past a pack of Marlboro Golds. Beneath it, folded tightly, was the stolen twenty. It slid back and forth between his thumb and index finger. Charlie's mind wandered back to 63rd Street. After the lights died, all that had been left to light the neighborhood was the full moon overhead. When the front window flashed thirteen times, the white glare was blinding. The Nova's windows were rolled up tight. He could barely hear the gunshots. For all his trouble, Dexter promised his brother another twenty when they reached their destination. Forty bucks would see him steady in the coming week.

"You can relax."

Charlie's hand jerked away from the stolen money. He could feel Dexter's eyes on him. He withdrew his hand from his pocket and returned his sleeve to his damp temples. The cloth did what it could, though not enough to diminish Charlie's growing self-consciousness.

"Everything went fine today. Nobody saw a damn thing."

"All that tricky, witchy shit worked *too good*," Charlie replied. "Both'a my headlights burned out, too. Had me peelin' outta there blind. What woulda happened if the cops pulled us over for some petty bullshit like that? What was I supposed to say, when the passenger sittin' next to me and his psycho girlfriend in the back seat are covered in—"

"Glad to hear you're suddenly the discrete type. I've been tellin' Bethany an' people over at the Mission that—y'know—there might be hope for you yet. But you gotta get that petty shit with Pops under control first."

"Ain't his t'begin with," Charlie howled. "That old fuck never earned an honest buck in his life."

"Yeah, an' half the neighborhood heard you shoutin' as much. Bitch about the headlights and the cops all you want, but new lightbulbs are cheap. The bond I had to post for Pop from his last arrest, on the other hand…"

Charlie's grip on the steering wheel grew tighter. That his brother had a valid point only made him angrier. He bit his lip.

The car turned onto 86th Street. The marquee of the old Loew's Oriental hung over an empty sidewalk. Although its lights were dimmed for the night, the black letters spelling out the former movie theater's new name were clear: *The Oneirological Process Mission of Brooklyn*. The marquee was a somber sight for Charlie.

After Dexter showed him how to bypass the fire exits without triggering any alarms, the brothers had sat through an entire day's run of *Temple of Doom*. Years passed. The building, in its repurposed state, was mournful. Over the past decade, Charlie had witnessed three of Bath Beach's cinemas draw their curtains for the last time. All three had been on 86th Street. None had been more than a five-minute flight from Adam Valerie's wrath. When the Loew's closed—the last of the neighborhood's venerable movie houses—Charlie found himself abruptly deprived of sanctuary. It was an afternoon spent wandering in grief. The Nova retraced those steps as the theater faded in the rearview mirror. Ultimo Delicatessen shined in the distance. The all-hours corner store introduced Charlie to movies on video tape. The owner rented them out. He even had a little, faded television hooked up to one of the new players. Getting chased out for watching the movies and never renting anything became Charlie's new past time. Eventually they gave up chasing him. One of the overnight clerks found another way to squeeze a buck out of Charlie.

"Y'know, that's another reason to lose that smack habit," Dexter continued. "You shoot every dollar you get your hands on straight into your arm."

"You of all people wanna tell me to *Just Say No*?"

"Well, it ain't like I can't speak from experience. I got cleaned up… got a job. A girl."

Charlie sucked his teeth. Sober or otherwise, the night's events did little to cast his older brother as the picture of success.

"Alright, you wanna keep the habit? Suit yourself. You can keep the bullshit fights. Keep smashin' car windows and tossin' ashtrays for pennies, too. You can either choose to start gettin' shit done— like me—or you can stay *Chuckie Cheese* forever."

Charlie's heart sank. The nickname made his vision flash red. It followed him from the 9th grade—not coincidentally the last time he attended school voluntarily. If it stayed confined behind the walls of James Buchanan High School, Charlie would have been grateful. But the world was small, and southern Brooklyn was a minuscule, insular microcosm adrift within. Paths crossed. Faces Charlie could not recall independently would turn toward him. *'Chuckie Cheese?'* random passersby would confirm amongst each other. *'Chuckie Cheese!'* they would cry in celebration. Dexter knew. At first, if he was present, he came to his little brother's defense. Charlie ground his teeth when he heard him invoke it now. He knew Dexter understood the sting. That made it more painful.

"I ain't no smack addict," Charlie growled. "If my memory serves, wasn't too long ago you weren't much better off. Not when dad had to lug you over his shoulder down to the E.R. to get your stomach pumped."

"I never said I was better than you. If it hadn't been for Doctor Glass, if he hadn't been makin' the rounds, spreadin' the word—"

"Or *preying*."

"Call it what you want, but sometimes a desperate person needs more than activated charcoal. I wasn't gonna kick booze just 'cuz I spent a couple nights dryin' out in Gravesend General. If Doctor Glass hadn't opened my eyes, you'da been Adam Valerie's only child a long time ago. That's what I've been tryin' to get through your head. The program the Doctor peddles to all the fiends and deadbeats, the folksy shit on TV, that's just scratchin' the surface. You say the word and I'll make sure the Doc puts you on the fast track with Bethany an' me."

"Sounds like you're tellin' me there's a monkey on my back," Charlie said. "An' Doctor Martin Glass—patron savior of downtrodden mopes such as myself—wants me to trade it for a demon over my shoulder."

Charlie sent an involuntary glance in the rearview mirror. There did not appear to be any malevolent spirits peeking back at him from the back seat. The passenger's seat next to him was a different matter. Charlie watched Dexter's nostrils flare. It was his brother's turn to fume and grate his teeth in frustration.

"You can be funny about it with me if that's how you wanna be, but watch your mouth," Dexter warned. "Bethany ain't so patient. She ain't afraid to make you a believer… the hard way."

Charlie's mind returned to when Dexter first introduced him to Bethany. They had wandered the artificial coast of Gravesend Bay in search of relief from the August heat. The receding sun inched behind the coast of New Jersey on the other side of the Bay, but the cement beneath their feet continued to broil. The journey ended muggy as it began when they reached the end of the path and found themselves in the parking lot of Ceasar's Bay Bazaar. With no relief found, they decided to test car door handles instead. Charlie was no stranger to the task. He could play it cool enough. After an hour, change adding to nearly ten dollars jangled in his pockets. Ultimately, he came up short. Bethany smoked him and Dexter both. Charlie did not see her yank a locked handle all night. She wandered from car to car, from one end of the parking lot to the other, solemn and impassive. If the pin was down, the lock still disengaged. Her pockets filled quickly, and not long afterward she started pulling stereos. When she squeezed a third one into her backpack, Charlie signaled to Dexter that it was time to throw in the towel. This decision was reached a moment too late. Charlie heard the oncoming rush of feet beating against the cracked asphalt.

Wheezing and blustering, the security guard zigged and zagged between rows of parked cars. The sight would have made Charlie buckle with laughter if his release from Spofford a week earlier had not been accompanied by a warning—a sincere *promise* in formal writing—to keep a bunk in the detention center open for him if he opted not to keep his nose clean. An electric motor screamed and then clattered to a halt behind him. The golf cart's suspension groaned as the guard's partner leapt out.

Charlie was ready to submit his wrists for as painless a cuffing he could wish when he heard Bethany's voice. The words leaving her mouth sounded strange, unintelligible. It was impossible to recall, fluency aside, when the stark impressions of what happened next dominated Charlie's recollection. Nor could he remember exactly from where Bethany drew the blade, but the horizontal line it opened along her opposing palm glowed vivid as the reddened wake left in the sky by the departed sun. The guards' pursuit must also have been distracted, Charlie reasoned, for some time passed where no one succeeded in tackling him to the ground. He did not know if they stood as transfixed. His own eyes refused to follow anything other than the red streams and heavy droplets sliding down Bethany's forearm. She shouted. They were similar or maybe the same words as before, but clearer. So clear, Charlie felt as though his ears were bypassed altogether. Her words were born and echoed and absorbed into his brain without passing his skull. They withdrew to the far corners of his mind and the world lurched a shade dimmer. Slowly at first, the lights towering high over the parking lot flickered and withered. Beginning over the spot they stood, darkness rippled outward in waves. Dexter yanked on Charlie's arm hard enough to peel his feet from the pavement just as the black tide broke against the backlit signs over each of the strip mall's storefronts. The three glided through the shadows before the guards could recompose themselves. When they rounded the corner onto Shore Parkway, Charlie pulled free of his brother's grasp. He demanded an answer—any kind of tether to reconcile a sound universe to that which he just witnessed. Bethany ignored him. She gazed out at the chaos she delivered unto the shopping plaza and smiled. Dexter spoke, but Charlie heard no answers there, either. He mentioned the universe and the unseen—about things that wait and things that dream. Charlie tried to resurrect his brother's precise words. It was those distant things, he remembered Dexter warn him, always listening for just the right invitation to traverse the chasm and impose their presence. Charlie guided the Nova away from 86th Street and onto one of the residential side streets. Months later, exactly what Dexter and Bethany were inviting had become no clearer, though they appeared engaged to the task full-time.

"You take care of your business," Charlie sighed, "Let me worry about mine.

The car was clean—nearest to clean as Charlie felt could be achieved under their present circumstances. Now it was time to settle up with the man himself. Though he had been promised compensation, Charlie was instructed to once more remain with the vehicle while Dexter and Bethany met privately with Martin Glass. Charlie found no complaints with such an arrangement. His hand returned to the money in his pocket. Twenty dollars slid back and forth between Charlie's fingers. Dozens of wants fought for primacy within his imagination's spotlight, each a far happier alternative to enjoying the presence of a man of equal parts new age evangelizer and dispatcher of dark deeds. One particular desire stood tallest. If all Doctor Martin Glass had to offer was a few bills more, that would be more than satisfactory for Charlie.

Tires shimmied against the curb. Charlie sucked his teeth and huffed at himself. He cursed his frayed nerves, fiending to the point of distraction. If Dexter held any criticisms of his driving, he kept it to himself. His attention lay elsewhere. Charlie followed his brother's eyes through the front windshield and toward a house past the side of the road.

Evidently long-neglected and overgrown, the two-story house rose over a double wide, wild copse of a yard. It was an antiquated archetype of the Victorian manors which, as decades passed, increasingly found themselves squeezed into the shadows of Bath Beach's more modern developments. The dense vegetation surrounding Doctor Glass's estate formed one last, desperate bulwark against time and the crushing gravity of the New York real estate market. Green shingles covered the façade—roof and walls alike—despite a few, sporadic exceptions where patches of decaying tar wore bare. Several window frames sneered jagged glass teeth instead of panes. Others were sealed by weathered patchworks of plywood. An octagonal tower jutted from the left side of the house and up through the covered porch. It loomed not much higher than the rest of the structure's sagging, gabled roof and the crowded, bare branches of unpruned maples. The house managed, barely, to survive the fate of most of its generation— summer retreats perched atop broad, stately lawns until forgotten by the Manhattanites who cultivated them. Where disinterested or absentee heirs failed to break their inheritances apart in the Surrogate's Court, time prevailed. The colony of seasonal retreats consolidated to a suburbia when veterans returned from fighting in the Pacific and Europe. They turned their backs on the crowded enclaves of the lower East Side and nearer tenement blocks of Bushwick and Red Hook in search of room to grow. Extended families followed and became neighbors on shared blocks. They all bought cars and demanded driveways. One plot of land could be carved into ten or twenty multifamily tracts.

As enduring survivors often do, the house became enigmatic—a local legend, unconquered and yet dilapidated to the point of seeming abandonment. Naturally, neighborhood children would whisper life into the monsters hidden within. Charlie passed by countless times as a child, breath held and legs scurrying, without imagining it was still home to a real, living person. When Dexter experienced spiritual rebirth and began to impress upon his younger brother a more sober, purpose-filled existence, Charlie learned the identity of the house's true owner. No formal introduction was necessary, not that any such offer had been extended. Not satisfied to merely swindle Charlie's favorite movie theater or live rent-free inside Dexter's head, Doctor Martin Glass inserted his face and voice into every other commercial interruption during the televised film marathons keeping Charlie company throughout the night. Charlie leaned on his elbow and stared through the driver's side window. His eyes travelled from one shattered window to another. He wondered if he would see that same face from the television staring back. Despite the certainty that he did not wish to find Glass's eyes gazing upon his own, the search persisted. Charlie had yet to observe any signs of life when he heard the passenger's door handle click.

"Just cool it for a while out here," Dexter said. "Bethany'n me gotta go talk to Doctor Glass. I'll let 'im know how good we did—how good *you* did tonight."

"Mm-hmm," Charlie replied. "Pleasure's all mine."

"You *did* do good. I'm hard on you, I know. But it's because, if you're ready to get yourself straight, I think there's a place for you in the grand scheme 'a things."

The night's residual adrenaline ebbed in Charlie's veins. It left corroded nerves in its wake as it drained away, and an undercurrent of nausea rose in his stomach. His mind screamed at him to get right—*soon*. As a result, Charlie did not hear much of his brother's praise, nor did he provide any response. When he managed to once more reassert control over his senses, he saw Dexter strolling toward a silver Camaro parked two cars ahead of them. Its own door opened. Bethany stepped out.

"Takes a lot more than some boosted car stereos to trade up to an IROC," Charlie mused to himself.

When Charlie last saw Bethany, quickly dropping her off behind the rented house she shared with Dexter in Gravesend, her straight, pale blonde hair was stained dark as mahogany. Not a splotch of blood remained to dye it now. She lit a cigarette as Dexter approached her. They spoke in low voices. Tobacco smoke mixed with steam as she exhaled into the freezing, early morning air. Charlie found his joints too rigid to crank down the window and his conscious brain too distracted to eavesdrop on the discussion. Suddenly, Dexter and Bethany's heads turned toward the house. Charlie followed their line of sight to the porch and nearly jumped when he saw the figure silently manifest in the house's doorway atop the front steps. The unilluminated yard was filtered from the light of the full moon by a dense and tangled ceiling of barren tree branches. Even with eyes strained, it was too dark to discern any features finer than a rough silhouette belonging to a tall man of average-to-slight build, hair neatly parted to the side and a clean-shaven jawline. Charlie recognized the shapes from television. Doctor Glass stepped back and held the door open for his guests as the three of them converged on the porch. Bethany and Dexter stepped inside, but the Doctor appeared to linger for a moment. Charlie could not see clearly enough to tell if Martin Glass returned his gaze. Charlie begged his eyes to move away. When this failed, he shuddered and slumped down in the seat.

Seconds passed with the urgency of idle hours. Charlie summoned whatever remained of his constitution. His feet pushed the rest of his body back upright in the driver's seat. The house's front door was shut. His brother, Bethany, and Glass were nowhere to be seen. Without so much as a moment's hesitation, Charlie's right hand found the gear stick. His feet shoved the gas and clutch and the car lurched away from the curb. The glow of Ultimo Delicatessen materialized in his mind. His nerves were far too numb to provide any reliable feedback, but muscle memory did what it could to pilot the car and shepherd him to the bodega.

86th Street was one of the primary arteries spanning southern Brooklyn. Beginning at the shore of the Narrows in Bay Ridge, it bent at an angle through Fourth Avenue and proceeded as an unrelenting, straight line through Dyker Heights. After passing Fourteenth Avenue, it divided Bath Beach to the south from Bensonhurst on its northern side. When the street reached the old Loew's Oriental Theater at Eighteenth Avenue, the elevated tracks of the D Line swept overhead from New Utrecht Avenue. The elevated train tracks continued until they dipped south along Stillwell Avenue to deliver riders to the line's terminus on Coney Island—but 86th Street punched ahead undeterred. It traced the edge of the Marlboro Houses before terminally fracturing in a five-way intersection with McDonald Avenue, Shell Road, and Avenue X amongst the decrepitude of Gravesend's industrial core, not far from the enduring two-by-two block ghost of that settlement's original layout. The particular segment which ran beneath the D Line, onto which Charlie now turned, was a magnet for unconventional nightlife. A crossroads alongside a 24-hour mass transit network, it was a natural haven for round-the-clock business. Boutiques and sundries extended their storefronts onto the sidewalk during conventional hours of operation. Long after sunset, unwavering—if not necessarily flattering—incandescent fluorescence poured down from the underside of the train tracks, inviting restless multitudes into second-story businesses and backdoor operations—after-hours clubs, bookmakers, massage parlors. Stoic men with broad shoulders kept watch by the never-shuttering entryways of indistinctly marked storefronts, peddling dope to folks they deemed too pathetic to be narcs. A live animal butcher specializing in poultry and goats rolled up its gates as Charlie drove by.

The Nova drifted away from the main road and crossed between the columns supporting the elevated track and into the service lane. The car was still at an angle when Charlie shifted into neutral and stomped down on the parking brake in front of Ultimo Delicatessen. He flicked the newly replaced headlight bulbs on and off several times, then waited. His mind screamed for the man on the other side of the store's greasy windows. The only notable response came from a goat, crying somewhere behind him by the butcher's shop. Impatience building, Charlie repeated the signal he sent toward the store with his headlights. What few portions of Ultimo's windows were left unobscured by iron security bars, sun-bleached cigarette advertisements, and excessively piled merchandise indicated only the fuzziest silhouettes of the persons and their activities within. Desperation seized upon Charlie as a third salvo erupted from the headlamps, hastier than those preceding it, and longer in duration. He scanned the roadway and his mirrors for bystanders, or—more importantly—cops who would have, by now, certainly deduced the nature of his intensifying indiscretions. Nothing stirred. When he was sufficiently confident that the coast remained clear, he glanced back toward the store. A blurry profile moved away from the counter and toward the front door. After an appraising pause, the door creaked open. A bell attached to the door chimed over the man's head. Puffy, pale features cast an unnatural contrast with the dark, tight curls of hair gelled against his scalp. If Charlie were inclined to grade dealers for customer service, Franco would have ranked dead last. The quality of his stock was unreliable, though his exorbitant prices could always be depended upon. Be that as it may, Charlie was in no mood—or physical control—to shop around, and as a matter of proximity and operating hours Franco earned his patronage by default.

"Will you hold your goddamned horses, already?"

Franco squinted at the car which had hailed him out into the night. His sneer faded when his eyes met the man behind the wheel.

"Well, look who it is," he crowed through the driver's side window, "*Chuckie Cheese*, the legend himself!"

What remained of the weak stream pumping through Charlie's veins ran cold. His mind wondered what would happen if he locked his arm around Franco's own, now perched along the top of the opened car window, shifted into gear, and mashed the accelerator. He imagined the unexpected ride would make Franco's smile disappear. If Charlie's foot held the accelerator down long enough, he would be searching for someone else to keep him supplied. As it was, Charlie could barely move as he was forced to endure Franco's small talk.

"Y'know, you gotta gimme a minute. I can't just drop everything to hop over the counter for everyone who rolls up to the door, flashing their headlights at me like a madman."

"Yeah, real sorry," Charlie croaked. "I know how long that checkout line can get at a quarter after four on a Sunday morning. Don't worry, though—wasn't plannin' on keepin' you long. So, how you doin'?"

"Don't worry about how I'm doin', my man. How *you* doin'?"

It was abundantly clear that Charlie was doing quite poorly. He was certain Franco saw the bullets of sweat running past his temples. He spoke through clenched teeth. It took every ounce of his remaining strength to form full sentences while suppressing his diaphragm's urge to heave.

Charlie chose to stop caring. He was in no shape to dance tonight. His hand dipped into the sweatshirt's pocket. His thumb cupped the money into the underside of his palm. There would be no need for Franco to read out the daily specials. Franco's left hand pulled away from their shake. His right hand dipped into the car and pressed onto Charlie's opened palm. He could feel the tight square of folded tinfoil resting in his hand as he clenched and pulled back down. The transaction concluded without money being counted or product being inspected. Franco could have passed him pure, uncut, powdered laxative. Charlie took that which he was given. Franco chuckled and stood back up. He hugged himself and shivered dramatically as he turned to walk back to the store.

"You stay warm now, y'hear? Take that somewhere real cozy. I seen too many good customers drop dead frozen on the streets on nights like these."

The greasy glass door swung open again. Franco laughed to himself as he strut through. Charlie watched his twisted mouth disappear inside. Where the cackle of a mirthful dope peddler should have been, Charlie heard only the continued bleating of the goat in the nearby butcher's store.

One solitary vehicle roared along 86th Street. Charlie's Nova screeched into a U-turn. He pointed it back toward the spot where he had dropped off his brother. His tire straddled the yellow line, thoughtfully considering the demands of urgency against recklessness as he navigated back to the side street. A few red lights were taken after preliminarily surveys for patrolling cops. Charlie made the final turn and nearly snagged his front bumper on another car parked on the side of the road as he careened into the empty spot in front of it. Rows of white knuckles reluctantly unlocked their grip from the steering wheel. The car's engine chugged as it idled. Charlie scanned the neighborhood for any potential witnesses to his not-quite crash landing not far from Martin Glass's house. The ancient, decaying estate still huddled between the leafless knotted maples. The only noticeable commotion came from the wind. It picked up in his absence, Charlie realized. He watched the tree branches scratch against one another in bursts with every gale passing down the block.

Charlie reached for the glovebox. From inside, he removed his kit and placed it on his lap. It was a small, black, rectangular bag rimmed on three sides by a zipper. Easily concealable, durable, well organized. Clean. Charlie imagined that any self-respecting heroin aficionado would have been proud to call a kit like his their own. He removed a spoon from within and unwrapped the tinfoil square he received from Franco. As was the case earlier, there was no time to examine the quality of the powder, nor was there an abundance of light in which to properly admire it. Charlie flexed the muscles in his arm to control the tremors and tapped a small pile onto the spoon. A moment later, Bic flames licked at its underside. The powdered heap sank beneath rolling bubbles. He burned what remained of his patience to let the liquid cool. The syringe's needle drank greedily and filled its chamber with a delicate amber glow. Charlie cinched the belt higher into his armpit and tied it off. Its edges dug into his damp skin as he flexed his hand. When a vein on his forearm bulged out at him, he was grateful. He did not look forward to the day when such a search would require him to remove his socks. The needle prodded the dilated blood vessel. He gritted his teeth to steady himself and pressed against his skin until it gave way. His thumb pushed down on the plunger.

The belt went slack. Charlie gasped, then sank into the car seat. The muscles in his neck melted and the window felt cool where his forehead slid down against it. Outside, in the cold night, stars strobed and flickered across the crisp, clear sky. Constellations and bands and clusters. A billion colossal, nuclear furnaces made the most of a passing moment to pierce the subdued artificial glow of the city with just enough power to reach across the void and lay a photonic finger down upon Brooklyn. Normally, the crushing immensity of it would have given Charlie a headache. But with his heart rate falling and, despite the cold universe smothering the world, he felt warmth rising from within. The stars in the sky began to multiply as more lights shot out from the corners of his eyes to join them. His breath adopted a tinny reverberation in his ears. The noise slowed and grew deeper while Charlie tried to put a finger on it. It morphed into something more familiar. Something recent.

"Mah-ah-aah..."

The muscles around Charlie's eyes twitched. He turned his head to direct his ear toward the world outside. While his heart pumped opiated blood through his body, he forced himself to listen. It was the same bleating he heard minutes earlier when he met with Franco. Charlie was immobilized—his limbs too sluggish and unresponsive to pick himself up and look for the source of the intrusive, bestial cry. It was not directly in front of him—that much his slack head could confirm. His eyes drifted to the sideview mirror just outside the window. A streetlamp not too far behind the car cast a singular spotlight down onto the center of the road.

"Maah-ah-ah-aah!"

A bright, white hoof reached over the threshold of the cone of light. Charlie watched in the mirror as an albino goat ambled into view. Light flared off the curls of its pure white fleece. Its nose and eyes glowed a ruddy pink. Charlie wondered what kind of butchers would allow such a striking animal to slip away from them.

The goat stopped suddenly and turned a pair of bright pink and red eyes to meet Charlie's hazy stare. Unable to fight the narcotic mixture pumping through his veins, his eyelids finally succumbed to their growing weight. Either a second or an hour passed and Charlie blinked hard before prying his eyes open. He found the circle of light on the road to be goatless. His eyelids shuddered and slammed shut again. An unexpected shock forced them open once more, and sent Charlie shooting upright in his seat. He reinflated his lungs with one quick, loud snort through his running nose. His heart raced. His arms extended outward, smacking his knuckles against the steering wheel, then returning to hug his chest as he flexed and stretched his shoulders. Charlie blinked a few times, glancing around himself suspiciously. He tried to gauge how long he had been out. His mind began to clear more quickly. The high was nearly gone. Charlie cursed Franco for passing off weak junk at a premium price. He cursed himself for getting suckered.

Charlie inhaled deeply through his nose. While his high drifted away faster than he would have preferred, no signs of withdrawal— no headache, no nasal congestion—appeared to remanifest. All things considered, he felt a way he had not in quite some time: he felt good.

The world around Charlie offered little in revealing how long he had passed out. The sky was still dark. The same stars still burned through the cold, dry air. Dawn gave no hints of approaching the horizon. The only light came from the same streetlamp behind him. Charlie held his breath to listen for the albino goat's wailing bleat. He reached up to adjust the rearview mirror, hoping to scan the area to find where the goat scampered off. The mirror swiveled leftward with a jerk and in its center stood a man draped in a billowing black shroud.

"Holy-Jesus-Fuck," Charlie shouted.

He stared at the figure. His mind raced, and among the hundred other scattered thoughts was the certainty, though not through any visual confirmation, that the invisible face behind the impossibly dark cloth stared back. Charlie spun around in the driver's seat to make direct eye contact with the stranger standing behind his car. He held his breath and squinted. Although standing in the center of the cone of light that beamed down from the streetlamp above, all he could see was the silhouette of a man wrapped entirely within a copious, yet thin veil. The material twisted and whirled toward the sky as if it were a pitch-black flame. Apart from this gown, the man beneath appeared otherwise unclothed.

"This crazy bastard's out here in February naked," Charlie thought aloud, seeking comfort in the sound of his own voice. "He's not… freezing?"

Exposed to the night, the nearly-nude man did not appear to shiver. For as long as Charlie watched, he did not move at all until, without warning, the figure's right arm rose perpendicular to his side and pointed straight out from his shoulder.

"Fuck this!" Charlie yelled.

He spun back around, grabbed for the gear shifter, and pulled downward. The shifter refused to move. Charlie's foot mashed the gas pedal but was met with silence. His eyes darted down to the ignition. The key was gone.

Charlie yanked at the door handle and pushed. He misjudged his composure. The asphalt rushed up toward his face and he sprawled onto the ground. Charlie's limbs frantically jabbed at the road until he found himself spinning around to face the mad man looming behind his car. The figure still stood ten or fifteen feet behind the Nova. His right hand stretched outward, freed from the black veil and hanging in the air. From his closed fist hung a long, slack, rope. Charlie could see it undulating, slithering. Whoever it was—*whatever* it was—it carried with it a snake.

"What the fuck d'you want, man? What kinda crazy bullshit is this? Who the fuck are you?"

Try as he could to focus, there were no identifiable features beneath the violently whipping veil. What was undeniable to Charlie was that the shroud now shifted downward where the figure's mouth should have logically appeared.

"That name will be yours to know."

Its voice was serene, distinctly masculine, and comforting—yet carried no warmth. Charlie could not place the accent on a map, but he knew it was not from Brooklyn. Despite the conditions of the season, no steam escaped from the stranger's mouth as he spoke. Nor, Charlie realized, had any steam escaped his own mouth when he shouted moments earlier. There was no ice left in the air at all. Charlie reached up and touched his face. Despite standing out in the open for nearly a full minute, he had yet to feel any effects on his body temperature. He looked upward. None of the barren tree branches canopying Martin Glass's vast estate stirred. Not far away, the stranger's shroud twisted and billowed as if gripped by a tornado.

When the figure began to walk backwards, Charlie's only surprise was that the sudden motion had not caused him to flinch. Within the comfortable void descended upon the frozen city, fear had departed his body. The figure continued to back away until its feet passed the boundaries cast by the overhead lamp. As the light faded from its veil, Charlie saw the material's hue change from pitch black to a brilliant white. Beneath, skin reflected an almost human pinkish-pale. Only the man's eyes remained black, now distinctly piercing through the sheer cloth and directly onto Charlie. Charlie looked down and realized his feet now hung slack several inches above the ground. His muscles relaxed, and he let his head tilt backward. In the sky overhead, the stars began to stir. They drifted and spun around a distinctly dark spot directly over the stranger's bald head.

"One who asks the darkness for truth must accept the truth the darkness reveals. Does this one seek to accept?"

"Yes," Charlie gasped.

There was a momentary lapse in his serenity where Charlie was unable to determine where such a response came. Before he could consider it for long, the stranger spoke again.

"When to our highest depths,
behind Heaven's glimmering coat,
With the churning, boiling madness
of Adam's children descending,
Bonded raiders with borrowed saddles
mounted upon manie a black goat,
Past barren Elysia gallop legion buckriders
o'er abyssal fingers extending."

A horrible odor surrounded Charlie as the figure spoke. Sulfur and rotting meat. The sweet tinge of organic death. Trying to distract from the smell, he thought about the voice. It seemed familiar, but remembering the owner proved difficult. It was someone Charlie had not heard from in years, belonging to someone at the tip of his tongue. Charlie turned back toward the voice. The person beneath the veil had taken on a new form. It was a middle-aged man, or maybe an old woman. Or was it a little kid? Charlie had difficulty focusing on any one individual feature before the rest would fade away. Just like its voice, it was recognizable but ultimately impossible to place. Whoever it was, the snake remained firmly grasped in its extended right hand.

"What do you mean?" Charlie asked softly, his voice growing drowsy in his own ears. "A black… goat?"

The figure offered no response, but the snake began to writhe more energetically, spinning like a helix. Its head lifted straight toward the sky. Charlie followed. The stars moved more distinctly, now spinning in greater numbers and at an increased pace. Trails of light bled from them toward the center of a hungry vortex. Thin, bright pillars rose from edges of the Earth's horizon, stretching up and joining the light being siphoned into the dark hole at the center of the spinning universe. The ground beneath the streetlamp dimmed as its own light was pulled away, falling instead into the sky. Charlie became aware that his perspective shifted by several feet. He looked down toward the dark asphalt which had grown more distant beneath him. His eyes turned upward again to follow the paths of light as they bled into the black whirlpool. An aperture grew in its center and expanded rapidly. Charlie peered within and, like a bird gazing down as it flew across the Grand Canyon, watched the yawning of a vast chasm beyond the cosmos. Ridges and ranges of light and darkness twisted and writhed. Entire mountain ranges and oceans drifted between one another until fading away to be replaced by fresh others in an unending cycle of erosion and construction.

Meanwhile, the world around Charlie grew darker as its own light continued to be torn away. The streetlamp, now below him, had nothing left to give. Its filament flickered and popped. Sparks fluttered downward and Charlie's viewpoint followed until both crashed down onto the pavement. He landed hard, knocking the air from his chest and the waning light from his eyes. He gasped as his diaphragm desperately pulled in frozen, winter air to reinflate his lungs. A cold wind washed over him. Charlie struggled to unfold his crumpled arms and perch himself back upright, but pain lanced his joints. Fingers locked onto his limbs. A pair of foreign hands reached under to pull him up. When Charlie opened his eyes, he was sitting upright again. Doctor Glass's stern expression was only a few inches past his own nose.

"Whatever they said, you should listen to them."

Glass whispered slowly and softly. With another yank, he pulled Charlie up onto his feet and spun him to rest against the trunk of the Nova.

"You should listen to what they have to say, because even though they do not always tell the truth... they will tell you what you need to know."

Clear as his mind had felt moments earlier, it was overstuffed with cotton balls now. Charlie stared at Martin, still unsure how either of them had arrived at this particular place and not nearly coherent enough to parse the man's words.

"Charlie, what the fuck?"

He heard his brother's voice. Dexter sounded beyond annoyed and much closer to enraged.

"Just for once... just for twenty minutes, can I leave you alone without you fuckin' yourself up?"

Charlie looked down to see his kit—the bag, the needle, the spoon—scattered on the ground not far from his car's still-ajar front door. The wind picked up the foil pouch. It tumbled and scattered its remaining powder into the night.

"Fuck me," was all Charlie could summon.

"We're done here," Dexter huffed. "I'm sorry, Doctor."

He scurried up to Charlie and dragged him around the front of the car to the passenger's side.

"No need to apologize," Doctor Glass said as he stepped onto the sidewalk behind them. "In fact, in light of your earlier requests, I must insist on treating him personally."

"Really?"

As Dexter lowered Charlie into the passenger seat, his glare intensified.

"He's a little more trouble than your regular deadbeat, is all."

"All the more reason I should oversee his care myself. A particularly complicated patient deserves special attention."

Charlie felt Dexter shove his legs into the car, then slam the door shut. Continued mumbling indicated that his brother's conversation with Glass was not entirely complete, but the fog banks rolling back over Charlie's mind made it impossible to follow. Before long, he felt the car rock as Dexter sat down behind the steering wheel and turned the ignition. Charlie's head returned to rest against the window as the Nova's tires spun over the street. He could feel the cold seeping through as he located his own reflection in the side view mirror. His skin was paler than ever. There was dried vomit matted into his peach fuzz mustache and the light blond whiskers that sprouted in patches on his cheeks. Where there should have been the reflection of an empty backseat just past his shoulder, he saw the shadow of a bald head. Scenes of exhaustion and narcotics—of murder and the cosmos—it all overcame Charlie and his body shut down.

Five

When the marked Chevrolet Caprice crossed the sidewalk into the parking lot of the Getty station, its undercarriage skidded across the pavement. Tabby winced involuntarily at the loud scrape and glanced at the odometer. Thirty-five thousand miles. She sympathized with the vehicle. Despite only a year on the road, its mileage was running far higher than the engineers at General Motors intended. The Radio Motor Patrol lifestyle to which the car was subject turned out to be a bit more demanding than most. When her tour of duty ended in another couple of hours, the keys would be handed off to the next two officers and the RMP would be ridden hard for another eight hours. The Sixty Fourth Precinct's shared fleet consisted of a dozen or so interchangeable Caprices and Crown Vics. One or two of the newest additions were always reserved for supervisors. The rest served interchangeably. Impersonally. They persevered service to the City of New York for three tours a day, seven days a week. After only a few years, a patrol car with even the most dutiful record of service would find itself barely fit to serve as a four-wheeled roadblock, unoccupied and parked to keep traffic turning toward a summer block party.

The glow from the 24-hour convenience store washed the blacktop pavement of the deserted parking lot nearly white. Tabby stood up and readjusted her gun belt, twisting and stretching, attempting to exorcise a crack from her vertebra. Hints of corrosion beginning to appear along the bottom of the car made her reflect upon her own service record, now one decade long. She wondered how much better she would fare.

Lucy's head popped up from the opposite side of the car.

"Time for a coffee break?"

Tabby turned and paused for a moment.

"How's that accident report coming along?"

Tabby had to suppress a smirk when she saw a bit of the energy drain from Lucy's face. Jimmy once lectured that idle rookies were the Devil's playthings. Most likely, someone else a very long time before told him something similar when he had his own reports to complete.

"Relax. Just tell me what you want. When I get back I'll help you with whatever you can't figure out."

"Oh, gotcha," Lucy said. "Coffee's fine. Milk, no sugar, please."

A bell jingled over Tabby's head as she stepped inside. The clerk at the counter failed to notice. He continued snoring while she sought out the coffee machine. She prayed that it would not be stale or burnt, but held her breath for neither. It was Sunday morning. Tabby reminded herself that while there might yet be some church-goers left in the world, the steady flow of commuters and the fresh pots of coffee they demanded would be few and far between this morning. Surrounded by an assortment of pre-wrapped muffins, donuts, and Devil Dogs, a half-empty carafe smoldered atop the coffee maker's burner. Tabby took two Styrofoam cups and poured. Only Lucy's cup received milk. Tabby preferred hers unadulterated.

Outside the gas station's grimy, cluttered windows, a van turned into the parking lot. With most of its panels covered in coats of yellow paint faded to a variety of degrees, it looked to be aging gracefully as Tabby's RMP. It came to a stop next to one of the two pumps and its door creaked and whined as it swung open. Out jumped a stout, older man balancing a stack of twine-bound newspapers beneath a plump, flush face. When he reached the gas station's front door, a gust of brisk, morning air carried him past the threshold. The rushing chill was enough to gently jostle the cashier from his slumber, but it was the stack of newspapers thumping down on the counter that lifted him an inch off his seat.

"Lenny! Jesus Christ," the cashier shouted. "I thought I was getting jumped by some punk skell again!"

"Hey now, you're good," replied Lenny. He jerked a thumb towards Tabby and continued, "After all, you got the *finest* here watchin' you count sheep."

Lenny grabbed two sticks of beef jerky from a jar next to the register and tossed a quarter onto the counter.

"Say, Officer. Georgie here doesn't hafta' worry 'bout any'a those strung-out thugs robbin' this joint, right?"

"Nope," Tabby replied. "Just the sober ones."

Lenny laughed and made his way back to the front door.

"You ask me," Lenny offered without solicitation, "you'd have to be crazy *not* be high walkin' 'round this city when it's dark out. What's the body count up to so far? We ain't even hit spring yet and there's already close to three hundred murders for the year."

A cup in each hand, Tabby approached the stacks of newspapers on the counter. The ink had barely dried judging not only by the smell wafting off the stack, but by the ink smeared up and down

Lenny's arms and chest. On the assorted front pages, The Times heralded the triumphant release of Nelson Mandela and the unexpected defeat of Mike Tyson, while the Daily News opted to cover Ivana Trump's public wrangling with her husband over his indiscretions with Marla Maples. Tabby raised the cup to her mouth, but stopped short of tipping it back. Word of the bloodbath on 63rd Street seemed to have occurred late enough to escape the Sunday editions. She wondered how long that would take to change once a city's worth of reporters drank their own morning cup.

"When the sun comes up… we may need to add a few more to the list."

Tabby's radio crackled.

"Receiving a wellness check in the Six Four," Central announced. *"Sector David, on the air? Can I show you responding?"*

Tabby glanced out the window. She looked through the Caprice's windshield and saw her partner's head bent down, buried an inch off her clipboard. As Tabby had inherited the driver's seat, the reports and radio transmissions were left to Lucy. From inside the convenience store, it appeared as though her partner was too engrossed in the former to hear the latter. Tabby rolled her eyes away from the parking lot and dug her thumbnail into the side of her radio.

"10-4. David read, Central," Tabby grumbled. "Georgie, how much for the coffees?"

"I can't charge you for those."

"It's alright, you don't gotta hook us up every time we stop by here," Tabby assured the cashier, raising the cup up to her mouth for another sip.

"No, it's not that. You guys—well, even you girls, too, I mean— are welcome here. But I can't charge you money for that in good conscience. That pot's been sizzlin' there since 7 P.M. last night."

The styrofoam cup sank with Tabby's arm. Caffeine was important, she believed, but a case of heartburn before sun up was one hell of price to pay to get through the night.

"I guess the price is right then," Tabby sighed. "Thanks just the same."

The door to the gas station swung closed until it resealed swiftly behind her. A singular, continuous wisp of steam circled the edge of Tabby's coffee cup. It twisted higher, stretching into the thin, cold air to be pulled apart completely. Tabby paused a few steps away from the gas station's entrance and turned. Styrofoam smacked against the bottom of the trash can and launched a narrow spout of black coffee just above the rim.

Tabby heard the steady, muffled beat before her hand unlatched the driver's side door.

"Well now I know why you can't hear Central," she said, plopping back down behind the wheel.

"What? Was she trying to get our attention?"

Tabby passed the remaining cup of coffee to her partner.

"Something like that. If it's alright with you, I'm gonna turn this down."

It was not a request, and no blessing was awaited. Tabby reached for the volume knob and brought the car's FM radio one notch above silent.

"Maybe next time Central needs us, we'll actually notice."

"Oh," Lucy replied. She brought the cup of coffee up high enough to obscure her face below the eyes. After a long sip, she tried—failed—to suppress the grimace twisting the sides of her mouth. "Sorry 'bout that, Officer Williams."

"You're good. And, for the love of God, don't call me that. Tabby is fine."

The patrol car turned out of the parking lot with just enough grace to avoid bottoming out a second time.

"Here," Tabby said. She passed one of the gas station's napkins to her right. "Sorry about the chicken scratch, but I had my hands full. Throw this address down into your memo book. Central gave us a wellness check."

Tabby did not need to turn her head to see the passenger's side of the car flourish with excitement.

"Forget this then," Lucy chirped.

Her partner's clipboard and the incomplete accident report attached thereon flipped onto the dashboard. She saw Lucy's hand stretching toward the emergency light controls.

"Someone needs help, let's get going!"

Tabby's own hand shot from the steering wheel to cover the controls.

"No. Relax. Just focus on one thing at a time. When we pull up, tell Central we're 84. Then, ask her to read back the details of the job. Lotta the time, it's just people who can't get their elderly parents to answer the phone. They want someone to pop in and check on 'em—if they can't be bothered themselves, that is."

"Huh."

Without conceding much excitement, Lucy chewed on the concept. She reached up and brought the clipboard back to her lap.

"But it could be an emergency, too… right?"

"Sure."

Lucy made several subsequent attempts to sip from her cup and keep her penmanship more skillful than that of a first-grader while the patrol car lurched and shook. When she finally threw in the towel in pursuit of either, Tabby was unsure whether to attribute it to motion sickness or acid reflux from the burnt drink. Lucy signaled their arrival over the radio and her grumbling voice provided no further evidence either way. The quaint, detached, single-family home betrayed no signs of life, which Tabby found none too unusual at 6:00 A.M. on a Sunday. Only a handful of the nearby homes had begun to exhibit signs of stirring. Some were illuminated by solitary kitchen lights while the rest of their rooms stayed darkened. Elsewhere, driveways harbored cars left alone to idle and warm up while their owners watched and steeled themselves inside living room windows.

"Caller says he hasn't heard from his grandfather in a few days," the dispatcher explained. *"First name Giuseppe, last name Tomasi. 84 years-old, lives alone, hasn't picked up the phone all weekend. Front ringer might be deactivated so the grandson says you can try the back door, too. He left a number, wants a call back once you've made contact with the resident. Advise if you need to get a bus rolling."*

"10-4, Central," Lucy replied.

Tabby felt a familiar stiffness near the base of her spine. Gripping the steering wheel, she twisted to the left. The tight muscles running along her spine protested, but she refused to relent. When she finally rung a pop from the misaligned discs, the sound was almost satisfying as the physical relief. Turning to her right scored her two more.

"Let's get this over with."

The night's bitter gusts fled as dawn approached, leaving behind a crisp stillness between increasingly sporadic breezes. It was a relief from the stifling warmth of the car and Tabby found herself feeling reinvigorated—the shift's illusory second wind. She knew it would not last. The sun would breach the horizon and her body would remember the trick being played against its nature. Her feet crunched over frozen, brown grass as she and Lucy made their way to the front door. The lawn displayed every sign of being diligently manicured before the onset of winter. Since then, snowfall had been neatly packed against the corners of the yard, scraped off of the walkways, and frozen solid to wait for the spring thaw. White lace curtains were drawn behind barred front windows. They stepped up to the front door. Tabby sniffed.

"You smell something?"

"Only the smell of the cold. In the summer it's easier, but this time of year you can never tell if anyone's ripening inside."

Lucy's jaw dropped. While she tried to produce a response, Tabby's hand reached for the doorbell. She stopped short of a pair of exposed wires poking out from an opening where a buzzer should have been.

"Come on, let's try the backdoor," Tabby said. "I don't wanna wake up half the neighborhood pounding on this one before the old man inside finally answers."

The driveway was empty. Near the middle lay a faint stain left by an oil leak, though an effort appeared to have been made over the years to scrub it from memory. At the rear of the driveway, atop a short, concrete stoop, stood the back door. Tabby stopped and waited silently next to the door, while Lucy watched curiously. She did not hear anything—did not see any movement in the nearby windows. If any living thing was on the other side of the back door, it gave away no signs of being aware of her. It was also possible, she realized, that they might also know how to keep an eye on her without making a peep. When Tabby was satisfied—or near to satisfied as she felt she would get—she knocked.

"Keep an eye on the windows. Looks like they're all shut tight, so if you see any movement in the curtains, you let me know."

"Yeah, sure," Lucy replied, scanning diligently.

After a second round of knocks, Tabby employed her flashlight. As was the case with the front windows, the door's panes of glass were covered on the interior by white curtains. Rather than shed light within, the white fabric mostly reflected the beam back into Tabby's eyes.

"Hey, Officer Williams—I mean, Tabby—come 'ere." Lucy whispered. "I think you should get a look at this."

Tabby stepped away from the back door. Her eyes continued to monitor the door while her feet carried her backwards, closer to where her partner stared up toward the side of the house. There was a small window not far from the door and just a few feet over their heads.

"I saw 'em drawn closed when we first walked up. The curtains, I mean. Then, when I looked back a few seconds later, there was a gap in between."

Unlike the others, Tabby could see that these curtains had indeed been parted slightly. The beam of Tabby's flashlight climbed slats of warped vinyl siding. It crossed the frame at the bottom of the sill. As it peeked into the house, the light spilled over the face of Giuseppe Tomasi staring back at her.

"Geez, what—" Lucy squealed.

The flashlight bounced as Tabby's arm jumped. A weathered palm and curled fingers shot over the old man's eyes, bleached by the light it sought to deflect. Tabby turned the light away from the window and turned it around toward her jacket. Silver light reflected off the shield on her chest. From the window, the man's hand slowly dropped and allowed his face to squint outward once more. Rheumy eyes twitched back and forth to Tabby and Lucy, then opened wider in recognition. In a frenzy, hands dug at the bottom of the window frame, grasped at the sill, and lifted it upwards.

"Oh, officers," Giuseppe shouted through the raised window. "I thought youse were those… *damn prowlers* again!"

"No, sir, Mr. Tomasi," Tabby replied. "We're just here to check in on you. Your family was worried—"

"Stay right there," he squawked before Tabby could finish. "I'm coming down to open the door."

The old man darted away. In a moment, a series of tumblers rattled and turn on the other side of the door and Giuseppe greeted them again. A warm burst of radiant-heated air caused his whisps of snow-white hair to flutter as the hallway behind him depressurized. Tabby found herself impressed by the plentiful follicles. She imagined they may not grow in densely as they had in past decades, but the hairline that framed the thin, wrinkled skin on the old man's forehead appeared reluctant to cede an inch. Despite the early hour, he was fully dressed in a brown pinstriped coat over a burgundy cardigan. A pair of rheumy eyes shined with relief and the early clouds of cataracts.

"Like I was saying, we're just here to check in on you. Your family's been tryin' to call you on the phone, but—"

"Why don't you two come inside?" Giuseppe interrupted again. "It's too cold to talk out here."

"Sir… that's alright. Everything looks *fine*, so we'll be sure to let your grandson know—"

"My grandson… mannaggia! I've been telling Michael for months about the problems 'round here, b-but he never comes."

One of Tabby's feet lost patience and descended the steps behind her.

"But you girls are here now… and I need to tell you about the *prowlers* we got in this neighborhood. Every night they're out here tryin' to get through my door!"

"Burglars?"

Lucy jumped into Tabby's periphery.

"They tried to break in?"

"Yes! Come in, come in."

Before Tabby could object, her partner rushed past her. She snorted, then grudgingly followed. She passed into a the dimly lit hallway while her eyes stared daggers into the back of Lucy's head.

"*Every night,*" Giuseppe lamented. "I keep all the damn doors and windows bolted, but every night they come and try to pry them open."

"When was the last time this happened," Lucy asked as she produced scratch paper in her hand. "Did they damage anything?"

"See for yourself!"

Giuseppe gestured along the length of the door frame while he held the door wide open.

"It's a miracle they didn't take the whole door off its hinges."

Tabby's second wind vanished. A tall column of boxes had been piled from floor to ceiling. It looked comfortable—if not entirely stable—and her shoulder found a place to rest against it. The entire structure only moved about an inch when the remainder of Tabby's weight joined. She watched her partner open an investigation into trespasses domestic and mental committed against Mr. Tomasi. As Giuseppe painted an elaborate picture, Tabby's eyes wandered around the door frame in question. There did not appear to be any evidence of attempts at forced entry—no cracks or splinters in the frame, no loosened hinges. When Giuseppe allowed the door to finally swing closed, she noted that the presence of quite extensive scratches into the paint around the doorknob and beneath the door's window.

"It's awful, what's happening to this neighborhood," Mrs. Tomasi whimpered. "First the Bronx, then Bushwick. Now I see the same things happening here. My sweet, dear Mable and me lived off'a Myrtle for years, 'til those awful people started tearing everything apart."

Tabby's eyes shifted to Giuseppe. The glare she had unleashed on Lucy returned to find a new target.

"We thought we'd be safer down here. But now my Mable's gone."

Despite the urging of her better judgment, Tabby failed to keep herself removed.

"Did you get a look at these people?" she asked. "How would you describe them?"

Giuseppe grew silent, lost in consideration.

"Well, it's hard to tell at night. They're just so dark…"

Mr. Tomasi glanced toward Tabby. In the moment before they darted to the ground, there was a flash of self-awareness in his eyes. Tabby watched Giuseppe endeavor best as he could to lift himself out of embarrassment and adjust his posture.

"That is to say… you two must be starving. Y'wanna come into the kitchen?"

"Oh, no," Lucy said. "But thank you. If we could just—"

Giuseppe took her by the hand before she could finish and guided her to the next room. Lingering behind, Tabby examined the boxes she had found more comfortable than she cared to admit. There were six of them, one on top of the other, each numbered by permanent marker. She leaned around the corner. Similar columns surrounded the kitchen table from which Mr. Tomasi pulled back a chair for Lucy. Giuseppe had accumulated a forest of box towers, each displaying various degrees of structural integrity. Tabby continued to count boxes as she made her way to join the table. Numbers eighteen through twenty-three and seven through eleven loomed nearer the table. A stack next to the refrigerator contained numbers thirty through thirty-five. The kitchen's sole light source, a lamp dangling from a chain over the table, could do little to overcome the many tall silhouettes cast across the room by each column. The numbers may have gone far higher. Tabby could not tell how many more stacks loomed in the shadows. As it happened, more troubling thoughts distracted her count. If just one pile were to topple onto an unsuspecting octogenarian, the aftermath would be debilitating. The exponential potential of a chain reaction in which each knocked over another could be deadly.

Tabby found herself wandering. The volume of her thoughts as she examined the room, and the physical presence of its many obstacles, muffled whatever small talk Lucy and Giuseppe were trading. The kitchen sink appeared to be empty and the countertops looked clean, either due to diligent care or lack of use. Vacant cupboards implied their contents had been transferred to several of the series of stacked cardboard boxes. Tabby heard the insulating liner crackle as she pulled open the refrigerator door. The lightbulb was burned out, but the contents were thin enough to parse without much difficulty. There were several browning, shriveled oranges. A tin of Sanka. Solidifed packets of sugar. It was a stretch to call any of it sustenance, and there was only one other object. Tabby felt her mind go blank as she picked up the chilled pinecone and turned it over in her hand.

At the kitchen table, Lucy continued to transcribe Mr. Tomasi's woes into detailed notation. Giuseppe's hands rested atop the table. His intertwined fingernails were immaculate, if trimmed a little too close. Tabby noted one exception. The tip of Giuseppe's left ring finger was wrapped in yellowing gauze.

"Whenever they're outside, they peep in on me through the windows. They'll duck down if they see you turn toward 'em. Oh, they think they're pretty clever. But I've got 'em figured out."

The feet of Giuseppe's chair shuddered across the linoleum as he pulled himself upright. He walked toward the sink. A small, rectangular mirror rested behind the faucet, leaning upright against the wall. Giuseppe picked it up and walked back toward Lucy, then bent down to demonstrate.

"This one and the one in my bedroom. I keep 'em pointed at the windows. Those bastards don't even know I'm lookin' right. Back. At 'em."

"Right…" Lucy replied hesitantly, her tone dimming. "So, what do you see in the mirrors?"

Mr. Tomasi's smile had grown wry as he shared tactical secrets with his guests. Now, uncertainty crept in. Frustration wracked his voice as he struggled to continue.

"I know 'em… from somewhere… but they're too dark for me to say who…"

"In the future," Tabby interjected, "you need to call us right away when this happens. We can come and help. That's why you need to get your phones working."

"No! That's the other place they get in," Giuseppe pleaded. "They can hear you through the wires. That's why I pulled the damn things out. The phone, the doorbell, the television set."

Giuseppe sat back down less gracefully than he had risen. Soon, his forehead rest against his palms. He rubbed his eyes and paced his breathing.

"Mable… Mable calls it the *'idiot box'*…"

A telephone hung against the wall behind Giuseppe. While the yellow, extra-long spiral cord twisted down to the ground from the receiver, the outlet at the bottom of the base where the two ought connect was empty. Among the piled, knotted cord, Tabby's fingers found the unplugged end. It slid into the bottom of the base with a satisfying *click*. She lifted the receiver to her ear. Even after confirming the dial tone, Tabby stood frozen. Balancing atop the base, level with her eyes, was the familiar shape of a pinecone.

Back at the table, Lucy appeared lost. Her pen had stopped scribbling a few minutes earlier. She looked at Tabby for help.

"Edward David Peter?"

Lucy looked more lost after Tabby's question. Tabby made a mental note to introduce her new partner to some of the more popular, discreet codewords. It would serve her well to learn how to communicate without detection around a potentially emotionally disturbed person. As it turned out, it only took Lucy an extra moment to catch on.

"Oh, EDP?" Lucy paused. "I guess that would explain… *some* of this."

Tabby backed out of the kitchen. She returned to the back door through which Giuseppe had invited them into his home. Her flashlight clicked on and returned to the damage she noticed in passing. Scuffs by the doorknob wore down through several layers of paint and into the wood itself to form a distinct circle. The scrapes near the window were similar, but extended over much longer arcs down to the ground. There was an odd shape disrupting those vertical lines. Tabby brought her flashlight up close to examine the foreign object. She passed the beam back and forth and an ivory glow bounced back at her. With her free hand, Tabby reached into her jacket. A blade flicked out from the side of her switchblade's handle. Its tip wedged into the deep scratch mark and Tabby swiveled it back and forth. After a half dozen careful turns, the object shimmied free and tumbled onto the ground. The blade returned to her pocket. Tabby stooped down, brushing along the floor until her hands confirmed that which it was she already suspected fell free. She raised her palm into the light and sighed at the chipped, severed fingernail.

"It's been a long day, girls," Tabby could hear Mr. Tomasi say in the other room. "I'm sorry, but I'm too tired to remember these things you're asking me. 'Til y'see it for yourselves, you just gotta believe me."

"Lucy…"

Tabby leaned into the kitchen from the hallway.

"Can you join me over here for a minute? I need help with something."

"Whenever I try to sleep… I catch 'em. Starin' at me," Giuseppe continued.

Despite Tabby's call, Lucy stayed focused on the old man sitting across the table.

"Are you sure you're feeling alright, Mr. Tomasi?"

Tabby watched her hand reach out to Giuseppe's.

"Lucy…" Tabby repeated more urgently, "It'd be great if I could *borrow you. Over here.*"

"If you want, we could take you to talk to someone—"

"I'm not crazy!"

Giuseppe howled. His chair flew backward as he jumped back to his feet.

"These people are everywhere! *They're trying to kill me!*"

Before her hands could reach his, Giuseppe locked his fingers around Lucy's wrists. Lucy rocked back in shock but was unable to free herself from Giuseppe's grip. Two columns of numbered boxes toppled as Tabby rushed forward into the kitchen.

"Come here, *damn it!* Come here and look at them. Look at what they've been doin' to me!"

Tabby grabbed the old man's hand and ripped it away from Lucy's forearm. She ripped a pair of handcuffs from the loop on her belt, but Giuseppe slipped free and stumbled out of the kitchen. Losing sight of him to darker depths of the house, Tabby turned back toward her partner. Lucy recomposed herself from her temporary shock and hopped to her feet.

"God *damn*. Where the fuck did that come from?"

"You should've seen that comin' from a mile away," Tabby scolded. "You knew damn well he was EDP and you're tryin' to hold his hands?"

"But he's, like, eighty-something years old, and—"

"Still out-maneuvered you," Tabby shot back. "Now stay behind me and don't *ever* do anything like that again."

The flashlight probed past the archway. Tabby tried to retrace Giuseppe's flight path. On the other end, through the living room's bay window, shades of faint purple began to stretch up from the horizon and bleed into the black of space. The faint radiance leaked into the house and revealed a dozen more of the black stacks made from the boxed-up artifacts of Giuseppe and Mable's life. It also betrayed the stooping silhouette of an elderly man behind the window's thin, white curtains.

"Don't let 'em see me," the shadow begged. "Saint Anthony, protect me…"

"It's just us here with you," Tabby urged as she approached. "We're here now and there's nothing that's gonna hurt you."

Tabby placed one foot ahead of the other and carved a wide arc around the room. She passed pillar after pillar to close in on the distressed man's flank. Her hand stretched out toward the cord hanging from the side of the drapes. Gently, she tugged downward. The curtains parted slowly and the rising light outside painted the room violet. Whether or not he knew it, Giuseppe stood exposed to the darkness and the approaching sun. He shrank until his knees sank into the carpet. He hugged himself with one arm and covered his face with the other. Tabby managed to draw the curtains fully without causing further disturbance.

"It's alright, see for yourself," Tabby reassured him.

With a regretful whimper, Giuseppe's arms loosened. The back of his hand fell to the ground by his feet. He looked up at Tabby. She felt her own muscles relax as relief and recognition seeped into the strike wracking the old man's face. His face rose, followed by his shoulders. When Giuseppe was upright, he turned to look at Lucy.

"I never meant…," he pleaded. "I'm so sorry…"

Before he could complete the sentence, relief began to melt away. Giuseppe's eyes drifted past Lucy to the wall behind her. His jaw shook. Though Tabby stood no more than a couple feet away, she could barely hear what he said as he spoke once more.

"Oh God, Mable. Jesus… help me. I'm so sorry. I need… I need…"

Tabby turned to follow his line of sight past Lucy to the far wall of the living room. Over the mantle of an antiquated fireplace hung the wide, ornate frame of a mirror in which the three of them stood. Giuseppe's eyes quivered. Tabby thought he was focusing on his own reflection. After a moment, she looked behind his reflection, through the living room's broad front window.

"Never alone."

"Tab," Lucy whispered. "You… do you see?"

Tabby counted heads. She saw Lucy's nearer the archway separating the living room and the kitchen. She saw her own face and Giuseppe's two feet away on her right. Through the window, the sun itself had yet to breach the horizon. Black shrubbery and a variety of shapely, stout bushes bordered the bottom of the frame. One particular shape rose more prominently. It was too dark in the limited light to make out any details finer than that the top of one shape on the lawn was too round, too dome-like to match with the other manicured plants. When the shape tilted back and exposed a set of shoulders, air sputtered from Tabby's mouth. The shadow developed the contours of a man's frame as its head rolled back and the shoulders continued to rise. Tabby watched it rise slowly and steadily—taller and taller until both head and shoulders crept over the frame of the window atop towering darkness. She flinched. Her eyes slammed shut for a moment until she could overcome the impulse and force them open. She strained at the scene in the mirror's reflection once more. The line of plants remained. The figure did not. Tabby stumbled forward and turned to face the empty window directly. The first sliver of true sunlight crawled across a deserted front lawn. Her hand felt numb as she reached for her radio.

"Six Four David, Central."

Tabby heard her voice shaking. She cursed at herself in her mind and steadied herself.

"Regarding that wellness check, we're gonna need a bus to our location."

Tabby was grateful to whomever originally installed the kitchen telephone. The force she employed to return the receiver to the cradle of its base could have easily sent both crashing to the ground had it been secured any less firmly to the wall. A moment earlier, Tabby had reassured Mikey Tomasi that his grandfather was awake and uninjured—however, he would still be transported to Gravesend General for psychiatric and nutritional evaluation. She made hundreds of similar calls in similar surroundings. It had yet to become an easy call to make. Most people reacted poorly when woken early to any sort of call from a police officer concerning a loved one. Mikey, on the other hand, seemed distracted from the details Tabby provided. After repeatedly confirming that his grandfather was being removed from the location, his questions mostly related to the condition of the house's interior. Tabby was unsure if he heard her relay the EMTs' suspicions that Giuseppe had gone without sleep or a true meal for more than a week. Ultimately, she fabricated an emergency requiring the call's end just as Mikey inquired as to the state of the downstairs plumbing. Tabby's only regret for the abrupt conclusion to their discussion was expediting the call she knew Mikey was already placing to his realtor.

Among those towers of boxes left upright, near the center of the living room, a pair of EMTs swaddled Giuseppe into white sheets atop a stretcher. Lucy shimmied stacks numbered forty-three through forty-eight and one through six away from the front door to facilitate their exit. Tabby approached Giuseppe. Tears tracks dried among the crevices of the darkened skin gathered beneath his eyes. In the time since the old man first turned his gaze toward the living room's wide mirror, he had not stopped mumbling. To say that what he saw pacified him seemed to Tabby a gross mischaracterization. He was too terrified for any action beyond reciting the same words, heedless to how hoarse his voice grew upon repetition:

"I flee not from your cuts," he whispered, "for even if you inflict more, nothing shall separate me from the love of Christ. My heart shall not be afraid."

Lucy followed the stretcher to the back of the ambulance while Tabby locked the house's front door from within and made her way out the back door. Before she descended the concrete steps to the driveway, she turned around to stand in the hushed house and judge its supposed emptiness. Until the ambulance and its technicians pulled up to the front of the house, the three of them had waited quietly in the living room, save only for Giuseppe's prayer. When Lucy saw the swirling lights come to a halt, she broke the silence:

"Should we tell them what we saw out front? When they get in here, they can keep an eye on the old man while we go have a look around."

"Let it be."

"But," Lucy stammered. "What if it's the prowler he was talkin—"

"That wasn't a *damn* prowler."

"So you admit it… you saw it too."

"If we tell them what we saw, the next stretchers are gonna be for us. Let it be. Some things you hold onto. You'll understand. Some things you gotta take to your grave."

When the EMTs knocked, they left it there.

In the intervening minutes, the sun crept higher to peek through bare tree branches and over neighboring rooftops. Lucy was already seated as Tabby climbed back into her car. Pulling away, Tabby could see out of the corner of her eye that her partner looked, for once, exhausted.

"Listen, ain't every night that's gonna be rough as this one," Tabby said. "You'll see more dullness than you know what to do with."

"I think I can handle dull. Worked that out in all the time I spent staring at basement walls, dreaming about the day I'd get to run around in the cold, gettin' screamed at by drunks and crazy old folks."

"Yeah, be careful what you wish for," Tabby chuckled as she warned. "You can't go diggin' too deep into some people's minds, y'know? The deeper you dig, the less you're gonna like what you find. Their problems bleed into you."

"Hmm…" Lucy offered in response. After a moment she turned back toward her window and muttered, "I guess that's one way to see things."

If it had not been the politest way Tabby ever found herself told to shove it, she might have been annoyed. She might also permit that she was too tired to push the point any further.

"You'll see. Grind through patrol on the midnights for a few more weeks—hell, a few years—and we can revisit those feelings."

Tabby received no further response. Glancing over, she realized Lucy had either nodded out or chose to look the part in order to shut her up. Tabby felt lonely. The radio's volume knob still rested near mute when her hand reached to turn it. She switched to the AM band.

"*—and if it's sales you're looking for this Presidents' Day, look no further than Ceasar's Bay Bazaar, where you'll find over five hundred independent merchants and factory outlets under one roof! Two full floors of quality merchandise, a seven-day refund policy, free parking, and low, low prices! Now, it's seven-oh-nine in the A.M. and here's your news on the nines…*"

On any other morning, Tabby would have left the radio dialed into music. She rarely listened to AM news radio stations like WNWS 990. Its personalities tended to rattle off nasally news briefs at a speed she found jarring, and at tight intervals she found needlessly repetitive. But this morning was unlike any other morning, at least not any in recent memory. Tabby was curious if the broadcast news cycle picked up on that which local papers had been printed too early to catch. The city was averaging more than thirty-five murders each week over the past year or so. Tabby considered that it was entirely possible for four dead and one critically wounded teenager to become lost in the statistics.

"Mayhem overnight in Bensonhurst!"

Possible, but not today, she realized.

"Five students from the Kingsborough Institute of Technology discovered shot in their own home following an apparent home invasion last night. Officials have yet to provide details on the perpetrator, but they have stated at this time that one victim is in critical condition at Gravesend General, while the remaining four have been declared dead. We're expecting official statements from police and City Hall shortly as a growing wave of murder and gang violence continues to menace the city."

The report was brief and included no mention of the bloody depravities Tabby knew would haunt her dreams.

"In sports: Iron Mike's title undisputed no more—"

Tabby turned the radio's nob again until it clicked. The Sixty Fourth Precinct's stationhouse loomed ahead. She circled the block, searching for a spot to leave their car for the incoming platoon so she and Lucy could bring the night to a close. This proved difficult as ever, with news vans hogging prime real estate around the facility. A phalanx of reporters gathered behind a tenuous, desperate semi-circle of barriers arranged around the building's entrance. They banded together, bundled into heavy winter jackets with steam rising from blue and white coffee cups.

"Circus in town?" Lucy asked.

"All three rings, looks like."

Parking was only discovered once Tabby grew desperate enough to expand the search by a few extra blocks. By the time they walked back, the reporters' attention angled up the building's front steps toward its main doorway. Captain Debois, the precinct's commanding officer, stepped out onto the top of the stairs. Tabby scowled when she saw Detective Vernon join him. The Captain opened with a brief introduction, not a word of which was audible to Tabby over the rapid shuttering of cameras. She only knew he was finished when he gestured to the detective standing by his side.

"Thank you, Captain, and good morning," Vernon began. "All the information we have so far is preliminary and subject to change as our investigation proceeds. In short, a little after midnight this morning, officers responding to a noise complaint discovered four dead and one critically injured student in their apartment's living room. All five victims appear to have been shot at close range by a perpetrator who is, at this time, still outstanding. We'll keep you updated on the status of the fifth victim as we hear more from the hospital, but as of right now we're keeping her identity confidential pending contact with her family. Furthermore, we're still assembling the details on the perpetrator and will release that information to you as soon as possible—"

A murmur grew within the crowd until one reporter broke interrupted Vernon.

"So, what *do* you have for us?"

"Are you saying this is the work of one perp," another interjected, "and it's not a gang?"

"We aren't confirming for now whether—I mean," Vernon stuttered, speaking over the questions. "In order to keep the scope of the investigation limited, we are actively looking for a perp matching a description given to us by a witness near the scene—"

"Detective, how many witnesses do you have at this time?"

"I'd really… rather not… uh, comment on…"

Vernon's face flushed red as he began to choke on his words. Captain Debois rolled his eyes and placed a hand on the Detective's shoulder. As the briefing descended into chaos, a reporter near Tabby turned to face her cameraman.

"Few details on the suspect this morning. Still fewer answers from the NYPD for the parents and families of the victims of what is already becoming known as the KIT Co-Ed Massacre."

Vernon's eyes scanned the crowd, begging for a question he could answer. When his eyes met Tabby's, he found a grin stretching from one ear to the other.

Report prepared by the 64th Precinct, New York City Police Department; Sunday, February 11, 1990:

New York City Police Department
Unusual Occurrence Report
PD 370-152 (Rev. 1-87)

Date: February 11, 1990

FROM: 1st Platoon Commander, 64th Precinct

TO: Chief of Patrol; Commanding Officer, Patrol Borough Brooklyn South; Commanding Officer, 64th Precinct

SUBJECT: Home Invasion and Subsequent Multiple Homicides Within Confines of the 64th Precinct; A/K/A "The K.I.T. Co-Ed Massacre"

DETAILS: (WHEN, WHERE, WHO, WHAT, HOW, WHY)

1. On Sunday, February 11, 1990 at approximately 0011 hrs a 10-10 was received via Communications Division concerning a residence located at 2356 63rd Street within the confines of the 64th Precinct. Details are as follows:

2. At approximately 0016 hrs, Communications received a call of a signal 10-10 noise complaint originating from ████████████████████, (718)████ ████, a 3rd party caller residing at ████ 63rd Street. (Caller, a neighbor, debriefed by Det. Vernon; ref PDU log #64-1990-0081 for details).

3. Patrol sector Adam (PO Antonio and PO Schilling) were dispatched to complaint by Communications at 0019 hrs.

4. The responding officers arrived 10-84 at 0036 hrs. Upon arrival, officers stated that they observed all lights in and around the location of occurrence and surrounding residences

to be inactive. Officers observed front door to 2nd floor apartment exhibited signs of especially extreme forced entry.

5. Officers noted detecting a strong odor of gunpowder and blood from outside premises, as well as an undeterminable number of sets of bloody footprints heading from front door to street. Officers requested additional units to scene at 0039 hrs.

6. Officers made entry into premises at appx 0040 hrs, and observed that all light switches were inoperable. (Req. submitted to ASAC ███████████, █████████████████ for specialized analysis. Results pending; contact Interagency Correspondence Unit for further info.)

7. Upon further investigation, officers discovered five (5) victims unconscious and unresponsive lying face up on living room floor:
i.   ALEXANDER, ANTOINE R. - DOB 02/22/1970
ii.   ISAACS, HOLLY E. - DOB 07/06/1972
iii. KOCHARIAN, CHERYL - DOB 03/17/1972
iv. ORMSBY, RONALD R. Jr. - DOB 09/01/1972
(All above T/O/D decl. 0057 by EMT Salvos, Dr. Kemp GGH)
v.   ████████████ - DOB █████/1971; aided removed to GGH unconscious, critical, likely to die.

8. All five (5) victims exhibited multiple ballistic wounds to head and upper chest area. Preliminary crime scene survey collected thirteen (13) spent .45 casings (complete recovery of ballistic evidence from victims and surrounding walls by CSU pending). Victims were recovered arranged in a spiral formation on floor of living room; on back, facing up, feet at the center of the spiral; left arm extending outwards overhead with left forearm and left hand curving further left.

9. Officers detected weak vital signs from one victim, ██████████ - DOB ████/1971. Officer Antonio provided first aid until arrival of paramedics. Victim removed to Gravesend General Hospital ER at approximately 0058 hrs. Ref. to Det. Vernon for interview pending stabilization and return to consciousness.

10. Upon further investigation, perpetrator made intentional marks to living room walls, written in █████████ (serological analysis pending): principally and repetitively references to "█████████" "██████" "█████████" "█████" "██████" "████████" as well as several other unintelligible markings. Additionally, several ornamental objects around the living room appeared to have been intentionally ████████ ██████████ (serological analysis pending).

11. Lt. Cordell and PO Melendez assigned as patrol supervisor and supervisor's operator arrived 0043 hrs. PO Daley and PO Williams assigned to patrol sector David arrived 0047 hrs, directed to provide perimeter security by Lt. Cordell. PO Daley disregarded instructions and left post without supervisory permission; entered premises and exceeded scope of duties by usurping responsibilities assigned to ME's office personnel on scene. As a result, PO Daley's actions caused himself to fall. Same thereafter complained of pain to lower back. Removed to GGH for medical examination and reassigned to limited duty within 64th Precinct station house until return to full duty granted by district surgeon. Disciplinary action pending by Lt. Cordell.

12. One witness was interviewed by Det. Vernon on scene, ██████████ residing at ████ 63rd Street. Witness stated to Det. Vernon that she is a neighbor ████████████████ location of occurrence. At approximately 2357 hrs, Sat. 02/10/1990 observed possible perp (white female w/ long blonde hair) in a double-parked car (dark color; unk. make/year; unk. if

two or four door sedan) in front of the location.
Description of perp and vehicle transmitted over
division.

13. Remaining rooms of location surveyed, no
additional damage or property theft indicated or
suspected at this time.

14. Premises are to remain secured and sealed
pending analysis by ███████████████████ and/or
clearance by the Commanding Officer, Patrol
Borough Brooklyn South. Strict compliance
ordered and anticipated.

15. All photographic evidence processed on
scene by PO Valentino, PBBS ECT; vouchered by
same as #1990-01094 through -01103; dupl.
provided to SA ██████████████, ████████████
███████████████

16. ICAD attached.

17. For your INFORMATION.

                              Leonard Cordell
                              Lieutenant

Entry posted to the Kingsboro Institute of Technology's Online Bulletin Board System; Tuesday, December 12, 1989:

```
-------------------------------------------------------------------
#  _______________________________________________________________  #
#    _  _   __________             __   ___   ___   __   __          #
#   / ,'   /          /          /    /   ) /   ) /  ) /  )          #
#  ---/_.'-------/--------___----/---/----/___/_/----/_/----\------  #
#   / \   ===  / /    /___) /   ')  /    )   /    )   /      \        #
#  _/___\_____/___(___(___ _/___/__/___/___/___/___/___(___/__       #
#                                                                   #
# Kingsboro Institute of Technology Bulletin Board System - Launched 1987 #
#                                                                   #
-------------------------------------------------------------------

===================================================================
[ M ] Main Menu       [ C ] Contact SysOp       [ S ] Search
[ R ] Read Messages   [ N ] New Message         [ H ] Help
===================================================================
Page [01/06]          [ PgUp ] Prev. Page       [ PgDn ] Next Page
-------------------------------------------------------------------
   Date    : 12/12/89 11:29
   From    : aalexande1970
   Subject : Historic Preservation and Digitization Project
-------------------------------------------------------------------
```

NOTE: This is the first entry in what I hope to be
an ongoing series preserving the massive library of
historical documents Dr. Lewis has collected throughout his career. The bulk consists of unpublished,
handwritten memoranda and journals which, as far as I
can tell, exist unreproduced anywhere outside the
slowly disintegrating stacks in the Institute's
basement. I believe this endeavor would be best
served not only transcribing them onto the library's
internal computer system, but by making them freely
accessible over the Institute's public BBS.

   The following is an excerpt from the journals kept
by Peter Hutchins, a colonial magistrate employed by
the Dutch West India Company as a liaison to
Gravesend, the first primarily English settlement
permitted within the area claimed for their New
Netherland. These entries date from late 1646 to
early 1647, long before this frontier outpost became
one of Brooklyn's many neighborhoods. They were recovered among the charred ruins of the last of the
grand old seaside resorts that gave nearby Bath
Beach, Brooklyn its name. In the spring of 1920, the

```
===================================================================
```

```
========================================================================
Page [02/06]              [ PgUp ] Prev. Page          [ PgDn ] Next Page
------------------------------------------------------------------------
```


Bath Beach Hotel was a pale shadow of its former stature. Many of its rivals succumbed to declining popularity over the previous summers, and now the last surviving resort's own Memorial Day opening was in doubt. In the early hours of March 26th its many rooms sat vacant, save for the hotel's live-in manager who noticed smoke rising from the building's wing closest to the waterline. No cause for the fire was ever determined, but when the fire brigade arrived just before sunrise, most of the structure was engulfed and collapsing, and the hotel's future was finally settled. That which could be salvaged was either sold off to settle the suffering resort's debts or scattered among the thrift stores and book-sellers of southern Brooklyn--much like this journal. With the land beneath the former waterfront hotel conveniently clear, it was only a matter of time before Robert Moses succeeded in pulling up the bottom of Gravesend Bay to sculpt a modern shoreline with room for the future Belt Parkway. How or why a diary this abnormal came to reside in an ordinary hotel manager's office in the first place remains a mystery.

   The world described by this journal seems as distant to the present as the memory of the seaside escapes lining Bath Beach. Both met the same fate: buried under time, progress, and the landfill dredged up from the bottom of Gravesend Bay. The salt marshes and thickets and stout brush forests; native generations, Dutch settlers, English settlers, and the enslaved; bayside resorts and the promises of therapeutic breezes advertised on the sides of horse-drawn trolleys. In Brooklyn, at least, this world has been almost completely obscured from everyday view. But at the height of the summer, you can still look out over that bay and share the same sunset with Peter Hutchins or the Gilded Age Knickerbockers who fled their sweltering Park Avenue, so long as you can overlook the six-lane highway. -A.A.

```
========================================================================
```

22nd of December, 1646
Another year with out that which one could
reasonably call a summer comes to a close. Autumn
brought a hasty, if not entirely fruitless, harvest.
I returned to the towne at Gravesend two weeks past.
Despite the poor yield, I find one dozen new families
now occupy lots at the southern end of the commons.
The commons themselves I come to find echo with manie
a strange whisper, for every person in lieu of
turning a field has turned a gossip! Reports preceding my return are that, despite our recent peace,
the Canarsees have evacuated their usual wintering
grounds altogether. It is believed they fled with
their own meager harvest in search of sanctuary of
any kind, far away. None among us can reckon why
they would deviate so suddenly from their custom or
how they would expect to escape the winter's
devastation, unless we are also to accept those other
popular murmurs and disaffections passing among the
towne that some other menace blights the land. Ever
more terrible accounts gather that the dunes and
marsh echo with profane howls and strange eruptions
of light during night's darkest hours, cycling and
swelling as the moon cycles. Perhaps the Canarsees
know something we do not. Perhaps, over those years
we have called peaceful, we have done little to prove
a friend nor engender a warning.
Not long after my return, I visited Lady Moody with
the Company's latest shipping schedules. My words
were first met with silence, then with weary counsel.
The Good Lady mourns how our summers dwindle as do
our harvests. "When people feel forsaken of the
Lord's bounty year after year," she lamented, "they
will eventually turn to other means for their
sustenance." To this I inquired, "And without the
Lord, where will they find spiritual sustenance?"
To my surprise, Lady Moody seemed suddenly quite
eager to hear me speak more of the shipping
schedules.

==

26th of December, 1646

Unexpected company greeted our departure from church on Christmas morning: six men from the Massachusetts Bay by route of the Narragansett Bay. If they were weary from that journey, their words and faces did not betray as such. They conferred with Parson Clemmons, to whom they were introduced by letter from a fellow vicar in Plymouth. Mr. Clemmons made assurances to Mrs. Moody and myself and curious others within the village that they are trustworthy and wholesome men of a goodly, Christian nature. In confidence, I believe the full intentions of this party and their arrival in Gravesend remains closely guarded behind their tight lips. I conducted my own inquiry with their leader, Mr. Jas. Sprague, who testified that he and his men are dispatched by the councilors of the Massachusetts Bay Colony. In his own words, they have been retained to locate and return some pernicious and possibly sinister fugitives encamped for a time along the Narragansett and now, as they presume, in flight south into our New Netherlands.   Mr. Sprague appeared reluctant to elaborate further when I pressed him as to the nature of the allegations against their elusive quarry. Despite his reluctance, I believe my eyes have found the answer, for I have seen among their bags and trunks a collection of muskets and gunpowder excessively robust for men who arrive bearing letters of introduction penned by clergymen.

All of this as other matters of administration demand my attention. Autumn has barely ended and the frost already reaches deep into the earth. I have advised that the men of the village increase their collection of firewood mind for the women to gather all kindling they may pass. Our reserves are fine enough that I caution against any more unnecessary worry, but the chill does not relent even on those rare days when the sun breaks through the gloom. As

such, this requires firing the village's hearths at
nearly all times. I have petitioned the Hon. Mr.
Kieft to purchase a shipment of more dried timber
from Fort Amsterdam or Breuckelen Towne. I await
from the good Director his response and guidance.

   31st of December, 1646
   Despite the introduction to this village of manie
new faces over the past year and those of our recent
guests from New England, whose presence still fans
the flames of common rumors, there came the discovery
two days since of an unexpected and unexplained
flight.   It would appear that Mr. Wm. Seymour, his
wife, and their two sons have departed amidst the
peak of the season's relentless cruelty. Their
absence from Christmas gatherings did not go without
notice, and several of the men were dispatched to
their farm, west of Hubbard's Creek. Parson Clemmons
set out on foot an hour after the sun rose and
returned to me before noon. His call at the
Seymours' door went unanswered, and an examination of
their fireplace found it cold and dampened by weeks
of neglect; however, their pantry was also neglected.
A hearty collection of maize and cereals sat
abandoned and undisturbed while a half-dozen bushels
of potatoes and cabbage turned to spoil. The home's
pantry appeared wholly disregarded in whatever haste
provoked the departure of Mr. Seymour and his family
from their home, as undetected it was at the time of
its passing and inscrutable the nature of the thing
remains today.
I pray, in private, that this discovery bears no
relation to another misfortune, news of which arrived
this morning. Though my request to our honourable
Director at Fort Amsterdam was graciously fulfilled
after some brief delay, the two carts he dispatched,
loaded with timber for the furnaces of our village,
were set upon by raiders. The shipment was observed

```
======================================================================
Page [06/06]            [ PgUp ] Prev. Page          [ PgDn ] Next Page
----------------------------------------------------------------------
```

passing through New Utrecht, but a farmer from one of
that towne's nearby estates found the two carts
dragged violently from their ruts upon trail and the
bodies of a pair of teamsters deceased and concealed
in an adjacent ditch. This much is common knowledge
already and, when digested alongside the
disappearances of the Seymours, has caused a pall of
general despair to descend around our village. I am
told, in confidence, of a bit more: that these
teamsters were not recovered in a state of wholeness.
There is evidence that the carts were led by exactly
two men when they first departed, but the state in
which they were left to be discovered unsettles me to
record, even in the privacy of my own thoughts and
this diary. It must therefore suffice to say that
their bodies, or the remains which most closely
constitute the bodies of the two men, were buried on
the spot, spared a return to the eyes of Fort
Amsterdam and, I pray further, from the details of
the written condolences which will extend the
Atlantic to their families.

I am further advised that a set of tracks leads
away from the road and presumably corresponds with
the route which the bandits diverted our stolen fuel.
As the news reached our village and the sun receded
toward the horizon, there were few volunteers willing
to form a party to investigate further.

```
======================================================================
```

Part II:
Katabasis, Kowaliga

Fri. 03/09/1990, 2329 hrs.

Six

"Behind me is the small town of Orpheus, New York. From where I stand, here on Mount Howard, it looks the very image of a wholesome, Christian America."

The mulleted television presenter extended a denim shirtsleeve and gestured over his shoulder while he spoke. In a far corner of the precinct's muster room, Lucy's eyes drifted away from the screen. As she half-listened to the video, her pen brought the pre-tour notations contained within her memo book up to the present.

"Hello. I'm Jeremy Gravel, and I served that small town as a deputy for fourteen years. During that time, I became aware of a quickly encroaching threat in the battle for the soul of our nation. When I parted ways with the Orpheus Sheriff's Department, I founded Mohawk Valley Ministries."

"Didn't he get shitcanned for pocketing money off crime scenes?" someone whispered near the center of the room.

"I heard it was either cop to that and retire, or get collared for selling the contraband he was confiscating," another officer murmured.

"Quiet!" Lieutenant Cordell shouted from the podium at the front of the room. "The sooner you *shut up*, the sooner we can get this over with and sign the damned Training Log."

The lieutenant held up a small box labelled *Antichrist in America*. When he flipped the video tape's cardboard sleeve, the color drained from his face.

"Run time… *seventy-two minutes?!*"

The sleeve tumbled onto the podium in front of him.

"Fuck me…"

"We have produced this instructional video lecture series to better prepare law enforcement agencies, like yours, to investigate and combat the growing menace of occult-oriented criminal behavior."

The deputy-turned-minister's image faded to a view of the Hollywood sign.

"Satanism is more than just the makeup affected by heavy metal headbangers and Hollywood punkers desperate to attract attention and invade the ears of our children. It is a multifront, coordinated menace

assaulting our families, our communities, and our way of life. Music, television, role playing games, and video games…"

A game of *Asteroids* now appeared on the screen, then transitioned back to a stern Jeremy Gravel.

"Are they really nothing more than the mere frivolous diversions they claim to be? There are many atrocities that remain unsolved in towns like Orpheus and, shockingly, even in your very own community. You, as members law enforcement, may struggle for an explanation to some of the seemingly senseless and depraved behavior you encounter every day. Today, we hope to shine a light on some dark traditions and beliefs gaining popularity at an alarming rate, yet are also regrettably protected by those who exploit our Constitution and its guarantees of free expression. We will explore some of these taboo doctrines in search for possible explanations to those heinous mysteries that haunt our caseloads."

The double doors to the muster room creaked open. Lucy's attention turned from her memo book to watch her partner, Tabby, slide in through a crack in the doors. The lieutenant might have noticed, had his face not fully planted into his hands, propped up by his elbows upon the podium. Tabby continued carefully across the room, tiptoeing over to the chair behind Lucy.

"What's this shit?" she whispered.

"You're gonna wish you'd run even later. The lieu' says it's part of our new training on account of, well… y'know… *murders.*"

"Cops like you and I recognize the potential for violence when we discuss cults like these. Not only are their practices and forms of expression difficult for us to comprehend, their deviant sexual behavior, limitless drug use, and lust for power reach a level we've never had to contend with before. Therefore, we will help you as investigators of possible occult-oriented incidents by considering their twisted motives through the lens of what we call 'abnormal sexology.' Remember: we are introducing you to perps who are vicious, revolting, and capable of inspiring fear in any community. Men must know to fear for the safety of their wives, mothers, and daughters—and women: for themselves."

"Yikes…" Tabby groaned. "Who approved this?"

"Shh!"

Tabby's former partner, Jimmy, turned around.

"It's just gettin' good."

Since returning from his injury, Jimmy found himself reassigned to administrative duties within the station house.

"You are likely to encounter Satanists as they progress through one of the three primary levels of devil worship:

"The earliest phase consists of dabblers. They're introduced to Satanism through heavy metal rock and roll music, video games, or role-playing games such as Dungeons and Dragons. They may insist to you that it's all innocent fun as it begins to consume their lives… and souls.

"At the second level we find true believers in the spiritual aspects of the dark arts. They have begun to understand that there is power in turning from Christ to worship of Satan, and even greater power in worshiping as a member—or even high priest—of a coven.

"And at the third and final level, these forsaken souls believe that the most fitting tributes they may offer their new dark lord are criminal acts of property destruction, violence… and even murder. The more heinous and depraved their acts, the more innocent their victim—the greater they honor their infernal master. The modern soldier of Satan may even believe that their continued, devout patronage will augment their criminality, granting them abilities of clairvoyance, manipulation, deception, and stealth far beyond those of traditional reprobates."

"Alright, enough!"

Cordell's face popped away from his hands. His index finger shot onto the VCR's eject button.

"Users of hallucinogenic or so called 'mind-expanding' drugs may be attempting to project their own consciousness behind the eyes of the infernal beasts of Hell themse—"

"Lieu," Jimmy said as his hand shot up into the air. "Quick question!"

Cordell paused. When he accepted that Jimmy would not be discouraged by glare alone, he extended verbal acknowledgement.

"Yes, Daley…"

"If we see the Devil, are we supposed to try and collar 'im or can we just go ahead and shoot on sight? Or do we need to call you first?"

"Call a priest. Hell, call the Ghostbusters, too. But if you're seein' demons, you'd sure as shit best not to call me," the lieutenant responded dryly. "Now, get outta my stationhouse. Fall out!"

Lucy tucked her memo book into her back pocket and followed the stream of cops out of the muster room and into the hallway. The hallway ran past several offices before it opened to the precinct's front desk and main entrance. Most of the offices were shuttered for the day, their doors locked, and windows darkened—with one exception. As Lucy passed by, she gazed in upon the provisional home of the task force established in the wake of the previous month's chaos. Days became weeks, and the windows peering into the task force turned opaque. They were filled with a curtain of clippings from tabloid front pages and articles meant to remind the officers and detectives within of their mission. *DEPRAVED KILLER SINKS CITY UNDER TIDE OF PANIC* read the headline of the Post from February 13th. It took less than a week for photographs from inside the apartment on 63rd Street to leak to the press. Black and white images of spiraling, bloody words and mutilated bodies filled the newspaper from corner to corner under the headline. Another one from the Daily News published a week later featured a more subtle shot of dried, bloody footprints on the sidewalk outside the house. *RUNNING WITH THE DEVIL IN FEAR CITY* read the headline, followed by smaller text which skeptically asked *LONE WOLF OR PACK OF DEVIL WORSHIPPERS?*

In the few remaining gaps between tacked-up clippings, Lucy saw the detectives still manning their stations. In the middle of the room sat Sam Vernon. His head lolled over the back of his chair while he searched for patterns on the room's white drop-ceiling panels. The department had pulled about a dozen detectives and uniformed patrolmen from their usual duties across nearly every borough. Their goal was explained simply: investigate and effect an arrest, then depart the detail with the city's gratitude. Not without perceptible regret, Vernon and his partner, Delavan, led the ongoing mission.

"Vernon looks like shit."

"Sure does," Tabby agreed cheerfully. "Almost as if someone slipped the extensions for every line in their office to the Morning Tribune's metro desk. Be a shame if someone snuck in and plugged the phones back in, too."

"Useless buncha' mopes!"

Lucy and Tabby both turned in time to see Captain Debois storm around the corner. They jumped backwards as the Sixty Fourth Precinct's commanding officer marched briskly toward them. His attention was focused elsewhere, however, as he brushed past them without breaking pace. Debois's palm slammed onto the task force's door. Vernon looked like he might get whiplash from the force that propelled him upright in his seat.

"Could I ask one of you assholes a question? How is it damn near midnight and I've got the Times on one line asking me if every stray dog is the victim of a gang of dognapping Devil worshippers, while One Police Plaza is on the other line champing at the bit to ream me out because last month's primary witness is now being *publicly* second guessed by one of my detectives?"

The walls of the task force could not sufficiently contain the captain's shouts, and soon his voice echoed throughout the building. The detectives assembled therein sat stunned, jaws hanging open. When none offered any response and Debois's frustrations failed to subside, he slammed the door closed behind him and approached Vernon. Though not presently the target of the captain's displeasure, Lucy realized she had become frozen as anyone else ahead of his path. A sudden yank at her shoulder broke the trance.

"Don't get caught snooping," Tabby said. "The last thing you need is a taste of that."

Lucy watched Tabby move away from the window, then rest her back against the wall.

"Listen in over here where they won't see."

Lucy followed her partner's lead and made herself inconspicuous as possible while the Captain's diatribe continued.

"It's been nearly a month. Murders for the past twelve months citywide are nearing two thousand. And yet, the only thing I ever hear about is these fucking kids, conjuring ghosts and getting blown away."

Vernon's head wobbled up and down as he knees failed to commit to standing or sitting.

"We might'a caught this case, Cap, but we didn't get a whole lotta witnesses to go along with it."

"What about the scene? The walls were splattered with evidence! Blood, bullets, gunpowder residue. Whoever did it covered themselves in enough blood to leave a trail fifty feet long from the front door!"

Lucy glanced over at Tabby. That night, while she was stuck at the Elysian Fields listening to the pandemonium playing out over her radio, she could only wonder how it looked inside that apartment. Afterwards, she read the same horrific gore in the newspapers and sensational television reports as everyone else. She also knew that Tabby had gone inside herself, originally banished to secure the perimeter but later called to action by her injured partner, Jimmy. Now that it was Lucy's turn to work with Tabby every night, she could not summon the courage to pry any details from her new partner.

"I gave you time," Captain Debois said, continuing his rebuke. "I gave you a whole squad of your own to lead and the best criminalistics lab in the country, but you haven't done a damn thing with any of it! A month gone and you haven't given me shit but for one witness who says she was still half asleep when she heard whatever it was she heard and didn't see a damn thing."

"Well, technically, sir," Vernon stuttered. "Her dog heard it too."

"Oh, that's fucking terrific, let me know when you get Fido in here for a deposition."

"Actually, it's Molass—"

"And then, you can tell the Daily News you're '*still seeking out more reliable witnesses*' again."

"I misspoke when I told them that. What I meant was—"

"Then don't say anything to anyone," Captain Debois barked. "If you can't keep your fucking foot out of your mouth, quit talking! At first this task force couldn't stop blabbing to the press. After that, you were spending the entire day getting your stories straight and correcting the record. Now that you've got the papers worked into a frenzy, you lock yourselves in here all day to hide from them."

"Hey," Lucy whispered. "You said you spoke to someone that night, right? They're saying she's the *only* person who knows anything?"

"Yeah… but it sounds like she isn't telling 'em what wanna hear."

"So, I'll give you one more chance," Debois continued. "Tell me, right here and now, what your next fucking step is."

Vernon's knees threw in the towel. He deflated into his chair. Nearby, someone cleared their throat.

"The girl…"

Ricky Delavan leaned forward and continued.

"Alice Weber. The staff over at General stabilized her, but couldn't do much more—she's still slippin' in and out of the coma, I mean. They're talkin' about transferrin' her over to some rehab center. We're gonna stop by tomorrow before the transfer goes through and see if she's in any state to interview."

"Thank your partner for bringing a few brain cells to work with him today, Vernon," Captain Debois said wearily. "If that girl wakes up, it could be the miracle we're looking for."

*　　*　　*

"*A witness to the murder of Yusuf Hawkins in Bensonhurst last August has resurfaced. Following a two-month disappearance, witness John Vento surrendered to FBI officials in Dayton, Ohio earlier this week. He returned to New York earlier today escorted by both NYPD and federal agents from LaGuardia airport to Kings County Supreme Court, where he appeared before a judge. According to Mr. Vento's attorney, his client still remains undecided as to whether he is ultimately willing to testify in the pending trial.*"

"Is it always like this?"

"Yeah. Sure. It always moves slow. It's always boring until you wish it still was."

"Something else. The volume of it all."

"That's a part of it. It comes in waves."

"*After numerous fierce exchanges in the streets of Bensonhurst over the months that followed Mr. Hawkins' death last August, something akin to calmness had begun to appear in the neighborhood—a tense reprieve while the wheels of bureaucratic jurisprudence ground infinitely fine, if slow as ever.*"

"So, you noticed it too?"

"It's hardly the first time. Always has. No idea why—"

"People are definitely getting worked up again, though."

"—not that I haven't heard some theories. Mostly they get on edge from what they read in the newspapers, not what they actually see during the day."

"What about us? The people out there, they're seeing it in isolation. They hear what they hear on the radio, what they see on the eleven o'clock news, but we're there each time."

"They can't see the forest through the trees."

"Now, shades of a new menace begin to emerge amidst a weary community. For more, we take you to our reporter Oswald Cohen, reporting live from Brooklyn."

"From the trees."

"Right. That's part of the problem—*context.* Just because it's terrible—*inhuman*—there's not necessarily anything supernatural, anything sinister about it. The results are no worse than any of the other mundane, less personal acts of cruelty people casually inflict upon each other with far more regularity."

"No worse? No worse than—"

"It all started a month ago in Bensonhurst: the senseless massacre of those five young college students in February still tests the uneasy peace of a community along the outer fray of Brooklyn."

"Granted. What I mean is that it doesn't come down to worse or better. The best detective I ever knew said *'it's all part of life's rich pageant, you know?'"*

"Was it Vernon?"

"What? God… *no.* He wishes. At the end of the day, all you get from worrying is distortion. Noise and interference. Without seeing the bigger picture, people fill in the gaps with their own anxieties. It's never really verbalized. Not directly. But still, nothing spreads quicker than fear of the unknown… especially fear of things that end up being nothing at all."

"Those two aren't always the same things."

"That's what I'm saying: *they* can't tell the difference."

"Can *we?*"

"And now, a month later and with no answers from the NYPD and City Hall, worry and impatience continue to spread beyond the borough and throughout the city at large."

"Mostly. Some of us. It's a question without any straightforward answer."

"Reports of cemetery desecrations and toppled gravestones…"

"Like when a tree falls in the woods?"

"Diabolical graffiti appearing on every inch of freshly scrubbed subway cars the moment they emerge from the underground…"

"No, that's just a *bad* question."

"And masked rituals by torchlight in city parks…"

"I don't think there's such a thing as a bad question."

"I'm reporting to you tonight from the intersection of Nostrand and Voorhies in nearby Sheepshead Bay where, late last night, police responded to what appears to have been an attempted dognapping *by a gang of five devil-masked—"*

The volume knob clicked off. The car lurched to a stop and Tabby's hand moved from the radio to the gear shifter.

"Good for you. I think there's plenty of stupid ones. And *wrong* ones?"

"Lemme guess: you think there's more than a few."

"Depending on the context—on *any* context—sure as hell you can always find plenty of people asking the wrong questions. Sometimes they accidentally stumble onto the right answer."

"And the other times?"

"Pray they don't come looking for someone to blame. Put us 84."

*   *   *

"And then, other times he'd come home late. It was like he knew when I would give up and go to bed. But this time, I… officer, I'm just so afraid."

The first step groaned. The next whined. The staircase leading up to the third-floor apartment rose sharply and turned continuous tight rights. Lucy watched the backs of Tabby's boots climb mere inches ahead but a full foot above her own. Mrs. Olivera was within earshot, but only the fluttering blue bottom of her nightgown kept her in Lucy's view as the woman lead them upward. A landing must have been reached, for the trailing nightgown disappeared while her worries still travelled throughout the hallway.

"This time, it's different. I just know, is all."

"When was the last time you saw him?"

Lucy still had a few steps left in her climb. Without any immediate response to the question, she was unsure her words reached much further than of her stride. Her partner might have heard, for Tabby echoed the inquiry.

"It's been two full days, now. A few hours more than two. The last thing he said was that he was on his way to see friends from James Buchanan High School."

"What grade is he?"

Lucy watched Mrs. Olivera from behind. Her slippers came to a halt under the exposed backs of her heels. She searched the dim ceiling and thought.

"Well, a sophomore, I suppose. On paper, still a freshman—but a sophomore If he'd finished the last year on better terms. If he'd finished it on *any* terms."

"But he didn't," Tabby said.

"No, ma'am. No, officer."

"So, if Robert ain't going to school anymore, how's he passing the time?"

"I always begged him. I tried to let him know how much I wished he'd just… show a little bit better judgment when it came to who he hung out with."

"Do you know *their* names," Lucy asked. "Where they live?"

"No," Mrs. Olivera sighed. "At first I was relieved…"

The woman began to walk forward again, slower than before, and came to a stop a few feet down the hall by a closed door.

"I used to bang on his bedroom door. He was becoming so reclusive. He'd only ever go out to buy those… *violent* funny papers. And new cassette tapes. I don't even know what sort of music Robert listened to. He'd stay in there all day and all night with his headphones on, miles away in those horror stories. One day, last year, I'd just about given up. I was watching the news. I thought he was in his room…"

Mrs. Olivera's hand grabbed the doorknob. Her wrist turned. Lucy felt the air shift. A breeze twisted around the stairwell behind her. She heard the heavy door on the ground-level entrance slam shut. A few moments later, the face of a young man rose over the top of the steps. Brown peach fuzz rested over his upper lip. His hair was a lighter shade of brown than Mrs. Olivera's bob, but shaggy and only slightly shorter.

"Ma'! What the hell is this? You brought over the cops, now?"

"She did," Tabby interrupted. "Watch your mouth."

"Robert!"

Mrs. Olivera sighed. There was relief in her voice. Lucy suspected something else, as well.

"Well, youse can call off the search. I'm only stoppin' by to grab my shit. Let search an' rescue know: from now on, don't bother lookin' for what doesn't want to be found."

As Robert Olivera pressed through the crowded hallway, he kept his head trained away from his mother. She opened her mouth as he stomped through the doorway and into the bedroom. After a moment, she closed it again.

"Robert," Lucy said. "You know we're here because your mother called. She was worried. If something had happened to you—if you'd been hurt—she wouldn't have known."

A dresser drawer creaked open. Lucy tried to angle her head into the bedroom to keep an eye on the young man.

"Let her worry. Wouldn't change anything. As it turns out, her baby boy is doin' just fine."

Lucy scoffed. She tried to prevent her annoyance showing, but she was not confident that her strained voice proved especially convincing.

"I dunno, are you? This whole thing is gonna be documented. Just because you popped up in time doesn't mean we aren't still taking a report."

Robert reemerged. That which he needed to collect had not taken long. The young man replied casually as he hurried back down the hallway.

"Whatever. What's another report in the file? Go ahead an' do what you gotta do, officer. *Ma'am.* And while you're takin' messages for the boys back at the station, let Jason know I'll see him in the same place, next week if he wants to haul me into Spofford for truancy. Hell, gimme a couple days' head start an' I can cook up some better charges for him than truancy this time."

Lucy felt her hands tense. Fingernails dug into her palms. She did not often feel compelled by principle to strike another person—much less a child in the presence of their parent. She looked toward Tabby to gauge whether her partner's energy mirrored her own. Tabby's posture was relaxed. Her mouth smirked.

"Sure, kid," Tabby said. "I'm sure *'the boys back at the station'* will be relieved to hear it."

Robert hesitated. His feet stopped momentarily, and his head turned back toward Tabby. At a loss for a reply, he sucked his teeth and began to work his way back down the staircase.

"Hold up, we're not through here."

Lucy heard her voice crack. Robert Olivera ignored her. She swore inside her own head.

"It's alright," Mrs. Oliver said softly. "Just… forget I called."

If the stairs groaned and whined during his descent, Lucy could not hear it over the stomping of his boots. The door below slammed shut. When the house was silent again, Mrs. Olivera continued.

"I did my best. I did what I could. I always will."

Lucy took a deep breath. The pages of a missing report slid back and forth between her index finger and thumb. She was grateful when Tabby broke the silence.

"You were saying? You saw something on TV?"

"Uhh, yes."

Mrs. Olivera's voice sounded weak. She paused to compose herself and return her mind to where she had left off.

"It was back when I could depend, y'know, that he was at least in his room. Sort of present, but not at the same time. Not emotionally. The only thing I had was that I knew—that I *believed*—was that he was safe."

While she spoke, Mrs. Olivera crossed through the doorway and into her son's room. As she followed, Lucy observed that the dimensions of Robert's bedroom were consistent with the stairscase, the hallway, and—presumably—the rest of the Oliveras' home: tight. Fortunately, Tabby did not budge from her position outside the room.

"It wasn't long after that boy got killed. Last August. I'm sure you remember. It was the first time they marched down Eighteenth Avenue, when the news showed up with all their cameras. When I first heard he was killed, I thought it was terrible. But I wrote it off. There's criminals in every neighborhood. I don't need to tell the two a'you that. Dangerous, vindictive people. Wrong places and wrong times. I've lived in Bensonhurst my whole life. I might not get out much… I may have been too soft on my children… but I'm not naïve. I *thought* I wasn't.

"That was 'til I saw my neighbors on the TV—people I saw every Sunday in church. I knew too many faces crowding those sidewalks. It brought out the worst in them. It brought out things that I'd told myself didn't happen anymore. Things left behind in the past. When they weren't laughing like maniacs, they were saying things they would've never otherwise dared. There were so many young men. Neighborhood boys. And in the middle of them, in the center of the camera, a face I missed so dearly.

"Their arms were draped over Robert's shoulders. They jeered. He jeered with them. I thought of how many times I begged him to leave his room, go out into the world. I said if he couldn't reconnect with the friends he had who were still in school, the ones he'd grown up with, then at least he could make some new friends. I heard my own voice replaying for me when I listened to the poison pouring from Robert's mouth for the whole world to hear. I felt stupid."

The sweat from Lucy's palms warped the blank paperwork in her hand. If smothered stress still forced her to massage it, her fingers would have long ground straight through its pages. As it was, her hand remained motionless while Mrs. Olivera spoke.

"I… wish I had confronted him about it," she continued. "I wish I could tell you who they were or where they could be found. I won't lie to you: I didn't want to know. But ignoring the problem hasn't worked, has it?"

Seven

"What do you see?"

Pressure radiated outward from Charlie's temples. The muscles surrounding his eye sockets strained as they fought to focus his vision. Rolling waves of electricity convulsed along nerves until they came crashing into one another. Charlie struggled to shield his eyes from the intense glare of the waning sun over the western horizon. Intrusive impulses begged him to force his eyes open and examine further. Streams of tears overflowed and tumbled down his cheeks. Gradually, shapes oscillated and merged, condensing into a scene between Charlie's fluttering eyelids.

"Focus… and tell me what you see, Charlie…"

His vibrating pupils continued to stabilize. The emerging world bathed in the intense sunlight. Charlie could hear traffic screaming past on a nearby highway. The Belt, he realized. Not too far beyond, waves roared as they broke against the sea wall. Charlie brought his right thumb and index finger up to his eyes and cleared away welled-up tears. He lifted his left hand before him to shield his face from the sun's glare. He was standing on the side of the road—Shore Parkway—not far from home. The local, one-way service road ran parallel to the highway, separated by a chain-link fence. An offramp fed highway traffic back onto the local roads of Bath Beach, and Shore curved inland alongside to accommodate until they intersected at Independence. Beneath the offramp, just across Shore, sat a small, windowless, red brick shed. Its simple rectangular form looked as though ancient tectonic pressure had long ago ejected the cubic structure up from within the ground itself. In the process of its emergence, the shed appeared to have pulled the natural carpet along with it, as a web of overgrown shrubbery, creeping vines, and mud clung tight against its walls. Charlie recognized the building immediately. He knew of many other identical buildings scattered along the length of the highway as it traced the shoreline of Gravesend Bay. This one, like all the others, featured a flat roof trimmed in gray-painted cement. A circle was engraved in the middle of the roof's trim. Two lightning bolts spread horizontally, one in each direction, extending outward from the orb to the right and left corners of the roof. The shed itself featured two doors approximately ten feet apart. The door on the right was solid and flat, and looked to be tightly sealed. The door to the left featured louvered panels with horizontal slats. Where its twin appeared shut tight, the louvered door sagged backward and left the entrance slightly ajar. Beyond this narrow threshold, a black, unlit interior stared back at Charlie.

Despite the persistent noise of passing cars, the highway, the road before him, and the offramp descending behind the shed all appeared empty. Charlie took a step forward and began to cross the street. He watched abundant greenery sway in the lazy breeze. One bush next to the shack's unlatched door shook swiftly. A young boy jumped out.

"Why'd ya' follow me? Go back home, Charlie!"

Without waiting for a response, the boy turned and darted toward the doorway.

"An' if you tell Pops where I was, I'll kill you!"

Charlie watched the shed's dark interior swallow the younger image of his brother. He remembered when Dexter would disappear for days on end. When he took another step forward, he felt an unsecured shoelace tug at the bottom of his other foot. As Charlie's balance shifted, the shed disappeared, and asphalt rushed up toward his face. He tumbled into the middle of the street. A bolt of pain shot from his elbow. Charlie propped himself up to examine it. Red beads of blood began to push up through scraped flesh. Turning the elbow over, he noticed the skin of his inner arm was smooth, unblemished by track marks. The palm which he had used to shield his eyes from the sun was smaller, too. Tiny fingers reached up and pushed the pair of glasses he had not seen in more than ten years back onto the bridge his nose. Charlie's head angled up. He looked at the shed again. Dexter was still gone, though the doorway was no longer empty. Instead, another figure stood there, only partially visible through the crack in the door and the louvered slats. It was a man. While Charlie recognized him, his presence in this memory felt wrong. Within the pitch-black interior of the small building, from more recent memories came the glowing white sheet, so thin it was nearly translucent. It was familiar, but out of time. It covered the stranger from head to toe and whipped into the air on currents Charlie could not feel. A pair of narrow voids where there should have been eyes burned through the material and came level with Charlie's much lower perspective.

"No," Charlie heard his younger voice whisper. "You weren't there for that."

"A shame."

The sound of the invisible traffic grew louder, but Charlie could not turn his eyes away from the figure in the dark.

"Who?"

"Pay tribute… and that name is yours to know."

The voice drowned in interference. Charlie's ears filled with the sound of rushing air and a roaring engine. He turned to the left and was greeted by the approaching chrome bumper of a yellow Volkswagen Beetle.

Charlie's eyes shot open. He bolted upright in the reclined chair. The air had grown thicker in the time since he let his eyelids slide shut. It was something more than just incense fumes. Everything around him felt damp and heavy.

A motor hummed softly behind him. The back of his chair rumbled. Before it could come completely upright, Charlie lifted himself up on his own. He held his right hand out in front of him, stiffened his fingers, and watched. Steady. There were no shakes. That he had not been high for several weeks would have been enough to render him helpless under normal circumstances, while tremors and convulsions wracked his body—the anxiety added from revisiting past traumas notwithstanding. He leaned back into the chair as it finally rose to meet him. Charlie felt calm. Artificially at peace. It was serenity with an expiration as indeterminable as it was certain.

Recessed ceiling lights slowly reacquainted Charlie's eyes with the apparatus introduced to him as a *'Dream Incubator.'* It reminded him of a dentist's office, motorized recliner and all, but instead of the overhead lamp, drills, and tray tables, the only other fixture in the room was a small altar resting against the wall directly across from where he was seated. Atop the altar was a bundle of incense sticks burning inside a jar. Next to this was a red, vase-shaped device from which water vapor billowed up into the air. Charlie had no idea what sort of liquid it contained, but it smelt like a cross between fireworks and low tide. Regardless, he was sure that in the right atmosphere, such as the one he now occupied, quite a lot of money could be billed in the name of new age-y aroma therapy. To the other side of the incense jar was a rectangular black box.

"Young Charlie. Tell me what you have seen in your dream."

Doctor Martin Glass emerged from the shadows at the edge of Charlie's periphery and walked along the right side of his chair toward the altar. Glass placed a lid over the top of the vase. When the last whisp of smoke evaporated, he turned around to face his new pupil.

"I hope you were able to hear my instructions while you explored. Now, let us discuss that which you remember."

Martin reached for the black box atop the altar. His index finger clicked a button on its top.

"Nothing special," Charlie replied dryly. "Just the same nightmare I've been havin' since I was six."

"A recurring dream?"

"Yeah. It's this thing with Dex. He used to run away a lot when we was younger. Sometimes Dad would beat 'im and he would just disappear. Whenever he came back, he'd catch another beatin' regardless'a how long he was gone."

"So, this is a memory of an actual event?"

"Right. I mean… it seems mostly like the actual thing. I still get hit by that car. But I don't think it's happenin' in the right place."

"Very good. Let us examine that incongruity," Martin said encouragingly. "Start from the beginning and walk me through everything."

Charlie closed his eyes and took a deep breath.

"I wasn't far from our house, maybe a few blocks down the road. It was hard to see exactly where at first."

"It was dark?"

"No, bright. Way, way too bright. The glare made me squint at whatever I was trying to look at. Eventually I could see it was this shack under the highway off-ramp. I think it's a sewer entrance or something. There's a couple of 'em by our place, all along the side of the road. We used to mess around in them a lot—just not on this day, if it's the one I'm thinkin' of. The way it really played out, that was when I got hit by the car a little further up the road. It was right after I tripped chasin' Dexter into Dyker Park."

"Do you remember anything else after that?"

"Nope. The car knocked me out. To this day everything's always been real patchy after that. Spotty, like. That's where the nightmare always ends, too."

"Possibly several negative memories being combined. That might be the product of physical and psychological trauma. It may also be the result of many years' worth of reinterpretation and distortion. What else was different this time?"

Charlie hesitated. The dream from which he emerged moments before had already begun to fade.

"I saw a yellow Beetle. A pretty old one. But the way it really happened, I'm pretty sure it was actually a Beamer. Dad got a pretty good settlement out of it. I mean, he blew through it before it came time to buy us any Christmas gifts that year. And he sold off most of the 'scripts the doctors wrote for me. But I got back at 'im. That was when I started coppin' his Valiums."

"Keep your mind off the drugs, Charlie," Martin sighed. "That is in your past now. Bring yourself back into the dream before it fades away. Try to think of anything else unique about this event you have relived so many times before. No matter how shameful or revealing you might think it is."

Charlie laughed.

"Listen, doc, with all respect—I ain't gonna lie t'youse. There ain't a whole lotta shame left about me—"

'A shame.'

The follicles lining the undersides of Charlie's arms stood on end. The icy feeling of the goosebumps made him shiver. He heard the voice from his dreams. He heard himself whisper and words tumbled from his mouth involuntarily.

"A… shame."

"Focus on that. Tell me what you saw."

Charlie felt his mind being pulled upward, out of the room. The scene replayed behind his eyelids. The brick shack set back from the road. The door Dexter ran into. The man in the sheet.

"There's this guy in the door. A man… I don't know, maybe not a *normal* man. But he's only covered by this thin white sheet and it's whippin' around 'im like he's on fire. Pure white. Even brighter than the sun…"

Martin's shoes squeaked as he shifted his weight off the altar and leaned in toward Charlie.

"What did He say?"

"'*A shame*'… that's what I heard. It was right after I saw 'im. I told 'im he wasn't there when this whole thing actually happened. And he replied that it was a shame. Then I got hit by the car… and here I am."

"And when you were spoken to… how did you feel?"

"Calm."

Charlie was surprised by how quickly his response materialized and how freely it left his mouth.

"Comfortable with the whole thing, for once," he continued. "Been wakin' up… cryin' and sweatin' from that dream for years."

Charlie's voice withered in his own ears. His mind caught up to his mouth and stopped him making mention of the wet bed sheets. He shifted subconsciously in his seat and confirmed that his jeans were still dry.

"Thinkin' back on the whole thing used to make me feel like shit. Now, though… I dunno. It feels like something's changed. He wasn't there, I *swear* it. But now it's like he always was. And so it's… different."

Charlie's eyes remained closed as he reflected upon the visitor to his dream. A mechanical *click* reverberated around the silent room. Charlie opened his eyes again and watched Martin extract a small tape cassette from the black rectangle on the altar. The pen in his other hand scribbled a quick note on its label and both fell into a pocket inside Martin's khaki sport coat.

"Excellent work today, Charlie," he said with a patient smile. "Now come along, we have to meet with the others and prepare for tonight."

On the inside, the Oneirological Process Mission looked like a high-end funeral home. It smelled like a library haunted by the spirit of stale popcorn. A few other hints of the building's past life as a movie theater still lingered around. As they left the room housing one of thirteen dream incubators, Charlie recognized the old Loew's concession stand, now remodeled with modern glass and marble fixtures into the Mission's concierge. The way everything had been previously persisted as a faint, parallel life within Doctor Glass's emerging operation. *Within*—perhaps *in between*, Charlie thought. Martin's pace did not slow for any similar sentimentality. Instead, his gait continued briskly along one of the facility's wider public hallways. The soles of Charlie's shoes chirped occasionally as he kept pace along the white faux-marble floor tiles. The high pitch echoed throughout the cavernous building.

"The brothers and sisters who so generously donate their time to keeping our facility clean go heavy on the floor wax at my request."

"Gotta look good for the donors and seekers, I guess," Charlie considered with a shrug.

"That is true. But as a practical matter, a lifetime in my discipline has taught me that it does not hurt to have a few extra reflective surfaces available to distinguish mortal associates from infernal ones."

Charlie's eyes shot downwards. He was not sure what he expected to find reflected in the floor. After a moment, he was not sure *why* he wanted to. Indeed, the floor shined like the surface of a mirror. The hallway's walls, its ceiling—all were adorned with mirrors or other such reflective surfaces. While Charlie continued the search against his own judgment, his gaze caught Martin's eyes reflecting back toward him.

"You are a part of something bigger now, Charlie," Martin said in a cold yet instructional voice.

Glass's brisk march came to an abrupt halt. Unnerving as his glare had been among the reflected light, the direct view turned upon Charlie was one of unparalleled intensity.

"Should that be for the betterment of all we are trying to accomplish in these halls... or otherwise. If you do not plan deliberately or act confidently when dealing with the darkness around you or within, it will overwhelm you. It *will* destroy you. It can smell your doubt and dig in with clawed hands. You will come to understand—that which hungers for all eternity tends to draw little distinction between that which is sacrificed and those who make the sacrifices."

"So, bitin' the hand that feeds?"

"There are ancient, powerful forces keeping watch over everything in creation. They are infinitely distant yet loom uncomfortably close across all time. Keepers of all knowledge, forever ignorant of the fleeting, turbulent ecstasy contained in each mortal life they are destined to consume. No, *'biting the hand that feeds them'* is a concept of little consequence in a universe to which your soul is already promised. It is primarily a question of time in the face of those both blessed and cursed to timelessness. But there is another, more perverse element sustaining our existence. Let us continue."

Charlie could not remember the advice of any spiritual leader that left him feeling near empty as those of Doctor Glass. In all fairness, he realized, he could not actually recall the last time he attended any form of religious instruction or worship. From what he knew of church—or, at the very least, its depictions in snippets on television or in movies—if it was not always especially inspiring or if the picture it painted of existence was essentially bleak, it was never as aggressively crushing. Nevertheless, when Martin Glass turned again to the depths of the Mission, Charlie found himself keeping pace a few feet further to the man's rear. Charlie found himself studying the doctor as he followed. The way he spoke, the way his voice sounded, the look in his eyes—they all predated his barely-wrinkled skin by decades.

"How long have you been at this?" Charlie asked. "This whole witchcraft… thing."

Glass did not skip a beat as he walked—however, the glance emerging over his shoulder caused Charlie to stumble.

"That's what, I mean…" Charlie stammered. "Bethany. That's what she's doing, right?"

Charlie did not know what it felt like when a person's soul was forcefully extracted from their body, but he was beginning to have some idea until Martin Glass's eyes softened. The man's head turned no further in Charlie's direction, but he could see the muscles in his cheek approximate what might have been a grin.

"Few would find *'witchcraft'* a complimentary phrase for serious activities, though it has been invoked with generous license to describe many diverse fields and traditions—typically, right before attempts at persecution or, ultimately, eradication."

"I… I'm sorry, I didn't—"

"I would never ask you to apologize for generations of errors and other mistruths compounded into the world around you. The world that raised you. Ignorance is only unforgiveable when it is wielded to forge more mistruth. *Honesty*, Charlie, is the language of learning. And learning is the only path to ascension, to salvation—to realizing a purpose for your soul. That is why I opened the Mission.

"What you have been programmed to call '*witchcraft*' is ancient as the first mortal eyes turning up to the heavens, reaching into the darkness, and understanding that they were being watched as well. *'Rather than slaving to the receding sun or dwindling campfire,'* they thought, *'instead of cowering for lifetime after lifetime, why not speak to the darkness itself?'* At first, it must have been terrifying to probe that great abyss. But there were many truths to be found in the black void between the stars and the ancient consciousness therein eager to feel the illumination of those probing dreamers. And the deeper they explored, the greater they dared dream, the more wisdom borne unto them.

"No, there is no such thing as *witchcraft*. Not in this place at least. I am in the knowledge business, Charlie, and no one has more knowledge to trade than those who watch eternally from within that abyss. Humanity's short, numbered days overflow with suffering, anger, and tragedy—all the energies immortals have envied and fought over for eons. For just a taste, the ancient masters in the void will gladly share their knowledge and their power."

"A taste? You mean… death?"

"Death is a natural and necessary consequence of life. A promise made by the universe. Fate. I mentioned earlier another element, and the question of time. It can be easy to see nothing but chaos when all you see is nothingness. On the contrary, the universe turns on rigid covenants. Gravity forges a nearly immutable hierarchy amidst so much power on such a vast scale. One power at a time reigns supreme, and the rest trickles down among ranks to every prince and duchess in its orbit, extending all the way down to legion knights and squires. Even the lowliest among them would tower over you or I, but they all have the same weakness. The same hunger. One that only mortal hands can deliver."

"Sacrifice."

Charlie bit down on his tongue. He had not meant to interrupt, but the word pushed past his mouth. When Doctor Glass did not immediately reply, he braced himself. Glass made a noise in response. Instead of correction—instead of any words at all, the noise resembled approval. Glass opened a door to a stairwell and Charlie followed. One flight down and their journey continued into the building's basement.

"A bargain," Martin Glass continued. "Not the soul itself, which fate never fails to deliver in a matter of time. Special dedication, on the other hand, is a premium. Agony. Passion. Despair. Raw energy."

"That's why we—why Dexter and Bethany—had to go to the house up on 64th Street?"

"Among other tasks I required of your brother and Ms. Ward, yes. That was part of a covenant. Those acts upheld our end of an agreement."

Charlie wanted to ask the question being begged. His mouth caught up with his growing sense of terror and resisted. Even along the basement corridor, his eyes landed on an approaching mirror. He wondered if his fear was showing. Before he could step into its frame, he looked away. He did not know if he should be thankful when Glass continued.

"Those bound by the eternal chains of universal gravity to serve under their masters may also serve those who honor the same. So long as these tributes continue, those princes and lieutenants of the great, dark crown near the center of the void become servants for hire. Their powers become ours—so long as our mutual benefactor stays fed."

"*Our* benefactor?"

Doctor Glass's pace wound down until he stopped by another pair of large, industrial doors. He extended an arm and braced a door handle.

"Theirs. Mine. *Yours.* I believe you have met, though you may not have been introduced. He who wields the viper in his right hand—"

Charlie swallowed hard. His mouth opened and words began to pour out once more.

"Covered, consumed by that white cloth," Charlie groaned. "A flame in the darkness. A shadow in the light."

Glass made no attempt to conceal the grin spreading across his face.

"It's true, then. *That name is yours to know.*"

Charlie's mouth opened wider as his jaw sank.

"That was the Great King of the Darkness," Glass whispered. "Our lord, Belial."

Charlie's skull throbbed. Familiar pains crept from his chest to his head. He felt eyes everywhere.

"W-well, is he here now?"

"Remember what I said: show no fear. He is always here. His loyal, infernal servants as well. Tonight's offering is another important milestone. We need their compliance, and they in turn demand obligation."

Charlie felt himself sinking into the polished floor. A restless, invisible kingdom of monsters rose around him faster than his sanity preferred. Even if he chose to leap off the wagon right now, flee the depths of Glass's renovated movie theater, and fill his veins with the first shit he could find topside, there was no hiding. Belial had his number, never any farther than the other side of his own drooping eyelids, with an army jonesing to tear him apart in his sleep.

"And that is why you must participate tonight," Doctor Glass continued. "We cannot ignore His interest in you. Not when there is much work left to be done before the true purpose of this Mission can be fully realized. I acquired a new patient recently. She lives only to dream now— a victim to an especially vicious trauma and a prisoner in her own body. But when one element of the mortal spirit is cut short, others compensate. In this newly adopted state, I believe that this subject's heightened abilities are a blessing to us. I have spent many decades searching for something that was unjustly taken from me. Hidden away by jealous and fearful men. But these men are lost to time, while I persist. Now, with her guidance and your blessed hands, I can seize that which is rightfully mine."

Charlie watched a new energy fill Martin. As he spoke, passion rose in his voice and his eyes darted all around Charlie.

"You are to assist Bethany. Some local racketeers entered into a contract for our services. Services which, by no happy coincidence, put us in the exact place where this very valuable object was stashed and forgotten so long ago. Out of duty and covenants to our client and dark benefactor alike, we must deliver. Blood must flow. That which is mine must be returned to me."

Charlie struggled to adapt to the strange inertia around him. He realized Doctor Glass had stopped speaking. When the man's eyes ended their frantic search, they came to rest squarely on Charlie.

"Great," Charlie forced himself to reply. "No pressure."

Martin responded by laying a hand on Charlie's shoulder.

"You are to strictly comply with every directive Bethany orders upon you. As long as you listen to her, you will succeed—and you will shepherd what I seek back to me."

Charlie took a deep breath. He thought of his brother.

"I won't let you down."

"I trust you, Charlie. You still have a lot of preparation left to do tonight. Bethany and your brother are back here preparing your tools as we speak."

Glass pushed the door handle and pressed his weight against one of the double doors. The boiler room smelled like shit and rotten meat. At the distant rear wall of the room, the Mission's gigantic furnace roared. They stood at the threshold, but Charlie could already feel sweat beading on the small of his back. A pair of tall, ornately decorated candles burned on either side of another small altar, similar to the one in his dream incubator upstairs. As he entered the room, Charlie passed by to get a closer look. Melted wax pooled around the base of candles. Latin letters and gilded crosses and images of Christ nailed thereon hung upside down, as the candles themselves had been inverted, and the wicks now burned from their upturned bases. Stacks of promotional flyers lie scattered across the floor in front of the altar. Charlie stooped down. He lifted one of the leaflets closer and recognized the name of a local nightclub:

The Rave Never Ends At

HALLELUJAH!

Atop the cellar's small altar sat an egg-shaped, brass container slightly smaller than a football. Its surface was pocked with small perforations through which a putrid haze billowed. A wisp of the smoke stung at one of Charlie's nostrils and sent him leaping and coughing backwards. His left eye winced as tears leaked out.

"God damn," Charlie shouted. "That smells like shit!"

"That's because it *is* shit," Bethany said as she approached the altar. "Among other things."

Bethany reached out and clutched a mass of chains extending from the top of the metal sphere. Suspended from the chains and now swinging slightly, a thicker and more potent cloud of the fetid gas poured out. Charlie smothered the openings to his sinuses with a shirt sleeve and backed away. Bethany began to rhythmically sway the brass vessel over a nearby workbench. A pair of handguns lie next to each other atop the table.

Not far away, Dexter stood over another workbench. A large, illuminated magnifying glass hung in front of his face from the end of an articulating arm. His attention was trained on an etching pen and a tray of bullets. Charlie walked closer until he was able to discern the spiral cuts Dexter carved at the tip of each cartridge. When each symbol was marked, his brother dropped the completed bullet back into the tray.

"Rise and shine, brother o'mine," Dexter chirped.

He mimed a time check on his watchless wrist, then looked up at Charlie.

"Pops always said you liked to sleep the day away, but this is ridiculous."

"Ha-fuckin'-ha," Charlie said as he rolled his eyes. "I'll have you know that I get more done in a single dream than you do jerkin' around all day."

Charlie turned to Doctor Glass. If his words reached the man, they left no obvious impact. Glass was full of encouragement when he spoke to Charlie, despite his intimidating demeanor. Great expectations had been clearly communicated, though the man remained cool most other times. Charlie heard Dexter say *aloof* once, though not where the doctor could overhear. With a twinge of paranoia, Charlie thought about the ever-present ghouls Glass had described. A world full of watching eyes. He wondered if their eyes were matched by similarly omnipresent ears. He felt a droplet of sweat trickle from his scalp, down to his jaw. The back of his shirt was nearly soaked through, and the clamminess was spreading. The sound of whooshing metal rose behind Charlie. He followed the noise back to where Bethany had been blessing the handguns. The incense container no longer swung gently beneath her fingers. Bethany's hands now whipped the chains from which the vessel hung, slicing figure eights into the air. The burning mixture within traced a blazing crimson glow over the array of weaponry as fresh air was force fed to the embers within.

"You sure you've completely woken up? You good?"

Charlie jumped when the hand gripped his shoulder. He replied to Dexter's concerned expression with a confidant scoff.

"Nah, y'know. I'm good."

Despite his best effort, the room began to spin. Charlie's lungs fought for oxygen in the thick, dark haze filling the bowels of Glass's Mission. The floor beneath his feet shifted and his body lurched backward. In a moment, Charlie found himself fortunate enough to have his downward trajectory interrupted by a slouching stack of decaying cardboard boxes. The flames of the desecrated Lenten candles flickered as turbulence continued to churn the air. Charlie struggled to maintain verticality. He counted the four shadows of himself, his brother, his brother's lover, and their mentor as they shimmied over the walls and clutter of the profane workshop. Then he found a fifth silhouette. It slowly climbed the wall behind the altar, lumbering forward until it towered over their own shadows. Something wet landed on Charlie's chin. He wiped at it with a hand, then retraced its path up to his eyes. More tears began to stream down his face—some from the stinging air, some from the calamitous shadow play clawing its way out of the darkness. He shivered under his sweat-soaked clothes and watched as the breath left his body in vaporous puffs. Although previously stifling, the temperature in the room now plummeted. Looking back up, Charlie saw the shape of their dark visitor turn slightly toward where Doctor Glass stood at the side of the altar. The profile of an apparently bald man emerged, licked by black flames burning high over its smooth head. Its mouth unclenched and its jaw dropped, continuing to flex and stretch sickeningly low, like a python unhinging before a meal. The veil of wriggling tendrils covering the figure grew brighter. Darkness itself combusted into a brilliant white inferno, then peeled away from the wall to loom above its mortal congregation. A pair of jet-black points began to extend upwards from the top of its previously smooth head. As they grew—twisting and curling backwards—the emerging rack of horns was encircled by a ring of similarly blackened, jagged thorns. When the coronation was complete their guest boasted a chaotically twisted crown of ebony spikes, splitting and forking to resemble the horns of stags, rams, and elk.

"Belial," Charlie gasped.

He tore his eyes away from the terrifying figure and turned his attention toward the continuing ritual below. By the altar, Martin Glass basked in the demon's furious glow while his mouth chanted words Charlie could not hear over the cacophony bombarding the room. Bethany's hand now extended directly over her head as it swung the metal vessel in a rigid orbit. The shape of the vessel disappeared amidst countless, seamless revolutions. The embers within blazed fiercely, radiating through the metal shell itself, and traced a bloody halo over her head. As it grew hotter, the escaping light strobed the room. With each pass of the beacon, Charlie noticed their guests multiplying. New silhouettes shambled higher onto the boiler room's walls. Though they bore lesser crowns and stuck to the shadows, they asserted imposing authority, nonetheless. Soon, Charlie counted a phalanx of inhuman shadows dancing grotesquely around the room. A scream pierced the air, though Charlie could not tell if it came from Bethany's lungs or the spinning orb itself. She grasped the chain in both hands and swung violently toward the ground. The vessel smashed into the pile of promotional flyers. When its metal shell shattered, it unleashed a shock wave of blinding light. Cinders and ash—smoldering excrement and burning paper—drifted down across every inch of the boiler room. When Dexter let his hand slide away from his face, he found the flames on the candles, the fire in the furnace, and the incandescence of Dexter's work bench all extinguished. Silence flowed back into the completely dark room, but for the sound of Charlie's heart pounding in his own ears.

The lull was broken by the silvery *flick* of a Zippo lighter. It hovered over the two ceremonial candles long enough for their wicks to reignite. When they did, the flames burned blue and a dim, azure light returned to the world. Charlie heard soft footsteps approach him from the altar. Flickers of candlelight reflected off a golden chalice, over which he saw the floating face of his brother. His hands reached out automatically and gripped the cup by its stem. Cradling the warm metal, Charlie gazed over its rim. Its contents were dark, and he could see a thick, crimson froth clinging to its sides as the rest of the liquid swished around within. Doctor Glass's face appeared. The doctor placed one hand on Dexter's shoulder. The next hand landed on Charlie's.

"Drink, Charles Valerie. Drink and be counted among His favorite sons."

Eight

"The security company finished installing them a few weeks ago. When they first gave me their estimate, I thought my parishioners would run me out of the diocese on a rail! Now, though... all I can do is thank the Lord for sending us that salesman."

Tabby sat in the back office of St. Anthony the Great and struggled to control playback of the church's closed circuit security cameras. Father Norman's disembodied voice spoke to her from the other side of the clutter piled atop his desk. His monumental gratitude for the state-of-the-art camera system—into which he apparently invested a considerable chunk of the church's funds— ignored the fact that the equipment had failed to actually prevent the criminality Tabby and Lucy were summoned to investigate.

"If only the cameras kept the church from notching the precinct another burglary," she sighed.

Tabby heard someone in the room suck their teeth. The priest did not betray any obvious offence from the remark. Tabby searched the black monitor in front of her. Over her shoulder, Lucy's reflection sent a look of stern disapproval in her direction. Before her words could cause the mood to curdle any further, Tabby continued.

"I suppose we'll just have to pray the video is clear enough to give us something to work with."

Norman's heaven-sent salesman had not provided any instructions on retrieving footage the cameras captured. Thusly, it fell to Tabby and the Bachelor's in Computer Science the Kingsboro Institute of Technology bestowed upon her over a decade earlier to discern that which she could while her partner navigated a pen around the usual checkboxes and blanks on the report. In under ten minutes' tinkering, it became readily apparent to Tabby that a lot had changed since the late 1970s. Security set-ups were rare in those days, and the banks and department stores that almost exclusively housed them employed skilled operators. Time passed and technology advanced to make video recording less cumbersome. Less exclusive. Progress introduced expanding capabilities to any old, consumer-grade VCR. This only frustrated Tabby more as she lost herself amidst the unending, branching menus of options that appeared as she clicked the machine's half-dozen unlabeled switches. It was possible the system was not working correctly. That or, as Tabby feared, she was getting old. Out of touch. The glare Lucy gave her said it all: *'You hairbag.'*

"So, Father," Tabby said without breaking her concentration on the screen, "any idea what kinds of totals we're putting down for the damages and thefts here tonight?"

"Let me think. The censer, the tabernacle... those were antiques."

Norman's chair groaned as he leaned back and searched the heavens for an answer.

"I'd say about a grand each. The graffiti on the altar and the pews, maybe a few hundred to remove. But those candles, I can't really say. Priceless, I suppose."

Tabby found a dial and spun it cautiously. She watched the timestamp turn backward until it approached the time of the church's last service the evening before.

"I'm sure. Unfortunately for us, government forms don't allow much for sentimentality. If something doesn't have a dollar value, it never existed."

"Members of the church worked on painting those candles for weeks before the start of Lent," Father Norman sighed. "As much wax and wick as it took to make the pair—and it couldn't have been more than a dollar apiece—they were worth more than the sums of either to those who gave their time to decorate them."

If her earlier comment stirred any offense in Norman, he had been gracious enough to spare her knowing. She sensed he grew less gracious as he continued.

"You can't put a price on faith."

Tabby's teeth squeezed the inside of her cheek. She pulled herself away from the video controls and leaned toward Lucy. She pulled down one of the sheets of paperwork with her finger and reached over with a pen in her other hand. In their proper place, Norman's own words were itemized: *Candles; Quantity: 2; Description: Tall, gold lettering; Value: $1.00 each.*

"So," Tabby asked, "you're sure that door was secure?"

"Well, we really haven't been tested like this in the past."

She handed the paperwork back to her partner and returned to the monitor. Tabby switched the display to a camera directed toward the front of the building, then adjusted the replay to 8x speed. The spools in the machine squealed. Strolling passersby accelerated to a brisk sprint. As the crowds zipped back and forth on the sidewalks, foot traffic began to thin. Eight o'clock advanced to nine and those lingering groups became outnumbered by individual stragglers, single-mindedly hobbling toward their destinations. When the timestamp in the corner of the screen reached 21:30, the street in front of the church became entirely devoid of human life. Another half hour passed in the span of a few minutes without so much as a single soul crossing into frame. Tabby sensed a presence looming over her shoulder.

"I think you've got a new problem," Lucy observed. "Either the picture on the TV is fading or there's a defect in the tape. Can you turn up the brightness?"

Tabby leaned back. The image did appear dimmer. She dialed the playback down to time's regular pace, then felt along the bottom of the monitor for any brightness or contrast wheels. She kept a close watch on the time displayed on the screen to make a mental note in case she needed to rewind. While the screen had gone nearly black, the timestamp blazed bright as ever when it reached 22:23.

"It's not the television," Tabby replied. "It's not the screen, either."

"Yeah," Lucy added. "Look at the lights."

Tabby searched the sidewalks for the halos of light beamed down from a trio of streetlamps lining the opposite side of the block. If they were there—fainter than ever—their light vanished entirely as another few seconds brought the screen a shade darker.

"The buildings. The windows, too. Everything's fading out."

"Hey, look," Lucy said. "Something's coming down the street."

A gray car entered the picture. Its headlights remained extinguished as it pulled up to the curb on the now pitch-black street in front of St. Anthony's.

"Can you make out that license plate?" Tabby asked, squinting at the screen as the car came to a stop.

"No idea. I can't even tell what make it is. Paint looks like some dull color. Four doors and a hatchback, but too small to be a station wagon. Unknown make, unknown year, unknown registration, I guess?"

Tabby sighed and shrugged.

"Yeah, sure. Jot it down with the time."

They watched the car idle for a few minutes until both front doors opened in synchronization. Two figures emerged from either side. The vague features of two light-skinned faces floated in the darkness over their uniformly black clothing. The pair approached the church and walked off frame toward the building's side entrance. Tabby's mastery of the surveillance system was improving. She quickly switched to the next camera and found her view transported to the church's side door without losing track of the duo. Their black shapes floated over the door momentarily until one of them pulled an object from within their jacket. The silvery outline of a hammer's head glinted briefly overhead before it swung down. It smashed the doorknob in a single blow. Fragmented parts of the door's lock bounced across the alleyway. The door swung open slowly and the pair of shadows disappeared within.

"You got any other cameras?" Tabby asked. "Anything on the inside?"

Father Norman shook his head.

"I'm sorry, officer. We figured those two would be enough to ward off any potential problems."

Tabby thought about encouraging Norman to throw a few more bucks from the collection plate at a better deadbolt. She bit her tongue. She had said more than enough already.

The exterior of the church became a static, if almost completely pitch-black picture as the clock continued to accumulate minutes. Tabby reached for the fast forward again. Time sprinted once more while she awaited any indication of the shadows' reemergence. Nearly twenty minutes passed before a crack opened between the door and its frame. Tabby pulled back on the throttle and the clock slowed. Quickly and casually as they arrived and forced an entrance, the pair exited and walked back to the car. A few unidentifiable spoils were tossed onto the vehicle's back seat before the successful burglars jumped into the front. The sedan sped down the block and out of the security system's memory. Tabby noted the timestamp one last time: 22:45. Before the clock could reach 22:46, a noticeable degree of light flooded back into the world. Tabby watched the streetlamps begin to glow once more. She thought about the house on 63rd Street. Her eyes again wavered over the bleak chasm inside its gaping, fractured front door. Dark as the unlit neighborhood surrounding it had been, an infectious gloom unfolded inside that place. A shiver pricked at the back of Tabby's neck.

"I think we're done for now, Father."

She suppressed the quiver in her voice. Tabby pushed herself away from the television screen and the troubling, complicated connections her mind searched for within.

"The tapes for these two cameras—can I ask you to make copies and drop them off at the Six Four for the detective squad?"

"Yes, of course," Father Norman replied. "But, it might take me a little while. This stuff is all Greek to me."

Tabby checked her watch. She and Lucy exited Father Norman's office and returned to the main hall of the church. She had made plans to meet up with her former partner at the Reno Diner a few blocks away at two o'clock. An elbow wedged itself between two of her ribs and prompted her to turn. She saw Lucy, gesturing with her flashlight at the church's vandalized altar.

"We've got all that stuff in the report already," Tabby said, dismissing the gesture.

She watched the beam of light rise over the altar.

"What about that," Lucy said. "What about *him*?"

During those intervening moments which evaded capture by Norman's cameras, red lines had been spray painted over every surface of the church's interior. The priest had already showed them most of the superficial damage before bringing them into his office to observe the recordings. The playback on Tabby's own recollection proved harder to control. Her eyes followed the spiraling paths of paint right back to the same month-old ones still fresh in her memory. She thought about the strange, unpronounceable words bleeding from every surface of the walls and ceiling that surrounded her as she pulled Jimmy back onto his feet. The chancel surrounding the church's altar was in not nearly as gruesome a state, though the injuries inflicted thereon prompted the same revulsion the longer she studied them. Her eyes climbed to the ceiling. She searched until she found the crucifix and prayed to never witness anything as grotesque again.

"Must be copycats…"

She heard the fear in her voice. She heard the skepticism and doubt reverberating from the words she forced herself to say. After the leaks to the press, there was little left to the public's imagination. As time went on, there was little she had seen which the rest of the world had not. The panic spread with ease through a dry, tinder city, and it pulled every creep from every corner of the city out of the woodwork. There were undeniably unique, telltale signs to the wannabes and nutcases—the signatures of bitter weirdos and artistic loners. Tabby had never felt herself as reluctant to detect the difference with ease.

"True, could be imposters," Lucy replied. "Spray paint's cheap. That wasn't what I meant, though. Sorry I missed it earlier, but I'll make sure to add it to the report."

Her partner's flashlight bounced around the cross suspended from the ceiling. The white marble body nailed onto it shined back—the same one which Tabby had begged deliver her from insanity a moment earlier. She felt lightheaded. The flashlight's beam flickered, and the red spiraling lines began to tighten and constrict in the many dim corners of the vast, stone chamber. In its absence, the receding darkness revealed its limitless capacity to conceal and preserve unimaginable monstrousness. No single image reproduced in the news coverage of what she had witnessed first-hand could ever speak to the weight of the raw gloom bearing down on her in that place. No mere imposter would ever know the cruelest, truest way to emulate it—could ever *understand*.

Beginning where nails were driven through his feet and extending upward along the cross, the body of Christ ended where its neckline affected a violent interruption. His thorn-crowned head had been removed. The breath escaped Tabby's lungs as her eyes refused to budge. When she felt a hand land on her shoulder, she gasped and clenched her teeth to keep from screaming.

"Woah there," Lucy cautioned. "You good?"

Tabby pulled as much fresh air into her lungs as her diaphragm would allow, then held it for a moment.

"Yeah, thanks," she replied as she exhaled. "Blood sugar's low is all."

"Good thing the next stop's the diner then, huh?"

Brief as it had been, Tabby could not recall a single detail of the half-mile she drove to the Reno Diner. Her patrol car found a space in the parking lot and, in a moment, she was squinting. The over-abundant fluorescence flooding the diner was amplified by the mirrored surfaces covering nearly every wall and every other checkered ceiling tile. It was easy to feel watched in such a place, Tabby thought. She caught an image of herself and, not far past, a man scrunching his face behind a pair of readers. His agonizing concentration, fixed to a dog-eared booklet of crossword puzzles, relaxed when his eyes flicked over the spectacles' metal rims. Jimmy Daley waved her over. He sat with his back against the diner's furthest wall in a well-worn leather booth, his well-worn uniform barely hidden under a well-worn ski jacket and a well-worn expression of impatience. As much as he attempted to conceal himself in the depths of the restaurant, even the most oblivious late-night patron could spot the old-school, Brooklyn patrolman from a block away. It was not meant to be a perfect disguise, Tabby realized—just a message. She understood the message: *'take your troubles to anybody else.'*

With only a few minutes remaining until two o'clock, the diner's sparse assembly of clientele were outnumbered by a crew of very obviously bored servers. Aside from Jimmy, Tabby, and Lucy following behind her, there was a couple sat in another booth by the restaurant's broad front windows. A few solitary patrons propped themselves atop elbows at the dining counter. All appeared to inhabit various degrees of waning intoxication, though the mood felt peaceable enough and steady, nonetheless. To Tabby, the stale, greasy atmosphere was a sanctuary compared to the vindictive gloominess seething and peeling off the walls of St. Anthony's—still clinging to the deepest recesses of her mind.

They passed a television set strapped onto an angled shelf on the wall. A cloud of vaporized frying oil struck the kitchen's ceiling and rolled over the rest of the restaurant. Pots and pans clashed violently. Tabby's stomach flipped. Mention of her thinning blood had not been purely deflective. She knew she needed to eat. She also knew she would need to reconstitute herself before her appetite would cooperate.

Tabby stepped aside. She motioned for Lucy to slide into the side of the booth opposite that which Jimmy was already deeply nestled. What little of his attention had not been absorbed into his book of word puzzles was just enough for him to idly graze on a half-ravaged patty melt.

"Sorry to interrupt your meal," Tabby greeted him.

"Save your apologies," Jimmy replied without hesitation. "I'm sorry you've gotta run around all night, wingin' it without my guidance and wisdom."

"Yeah, it's really falling apart out there without you."

"Sounds like. I blame me, too."

"So modest. But selfish, really. When are you gonna step away from your little desk and save us all?"

Jimmy held up his hands in surrender.

"Relax! You can't blame Superman for needin' to take a break every now and then. But, just to show you that I haven't forgotten all the little folk, lunch at the Fortress of Solitude is on me."

Jimmy turned to Lucy.

"And you—what can I get for my spittin' image replacement?"

Lucy seemed more inclined to blend in with the scenery than insert herself between Tabby and Jimmy as they went back and forth. She was surprised by the sudden acknowledgement.

"Uhh… just a bacon, egg, and cheese on a roll?"

Jimmy looked at Tabby and shook his head in disapproval.

"*Just* a bacon, egg, and cheese… on a roll?" he howled as he turned back to Tabby. "Whatsamatta with you? You forget to feed your rookie?"

The back of Jimmy's booth lurched as his body turned to the diner's counter.

"Hey, Judy! Baconegg'n'cheese for the kid! On a roll—a *buttered roll*. Tabby, what're you havin'?"

Tabby admired her coworkers' appetites. Her own stomach had yet to forgive her mind for negative vibrations it refused to let lie in St. Anthony's.

"I'm good. I'll work on the free pickles and coleslaw if anything."

The eyebrow climbing Jimmy's forehead may have indicated genuine concern. After nearly a decade, Tabby still had not figured the precise line where her old partner's sarcasm ended.

"I just want you to know, broken a wretch as you might now find me, Tab—I ain't completely destitute. Whatever you want, I got it."

"I know you're good for it. What can I say? I come for the show more than the meal."

Jimmy's face morphed into a mug that bordered on Vaudevillian. As he jabbed a thumb in Tabby's direction, he turned and winked at Lucy.

"She misses me."

"Sure," Tabby sighed. "Something like that."

Tabby looked down at the table. A copy of the Morning Tribune served as an improvised placemat for the dwindling remains of Jimmy's sandwich. The back cover of the tabloid boasted the top story of the sports section: *NO WAY, FAY! Players' Assoc. Rejects Deal—Spring Training Lockout Continues.* Tabby's index finger shimmied the newspaper from beneath Jimmy's plate and spun it over to her side of the table. She flipped it over to inspect the front page's headlines. What she saw pulled a disappointed snort from her nose. The hysteria—and the press' fixation—showed no indication of slowing: *SATANIC PANIC ALONG THE ATLANTIC: Wave of Devilish Delinquency Batters East Coast!* Tabby did not follow baseball. She flipped back to the sports section, anyway.

Her head fell into her hand as her elbow leaned against the table. The television mounted to the wall was angled near enough to give her a partial view of its convex glass screen. Joe Namath heralded a sale on Laserdisc players at The Wiz. When the commercial faded away, a new the face emerged from the darkness.

"When you gazed out through your front door this morning," the man on the television began, *"did you feel like a strange, new world was staring back at you?"*

"Oh, my favorite quack," Jimmy chimed in. "I love these middle'a-the-night, new age fruitloops."

"My name is Doctor Martin Glass, my brothers and sisters, and I am here to let you know that I felt the same way. Established order erodes under the pressures of a constantly turning universe. We bear witness as eons-old traditions have begun to flail in the face of impending extinction. An inscrutable, new millennium approaches. As do ancient, reawakening truths and the wisdom they yearn to offer us. They surround us. They are within us. Brothers and sisters: what if I told you that the universe lies in wait, awaiting your call?"

"Why do I get the feeling that call ain't toll free?" Jimmy asked.

"The natural, destined lifespan of even the fittest, most tenacious among us is fleeting. Through my studies in the field of Chthonic Dreaming, I have spoken directly with the undying, eternal universe. That is why from now until Easter, I will be offering copies of my book, Chthonics, for all who attend one of my free, daily introductory seminars at the Oneirological Process Mission. Each one of you who enters our Mission will be treated to a free, private, one-on-one Dream Survey. We are also proud to offer a multi-volume collection of inspirational and educational seminars on VHS cassette, which we invite you to share with friends and loved ones. Chthonic Dreaming can open your mind and teach you not to fear the changing world around you—rather, you shall embrace it! You can awaken the dormant spirits in the universe. You can awaken that which lies sleeping within you."

"That's how they getcha…" Jimmy continued his commentary. "It's like I always say, kids—there ain't no such thing as a free lunch."

Tabby rolled her eyes.

"Isn't that why you came here," she asked. "For your *free* lunches?"

"Hey, hush you. I tip…"

"Sure—tell me what's fifteen percent of *nothin'*."

"I've seen that guy's commercials before," Lucy said. "He's from around here, right?"

"Yeah," Jimmy replied. "That Glass kook bought the old Loew's Oriental a year or two ago. Got himself a real *sharp* head 'a hair and a nice set to shoot those commercials, too. Truth is, he's been mopin' 'round this neighborhood since forever. Hell, he was creepin' up an' down Stillwell Avenue back when you were still in diapers. More into the hippy, freak scene back then, though. I guess he musta drifted off somewhere for a while—found a new way to sell the same ol' *new age-y* crap. Must've been twelve—no, thirteen years since I last seen his mug. Guy ages well, I'll give 'im that much."

Tabby found it hard to believe a word Jimmy pulled out of his bag of stories and legends. That was not to say she was disinterested. When he stopped to artfully maneuver the deteriorating pile of patty melt into his mouth, her attention returned to the television screen. Doctor Glass was gone. An old episode of *Dance Fever* took his place. Unlike Glass, the rerun had not aged well. When Jimmy continued to reminisce, Tabby's attention returned to him without consent, nor objection.

"We dealt with a lotta messed up stuff back then," Jimmy continued, "but the job is changin'. No sir—ain't what it used t'be! Really tears me up inside thinkin' about the world you kids are gonna have to deal with. Once the Puzzle Palace gets my walkin' papers, I'll be sittin' on a beach in Boca Raton, sippin' pina coladas courtesy a' the Pension Fund."

"That's beautiful, Jim," Tabby said, then turned to Lucy. "Watch. It's like clockwork: you get an old hairbag of a cop talkin' about how much shit's changed—how much they don't recognize the world anymore—pretty soon they'll dredge up some stories about *the good ol' days*. They're mostly true, sometimes. Mostly."

"Did I ever tell you about what we had to go through back in '77? The blackout? The Son of Sam?"

"No, not never," Tabby replied dryly. "Not even once."

"What a shit-show, lemme tell ya. When we weren't chasin' looters down Flatbush, Beame had us workin' 'round the clock, runnin' after shadows, night after night. They had us lookin' for a guy who no one knew what he looked like—and even then, it turned out they had us goin' about it all the wrong ways. Everytime the brainiacs downtown or at the task force came out with a new composite sketch, the next witness had us lookin' for a completely different sonuvabitch! I bought myself a new car with all the overtime I clocked throwin' longhairs up against a wall and prayin' I actually found a forty-four each time I tossed their pockets."

"Was it a Cadillac?" Tabby asked with a pronounced lack of wonder.

"You bet your ass it was a goddamned Cadillac! And that shit was *cherry*. Still got it, too. Anyway, it was nuts. Everyone suspected anyone else while it was goin' on. People were droppin' dimes on every loner and weirdo they knew. Hell, I'm pretty sure I saw that Glass guy got picked up by the squad a couple'a times. And then, just like *that*—"

Jimmy paused and snapped his fingers.

"All over. Hundreds of suspects brought in for interviews. Months of searching by the best of the best. None of it mattered. One night, an ordinary beat cop wrote a Ford Galaxie a ticket for parking on the pump. One of a million that gets written every year. The cop even forgets to turn the damn summons in for almost a week. Everything changed when they noticed a car registered to some creep up in Yonkers getting' ticketed a block away from the most recent shooting. Next thing you know, they're scramblin' up there to pull Berkowitz outta his rathole and he cops to each and every shooting."

"And now here we are," Tabby added. "Thirteen years later. Another crime spree. Another task force."

"Cheer up, kid. Once again, we've got the best and brightest leading the way. Your favorite partner is hot on this new psycho's tracks!"

Tabby's back swayed into the plush booth behind her.

"Why would you bring *him* up?"

Jimmy's hands rose defensively, open palms splayed toward Tabby on the other side of the table.

"Sorry, I slipped. Didn't realize that nerve was still raw."

"I didn't know you were on the task force," Lucy said.

"Yours truly? No, her *other* favorite partner. Detective Vernon—well, technically *Officer* Vernon at the time."

"Technically and *rightfully*, but even that's up for debate," Tabby groaned.

Jimmy leaned over the table. He cupped a palm over his mouth and directed his voice toward Lucy—though this did little to prevent Tabby hearing him whisper.

"Your esteemed mentor used to be what we like to call… '*a worker.*'"

"What *do-nothings* like to call '*a worker*,'" Tabby shot back.

"Never heard her say '*no*' to anything. Never saw her go home on time, neither. Pretty sure she never went home at all. I swear, you could see the reflection of a gold detective's shield glowing behind those bloodshot, rookie eyes. Ten years ago, the Six Four was takin' a beating on car thefts—highest GLA's in the borough."

Jimmy's hand fell away from his face. He jabbed a thumb in Tabby's direction.

"'Til one smart cookie cracked the case. She tracked the whole thing back to a scrapyard down off'a Cropsey. The perp had an unregistered tow truck—used to go out and hook up whatever he wanted just after midnight. Before sunrise he'd have the whole car chopped for parts. This one over here caught him red handed unloading a brand-new Ferrari off the back of his truck. He tried to run. *Tried.*"

Tabby's eyes shot open. An old pain nagged at the base of her spine.

"I had just pulled up when she tackled 'im, too," Jimmy continued. "Jumped 'im hard enough to knock both shoes off."

"Too hard," she said, trying to ignore the old injury.

"Right after she slapped a pair of bracelets on the perp, Vernon took out his radio and called a bus for her."

"That bad?" Lucy asked.

Tabby remembered the concern in Sam Vernon's voice. She remembered being convinced.

"When I was in the back of the ambulance, he said he was '*taking care of me.*'"

"Took care of your perp, too. Signed his own name over all the arrest paperwork. Fielded every call when the DA's office rang."

"Real *thoughtful*. Even after I was cleared by the department surgeon, Sam made sure I never had to miss a day on patrol to make a court appearance. He was nice enough to invite me to his promotion ceremony, though."

"Shit," Lucy said. "I heard he was an asshole, but that's just completely miserable."

"I wouldn't call all that *complete* misery," Tabby replied, "but whatever he's gotten himself into now looks close enough. What goes around, comes around."

Jimmy waved a hand dismissively.

"He's an apple polisher. In over his head and gettin' what he deserves if you ask me. Hopefully someone with a few spare brain cells on that team of his actually figures out what's goin' on before anyone else gets hurt."

"Maybe," Lucy said. "Or they'll find just grab someone to pin everything on."

After a long pause, the conversation strayed. Samuel Vernon's name and the credit he did not deserve were not revisited, nor was any talk of work at all. Tabby stole a few stale french fries and her lightheadedness faded. The remaining discourse was sufficiently innocuous to the point where she could not remember any particular details as a busboy cleared the table.

"Thank you, Officer Daley."

Jimmy's forehead wrinkled at Lucy's gratitude. He followed this with another concerned glance toward Tabby. It lasted only as long as he could stifle laughter.

"She does that," Tabby informed him.

"No problem, I'll let *Officer Daley* know. Thanks for tryin' to keep the meal classy, but *Jimmy* works just fine."

"I mean it though," Lucy continued. "At least it's been quiet enough for us to have a nice meal."

Hairs stood at attention on the back of Tabby's neck before the word finished leaving Lucy's mouth. She held her breath while her attention involuntarily turned to the radio. Jimmy's smile faded. Tabby knew her own expression must have match his seriousness when Lucy looked between the two of them

"She does that, too."

"What? Did I say something?"

"Oh yeah," Jimmy chuckled. "You said the one thing. The Q-word."

"You mean *'quiet?'*"

Tabby winced.

"Yeah, that's the one," she grumbled.

"Six Four David, on the air?"

Tabby did not know how every Central managed to hear a cop either compliment or complain about—acknowledge in any way— the peace they were experiencing. Whatever metaphysical power the word *'quiet'* carried, it never failed to bring such peace to an end. Jimmy looked just as delighted as Tabby knew she appeared deflated. In all their years working together, she knew she must have made the same mistake at least once and inspired similar grief. Now he enjoyed his opportunity to revel at very long-term karma bearing interest.

"We're receiving a call for a missing EDP in your sector. Can I show you responding?"

Tabby turned to look at Lucy. Her face was red with sudden understanding and guilt. The rookie raised her radio to her mouth.

"10-4 Central. Show us going."

Jimmy departed for the station house to resume his newfound position monitoring the Six Four's landline. Tabby and Lucy returned to their car. Tabby blinked hard. She still felt as if her head was miles away from where she needed it to be. Despite her best efforts, it remained elsewhere, distracted by a puzzle her brain was relentlessly fixated on piecing together. The extraordinary violence she saw in the church refused to dissipate, as did the pair of figures entering St. Anthony's on the security tape, their identities completely and inexplicably obscured. She thought about Jimmy's younger days—the perfect storm about which he waxed so sentimental. Something he mentioned refused to fade away with the rest of their conversation. Tabby remembered Jimmy's words and the futility of chasing shadows at night. She wondered how regularly the cop who ticketed David Berkowitz forgot to hand in the other, less infamous summonses he wrote.

Nine

Charlie dragged his right thumb and index finger along the ridge of his eyebrows, then traced the edges of his eye sockets. Nerves were beginning to get the better of his motor functions. The tips of the two fingers massaged the damp flesh around his eyes out toward his temples, then slowly reversed back toward his nose. He pressed deep on his closed eyelids—deeper, squeezing to the back of his skull. Charlie released, then rubbed in slow circles until a monochromatic kaleidoscope pinwheeled out of the darkness. It spun like a cyclone until it began to fade. His arms crumpled down onto his lap. Eyes reopened, the murky haze dissipated quickly, and the dashboard of the Camaro returned. Black with red trim. Leather seats with red stitching. As the car turned a corner, the light of the full moon shined in to reveal red carpeting.

Charlie had been the driver last time. Now he sat in the passenger seat while Bethany circled the block. A cramp lanced his stomach. It was a repeat of the same routine he had gone through weeks earlier. Charlie could not remember withdrawals coming back this quickly, though he could also not remember what it was like to remain clean long as he had. It was no easy endeavor, but he resisted making any trips to Franco—had not so much as glanced at his medicine bag in a month. He had assumed the worst was over. Now, the emerging signs began to scare him. He chalked it up to the mounting expectations of Doctor Glass, and perhaps those of his brother as well. Bile and electricity passed from his stomach to his brain, then out to the tips of every finger and toe. He left the dream session with Glass feeling almost serene. Afterward, he drifted along behind the man and down into the basement. The ceremony. The shadows. Their crowns. Belial.

Whatever he drank from the cup left him feeling queasy, yet hollow—sickened, but without any poison to purge. Charlie thought about the taste of blood. He winced and shook his head, then tried to focus on the plan for the night. Plans were simple when you broke them down, only looking at each step in isolation: get in, retrieve that which Martin requested, and get outta there. In the end, Charlie would get paid. It was not the least among the motivations which drew Dexter back to the Oneirological Process

Mission, but it was often the simplest terms Charlie's brother could employ to entice him.

The Camaro came to a stop along the shoulder of New Utrecht Avenue. A hundred feet away, on the opposite side of the street, an electric neon cross flared in the cold, dry air. It was attached to the highest steeple of the former Reformed Church of the New Netherlands. Sharp, sacred angles and gothic accents menaced the sky. Its brownstone facade looked freshly pressure washed. Multicolored neon letters flashed down the length of the illuminated crucifix to exclaim *HALLELUJAH!* A pair of heavy, wooden doors beneath the sign swung open to pour a herd of twenty-somethings onto the sidewalk. The rhythmic commotion within trickled out onto the sleeping neighborhood until the doors closed once more and left only the DJ's deep rumbling bassline in its wake. Amber street light mixed with the pulsating neon glow of the electrified cross while Charlie watched streaks of fluorescent yellow and orange bodypaint glisten on the skin of women who seldom crossed the river to his own outer borough. They shivered in the early morning air, trading joints and clove cigarettes back-and-forth to young, howling, drunk men. Charlie's hand reflexively gripped the barrel of the .45 in his jacket pocket.

"You awake over there?"

Charlie jumped, caught off guard by Bethany's voice. She sounded impatient.

"Y-yeah," he stuttered, swallowing hard to freshen his unexpectedly dry mouth. "Just going over some stuff in my head."

Charlie turned to face her. He was unaccustomed to seeing his brother's girlfriend in anything close to the club kid camouflage she adopted for the evening. An oversized, white t-shirt-turned-crop-top. Acid-washed jean shorts over fishnet leggings. Manufactured distress and affected tears and rips. At least the Doc Martens—the only reliable members of her usual rotation—were practical, if slightly intimidating. For Charlie's part, he lacked any clothing either expensive or hip enough for a night of clubbing: jeans and a black hooded sweatshirt under a no-name windbreaker, all from the Telco clearance bin. The suggestion came from Bethany. She seemed confidant it was as much effort as would be required of Charlie to blend in, become forgotten, and proceed from the front door to the end of the night without anyone remembering he was ever there.

"When we get in there, you don't talk to no one," Bethany said, repeating the ground rules she, Dexter, and Glass had already laid down. "You just follow me and don't stop for nothing."

Charlie tried to remain focused as she continued. His stomach gurgled while he struggled to maintain the appearance of attentiveness in the face of Bethany's instructions. The pangs were distracting enough without the added guilt of feeling as though his weeks of suffering had been for naught. An object the size of an egg dangled from the Camaro's rear-view mirror. Charlie had not paid it any attention until now as his mind began to wander. Only when it managed to pulled him away from Bethany's speech entirely did the decoration's full nature become clear.

"Jesus," he mumbled.

The face of Christ stared back at him, thorny crown still unmistakable despite the added layer of red paint covering the messiah's face. Charlie assumed that it was paint. He noticed other creative flares as well. The eyes had been blacked out. A pair of nails had been hammered in between the crown of thorns to add a nasty pair of spiky, metal horns. In effect, the son of God looked to be showing signs of demonic possession.

Charlie shivered as an involuntary laugh twitched out of his clenched jaw.

"Glass teaches arts 'n crafts, too?"

"Will you shut up and listen?" Bethany snapped. "Have you heard a single thing I've told you, or am I wastin' my breath?"

Nervousness crowded the already uneasy atmosphere of the car. Charlie shivered again. He felt the air growing colder. In the year or so he had known Bethany, he had yet to hear her spare him more than a half-dozen words at a time. Now that she was directly addressing him, he realized the warmth in the car had, in fact, fled. Framed as it was, the question of Charlie's presence—physical or emotional—was fairly fluid, and due in no small part to the chemical deficiencies besieging his nervous system. Frustrated at his inability to summon some response he could be in any way confidant would not turn him into the night's first sacrifice, he exhaled and watched a puff of steam vaporize in the now frozen air filling the car. In no uncertain terms, Charlie had been told he was hopeless by many sources in a vast spectrum of contexts—not the least often by Dexter. The futility of his cause was cemented when, rather than threaten him further or perhaps cut losses and eject him from the car, Bethany simply turned in the same direction. Charlie heard her teeth grind against one another as her jaw clenched tight. She resigned herself to join him and stare out the Camaro's front windshield in silence.

Charlie returned to the Christhead floating over the dashboard. The black eyes stared back at him. He reached up and unlooped the string that suspended the ceramic head from the rearview mirror. It was lighter than he expected. When knuckles rapped at the window to Charlie's right, his hand jerked, and the head flew into the air. Dexter had materialized while Charlie's attention wandered, and now his older brother braced his forearm against the car's roof.

"You two look like you're ready to dance the night away," he laughed as Charlie cranked the window down. "Or maybe snuff some yuppie scum instead?"

"No pressure or anything," Charlie replied.

Charlie did not need to look away from his brother to know Bethany now turned in his direction. He could feel the daggers she stared into the back of his head. He saw Dexter glance past him, then return with a sterner expression. Needles pushed up through Charlie's skin as the mercury dropped further. A wave of bile leapt up his throat. His hand still buried deep within his jacket pocket, Charlie rubbed the grip of the gun.

"You're gonna have Bethany with you. Just stick to the plan and do whatever she tells you."

"Yeah… I gotcha," Charlie said, eyes closed as he exhaled deeply. "I'm just tryin' to keep my stomach down. Whatever I drank before just ain't sittin' right."

Dexter chuckled.

"Relax. That was just pig's blood. Dramatic, I know. It don't taste too great, neither, but it's part of the Doctor's repertoire. Besides, it ain't nothing you haven't had in a pork chop. Trust me, I prepared it myself."

The doors to the club opened once more and the crowd on the sidewalk grew larger. They were covered in sweat and body paint, radiant in the crisp, early morning. Charlie could hear the dryness in his mouth as he spoke.

"So… who is this guy, anyway?"

"Mervin Zero," Dexter responded. "He's the owner of the nightclub—the name on the liquor license, at least. Bought up this old wreck of a church, installed some new lights and a sound system. Christened it *Hallelujah*. Cost a lot of money. He borrowed from the kind of people who don't send you a past-due letter when you miss your payments."

"Must owe a lot if they want the guy rubbed out," Charlie added. "Let me guess, Glass takes his cut once they liquidate the club?"

"A big cut," Bethany added. "Too big to risk on some deadbeat skell fuckin' everything up."

Frigidity and unease aside, Charlie snapped.

"Don't call me no fuckin' skell!"

"Who d'you think you're foolin'? Once you get your share—assumin' you don't get us all killed, *or worse*—I don't care if the whole thing goes straight up your arm. I just need you to clear the smack from your head just long enough for us to get through this."

"I told you guys, *I'm clean*. Have been for a month."

"That why you've been chokin' back dry heaves for the past hour? I've been ready to shove you out the door before you lost your lunch all over the insides of my car."

Frustrated, Charlie pushed himself firmly against the back of his car seat. He did his best to avoid making eye contact with Dexter. If any fraternal judgment awaited him on the other side of the car window, he was unprepared to grapple with it.

"I ain't touched any'a that shit," he repeated.

Charlie thrust a flattened, downturn palm out in front of him. "Look!"

He fought against the tremors creeping down from his shoulder. It was a vain gesture, and effect of his wavering hand was less impressive than he hoped.

"Nice try," Bethany sighed. "Like I said, doesn't change nothin' if you use or if you don't. But I came here under expectations tonight. The Doctor has his oath to keep, and I got mine. Blood's gonna be shed or there'll be hell to pay. If makin' it to see the sunrise means it's gotta be *yours*—"

"Charlie's gonna be fine, ain't that right?" Dexter interrupted. "Us Valerie boys don't fold for nobody."

His clear ignorance—willful or otherwise—of their shared family history aside, Charlie was nonetheless thankful for his brother's confidence.

"I believe you," he continued. "I know you're gonna keep your head on straight. Enough arguin'. Time to get out there and break a leg."

Before Charlie could offer Dexter any gratitude, his brother was already on the move. Per the plan, he would act as lookout while Charlie followed Bathany inside. After a few brisk, silent strides down the sidewalk, Dexter crossed the avenue to take point. Charlie heard the driver's side door creak open. He turned to watch Bethany jump out.

"Get up," she ordered softly.

Charlie's hand ached. He did not realized how tightly he had gripped the gun in his pocket until his fingers unclenched. Charlie pulled at the door handle and gave it a shove with his elbow, but underestimated his fluctuating muscle coordination. The Christhead still hid within his other palm and prevented him from maintaining a sufficient grip on the door, allowing it to fly outward without slowing. Bethany's muscle car rode lower than most. When the door passed over the high curb to the sidewalk, its metal edge scraped along the top of the pavement and etched a trail of silver paint. Charlie leapt out of the car. He shoved the ceramic head into his sweatshirt's pocket and grabbed the top of the door to jimmy it loose. The noise of the door scraping free of where momentum embedded it echoed over the nightclub's low, bassy rumble and the gaggling din of clubgoers not far on the other side of the street. A few heads briefly turned in his direction during the struggle, then lost attention. Most returned to cigarettes and flirtation, but one head stayed facing him. Bethany's narrow pupils issued an unspoken, final warning in his direction. Charlie bowed his head and pulled up the hood of his black sweatshirt.

Muffled music filled the night while wobbly knees carried Charlie over the asphalt and closer to the crowd. The heavy doors swung opened. Noise bellowed out. Rhymes and wails which Charlie could not understand belted over drum machine strikes and heavily distorted bass chords. A small group of young women shivered near the edge of the sidewalk. They danced for warmth when they heard the song. Some ventured their own approximation of the incomprehensible lyrics. Charlie climbed onto the curb and walked toward the entrance beneath the enormous, vibrant electric crucifix. Despite the advanced hour, a pair of doormen towered over a restless column of prospects gathered by the entrance. The hopeful crowd shifted and shivered beyond the velvet ropes while the deliberating bouncers made visual weight, passing over those found wanting. Charlie caught up with Bethany as she steadily approached the rear of the eager throng.

"For a guy who's havin' problems keeping up with his bills, Mr. Zero doesn't seem to have any trouble drawing a crowd."

If Bethany heard Charlie's commentary, she offered no acknowledgment. It might have been too loud. More likely, he realized, she was too focused for small talk. By the front of the line, a pair of men in their early thirties griped at one of the bouncers.

"Aww… c'mon, man."

"Yeah, these chicks are fit tonight, boss!"

"Right on," the doorman replied. "That's why they're comin' in and the two'a youse are stayin' out here. *Boss*."

He motioned for a group of three women to proceed inside while his partner pulled on one of the ornate, wrought iron door handles. The ancient, double doors parted. The warm blast of chaotic, computerized notes that wafted over Charlie smelled like sweat and ecstasy. The wave receded as gravity returned the opened door to its frame. Bethany elbowed her way past the rejected men as they shrank in disgrace. The Bouncer gave her a once over, then let her through without challenge.

Charlie felt sweat trickling down his back as he approached the entryway. He cursed the mission's planners for overlooking his magnetic tendency toward immediate and firm social rejection. The universe had been nothing if not emphatic about this throughout his previous twenty years.   He made a point to highlight this potential hurdle with Bethany and Dexter when they first discussed the night's activities. Believed or not, his concerns were dismissed outright.

Charlie's heartbeat began to pound inside his head again. The inescapable bassline was not helping. It grew more intense as he neared the doors. Every block of stone in the centuries-old structure vibrated and hummed, promising a much more powerful barrage to anyone who passed its guarded front doors. Charlie's blood pressure was spiking and the reverberations inside his skull hammered harder.   Another dry heave tickled his esophagus. Charlie turned to his side, away from the crowd, to exorcise it without drawing any attention. As he covered his mouth with his right hand, he realized it was more than a reflex pushing up his throat. Before he could stifle its momentum, the contents of his stomach slammed into the back of his mouth, flooded his sinuses, and poured past his teeth. Blinded by tears, Charlie choked when his diaphragm tried to pull air in spite of the torrent of bile and fluids still cascading onto the sidewalk.

"Oh my gawd!"

"Look at this fuckin' mess—"

"Whadda jerk…"

Audible gasps and other pedestrian revulsion joined the deafening heartbeats and penetrating soundtrack assaulting Charlie's skull. The veins under his flush forehead bulged while aftershocks left his muscles quaking. When his stomach found nothing to make the continuing heaves productive, he cleared the tears clouding his vision.   Charlie's throat remained tightly constricted. He gasped as his lungs tried desperately to reinflate. He surveyed the scene through bloodshot eyes. Dark vomit pooled around his feet. A foamy, scarlet sheen reflected around the puddle's edges.

"Well, fuck me," rose a singular, deep voice over the general displeasure. "If it ain't *Chuckie-fuckin'-Cheese*."

The name sent a fresh chill travelling from Charlie's head to his toes. His throat relaxed. Irritation cleared the sickness and unease from his body. His windpipes, still tender, wheezed.

"Do I fuckin' know you?"

"Everyone who went to James Buchanan High School in '85 remembers Charlie Valerie," the bouncer replied. "Most likely to drop out, burn out, and O.D. in a McDonald's bathroom."

Vivid as his own memory still appeared to live in the bouncer's mind, Charlie could not place the man's face. Six-foot-whatever, local accent—he could have been anyone from among a few dozen people who made Charlie's life a living Hell from kindergarten to freshman year at New Utrecht.

"*Chuckie Cheese!* That's where I know him from," a girl in the line squealed. "Remember, the one I told you about? I haven't heard that name in years!"

Charlie's fist clenched. His sleeve cleared the residual saliva and vomit out of the peach fuzz sprouting at the corners of his mouth. Being involuntarily dragged down memory lane erased several negative emotions. It introduced a couple more.

"It's been real nice catchin' up, *Chuck*," the doorman continued. "But this joint's already got more than enough dope fiends mopin' 'round the bathrooms all night long. How 'bout you make way for some of our more distinguished guests who ain't dressed like the squeegee man?"

With a snort, Charlie hocked what remained of the stomach acid and mucous caking his throat. The thick wad of spit splashed onto the sidewalk a few inches shy of the bouncer's black shoes.

"I'm good for the money, asshole."

Charlie jammed a hand into his pocket and pulled out the pair of hundreds Martin had furnished him.

"So shove the comedy routine and don't quit your day job."

"Fuckin' junkie runt," the bouncer roared. "Am I supposed to be impressed by a couple bucks? I don't gotta do shit for some little loser like you just 'cuz you flash your pocket change in my face. How's about you get lost before I stomp your filthy mug."

When Charlie rediscovered the feeling in his fingertips, he found they had been fondling the trigger of the handgun in his pocket. The line shifted to cut him off from the doorway. The girl who shared the memory of his nickname stepped up and presented her driver's license to the bouncer. His flashlight passed from the photo identification, climbed up her legs to her face, then returned downward to her chest. He squinted. The flashlight's bulb dimmed, then flickered. Charlie's eyes looked up toward the door. At some point during the exchange, Bethany returned. She held the double doors open and glared in the bouncer's direction. Her lips moved, forming quiet words not meant for any of their ears. Frustrated by the flashlight's lack of cooperation, the bouncer gave it a quick smack against the heel of his palm. The bulb continued to flicker until the dim light from its choking filament withered to an orange cinder. The bouncer turned the flashlight around and pointed its lamp up to his eyes for closer inspection. Charlie watched Bethany's hands clench. In a moment, light stirred once more within the struggling bulb and grew until it burned far brighter than the device's original design or natural capacity. When the flashlight could no longer contain the beam, a shower of sparks and glass burst into the face of the stunned doorman. Charlie watched over his shoulder as the man grabbed at his face and howled. He refused to allow his own scurrying feet to slow as they carried him over the nightclub's threshold.

A balmy gust slammed into Charlie when he stepped into the vestibule. His eyes strained to adapt to the chaotic environment. Despite—or perhaps *due* to—the strobing, dazzling lights, the inside of the church seemed darker than the sidewalk behind him. Charlie wove through the looser groups meandering by the entrance toward Bethany. She stood at the edge of a massive, multi-tiered dancefloor. The entire nave of the church was a dense, shapeless sea of writhing bodies. From a lofty pulpit, the DJ fixed his attention on his turntables, indifferent to the adoration and reverential palms thrust in his direction. Waves of colored light rolled over a sea of silhouetted heads—churning and sinking and resurfacing. There was only one steady source of light to pierce the swirling void that filled the chamber to its vaulted ceilings. Beyond the peaks of the towering, stained-glass windows, a brilliant, full moon peered down on the church's new communion.

A hand seized Charlie's forearm. He jumped, eyes snapping back down. Bethany's face stared at his own. A cyclone of primary colors twisted and strobed over her, but her eyes drilled through the fluctuating light. Whatever words she growled at Charlie could not compete with the noise filling the room. She might be able to speak to ghouls at the other end of the universe, but breaking the din of a pitched rave was a different task altogether. Aware of the struggle, she slowed her speech down and exaggerated the formation of the words.

"Stay. Behind. Me. And. Keep. Up."

Charlie nodded.

He dodged and slid where openings appeared in the crowd. Charlie followed Bethany along a right angle around the edge of the dancefloor. They passed by the bar. A couple of especially unengaged bartenders surveyed a disinterested crowd for any potential orders. A woman leaned over to shout for their attention. The barman's hopeful expression soured. He shoved an empty glass into the icebox until it was full to the brim with crushed ice. A stream of water shot into the glass and he grudgingly thrust it across the bar into her hand. She popped something into her mouth and washed it down with the water, then returned the glass to the bar and walked away.

Where the bar ended, a restless and exhausted line flanked the wall. Dozens of people stood shoulder to shoulder, anxious hands fidgeting and shuffling folded twenties and hundreds. Bethany traced a parallel path and turned the corner. The steady beat coming from the club's amps diminished to a degree as Charlie followed in her into the smaller hallway. Music subsided to the jabber of restless conversation between patrons awaiting their turn to enter the restrooms.

"It's not the best shit," a man testified, sweat soaking through his blue button-down, "but it's the best we're gonna do on this side of the river without taking our chances on Flatbush."

A girl twenty years younger than him in an oversized, ripped sweatshirt slid down the wall and landed on her own crumpled limbs.

"Whatever you say," she sighed. "It's barely two thirty—still way too early to crash."

Bethany continued toward an unmarked door at the end of the hallway. Her hand landed on top of the door handle and pressed down gently. When she turned back around, she looked through Charlie. When she was satisfied, she locked eyes with him. She raised a finger in front of her mouth and pushed the door.

The musty odor that travelled up through the stairwell was a stark contrast to the lively, dewy mist of perspiration and alcoholic residue that filled the dancefloor. Charlie found something close to comfort in the familiar scents that accompanied him into the structure's basement: stale, aging wood, a tinge of mold, with a twist of sawdust and renovation. As the door slid closed behind him, the DJ's notes withered to a distant, rhythmic thudding like that filling the neighborhood outside. Dim light provided by the bare bulbs affixed to the ceiling revealed the staircase was made of fresh, new wood. Bethany's feet managed to descend the wooden stairs without a single creak. Charlie focused on setting his own feet down in the same spots she stepped. To his surprise, he was able to keep his own descent as stealthy.

The stairs landed on the side of a wide hallway. The pathway along the hall's floor would have been as wide were it not for the palates of unopened alcohol lining either wall up to the ceiling. Bethany stalked the corridor with Charlie a few feet behind. The passage turned to the left and opened into a larger room. Bethany crouched down beside an improvised wall of beer kegs and craned her head around the side. Charlie stooped next to her. He peered over the top of the kegs to see what earned her attention. A few yards away he saw a white, leather couch. Propped on top of its nearest arm was a pair of purple-socked feet. Bethany turned toward Charlie. She gestured with a shake of her head toward the resting man and whispered.

"That's our guy."

A new beat joined the bassline overhead. Footsteps travelled down the hall behind them. They grew louder at a determined pace.

Charlie instinctively pressed himself against the wall of kegs and shimmied back to a shadowy corner. In a moment, Bethany's elbow pushed him tighter against the wall to share in his concealment. Her frustration was obvious. Their unexpected and unwanted visitor passed by without pause.

"Merv!"

The man called out to the couch, then smacked at one of the feet.

"A couple 'a the guys from the Vanderveers are circlin' the block. Might be plannin' to throw their weight around an' step to the Marlboros crew that's workin' the bathrooms."

The man on the couch grumbled. In a single breath, aggravation turned his grumble to an impotent growl.

"—so damn sick'a these fuckin' pill-poppin', yuppie kids!"

Charlie found a crack between the kegs to monitor the scene. Mervin Zero's feet swung off the couch as he spun himself upright.

"It's bad enough I can't turn a buck off 'em at the bar, now they're gonna invite a turf war right in the middle of the dance floor."

Mervin shoved the exaggerated width of his jacket's shoulder pads deeper into the overstuffed, white leather couch behind him. Despite his recent repose, not a wrinkle showed in the oversized, silvery, silk fabric of his double-breasted jacket. He ground his bared teeth. A hand flattened the greasy strands of hair escaping the tight, thin ponytail at the back of his head. Charlie could hear the tempo of the music upstairs pick up as the DJ mixed into the next song. Dust shook down from the rafters and drifted toward the raw cement floor as dancers overhead oscillated to a new beat.

"Well, what're we gonna do?" the other man asked. "We told 'em they could work the club long as they stuck to the bathrooms where the cops wouldn't catch a whiff of 'em. Now that they're makin' a killing, all the other local crews are startin' to take note."

"It's this generation. Trust fund junkies. Club kids. Booze and a healthy bump ain't good enough for 'em anymore. If they ain't chokin' down E, they're passing out on K."

Pounding feet and strengthening basslines shook down greater crumbs of plaster onto Charlie's scalp. He turned away from Mervin and his associate to get a read on Bethany. At some point during the conversation, she pulled her own firearm out.

"It's bad enough I've got every greaseball on Eighteenth Avenue breathin' down my neck and unloading ten times the booze I can't actually sell into my basement every week. Whenever one of Gentile's trucks shows up it erases whatever we managed to take in over the weekend."

The commotion above Charlie sounded like it was growing into a stampede. Before long, Mervin's list of complaints faded behind what seemed to be early indicators of the imminent collapse of the dancefloor onto their heads.

"I'm tellin' youse—it's only a matter 'a time before one of these idiot gangbangers or Gentile's goons decides to turn this place into a shooting gallery—"

Two more loud beats from the DJ synchronized with two flashes in the basement. Charlie pulled his hands down from his ears and looked at Bethany. A trail of smoke rose gently from the barrel of her .45 Glock. Mervin Zero pushed himself deeper into the plush couch as he watched his assistant crumple face first on the basement's stone floor. When his mind restarted, Mervin turned with a shudder to where Bethany stood upright, no longer concealed. For reasons he could not explain, Charlie stood as well. He looked back and forth at the standoff. The verse came back around. Two more beats from the party upstairs. Another volley of bullets erupted from Bethany's gun. A thick mist of red blood sprayed across the couch's white cushions.

Charlie's ears rang. He checked over his shoulder toward the hall from which they entered. The shock to his eardrums made it difficult for him to assess whether anyone had been alerted to the noise. He turned around and looked at Bethany.

"Don't worry about that," he read on her lips. "Just work quick."

Charlie walked over to the couch. He did not need to examine their bodies too closely to confirm both men had expired. Bethany produced and quickly donned a pair of latex gloves. She moved over to the couch and jostled it away from the wall, then groped along the exposed, unpainted sheetrock. Charlie remembered his own pair of gloves. He pulled them over his hands and continued to scan behind him for any more unwanted guests. He stooped next to Mervin. The man kept his wallet in the right front pocket of his silver silk trousers, which Charlie now withdrew for examination. It was full of credit cards bearing the names of lenders Charlie did not know, but proved ultimately cash poor. He checked the man's jacket next. The inside pocket bulged. From within, Charlie pulled out four tightly spooled rolls of hundreds. He admired his bonus and returned the wallet to where he found it.

A loud crunch sent him jumping upright. He turned to the wall behind the couch over which Bethany had been running her hands. The bottom of her fist crashed against the drywall. A tear began to form. She clawed the flaking material away until a bigger chunk peeled loose to reveal the structure's original, stone foundation. Bethany traced her finger around the outline of one of the stones. Charlie leaned over the couch to examine the exposed bricks. He squinted and saw markings—a small, inverted cross with two upside down letters etched beneath:

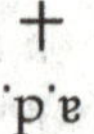

Dust and debris trickled to the ground. Bethany's fingernail dug a deeper line around the stone. She shoved the tips of her fingers behind the corners and began to jimmy the brick loose. A puff of dust flew outward when the brick finally budged. Charlie reached down over the back of the couch to help pry it away from the wall. With a shudder, the stone tipped away and tumbled onto the cement floor. A black cavity stared back at them. The dimly lit basement spared little light for the crevice. Bethany reached inside with her right arm. She braced herself against the wall and manipulated her shoulder through the slight opening. Her face remained blank while she rummaged through the darkness.

"So, this thing Martin wants," Charlie whispered. "What is it exactly?"

Bethany let a heavy puff of air escape through her nose.

"You wouldn't believe me if you didn't see it with your own eyes."

Suddenly, her expression changed. Her arm froze and her eyebrows climbing higher on her forehead.

"But I'll be damned—the thing's exactly where he said it'd be."

Bethany used her free hand to push away from the wall. As it reemerged, she cradled something in her other hand. Charlie watched her bring the object into the light. It was round, wrapped firmly in stale, yellowed cloth. Bethany stood up and turned it over in her hands. She smiled and, without warning, gave it a swift one-handed toss toward Charlie.

"Woah," he sputtered in shock. "Careful."

"You'd better be. That thing's gotta be pretty fragile after a few centuries."

Charlie held the wrapped object between his two hands. It was surprisingly light. Familiar, too. He rubbed one of his thumbs in circles over it, idly sussing out the contents. A nearly uninterrupted row of teeth teased his thumb. He cautiously pulled one of the corners of the linen wrap. The cloth encircled the object a few times before it finally pulled away to reveal a hard, porous surface with a dull, yellow-brown sheen. He pulled back a little further and a pair of empty eye sockets stared back at him.

"Fuck. Fuckin' *shit*. Why do I gotta carry this thing?"

"Are you serious," Bethany replied impatiently. "Look at this stupid outfit I gotta wear."

Charlie complied with a quick, reluctant scan, then quickly returned his eyes to her face.

"Do you see a single functional pocket anywhere, let alone somewhere to hide a goddamned *human head*?"

He did not. Without any further protest, Charlie tucked the ancient skull beneath his hooded sweatshirt and pushed it up into his left arm pit.

Dim, alternating stripes of yellow and blue light seeped past the door frame at the top of the staircase. A crack opened in the doorway wide enough for Bethany to disappear back into the club's bathroom hallway. Charlie slipped in after her, then gently guided the door closed again behind him. It felt like an hour had passed since he first descended the staircase. If the seemingly undiminished lines which led to the bathrooms' entrances were any indications, it might not have been more than five minutes. Whatever the case, neither their return nor anything which the two caused to transpire below invited any obvious public inquiry or panic. Music still blared. Bass still thumped. Patrons in search of narcotic stimulation looked bored and, to varying degrees, impatient. Charlie had never imbibed party drugs any more frequently than the opportunity to freely dabble presented— keeping up with his poison of choice demanded enough—but he could relate to their mindset. He was certain that none of these people were of a mindset which made them more than vaguely aware of the young man wearing ill-fitting, clearance-rack clothes and staring at the ground as he marched past. The guilt on his face was far less unfashionable. They were all sinners congregating in this corner of the former Reformed Church. Whether or not it weighed heavy as the package under Charlie's arm, the burdens on their own consciences begged to be lightened with the neatly folded bills cupped tight into their rigid, damp palms.

Charlie felt eyes on him all the same. He fixed his own gaze to the ground, but after a few seconds his head would bob back up and find someone to lock eyes with. He jerked away and studied the pattern on the carpet as he continued to walk. After a few paces, the cycle repeated.

The skull felt warm. It burned through its ancient wrappings and radiated directly into Charlie's gut at a frequency which only further agitated his trembling constitution. His throat tightened. Not wishing to repeat his performance from the club's entrance, Charlie made a sharp turn and huddled against a wall to conceal any potential regurgitation. He felt the wave rising within. The first dry heave gripped his chest, then released. After the fourth, longest convulsion, it became clear nothing would be produced. The nausea subsided, but the club's amplifiers felt as though they had been relocated to the front of Charlie's brain. The deafening thumps squeezed the passageways and cavities of his inner ear. He felt his collar tightening. Warm droplets of sweat tumbled down his face and glued his sweatshirt to his chest.

"You good, boss?"

The voice cut through music and strobing eardrums effortlessly. Charlie pried his eyelids open and turned back toward the hallway. His eyes swiveled, searching for Bethany. He found only strangers.

"Yo, boss," the voice repeated. "No need to bottom out if you've got the green. Take a step inside my office."

Charlie looked up and saw a pair of purple, velour track pants towering over him. A Mercedes Benz hood ornament swung from a thick gold chain draped over a teal and white windbreaker. Charlie's hand covered his eyes when the bathroom door parted behind the man and unleashed a flood of fluorescent, white light into the hallway.

"Come on, my man. Be young. Have fun."

Charlie's feet complied without awaiting his approval. The nausea was gone and all that remained was pain. His pupils were slow to adjust to the disproportionately bright lavatory. He pulled his hand away from his face without waiting and felt the front of his jeans. Rolls of money. He was starving and Mervin Zero furnished the means, albeit posthumously. The bathroom door swung shut behind him. Every stall flanking the left wall was occupied. Two-to-three pairs of shoes stood in circles behind each stall door. The right wall was lined by a long, white marble countertop and one continuous mirror up to the ceiling. A woman perched atop the counter between two sinks. Artificially red ringlets tumbled down the sides of her head and onto the shoulders of her black, leather jacket. She leaned on her left hand, while her right was busy pressing a credit card down flat onto the counter's marble surface. The card crunched and shuddered until it came flush with the countertop. She lifted the card back up to reveal white powder and ruptured pill shells. Charlie's mouth began to water. His hand dove into his pocket. Nervous fingers fished out one of the bundles of cash. He did not remember walking over to the sinks but found himself standing directly in front of the woman, nonetheless. The edge of the credit card chopped and then ground the pill into fine, even powder. Charlie slipped one of the hundreds out of the roll and handed it to her. Without hesitation, she took the bill and rolled it into a straw. She turned her head up to face him. Green eyes locked with his. She cupped the back of his hand, turned it over and placed the rolled up hundred between his fingers. His eyes remained frozen in place. There was a fire emerging in the massive mirror behind her. The black tendrils grew higher, filling the periphery of Charlie's vision until his was free of her charm. Most of his own reflection was blocked by the back of her head. Behind what he could see of his shoulders, in the center of the luminous bathroom, stood a towering inferno of shadowy cloth. The billowing tempest rippled violently toward the ceiling and teased the silhouetted, demonic frame of King Belial. Charlie watched his own jaw drop. He saw himself jump backwards and spin, knocking into the woman on the counter. Her hand jerked away and sent the makeshift rolled straw tumbling.

"Yo, what the fuck?" she snarled. "Gene, why'd you bring this spaz in here?"

Charlie could not stop himself spinning in circles, scanning the room. The bathroom appeared devoid of any unexpected guests, though several of the stall doors parted inquisitively. Gene sounded impatient.

"Man, just buy the shit or get the fuck out. I don't need some junkie disrespectin' my place of business."

"Whom the light never touches," a voice bellowed in Charlie's head, *"must now rise in the darkness."*

The speaker did not need to yell. Its deep whispers managed to rise above all the ambient noise of the nightclub and assert primacy within every cavity in Charlie's skull. Charlie turned back to face the sink, back to the ten-foot-tall demon still standing in the bathroom mirror. His shadowy shawl parted at the sides as both of his hands rose in the air beside him. The black tendril of his snake writhed, dangling from his right hand. Belial's jaw began to sag lower, mouth opening to speak.

"Speak my name, black buckrider. Rise with my tide and ride high."

A convulsion spread out from somewhere deep in Charlie's core. When it reached his lower extremities, his legs scrambled in animal fright. His elbows flared outward, arms gripping the package firmly against his ribs and shifting his mass toward the bathroom's entrance. As Charlie turned, he felt the weight in the pocket of his pullover sway until something within tumbled free. A clatter echoed from the floor tiles. The bathroom hummed with gasps of shock and anger. He did not hesitate. Despite the commotion, Belial loomed terrific as ever in the porcelain behind Charlie. In a full sprint, his free palm smacked the back of the bathroom door. It swung open and crashed into two clubgoers perched just outside the door frame to await their own turn in Gene's office. Charlie could not waste time to turn back and offer them any apology. He barreled down the hallway back toward Hallelujah's main chamber. Another dark shadow materialized around the corner to stop him in his path, though he was moving too fast to completely break stride. Momentum brought him into a collision with the new figure. It seized Charlie by the arm and neck and lifted his feet off the ground. A moment later, a burst of cold air ripped away the balmy heat radiating from the dancefloor. The bouncer growled as he heaved Charlie through the club's front door.

"I knew I'd find you, you fuckin' freak!"

Beneath the glowing, crimson cross, Charlie crashed down onto the sidewalk. The stale sweat permeating his clothes turned frigid and constricted against his skin.

"Beat it, *Chuckie Cheese*. Next time I catch you anywhere near this block, your next stop'll be the hospital."

Charlie's feet found footing while his hands confirmed the package beneath his arm had not come loose.

"And don't think I haven't noticed that deadbeat alcoholic brother a'yours creepin' 'round, too. I'd tell him and the rest'a your white trash family to drop dead, but I didn't see where the clown fucked off to."

"Probably off t'fuck your mother," Charlie croaked.

A sharp crack filled Charlie's ears a split second before stars crowded his vision. The bouncer's knuckles dug deeply into his jaw. He did not notice the pavement rushing up at him until it slammed into his back. Somewhere beyond the ringing echoes that filled his head, Charlie heard a dry thud hit the ground and roll past his sprawled feet. He checked his left hand and found that the second fall had not ended gracefully as the first. His fingers clenched only the corner of the unfurled cloth wrappings which previously concealed the disembodied head. Looking down past his feet, he saw the brown skull tumble to a stop beneath the horrified, frozen faces of the crowd gathered outside the club's entrance.

"Is that? Yeah, that's a—"

"—can't be *real*, can it?"

"Wh-what the fuck," the bouncer stammered. "What the fuck is that?"

Charlie shimmied back up to his feet. He stared at the skull and slowly unclenched his throbbing jaw to speak. At a loss, only warm air rattled out of him. A panicked hand shot into the pocket of his hooded sweatshirt, fingers searching desperately for the comforting grip of the Glock. His stomach sank. Memory brought him back to the club's bathroom—back to his panicked flight. He remembered turning and the sudden lightness in his hooded sweatshirt's front pocket. The sound of metal and plastic clattering onto the bathroom's tiled floor replayed in his ears. As many times as his hand searched the inside of the pocket, all he felt between his thumb and fingers were the ends of household nails and the ceramic likeness into which they had been embedded.

Charlie's motor functions fully escaped his waning capacity for rational thought. He grabbed the disembodied head of the messiah by the crown on the top of his head and shoved the round, fractured neck outward from within his pocket. It formed a cylindrical point as it strained against the fabric.

"Back off," Charlie screeched. "Everybody just… back *the fuck* off!"

To accentuate the simulation, he made several sharp thrusts with the simulated handgun barrel toward the speechless onlookers. A moment of clarity blossomed in his mind. Charlie saw himself. Dazed and desperate as he was, the absurdity of the scene he was making was undeniable. He cursed himself for making an even bigger fool of himself.

"Woah, easy there fella," one man urged. "We ain't seen nothin'! We swear!"

"Oh my God, Georgie," another woman squealed. "He's got a *gun!*"

Charlie watched as the circle of assembled spectators widened. Wherever he pointed, restless torsos shifted aside the sights traced by his simulated weapon. His confidence stirred. He heard his own voice returning.

"Who's the freak now, you fuckin' assholes?"

While the crowd stayed glued to the spot, Charlie could not manage the growing din of terror. Cries of *"Gun!"* grew louder, a chorus echoing over the street. That the trick worked at all left him still dumbfounded. It had, in fact, worked too well. In a matter of seconds, its momentum exceeded his grasp.

"Police!"

The shout came from the other side of the street and landed on Charlie like a bucket of ice. Its femininity surprised him, as did its nervousness. But its sincerity was clear.

"Don't move!"

Charlie's lungs emptied on their own. His attention oscillated somewhere inbetween the unexpected gravitational shift in his simulated stand off and the unwrapped, fully decomposed human head still lying on the ground a few feet away. It leaned on its side, resting against one of many fissures in the fractured cement. A pair of empty eye sockets stared back at him, waiting for him to make a decision. The fresh image of Belial, imposing and magnificent, burned like a black flame in his mind.

'*Speak my name, black buckrider.*'

The phrase returned to Charlie's head.

'*Rise with my tide and ride high.*'

"Your hands," the voice behind him barked. "Let me see your hands!"

Simple instructions. Complicated response. Charlie listened to the very urgent, very officious demands echoing against the back of his head. Doctor Martin Glass made demands of him as well. Doubt entered his mind. Doubt that he could escape this situation with the package Glass wanted so badly. Doubt that he could extract his hand from his pocket without getting himself shot before he could reveal the illusion.

The police officer behind Charlie continued to rattle off directions, but the blood pounding between his ears was too deafening to indulge his comprehension. Slowly, rigidly, he pulled his right hand out of the sweatshirt's pocket. The tips of Charlie's shoes pivoted beneath his toes. One long revolution swung his view around to give the voice a face. She looked familiar. She looked terrified. Her mouth was still moving, he realized, but he could not hear a word she was saying. His right hand rose toward the sky. Fingers peeled away to reveal the desecrated, inverted Christhead within his palm. The expression on the other side of the barrel rose to meet the ceramic figure's gaze and froze solid. A sudden, mechanical shriek was quickly followed by the howling eruption of the crowd surrounding them. Charlie watched the cop's eyes squint as brilliant red light filled the world and a flash tore open the sky above them both.

Ten

Male, med. complexion. 6'5", heavy build, appx. 270 lbs. 50 y.o. Last seen w/ salt & pepper hair pulled back into ponytail, receding hairline. Unk. clothing desc.

Lucy glanced over her notes. The tip of her pen retraced the words she managed to transcribe from Central's brisk relay of the 911 call. Her radio ear was improving. Most of the dispatcher's words were immediately intelligible—some definition remained elusive behind unfamiliar jargon or exhausted vocal cords.

Last seen at Elysian Fields around dinner time, appx. 1900 hrs. Facility admin called, stated patient absent from rm. during midnight headcount.

Lucy had not set foot inside the Elysian Fields Adult Rehabilitation Center in a month. After the countless nights she spent cooped up in the building's basement, she was confident a much longer absence would be required before the place ever began to diminish in her memory. She could still smell the cafeteria, its walls stained by tobacco smoke and sweating nicotine residue. Her imagination conjured up a face when she reviewed Central's description. One of the facility's residents introduced himself on that visit which turned out to be Lucy's last. Central might have mentioned a name when she assigned the job. When it failed to materialize in Lucy's memory, she thought about the sights and sounds and odors of the Elysian Fields.

"Turn the dome light off."

Lucy was pulled out of the rehabilitation center in her mind and returned to the passenger seat of the Caprice.

"Quick now," Tabby continued. "Look over there."

Lucy looked up at the miniscule bulb beaming between rifts in the vehicle's sagging fabric ceiling. Little wattage needed be shed to illuminate the car, nor to blind them to the darker world beyond. Lucy's hand jabbed the switch drand the darkness stood nearer without hesitation.

"You see something?"

"Over there."

Tabby's finger peeled away from the top of the steering wheel and traced a line down New Utrecht Avenue. She toggled the headlights, hugged the shoulder, and let the accelerator ease.

"Behind that van. See anyone familiar?"

Lucy scanned for whatever attracted her partner's attention. Rows of empty, dark cars lined the road's two lanes beneath the elevated train tracks. No untoward disturbances or movement of any kind emerged in the largely static scene. Even the few meager, barren trees surviving on the sidewalk caught no breeze to make them sway. If a single, living creature was out there, it devoted no small part of its energy toward remaining undetected. A pair of headlights appeared in front of them. The car made a right turn from a side street about five blocks away and entered the oncoming lane. The stretch of roadway beneath the train tracks was only sparsely lit. With their own headlights extinguished, the approaching car flooded the street as it rolled nearer. Lucy saw the silhouette growing between parked cars until it washed over the sidewalk.

"Yeah," Lucy said slowly. "*Him.*"

If the man was aware he was being watched, he remained motionless. Without much of a struggle—without being able to see more than a sliver of the side of his face—Dexter Valerie's name returned to Lucy. He stood at the edge of the street with his back to them, his shoulder perched against the corner of the elevated track's support column. A pair of parked cars provided cover while he watched a crowd loitering under an array of red, neon lights not far away.

"What do you figure he's doing all the way up here?"

"Nothing constructive, if I had to guess," Tabby replied. "Hopefully, someone'll call the cops—tell 'em one of the Valerie brothers is creeping on girls leaving the nightclub."

"But *we're* the—" Lucy started. "Ah. Funny."

"Don't tell me you aren't curious."

"You're right, I won't. Sounds like you're still looking for a new shot at that gold shield."

"Hate to break it to you, but the P.C. doesn't go around handing out awards for collaring Valeries. Maybe a firm handshake if our man right here has a couple of those girls tied up somewhere. Either way, I'm not especially confident that's the type of reward to make up for the damage that's been done. I could still make detective before I retire—hell, I could just study for the Sergeant's exam and make rank the easy way. It won't change that Vernon got a free ride on me."

"That's on him. Stop taking credit for his shitty behavior."

The driver's seat groaned. Tabby pushed herself higher and sighed.

"You'll see. Where you're at, the playing field still looks level. Wait 'til you start asking about all those greener pastures and getting told 'no.' Wait 'til you find yourself left in the lurch when all you asked was 'why not?'"

"After everything you've seen, how is being told 'no' the scariest turn the day could take? How many people get burned out on this job just because nothing scares them more than rejection and bosses? You never hear anybody talk about what else they'd rather be doing, or what they could do to make the next day less miserable. But you'll find plenty of people pointing the finger at everyone else after they burned out and gave up on themselves."

"Starting to get cold feet being stuck with a *burnout* like me?"

"I didn't mean it that way. And I might not be as naïve as you think. I know I'd still be on the same footpost Cordell buried me if he could spare the resources. I'm making the most from what I've been given."

"Gee," Tabby laughed. "Thanks."

Lucy bit her tongue. Any more backpedaling and her partner's amusement might turn to genuine offense. When she looked back toward the street, her stomach went cold. Dexter Valerie turned and their eyes met. With a hard blink, he shoved himself away from the steel column. He was too far for Lucy to hear his words, but his frustration spelled them out clearly:

"The fuckin' pigs."

The Caprice's brake pads squealed as they released. The car rolled forward, slowly.

"Oh well," Tabby sighed. "If he knows we're here, let's at least make sure he knows it's time to hit the bricks."

Dexter kept his shoulders tight, arms pushed deep into his jacket's pockets. Puffs of steam billowed from his nose and lingered in his wake. He showed no interest in any exchange with Tabby as her hand cranked the car's window lower.

"Caught you at a bad time?"

The brakes chirped again and the car shuddered to a stop. Tabby sat upright, cranked the shifter into park, and made a quick jerk to her left. She twisted until her vertebra responded with a pair of audible realignments. When she repeated the stretch to her right, her spine permitted one more dull pop.

"Guess we're doing it the hard way," Tabby sighed.

Lucy was accustomed to watching Tabby exit the car at a leisurely pace. Now, she was upright and crossing into Dexter Valerie's path no more than a second or two after shoving her door open. With an abrupt spin, the older Valerie brother turned away and began to sprint. Lucy rose from her own side of the car.

"Alright, not so fast—"

"—*you fuckin' freak!*"

Though it came from over a block away, the shout was loud enough to interrupt Tabby's warning to Dexter Valerie. Both officers turned to look. The crowd in front of the nightclub hummed as people backed up, widening into a circle near its middle. A giant cross trimmed in red neon lights glowed over the brewing disturbance. When Lucy turned back to her partner, she saw that they were now alone. Free of their attention, Dexter had disappeared completely.

"Shit," Tabby grumbled. "That creep dipped and now this."

"Whatever *this* is."

"Last call. There's always somebody ready for a fight when they know they're about to be cut off."

The crowd backed away just far enough to not risk becoming part of the action while maintaining an excellent view. The wall of onlookers thinned as it expanded in time for Lucy to see the frame of a gangly, young man launch from the club's doorway and crumple onto the ground.

"C'mon," Tabby said. "Let's clear 'em out—make ourselves known before it turns into anything worse."

Tabby slumped back into the car at a pace Lucy found more typical. Lucy lowered herself and monitored the developments from her window. Mobile once more, the Caprice rolled up to the next intersection. The man on the sidewalk pulled himself back onto his feet.

"Roll down your window," Tabby said. "Time to let 'em hear that big, bad cop voice."

Lucy turned the window crank and cleared her voice as the two men continued to hurl insults at one another.

"Ah-hem," she coughed. "Time to break it up, guys."

If the younger man on the sidewalk heard her instructions, it did nothing to stop him shouting back to the man who sent him flying through the air.

"*Probably off t'fuck your mother.*"

The much larger man lunged forward in a single stride and buried his fist in the young man's cheek.

"That's showin' 'em, kid," Tabby grumbled. Her hand patted Lucy's shoulder to offer mock reassurance. "Very intimidating."

"Ah, fuck," Lucy said. "Assholes didn't even hear me…"

Lucy jumped out of the car. As she neared the edge of the sidewalk, she could see the younger man sprawled across the concrete once more. A long, dirty blond rat's nest of split ends tumbled down from the top of his head to hug a familiar face. Gasps arose from the crowd, but their attention was no longer focused on either of the two men. She followed their gaze for a few feet. A brownish, round object tumbled away from the smaller man. Before she could make out precisely what it was that he dropped, he was already scrambling. Upright, he paused. For a moment, both he, Lucy, and the crowd lost themselves in the pair of bony eye sockets staring up from the concrete. Entrancement gave way to murmured debates, then shouts of conclusive disgust. Freeing her own gaze, Lucy's eyes returned to the young man's face. She searched through her memory until she saw his hand lunge into the front pocket of his black hoodie. After some momentary fumbling and jerky hesitation, the heavy cloth of his sweatshirt pressed out toward the crowd.

"Back off! Everybody just… back *the fuck* off!"

The object pressed outward. From a distance, its menacing end very much resembled the round barrel of a revolver. Genuine article or imitation, it was having an indistinguishable effect on the assembled bystanders over whom it swept. A woman yelled, confirming what was on Lucy's mind as she snapped open the leather strap securing the back of her own firearm.

"He's got a *gun!*"

He was distracted. He did not notice as Lucy bent her knees and pulled her arms up in front of her.

"Who's the freak now, you fuckin' assholes?"

"Police," she shouted. "Don't move!"

The world stood still. Her vision narrowed to a pinhole no wider than the .38's sights. Not far beyond the barrel, the young man's shoulders slumped.

"Y-your hands! Let me see your hands!"

Was it a scream or was it a whisper? Lucy prayed the words landed at all, but continued to rattle off directions, nonetheless.

"Don't move, I said. Take your hands out of your pockets!"

She was only partially cognizant that commands tumbled from her mouth faster than she could arrange them coherently. Momentary self-awareness of her contradictory instructions fled as the shoulders beneath the black sweatshirt began to pivot. Lucy's eyes moved down. The man's revolution continued until the protrusion still concealed within his pocket waxed into her vision.

"No, stay turned away. Let me see your *goddamn* hands! Do *not* turn around!"

Panic took over. The bridge between her mind and muscles splintered into a hundred conflicting impulses. The tendons in her hands quivered, then tensed. Her grip tightened and squeezed the revolver' trigger closer to her palm. Her jaw clenched as words continued to press through her teeth.

"Just let me see your hands and *stop moving!*"

The world was getting darker. As Lucy spoke, she realized she had shouted away the last of her fresh oxygen. Her contracted diaphragm refused to allow any new air into her lungs. Nerves and limbs drifted miles apart as the young man yanked his right hand out of the hoodie. Both hands rose high overhead. Fingers uncurled to expose a second pair of eyes, tiny and inverted. A waterfall of ice washed over Lucy and sent shivers from the top of her head to the tip of the finger still pulling tighter on the trigger. She watched the hammer at the back of the gun teeter at the edge. What exactly was cupped in the palm of the man's hand, Lucy had no idea. A weapon it was not. Crushed beneath the weight of realization, Lucy's hand finally surrendered its death grip on her revolver. Her index finger released. When her mind began to approach something resembling normal operation, her memory returned. The apartment, their argument. The father, his sons.

Charlie Valerie.

But his eyes were wrong. Darker. Colder. Reflections of Hallelujah's glowing red cross floated inverted within two wide, black pearls on the face of a cornered animal. His figure became a silhouette. The sky over him was turning bright and red. Lucy ordered her eyelids to stay open long as she could bare. She looked up and watched the blazing neon trim on the cross swell. It grew from an impossibly brilliant crimson into a pure, blinding white explosion. Lucy covered her face and ducked down as the explosion filled the air. Without awaiting the order, her legs dove behind the trunk of a car parked on the side of the road. The screams of the crowd twisted and fused with a thunderous volley of high voltage bursts. Sparks and shattered glass rained down as the letters spelling *HALLELUJAH!* could no longer contain the energy pouring forth and exploded one by one. Lucy felt debris and shrapnel pelt her arms and desperately tightened her hold on the cover around her. When the barrage began to die down, she looked up. The last of the neon letters popped off while a steady blizzard of sparks twinkled and faded, drifting lazily onto the street below.

In the vacuum that followed the fury, Lucy pulled herself up. She scanned the sidewalk for Charlie. He had adopted a similar pose to her—the mop of his hair shielded by crisscrossing arms. Lucy took a step forward. The silence came to an end. An engine roared behind her. The headlights of a silver Camaro flooded the entrance of the unlit nightclub. Tires screeched to a halt. Thin, pale strands of hair billowed in the breeze as the car's driver leaned out of the window.

"Pick it up," the driver yelled, "an' get the fuck outta here!"

Charlie did not hesitate. The younger Valerie brother flew into action. He scooped up the brown skull from the ground as his sneakers pounded the pavement.

"Hey, stop!" Tabby shouted as she emerged from the front end of the same car Lucy hid behind.

"Eat lead, pigs!"

The woman from the Camaro shrieked and leaned even further through her window.

"Try 'n catch this!"

Tabby's interest in the second Valerie brother met a similar end. A series of blasts cracked from the window of the Camaro to the sky above. The woman and her handgun bounced back into the car. Smoke burned from the tops of its spinning back tires. The remaining bands of bystanders broke into a final, fearfull stampede and filled the sidewalk with chaos. Lucy twisted and weaved, angling for a view through the scattering crowd. When she found Tabby, she was already halfway back to their patrol car. The Camaro begged for traction, drifting past in a wide arc until it launched itself down the road. Lucy's gunbelt refused to synchronize with her footsteps, but her boots tore across the street without haste.

"Get in the car," Tabby yelled, "and don't lose sight of her."

Lucy latched onto the passenger door's handle, swung it open and vaulted onto the seat. The tip of her boot squeaked against the pavement when the car charged forward. Lucy fought against momentum. She braced against the vehicle's frame to pull her own door shut as Tabby leaned into a U-turn. Lucy yanked at the portable radio still clipped to her gun belt. She raised it to her mouth and jammed her thumb into the transmitter button.

"This is Six Four David, Central! Northbound, New Utrecht Avenue."

Her lungs had yet to fully replenish her blood's oxygen levels spent on desperate pleas with Charlie Valerie and the subsequent sprint to the Caprice. If her voice sounded nearly spotty over the radio band as it sounded to Lucy's own ears, it may have failed to constitute much more than panicked yelling. She tried to meter her breathing. The transmissions might have been helpful. They might even have been accurate. There was no more time to catch he breath, and her best would have to do.

"Shots fired from a muscle car. Two doors. Silver."

The Camaro had a four-block lead. Its distant taillights flared and curved to the left.

"Which unit is raising Central?" The dispatcher's groggy voice indicated some surprise and no small amount of annoyance. *"10-5 that transmission."*

"Northbound on New Utrecht, it just made a left onto…"

Lucy's eyes darted. Corners passed before she could focus. When street signs caught any light, they raced past her as brown blurs.

"Sixty-Fifth," Tabby added. "It turned westbound."

"Westbound on Six Five Street, Central," Lucy repeated.

Lucy felt her lungs begin to catch up. She tried to orient herself.

"This is Six Four David, following a silver Camaro involved in a shots fired—"

Central had responded quickly. The rest of the precinct took a moment longer to compute the sudden noise. When they caught up, they fought for airtime.

"Six Four Charlie, Central! Show me going—"

"Show sector Adam backing! 10-5 the locatio—"

"This is Six Four Lieutenant. Redirect all sectors to—"

The voices of Lucy's coworkers stumbled over one another. One would cut off another, then fail to complete a full sentence before being interrupted themselves. The channel's dispatcher fought to maintain order.

"Clear the air, units! I'm showing all units redirected to back Sector David. Sector David, please 10-5 your current location."

The steering wheel twisted and spun between Tabby's hands. She mashed the gas and the Caprice peeled into an abrupt lefthand turn through another intersection.

"We're on Sixty Fifth Street, heading westbound from New Utrecht."

Lucy searched the horizon and soon found the Camaro as a lone set of taillights. The four-lane roadway was barren, making it easy to keep track. It also provided Tabby ample room to test the limits of the NYPD's motorpool—eight aging pistons rolled out of a General Motors plant three years past, but already much nearer retirement and a resale auction than its original delivery. Heavy as Tabby's foot was, they were no match for the IROC and had yet to close a fraction of the distance they tailed. It sailed effortlessly around another corner without as much as a flare from the brake light.

Lucy's radio continued to roar with confusion. Regardless, her thumb jabbed at the button on its side.

"They just turned again. That's gonna be…"

She closed her eyes and summoned a compass in her mind.

"Northbound, Twelfth Avenue."

Tabby eased off the gas and swung wide to the left. She reeled the steering wheel to point the car's nose to the right. Her foot returned to the accelerator. Lucy found both her forearms planted against the car's frame and dashboard as the hard turn tried to forcibly remove her from her seat. Adrenaline mixed with G-forces. The car filled with the smell of smoldering brake pads and burnt rubber. It was apparent their incremental gain had not escaped the attention of the Camaro's driver, who now began another turn in an attempt to throw them off. Tabby managed to push their car within a half a block of the Camaro when it dipped once more to the left.

"Twelfth Avenue, now westbound onto Sixty Second Street…" Lucy's voice trailed off in awe, then returned. "… in the wrong direction."

The vehicle they were pursuing skidded defiantly past a one-way traffic sign.

"Fuck," Tabby growled.

"Are we gonna follow? Is that the best way?"

Tabby sighed. Her shoulders had relaxed or, perhaps, slumped when she saw the Camaro disappear around the corner. She shot up in her seat. Her hands gripped the steering wheel again.

"It *can* be, as long as we approach with a very open mind… and a light touch."

Lucy sank into her seat. Her fingernails buried themselves in the passenger door's armrest. Their chase had been blessed to cover unoccupied, predawn roadways thus far. A silent prayer entered her mind as they rounded the corner themselves. Lucy saw only the red flare of the Camaro's lights without any oncoming headlights ahead of it.

"See?" Tabby wheezed. "Easy as pie."

Intersections whizzed by. The Camaro never slowed, but the Caprice's front end still dipped as it slowed before crossing into each one. Lucy was grateful for her caution, if frustrated by the gap which widened their pursuit.

Their target's taillights flared once more. A halo of white light crested over the muscle car's roof. A pair of headlights had entered their path. The Camaro skidded and gave up a great deal of momentum and territory before it swung left of the oncoming vehicle. Lucy saw the streetlamps shimmer, then flickered slightly. They gained ground for a change and swerved right of the now stopped, nonplussed car.

Lucy looked down at the Camaro's bumper. It was close enough for the blurry lines on its license plates to resemble individual digits.

"Robert… Four… George. Three, Two, Two. Again, silver Chevy Camaro. '87, maybe '88—"

"This is the Six Four Lieutenant, Central!"

Cordell plummeted from the airwaves into the middle of Lucy and Tabby's car.

"*Have all units terminate this pursuit,* forthwith. *Units are ordered to terminate and stand by.* All units acknowledge!"

"Fuck that," Tabby growled. "Too close."

Lucy hesitated. She had enjoyed her time off the lieutenant's radar. He was likely to bury her for good if the chase continued. Her finger brushed over the radio's transmitter. She raised her hand to her mouth. At this point, Cordell would bury her, regardless.

"Westbound, Six-Two Street, toward Eighth Avenue!"

The IROC carved a path to the left as it entered the next intersection. The view which was revealed when it listed to the edge of the crossroad was that of their path ending entirely on the other side of Eight Avenue. Sixty-Second Street was coming to an end whether their brakes permitted it or not. A bright white streak of light ran down the Camaro's silver paint. A city bus heading southbound skidded into the intersection from their right. Smoke hissed from its tires as the driver struggled to halt its momentum. The fleeing car corrected its leftward motion and drifted in a wide arc no more than a few inches shy of the bus's front end.

"Northbound, Eighth Avenue," Lucy shouted.

The bus's driver leapt from his seat and yanked at the door's lever. He stumbled out onto the street and gesticulated madly, lobbing obscenities at the car that nearly hit him while Tabby and Lucy trailed in its wake.

"Going west again… Six-Oh Street."

The Camaro bucked as it slammed into third gear, straddling the double yellow line and gaining ground faster than the automatic Caprice could ever dream.

"Northbound, Fourth Avenue!"

Green lights twinkled at them far as the flat and level roadway would reveal. After a few blocks, the Camaro swerved and crossed between the Avenue's cement dividers. Lucy watched it barrel ever fast, now separated from pursuit by a concrete barrier and headlong into oncoming traffic. Not much time had elapsed, though morning approached by the minute. Others joined the roads, entirely unaware of the potential disaster which could bring their morning commute to calamitous end. The muscle car veered over dividing lines between bewildered southbound traffic. As it bobbed and weaved, Tabby maneuvered their patrol car nearer on their own side of the avenue.

Waves of cycling traffic lights passed by, disregarded altogether by the Camaro and crossed with diminishing precaution by Tabby. Lucy gripped her seat and watched ambers change to reds. She blinked to clear her eyes. The lights around her blinked on their own. She watched the next traffic signal. Green and amber and red mixed erratically until they danced between the strobing, sulfuric streetlamps surrounding them. Entire side streets fell dark, then flared to life again, burning brighter than ever. Neon signs suspended from the sides of sleepy buildings and hanging in the windows of shuttered storefronts crackled and fluttered. A compact car crawled onto the avenue from Fifty-Fourth Street. Lucy could see the dazed look on its driver's face, dazzled by the ambiguous and chaotic traffic signals. It crossed into the intersection no less than fifty feet shy and dead center of the Camaro's roaring engine. Tires squealed. The compact came to an immediate halt in the middle of the intersection while the Camaro drifted around its trunk. The Camaro's driver hit the gas and spun the wheel to maintain control. While they cleared the compact, they were too distracted by the near-miss to account for the box truck sprinting along the opposite direction. The Camaro made an abrupt, sharp turn to the right. A split-second later, its front end connected and crumpled against the raised cement edge of the avenue's steep divider. The Camaro's trunk rose into the sky when its front could no longer direct its weight forward with the rest of the vehicle's energy. Back overtook front, then pulled the remaining mass, end-over-end, tumbling across the rest of the avenue while Lucy and Tabby passed beneath.

Tabby slammed on the brakes and the Caprice swerved. What brakes could not accomplish in bringing about a full stop, the rear bumper of a parked car succeeded following a sharp crunch. What followed was the sound of an avalanche of twisting metal and a torrent of concrete debris. It was not from their own collision, Lucy realized. When the cacophony died away, all she could hear was the sound of the Caprice hissing and her own throbbing chest.

"Shit," Tabby cursed as she exhaled.

Her partner glared at the steering wheel while she rubbed her forehead.

"What about you, you good?"

Lucy's hands instinctively groped for signs of obvious damage. Her legs looked fine and, as an added bonus, she could still feel her toes. Early indications seemed to reveal their own crash had been relatively minor, although steam was now screaming from beneath the Caprice's crumpled hood. Lucy heard a wump and a groan from the driver's side. She saw her partner wrenching the door's handle open, trying to force it open. Metal whined against metal as it refused to budge. The crash had pushed in the patrol car's front end and pinched the hinges of the driver's side door. With a lesser if not altogether inaudible protest, Lucy swung her own door open and pulled herself up onto the street. She found her stance wobbly and leaned against the side of the car.

"Follow me. Hop over onto my side."

She did not turn completely to offer Tabby the invitation. The scene outside the car was difficult to ignore. A whirlwind of smoke and steam raged further down the block. Lucy steadied herself and contemplated the underside of what was left of the Camaro. The awning of a wholesale operation into which it was now partially embedded sagged and groaned. Wedged with its passenger side to the ground between a pair of stairwells leading down to the Fifty Third Street subway stop, the car's front tire still slowly spun in the air. Lucy spotted another tire not far from the axel it had dislodged, tangled amidst the remnants of the neighboring shop's roll down gate.

"Be advised… crash at Fourth Ave, Five Three Street. Vehicle stopped at this time."

"Six Four Lieutenant!" a voice growled over the radio without delay. *"Units are ordered to stand by."*

Lucy's arm fell slack, pulled down by the weight of the radio in her hand. The wreckage of the Camaro hissed. She pushed herself away from her own car and walked over slowly. Her right hand climbed to rest on the back of her holstered gun.

The lighting along the block appeared to have stabilized from its chaotic rhythm during their pursuit. The most glaring exception were the traffic signals, which had either reverted to blinking red and amber or had ceased to function altogether. Otherwise, only the occasional, residual spasm and flicker rolled across the grid. The subtle palpitations reminded Lucy of heart beats.

"Ugh."

Tabby groaned behind her. She shoved herself over the center console and tumbled through the passenger's door. When she stretched upright, Lucy noticed a dark line dripping down the side of her partner's forehead.

"You sure you're alright?"

"Oh, that…" Tabby's voice filled with a hoarse laugh. Her hand swiped at the blood trail. "Remember to wear your seatbelt."

Lucy flicked her head toward the Camaro's remains.

"Tell that to *her*."

"Yeah," Tabby agreed. "We're done here. That's gonna be a D.O.A., no two ways about it."

The gnarled, metallic whine that twisted its way from the remnants of the sportscar made Lucy jumped backward. She watched Tabby's eyes go wide as she rocked her own handgun backwards in its holster. In a second, her partner's firearm levelled on the wreck. The car shuddered, then sank down a few inches. Its frame scraped down the side of the subway entrance to rest more firmly against the ground. Tabby's gun eased downward.

"We gotta be sure," she said. "I'll take the right, you cover the left."

Lucy nodded. She forced a foot forward. The car shuddered again as it continued to settle. She listened for movement or any evidence of life whatsoever escaping from within. Tabby put a foot up on the sidewalk. Her eyes remained fixed on the car's upended windshield. Lucy watched her partner's shoulders slump when she was a few feet away. With a sigh, Tabby shoved her revolver back into her holster.

"That's the end of that—whatever *the fuck* any of that even was. What a senseless mess."

A metallic shriek pierced the air, squeezing needles out of Lucy's forearms. A dark hand shoved aside the door atop the wrecked car like the hatch on a submarine. Without hesitation, a shadow leapt upward and landed on the highest point of what remained of the silver muscle car. The pulsations still seizing the streetlights deepened into dark tremors. Lucy, frozen in place, stared through the darkness at the eyes of the pale-haired woman. The lights convulsed, then flared brighter. Through squinted eyelids, Lucy watched the woman turn into an impossibly quick, shadowy blur. In a single stride, she leapt down the car's capsized underside, around the side of the subway entrance, then down its stairs. Lucy reeled. She remembered the shots fired at the sky in front of the club. Her hand found the grip of her gun.

"You ok over there? What was that?" Tabby sounded baffled as she called to her younger partner. "Hey! Where the fuck are you goin'?"

"She's running," Lucy yelled as she raced toward the subway entrance.

"Who?" Tabby shouted. "What do you mean? Stay here!"

Lucy's feet pounded down the steps. As her view came level with the subway station's mezzanine, she scoured the tiled hallway for any sign of the fleeing woman. The hallway widened into an empty ticket checkpoint. Lucy saw no movement on the other side of the turnstiles. The station's fluorescent bulbs flickered. Straight ahead of her, a shadow sprinted into the hallway leading to the station's exit on other side of Fourth Avenue. The soles of Lucy's boots squeaked as she pulled herself back into motion. Her feet skipped every other step on the staircase as she climbed topside, this time on the opposite side of the avenue from the still-smoldering Camaro. She was gaining ground on its driver, who now sprinted up the sidewalk past the drawn roll-down gates of the avenue's dormant businesses.

"This is Six Four David, Central."

Lucy gasped as she brought the radio to her mouth. She strained to keep herself calm. What sounded like a banshee roared at her, as feedback filled the airwaves. Lucy released the button, then mashed it down again.

"Suspect, white female. On foot, Northbound, Fourth Avenue."

Lucy spun around the side of the subway's entryway and resumed her pursuit. The weight of her gun belt shifted and listed, throwing her stride off with each step. Metal buttons and leather flaps popped open. Her perp had no such burdens and moved as if wholly weightless. Lucy's lungs burned. The woman was no more than a blur. At the next intersection, she disappeared to the left, eschewing the wide roadway for a narrower residential corridor.

"Westbound on Five Two."

Her words echoed back at her over the radio, but the voice sounded more mocking than her own. Distracted by the delay, she momentarily lost track of her target. Out of the corner of her eye, Lucy spotted the woman crossing between a row of parked cars to the other side of the street. She followed, but stumbled as she shimmied between fenders to get onto the sidewalk.

"Third Avenue."

The narrow, residential block opened wide as Lucy careened into the intersection. An elevated highway ran down the center of the avenue to form a broad, concrete and steel canopy over its median. For a brief moment, the woman was in Lucy's sights. When she crossed the intersection, the figure disappeared between the raised expressway's support pillars.

"Northbound, I've got her beneath the Gowanus!"

Lucy could do nothing to consciously stop her feet if she tried as they carried her under the highway. The wide, concrete space was littered with vacant automobiles. Unevenly parked at irregular angles, they straddled the invisible lines of extremely informal parking spots. Some were left overnight. Others appeared subject to far lengthier neglect under accumulated layers of soot and brown, streaked windows. Lucy forced herself to examine her surroundings. A chill washed over her. The silence and stillness forced her to confront her own exposure. She had lost sight of an armed suspect. Worse, she wandered into the middle of a hundred potential hiding spots. No foreign footsteps arose from the deserted landscape. No shadows breached the light of the lamps dangling from the steel-reinforced beams holding the Gowanus Expressway aloft. Lucy clenched her teeth. She tried to stifle the noise of her own breath as her lungs sought to recover from the pursuit. In the overhead distance, the eighteen wheels of a tractor trailer truck approached.

"Fuck."

The trail was cold. While Lucy debated throwing in the towel, she felt a twinge of pain from the crook of her right index finger. She turned her palm over. A red blemish pushed up from beneath her skin. She could not recall slicing or burning it at any point, but an unmistakable red line had manifested. The wound bisected the joint of her finger. Lucy traced her steps backward through the night until she found herself staring down the sights of her revolver—staring at the back of Charlie Valerie as he turned to face her. She remembered the straining fabric of his pocket he used to simulate a gun. Lucy was unsure of the moment she determined it was not the genuine article. She was unsure of the moment she made the decision not to shoot. The red line crossing the inside of her index finger made her unsure exactly who it was that controlled the hand which nearly tore a hole through Charlie Valerie.

Lucy's guilt was pierced by a shriek as her radio flared. A blast of feedback and static bounced off every inch of lifeless metal and poured stone around her. When the ringing subsided, a sigh escaped her exhausted lungs. The median beneath the highway ran from one horizon to the other. Dim, coppery lamps illuminated columns of cars and trucks. Lucy turned around. She looked to the north and studied the distant end of the median. She blinked hard. It had grown closer. Lucy trained her eyes into the distance. The highway began to rumble as the sound of the oncoming truck grew nearer. A frigid chill blossomed in the pit of her stomach. The horizon lurched forward. Her eyes refused to comprehend— refused to budge. She watched the corridor of light shrink once more as the next overhead light withered and ushered the darkness a step closer.

Lucy shifted her weight to her back foot and took a step. The rumbling overhead contorted as it strengthened. She assumed it had been a semi barreling down the highway, but its morphing pitch no longer matched. A scream rose over the thunder. The highway quaked atop its support columns, channeling its vibrations into the ground beneath her feet. Dust and pebbles sprinkled down inside the diminishing beams of light. The next set dimmed and died, followed by another. Lucy's mouth let out a low whistle. The intervals between the dark wall's steps shrank and the sound from each popping bulb grew louder.

The darkness was a block away. A few seconds later, it had marched halfway to the next intersection. Lucy broke. Her feet scrambled. As she pivoted toward the still-lit block behind her, she checked over her shoulder. It was still gaining ground. Before she could turn back to face the same direction she sprinted, the tip of her shoe dug into something hard. All she could see was the ground rushing toward her face. Lucy grunted. She fought back against her impulse to curse the brick dislodged from the median's pavement.

"For our desires, for your charm. We swear this oath, we raise an arm."

Obscenity melted away. Lucy's head twisted as she searched for the source of the whisper. She froze when she saw the silhouette a few yards away, in the center of the intersection.

"Lift us nearer your peerless might, and in your honor rule the night."

A crack snapped through the air. The whispers swelled as Lucy tried to find footing. From the slightest breeze came a wall of wind howling around her.

"No longer our fathers' wayward ones, we are the Devil's favorite sons..."

A black tide washed across the ground and ran over her fingers. It splashed over the cars and the pavement, drawn along the road toward the soft-spoken shadow. When it ran under her, it engulfed the rest of her world. Every remaining light Lucy could see disappeared. Only one thing shone in her vision: a slender, young woman, in the same place the shadow had stood a moment before. A frenzied blaze of long, straight, platinum hair whipped around her and twisted like a bonfire into the pitch-black sky. It wrapped over her like a sheet to obscure her face, but Lucy recognized the driver from the Camaro. The woman's right hand rose at her side. In it, a long, black object slithered and twisted. Lucy squinted. Before she could fully comprehend the nature of the snake in the specter's hand, the writhing creature stiffened and shrank into the shape of a black handgun.

"Hail, mighty King Belial."

Lucy's hand made a frantic dive for her holster. She tore out her revolver, rolled to her side, and jumped up onto her knee. A loud blast cracked through Lucy's eardrums. An explosion of red and white spinning lights drove her forearm up to shield her eyes. The world erupted in light and electric chatter.

"Six Four Lieutenant, Central. Show me 84 with Sector David. *Absolutely no further.*"

Lucy lowered her arms from her face to see a new silhouette rushing toward her. A hand dove under her left arm and ripped her upright.

"Holster that fuckin' gun, rookie, and tell me *just what the fuck you think you're doing?*"

Conflicting waves of relief and dread crashed against each other in Lucy's head. She stood face-to-face with a very obviously infuriated Lieutenant Cordell.

"Lieu, it was the woman with the gun! She jumped from the car, and I followed her here. She was right here, you had to have seen h—"

"Damnit, Madrigal, how stupid do you think I am? Don't think for a second you're gonna pull the wool over my eyes! Your partner—your *injured* partner, who you left behind—is sitting next to the *dead-fuckin'-body* of that woman right now. A woman who is dead, by the way, because you two can't obey a direct order from your *superior*."

Lucy felt the ground spin away from the soles of her boots. She had only seen one person in the car. And she had watched the same person jump out of its wreckage after the crash.

"Lieu, I'm sorr—"

"I said… *Shut. Up*,"

The lieutenant's face trembled as his teeth clenched behind his lips. High pitched screams began to appear in the cracks in his voice.

"Always with you… always with the *disrespect*. I hear it in your voice every time you open your mouth. You're done."

Lucy's throat tightened. Her mind raced for the right response. Before any such words could materialize, her mouth ran with whatever it could find.

"Again, I'm sorry, I'm not tryin' to be disrespectful. I just did what I thought was best. Y'know, what was best *at the time*. She was dangerous. She was armed, letting off rounds. I swear to you, I saw what I saw…"

Lucy forced her neck to look up. Cordell's indignant rage appeared undiminished.

"…but, I understand," she continued. "I understand if I need to take a hit for this."

Cordell's face finally loosened. A laugh burst from his lips and sent a drop of spit to land on Lucy's cheek.

"*A hit*," he repeated. "You think you're gonna take *a hit* from this fuckin' mess? Your partner, yeah sure. Disobeying radio transmissions, engaging in an *explicitly* unauthorized pursuit. I'm gonna make sure she doesn't hold onto another vacation day until she decides to retire."

Lucy's limbs went cold. She had been on thin ice with Cordell already, ever since the Christmas party. There was still nearly a year left in her probation. Not much stood between her and immediate, unappealable termination.

"You, on the other hand, are going to be escorted back to the station house so we can safely lock up your firearm and shield, and commence your suspension without delay."

Melendez's eyes reflected sympathetically in the rearview mirror. Lucy glanced at her rolled up gunbelt and the butt of her revolver inside its holster. It sat now atop Lieutenant Cordell's lap. She slumped in the back seat of the supervisor's patrol car. A halo of fog spread out along the back window from where her head rest. She lost count of the blocks that passed by and without seeing a single light bulb left functional. Her mind was miles and months away. Lucy thought about her first tour of duty after the night of the Christmas party. The lieutenant called the room to attention and prepared to begin reading the roll call. She had not seen him since abruptly leaving the party. When he arrived at Lucy's name, he stared at her appraisingly.

"Madrigal. You'll be drivin' me."

She thought she made her rejection explicit enough. Less than twenty-four hours later, he still scheduled her to drive him. Before moving onto the next officer's assignment, he studied her face. He waited for a reaction. Whispers and glances grew. Lucy felt her face redden.

Roll call resumed and she spent the remainder planning her next moves. She chose every word carefully. When the muster broke, she approached him.

"Sir, I was wondering if I could work with Melendez or maybe Schilling tonight. His partner is out on vacation anyway, so I know he needs someone to work with until Antonio gets back."

The lieutenant squinted. A faint smile tugged at the edges of his lips.

"Huh," Cordell laughed. "Don't you think I know what's best for you?"

"It's just that I—y'know—wanted to start learning on my own. Working with the other cops. I think I know enough by now to—"

"If you knew anything at all, you'd know how foolish you sound."

Lucy was stunned. Cordell's collar grew visibly tighter as blood rushed to his face.

"Are you questioning my judgment and experience?"

"No, I just thought—"

Lucy tried to reassert some control over the conversation, but was cut off again.

"Do you have any idea how *grateful* you should be? Ask anyone here. They'd give anything to have what you got. What you *coulda'* *had*. In my day a rookie didn't speak 'til they were spoken to, let alone get to drive a lieutenant. Especially a woman. Back then they'd have never let you outta the building."

Lucy did not drive the lieutenant that night. On the printout of the roll call, a line was struck through her assignment. *Special Post*

#99 was scribbled over it. Lucy remembered the last of the late-autumn breezes blowing over her. Cordell finished chalking off a circle in the middle of the sidewalk. The wind shifted. The temperature dove a few degrees.

Lucy shivered. Slouching in the back of the lieutenant's car, she listened to Central clear the air. The dispatcher drew the attention of every unit to an emergency announcement.

"Be advised, as per the borough's commanding officer, a citywide mobilization of all units is now in effect. All electrical light and machinery located within three blocks of Third Avenue and Fifty Second Street has been completely disabled. A power surge has spread across all precincts in Brooklyn South, as well as several commands in Queens and Staten Island. All units are directed to contact their Desk Officers forthwith for emergency reassignment within those affected areas."

The car's brakes squealed. Lucy's window came to a stop next to the wreckage of the Camaro. Deserted when she saw it last, the surrounding sidewalk now buzzed. Gas generators hummed beneath mobile flood lights. Silver paint and twisted metal glowed beneath them. The air bordering the scene swirled red, white, and amber.   Lights spun from the tops of emergency vehicles dispatched by a dozen different agencies and representatives of every level of government over the City of New York. An officer sat on the back bumper of an ambulance. She cradled an ice pack against her bandaged head. Lucy felt her eyes sting.

"Tabby…"

Her partner looked up. Tabby forced a weary smile, but a shudder made her gaze waver. Lucy's view shimmered. Her eyes stung. She broke away, looked down, and shoved the heels of her palms against her eyelids. Warm water trickled around her fingers. The tears flooded the crook of her right index finger. A familiar burning sensation returned. Lucy turned the palm toward her face. In the darkness of the back seat, the mark radiated, glowing dimly red.

Shouts rose on the sidewalk nearby. A sudden commotion erupted among a gaggle of suited men bundled tightly beneath long, winter trench coats. They stood a few yards away, next to a van marked for the Office of the Medical Examiner. Lucy recognized one of the men behind the meat wagon. Sam Vernon kneeled next to a stretcher draped under a white sheet and pulled it up by the corner. In his other hand, he held up a photograph. His face passed back and forth between the picture and the uncovered body. The detective let the sheet drift back down. His face turned upward. The lines on Vernon's forehead faded as he looked at his

colleagues. The car started to roll forward again. As they passed by, Lucy could read Vernon's lips.
          "Boys, we got 'er."

Eleven

Charlie's throat was raw. His labored struggle to breathe hardly registered over the sound of his heart pounding between his ears. The last clear thing he remembered hearing—not long after the deafening bursts of each tube of neon lighting attached to *Hallelujah*'s façade mere feet away—was Bethany shouting for him to run.

His knees buckled. For not the first time that night, the frozen concrete rushed up toward Charlie. After the initial sting subsided, he lay there, catching his breath. Wind whistled in and out of his contracted larynx. Icy fingers pressed up from the coarse ground into the overheated pores of his flush face. The break was abrupt and unplanned, but sorely needed. Gradually, the muscles in Charlie's arms resolidified until they could right him. When his top half was vertical, a tremor spread from deep within his chest. It wrapped around his body until it manifested into a cough and, quickly, a fit of them. Charlie pressed his tongue against the back of his throat. He sucked deep through his nose, then ejected the accumulating matter out of his mouth onto the sidewalk. A wisp of steam drifted away lazily until its drifting molecules pulled apart into infinity. His throat relaxed. The whistling of his breaths died down. When his heartbeats retreated from inside the walls of his skull, Charlie found the world quieter. In ten years of earning their attention, he had never known cops to pursue with any excess subtlety. Charlie checked the horizon to either side. There were no blinding lights peeking around any corners. No sirens cried in the distance. He had no idea when he lost them, much less how. Satisfied—moreover, surprised—that the coast was clear, he sought the nearest street sign, unsure where he lost his own track.

85 St

21 Av

A little over a mile and a half from the club without slowing. Charlie pressed his palms against the concrete and shoved his back against the side of a building. His legs uncurled beneath him and splayed across the sidewalk toward the road. The serenity of his respite was already receding, peace melting away to a growing ring in his inner ear. His eardrums had not suffered any ruptures during the gunfire outside the club, nor in the explosion which preceded it, but something effected them, nonetheless. Charlie stretched his jaw. He took a deep breath and tried to turn it into a yawn. His left hand cradled the disembodied skull still tucked beneath his sweatshirt. The other hand found the desecrated Christhead in the hoodie's pocket.

Charlie remembered Bethany. Her order to grab the skull and run was not immediately complied with, but once he was in motion he did not stop. He did not need to see the Camaro in motion to know when it hauled ass in the other direction. For every beat up, shit box car he ever saw the cops roll up in, he had yet to see a single one that could match Bethany's IROC. Unfortunately, Charlie knew cops did not keep to one-on-one when they gave chase. Not for very long, at least.

On their own volition, Charlie's eyelids slid together. In the moment before he forced them open, he slid into a darkened world punctuated only by the occasional shooting star. Even peeled wide, Charlie chased the specks of light drifting around his field of vision past the borders of his periphery. His blood stream was still starved for oxygen. Not far from his numb diaphragm, Charlie's stomach began to contort. He thought about the bathroom and white lines— the angel cutting them and the king of all beasts over her shoulder. Next to the ceramic head, he felt one of the rolls of bills he liberated from the late Mervin Zero.

Charlie pulled his hand from his pocket and rubbed his eyes. The world beneath his eyelids still flickered. He was exhausted, but his mind was nowhere near settled enough for sleep. When the world began to slip into darkness again, fingertips pulled at the sides of his face and pried back the skin around his eyes. He craned his neck and looked up at the sky. The streetlamp over his head could barely emit enough light to reach the ground. Charlie watched it undulate, wavering brighter, then dim again. A low rumble was rising somewhere beneath the steady ringing in his ears, building deep within his chest. His head slowly returned to the street around him. Storefronts lined the avenue. They were all shuttered for the night. Those left to await the morning with minimal lighting behind their rolled-down gates similarly flickered and waned. The traffic signal hanging over the intersection cycled from green to amber to red, then immediately green again. It looped over again without pausing between phases. Charlie shivered and found himself upright once more, with no memory of lifting himself off the sidewalk. He hugged the skull under his arm. The noise grew louder and sharper, from a rumble to a roar. It rushed toward him from the edge of the western horizon. Charlie's ears popped, ringing no more. The air around him shifted, sucked toward the approaching fury like undertow until it swept back over him in a frigid wave. The world hemorrhaged around him. He watched the traffic light strobe spasmodically as it twisted in the wind. It flashed amber and green—green and red. All three at once and then none at all.

The roar drifted away on the fleeting wall of wind. Every surface of the world surrounding Charlie was abandoned to darkness. The streetlamps had all disappeared. The traffic signal bobbed and swiveled over the road, present only in negative space between Charlie and the brilliant sky above. Innumerable stars glared down over Brooklyn, so dense and vibrant as to render their tremendous distance trivial. Dense bands and twisting rivers of light wrapped around ever more massive, piercing cosmic beacons. The dam of the city's baseline radiation had broken, washed away with the screaming tide. Now the unfiltered cosmos pored over the land and the eight million souls dwelling thereon lie naked before trillion upon trillion celestial eyes. The sight was breathtaking for Charlie, but he recognized the prelude to much more terrific dimensional revelations still fresh in his memory.

Ultimo Delicatessen stood beneath its unilluminated sign a block away. It looked cleaner, Charlie noticed, without its interior lights glowing hazily through the store's grease-stained windows. Only a faint red glow escaped through the front door's glass panes. The entryway offered no resistance to Charlie's hand and swung inward. A bell jingled overhead. A voice called out from the abyss.

"Hold your horses right there, pal. We ain't doin' any business right now, if it wasn't obvious."

Charlie's feet came to a halt. The only functional source of light in the room came from an emergency exit sign, still running on reserve batteries, hung over the door to the deli's rear stockroom. The source of the voice came from the front counter, just beyond the meager light's reach. Charlie kept still. He felt it safe to assume the call had travelled over open sights. Moreover, he reckoned any respectable drug dealer would know the layout of their own operation well enough to engage unwelcome intruders under even the poorest of conditions.

"I ain't here to rob youse, Franco."

Charlie found a plastic lighter in the pocket of his jeans. He raised it to his face, and scraped down on the igniter. The flame floated a few inches below his face.

"Oh… it's you."

"Don't sound *too* disappointed, big guy. I thought you was open all hours, anyway."

"There's a fuckin' blackout goin' on, if you hadn't noticed."

Something metal clanked down onto the Formica countertop by the register. The muscles in Charlie's upper back loosened.

"You know," Franco grumbled, "you really are more trouble than the regular deadbeat."

While the tension between him and Franco eased, Charlie felt the passing seconds slow to a crawl as he spent them listening to the dealer's gripes. Not once had he sought Franco for the rewarding socializations. His visits to Ultimo Delicatessen were a consequence of basic necessity. Desperation. The extenuating stress which inaugurated this particular meeting did little to diminish the hassle of the usual song-and-dance. Worse, there was an added feeling of déjà vu from Franco's words which sent a chill through Charlie's limbs as his fatigued ego parsed them.

'He's a little more trouble than your regular deadbeat, is all.'

Dexter.

His own brother had described him the same way to Glass. He long accepted the world saw him as a joke. It still stung when the barbs came from someone Charlie looked up to for protection—someone he owed his survival to more than to his own father. Replayed moments of Dexter's dismissive tendencies kept Charlie's mind from sleep some nights. Failing to actually be there when Charlie needed him most was worse. Bethany came charging in with a distraction that allowed his flight. Dexter was assigned as the lookout. Charlie could not recall his face among the panicking crowd from which he fled.

'I'm just tryin' to keep my stomach down.'

He still ached, more direly than when he last saw Dexter turn from the Camaro's window. The last drops of his body's naturally produced adrenaline had long disappeared. In its absence, his brain ran on fumes—alongside his oldest and most painful memories.

'Relax. That was just pig's blood.'

Perhaps not just memories. Charlie could not remember his last meal which had not been unwrapped from cellophane. Though insubstantial, the pig blood turned his stomach in a bad way for a night like this. Charlie had not felt the itch for weeks, nor the sickening penalty for trying to ignore it.

'Whatever I drank before just ain't sittin' right.'

The flame on Charlie's lighter blew out. The deli was only dimly red once more, but the lingering imprint in his vision from the flame resembled the golden cup in Glass's basement. He slammed his eyes shut, then rapidly fluttered his eyelids. The image was reluctant to melt away.

'Go back home, Charlie.'

When Charlie opened his eyes, the flame and the cup were both absent. He saw the windowless brick shack by the side of the road.

'An' if you tell Pops where I was,'

The voice was that of his adult brother, standing in the same doorway.

'I'll kill you.'

Charlie squeezed the roll of cash in his pocket. His ear drum hummed. Those few parts of his mind not yet ceded to jealousy and anger shouted at his rigid nervous system to complete the transaction.

'You can either choose to start gettin' shit done—like me—or you can stay Chuckie Cheese *forever.'*

The humming grew to a ring, amplifying louder until a scream reverberated through every corner of Charlie's head. He stumbled up to the register.

"Hello?" Franco yelled. "Hey, *Chuckie Cheese*! I haven't got all day, already. What's it gonna be this time?"

The scream disappeared. The roll of cash slapped onto the counter. Charlie's hand bolted back up. He saw the entire store lit in an instant, awash in bright, white light. When darkness flooded back into the world, the shocked expression on Franco's face hovered over the cash register. Beneath the cloud of sulfur and smoke expanding across the store, a bloody mist unfurled. A second hand slammed down on the counter. Fingers probed and scurried as they searched for the firearm they remembered setting there a minute earlier. Charlie's arm stayed level and his hand squeezed the trigger four more times. Over four frames of light, Charlie watched Franco crumple until all that stood behind the cash register were cigarette displays spattered red.

Charlie rediscovered voluntary muscle movement as his lungs gasped for air. His right arm quivered, then swung down to his side. He squatted and perched his elbows atop his knees. His jaw stretched, trying to clench his ear canals shut, as he exhaled through his nose. The sensation that his ears had been packed with cotton balls lingered. He was flying blind once more, and deaf as well.

"Fuck..."

Charlie ducked lower. He sucked in his stomach and buried the muzzle of Franco's revolver behind his waistband.

"Fucking *fuck*."

The deli's tile floor was cold. Gritty patches that had not known the attention of a mop in years clung to Charlie's palms. He scraped hand-over-hand past the candy bars and packs of gum displayed beneath the register. When he found the edge, he paused. The butt of the revolver rested beneath his right palm. Sparks spun from the lighter in his left hand. A thin flame extended upward. Charlie leaned forward. A dim, coppery glow flickered as it spread over the surface of the black puddle expanding across the tiles behind the counter. The pool of blood extended from a pile of haphazard legs and baggy clothes steeped in dark, crimson splotches. Beneath a cluster of dislodged cigarette cartons, Charlie locked onto a pair of wide eyes. Franco's mouth lolled open, motionless.

Potato chip bags and snack wrappers crinkled and tumbled across dirty floor tiles. Charlie pulled a cardboard tray down from the shelf over the register. He tore rolls of scratch-off tickets out of their dispensers. The skin on his thumb burned as it throttled the red button on the side of his disposable lighter. Franco's pockets had been turned inside out. The dealer was smart enough not to carry narcotics on his person when it was not necessary. Charlie was ravenous.

"I ain't leavin' here, asshole..." Charlie hummed to the body piled next to his feet. "Not leavin' 'til I find that *goddamned* stash."

A spinning ray of while light sliced through the filmy streaks on the store's windows. A red flash followed shortly thereafter. The lights spun across the pitch-black room again, repeating faster. Charlie's knees bent. He kept his head level with the counter. Emergency lights were approaching the store, unaccompanied by the usual warning of sirens. Charlie continued to lower himself until something cold and wet began to seep through his jeans. He looked where his knee touched the ground. Franco was slouched down next to him, fluids still slowly seeping out of him. Charlie froze in place. He watched the swirling lights wrap around the perimeter of the store. Along the left-hand wall, atop a shelf over the display freezers, were shelves lined with narrow plastic boxes. The white light passed over them. Each plastic case had a label over its spine. Most looked like they had names printed by a computer. A few looked handwritten. The passing lights dwindled until only the exit sign once more illuminated the store's selection of rental videos. Charlie exhaled. The denim covering his knee peeled away from the coagulating blood as he stood up.

The lighter passed over the white labels lining the video cassettes.

A Clockwork Orange, Airplane, Apocalypse Now.

Charlie followed the row, unsure of what should have been sought. The corner store's rental library was nowhere near expansive as the bigger, chain video stores. Nor, Charlie noticed, as current.

Halloween, Harold and Maude, Jaws.

One Hundred and One Dalmatians, Peter Pan, Pinnocchio.

The collection covered the hits. The boxes were scratched and the art filling the protective covers faded. From experience, Charlie knew the reels and strips of tape within were just as worn. He had been forced, on more than one occasion, to carefully extract and respool several cassettes on loan from Ultimo's after they decided to unravel inside his VCR.

Further along, the plastic cases transitioned from semi-transparent to black. Charlie's hand reached up to the adult section, then paused. Porn would be too obvious—let alone, pulled down more frequently than the rest. His eyes travelled back down the alphabet. Something did not fit.

Raging Bull, Risky Business, Rocky.

Saturday Night Fever, Staying Alive.

Charlie stopped. The image of John Travolta inhaling a slice from nearby Lenny's stared down at him from the edge of the box. He sidestepped to the beginning of the alphabet and scanned the titles one more time. Charlie's hand shot up on its own. It yanked at the edge of one of the tapes, then flipped it over.

The Boy in the Plastic Bubble.

Charlie never knew what it was like to be popular as Vinnie Barbarino. In the brief time he attended James Buchanan High School he passed through the same doors as the Sweathogs and fell victim to several uncannily similar meatheads. Whereas Charlie dropped out, John Travolta moved on from his fictitious version of the school and eventually earned a place in disco immortality strutting down the nearby sidewalk outside Ultimo Delicatessen. Charlie knew that, in between the two roles, the actor appeared in a disaster that could have easily doomed them to the same path. In the event anyone came into the corner store looking to throw a little Travolta in their VCR and found *Saturday Night Fever* already spoken for, he was certain they would always settle for *Staying Alive* over an evening the bubble boy. Poor a film as the former might be, it came nowhere near the travesty of an immune-compromised protagonist clad in an air-tight space suit with a limited supply of oxygen settling a schoolyard dispute via push up contest. Charlie jiggled the case in his hand. The cardboard sleeve inside shifted, but nothing of any substantial weight rattled around. His thumbs and index fingers clawed at the tabs on the sides of the case. Unfastened, the plastic case dropped from his hand and clattered against the ground. Charlie turned the sleeve over. The flame from his lighter danced across the surfaces of dozens of plastic baggies stuffed with hundreds of white decks of heroin.

The lighter offered little light as the supply of fuel within ran lower. Its flame had shrunk noticeably since Charlie began his search of the store. Aided by what limited illumination it could still provide, Charlie's eyes ran down the length of his forearm as it held the repurposed VHS box. Tiny hairs pricked through goose flesh. The air pressure in the room shifted and, for a moment, the tiny flame flickered near death. Charlie's heart sank when the bell over the Ultimo's entrance chimed. A silhouette appeared at the edge of the world outside.

"Charlie… what're you doin' in here, bro? What the fuck's goin' on with you?"

Charlie's turn ground to a halt. He had been more eager to see the intruder before he recognized Dexter.

"You weren't at the meeting point," his brother continued. "We went over it, again and again. That's what you were supposed to do—*where* you were supposed to go. Not… *here*…"

"What I was supposed to do," he echoed. "What about *you*?"

"What *about* me?"

"What about our lookout? Where were you while I was gettin' rocked by that meathead bouncer? When Bethany was gettin' chased by the cops?"

"I've been runnin' around Bensonhurst lookin' for the two 'a youse for mosta' the last hour. Now I find you tossin' your dealer's joint an' you wanna cop an attitude with me? And don't gimme none 'a your fuckin' *concern* 'bout Bethany. Don't you know how I was able to find you here? You think I don't know what it *smells* like in here?"

"I dunno, Dex. You tell me."

"Like Bethany said, whatever the fuck you do with your share— whatever other deadbeats you decide to blow away now that you finally found a pair of balls—that's your business. I can't play your fuckin' babysitter forever. But when Doctor Glass needs something—"

"You don't give a fuck about me," Charlie groaned.

"*You* don't give a fuck about you. I tried. The doctor tried. Even Dad… in his way. But you of all people can't even say as much for yourself. How many times do you expect the world to keep lettin' a fuckin' reckless junkie like you burn it, Charlie?"

"Dex," Charlie replied. "Don't fuckin' call me no fuckin'—"

A pair of feet stomped from the front door and down the aisle to the freezers. Dexter's face soared over Charlie's head into the dull red glow of the emergency exit light.

"*Junkie*," Dexter spat. "Fuckin' deadbeat, skell of a fuckin' junkie."

Silence filled the room. Charlie's eyes closed tight as his ears began to burn. Electric impulses shot down his arm, teasing his hand toward the gun tucked into his waistband. A hammer clicked backward as the cylinder of a revolver rotated into place. Charlie's eyes flew open. Even in the dimly lit store, the outline of the gun hanging along his brother's side was unmistakable.

"Charlie, you had one simple thing to do tonight. I pray right now—I pray *for you*—that between all 'a your fuckups and whatever it was that you did in here, you managed to keep yourself from losing what Doctor Glass needed you to get outta th'place—"

"It's a skull."

"What? Whose skull?"

"Fuck if I know," Charlie snorted. "Some jerk who couldn't keep it on his shoulders."

With a flick of his chin, Charlie gestured toward the front counter. The room's limited light traced the ridge of a skeletal brow next to the cash register. Dexter's shoulders pivoted, then slouched away toward the disembodied head keeping watch over the room. After momentary consideration, Dexter shrugged. He wrapped the skull in the unraveled cloth it rested upon and tucked it under his free arm.

"Charlie, after what happened tonight—"

Charlie looked at Dexter's back, the gun still hanging from his right hand. Another hammer cocked. The barrel of the little .38 to which his hand had beaten Franco's drew a line from Charlie to his brother. Dexter let out a loud sigh, then tucked his own gun into the front of his belt.

"I guess there's nothin' left to say, then."

"You're right. I guess not."

Charlie quivered as he spoke, forcing his voice to stay steady. He could not gauge how effective it had been. The sting overtaking his eyes was enough of a distraction. Dexter turned away from Charlie, for which he found himself grateful. Tears streamed silently down his face. He could not let Dexter see him cry. It may have meant prolonging the painful farewell—or resorting to more agonizing means to realize its conclusion.

The bell over the deli's store rang. Charlie leaned back against the store's freezers. The cool glass doors slid up along his back as he collapsed onto the ground. He felt like a wild animal. He knew that was all Dexter had seen in the middle of the blood-soaked, ransacked store. Not a little brother—an uncontrollable monster. He had been ready to put Charlie down as such, if it meant Glass's satisfaction was on the line.

More than anything, Charlie felt lonely. He could barely hear his brother's footsteps as they blended back into the city's ambient buzzing and missed him already. The only person Charlie missed more was the young man whom their father carried over one shoulder from their apartment all the way to the emergency room. That brother died, but not of the alcohol poisoning that necessitated hauling him to the hospital. The true Dexter never returned after his first introduction to Doctor Martin Glass, though even that sober young zealot had been better than nothing. Charlie wondered who would love him now.

When Charlie's knees could sink no further, he punched the tile floor. Pain shot past his elbow. He punched the same spot again, then a third, fourth, and fifth time. He thought about the shiny, polished tiles in the Oneirological Mission and the doctor who warped his childhood theater. Charlie focused on visions of the man's paranoid face reflected over the facility's every gleaming surface. He repeatedly beat his knuckles into the floor until each subsequent punch returned a lesser report of pain.

The box the bundled glassines of heroin sat less than a foot away from the bloody mess his fist left behind.

Needles hid among other medical supplies offered for sale.

A Pepsi cap twisted eagerly into Charlie's palm.

The lighter's fork sprang back up.

The plunger squeezed down.

An empty syringe clattered against the floor.

Charlie's body outpaced his nervous system, released a long sigh, and unfolded across the floor. Everything around him was covered in a faint, red sheen. As his eyes gradually adjusted to the conditions, the light from the store's emergency exit sign extended its reach. From where he sat on the floor, the lower shelves around him were stocked with what appeared to be the corner store's least-perused goods. Unsold holiday decorations, 6-packs of white wife beaters. Patron saints and biblical scenes painted onto prayer candles peeked over the edge of a cardboard tray. Charlie had not been raised alongside any routine religious enrichment, nor could he summon a single memory of his father being sober enough to keep himself upright during the hours traditionally reserved for Sunday services. The faces looked typically saintly, nonetheless— bearded men, ornate halos, instruments of symbolism held aloft in outstretched hands. Scenes of terrific magic and miraculous demonstrations. Saint Michael with his sword drawn. Padre Pio, hand bleeding as he manifested stigmata. More *Our Ladies* than one could count making appearances at every corner of the globe.

Saint Jude, Charlie read. *Patron of lost causes. Brother to the son of God.*

Making his way down the row, Charlie's eyes spotted the man himself. He rubbed the small, porcelain head in his pocket and remembered its face, dangling from Bethany's rearview mirror. The image on the candle was more conventional. Jesus held nothing in his right hand, just an open palm extending outward in a gesture of peace. His left hand was held by his chest, where two powerful streams sprayed onto the ground. One was pure white, the other bloody red. It reminded Charlie of a scene he could not attribute to any one particular film—of a Roman soldier with a lance, walking away to let the man on the cross bleed out and die.

Franco's junk was taking too long. Charlie shivered. The store was quiet. Lonely. Charlie addressed the empty room.

"…all the time in the world… and enough poison to finally send me out of it."

The ritual repeated. Another glassine envelope emptied into the singed bottlecap. Another pile of powder disappeared beneath a boiling tide.

"Oh, fuck," Charlie groaned. "Fuckin', Jesus… Christ."

The second set of waves hit hard, swelling stronger with each new surge to wash over Charlie's body. He fought to stop his eyes rolling to the back of his skull. Desperate, weakened fingers scrabbled and groped at the cold, damp skin of his face, struggling to reconnect with the audience of patient, holy icons. His eyes twisted back and forth over the candles in search of his new friends and protectors. There was no shortage of the stock filling the shelves in front of him. Rows upon rows of white candles sat within tall glass jars. Each one was blank. No labels, no faces. Only clear, unlabeled glass tubes. Charlie's heart skipped every other beat. A haze of dope descended over his conscious mind while his eyes spun wildly. Resisting the backward roll, he fought to keep up his search—the saints, Christ. Dexter. Anyone.

"Dexter. I ain't… ain't no monster…"

A sharp jerk and Charlie's muscles collapsed. His eyelids drifted down on their own.

Everything was dark until it was not. A spiderweb of red capillaries filled Charlie's vision. His eyelids shot back open, then immediately clamped shut with the aid of his palms to shield him from the fresh light. The world hummed. Charlie struggled up to his feet. Legs stiff, he braced himself on the nearest refrigerator. He could feel the motors in the store's display freezers buzzing. Everything was coming back on.

Charlie pried his hands away from his face and beheld the store through squinted eyes. Despite his bumbling around in the dark, he was impressed by how orderly everything still looked. The television by the front of the store clicked back on, its image flickering and then expanding to fill the convex, glass screen. A board of Keno numbers slowly appeared.

His eyes drifted down from the TV screen and stopped over the front counter.

Franco.

The lights were back on. The world would begin to return to normal. Time was short, as was the darkness to keep him hidden while he cleaned up the dealer's body. Another visitor with more conventional views on murder than Dexter might cause the door's bell to jingle at any moment. Charlie decided not to wait. He looked back at the ground where he had been sitting seconds before. The deli's harsh fluorescent lights still rendered him partially blind and unable to locate the stash he worked so hard to discover. He could not afford to delay his flight wasting more time to let his eyes readjust. His best bet was to put as much distance between himself and what remained of Franco.

Charlie shifted on his feet and began to lumber toward the front entrance. The muscles around his eyes strained. He brought his left hand up to massage his temples and found shade beneath his sweatshirt's black hood. Along his rolled-up sleeve he saw the usual tracks and a nasty new scar. Charlie looked closer. Where he shot up, his skin had already begun to bruise. The two spots where the needle dug in were pitch black. With a fingernail from his other hand, Charlie picked at the damage. When he reached the door, he stopped, abandoning his flight. He turned back to the counter again. Reams of lottery tickets and scratch-off cards still filled the bins by the register. Cigarette cartons lined unbloodied shelves. Charlie took a step closer, eyes locked on the counter. His neck craned. His pace quickened. Franco's lifeless torso never crested over the horizon of the countertop. Charlie's hands landed flat on either side of the register as he lifted himself up. He landed back on his feet and shoved his hand into the pocket of his hoodie. The weight of Franco's revolver remained, but the Christhead was gone.

Adjusted or otherwise, Charlie's eyes remained open wide as his head would allow. Images of an unbearably well-lit and pristinely undisturbed bodega flooded in. Charlie's lungs deflated. He froze in place until he could force his mind to start up again. He needed to find a mirror.

Charlie looked around frantically. Every corner of the store was piled to the ceiling with merchandise and every available wall was lined with densely stocked shelves. Over the register, an automated game of Keno glowed on the television set. One-by-one, pixelated balls flew in arcs from alternating corners of the curved glass screen and landed on the numbered board below. Charlie walked up to the television and reached up with his free hand. His fingers rattled against the set's dial. He steadied his arm and took a deep breath. The dial turned with a heavy *clunk* and the Keno board shriveled into darkness. Charlie was left with the unlit, black glass screen. He watched his own eyes twitch back and forth in the reflection. The store behind him appeared empty but for the panicking boy in the center of the black bubble.

Charlie spun around and ripped a display stand down. Bags of beef jerky and mixed nuts scattered across the floor. His hand dove for the revolver, ripped it from the sweatshirt's pocket, and brought it level with the television screen.

"Come out, you demon son-of-a-bitch! Get on with it already!"

His index finger jerked back on the trigger.

"You're here! I know you are!"

The last thing Charlie saw before his eyelids slammed down was the ball of fire erupting from the barrel toward a shattering television screen. The shot echoed throughout the store and brought the familiar tinnitus back to his ears. And then it evaporated. His ear canals cleared. Charlie slowly opened his eyes. A Keno ball flew from the edge of the screen, over the curved, unblemished glass, and landed on the number nine.

What felt like a static shock popped somewhere near the center of Charlie's brain. It took a few seconds for synapses to resume their normal routines. A loose trail of drool at the corner of his mouth informed Charlie his jaw hung open. Shortly thereafter, he noticed how much lighter his right hand felt—emptier, too. He looked down and found his right hand empty. The .38 was nowhere in sight. Charlie staggered backward and knocked into the display rack he threw to the ground a moment earlier. Though the rack remained, the snacks which had either flown off or remained tenuously hooked onto it were gone. Charlie's fingers caught the top of one of the many shelving units that formed the store's aisles and managed to keep him upright after some rebalancing. He leaned into the bare, wire framing. These places too had been emptied of the products they previously featured. As his view rose, Charlie found every shelf across the deli barren. The junk food and cigarettes, the Crazy Horse tall boys and six-packs of Bartles & Jaymes in the freezers. Even the Travolta flicks and the pornos. From the center of the empty store, Charlie stumbled, dazed. His palm landed flat against the higher of the front door's two glass panes. Every bulb in the store burned bright as they could, while 86th Street remained under cover of complete darkness. Charlie pushed. The door swung open without resistance or sound. He looked up as stumbled into the night. Ultimo's jingling chime was gone, too.

Immediately as it wriggled into his nostrils, the night air brought Charlie's mind back to the circus. It was apparent that the streetlamps lining 86th Street had yet to come to life with the same power returned to the deli. All the same, the scene was brighter than Charlie remembered, touched by a glow that gave the street a new dimension. A breeze from the west blew over his left cheek. He looked up. The overhead train tracks were gone.

The wrong door—the back door, perhaps. Charlie was sure, gripped by panic in his escape, that he must have barreled through the nearest exit he could find instead of the one which would correctly return him to the street. He sighed, embarrassed but relieved, at the mess he was becoming. Too much of a mess to believe his own eyes. Disorientation and hallucination, he told himself. Nerves and narcotics.

The urgency of his circumstances remained unchanged. Charlie tipped his nose to the sky and let his lungs fill. More strange air. After a long pause, he gathered himself, turned, and reached for the handle of the door through which error brought him. His knuckles rapped against a loose glass windowpane. The door stood apart from where muscle memory placed it. Charlie took a step back for a wider view. The building he stepped out of—one in an unbroken sequence of store fronts stretching the length of the block's 86th Street side and a good portion around the corner on Bay Parkway— had been replaced with a solitary, wooden house. The door which Charlie reached for was replaced by the right-most in a matching pair of bay windows. The ceiling-height windows obscured by grease, cigarette ads, and sun-bleached boxes of cereal were gone. On the other side of the wood-framed glass panes were reams of textiles and stacks of folded clothes. Woolen hats with curved brims filled the other window's display. Charlie lifted his head and searched for the corner store's sign. As with every other trace of Ultimo Delicatessen, a much broader, wooden sign hung in its place along the side of the building's shingled walls. Ornate, hand-painted letters advertised another business entirely:

Wm. R. Speir & Son
Drapery, Finery, Millinery

Charlie reeled backward on his feet. His back found something dense and cold to slam flat against. What he saw exceeded mere misdirection or drug-induced delusion. The two-story, wooden structure housing the clothing store was the only finished building on the block. The elevated train tracks and garbage-strewn 86th Street which ran beneath it were nowhere to be found. His sneakers thudded atop a dusty, uneven sidewalk. Its abrupt curb sank into a muddy gutter out of which gradually emerged a cobblestone street. Light flickered overhead. Charlie leaned forward, turned around, and looked up to the top of the post he landed against. Wide at the bottom, like the trunk of a tree, the cylindrical cast iron column tapered as it rose into the sky. At its top sat a hexagonal glass box. A delicate, amber flame danced within.

It was warmer than Charlie remembered, too. The air was crisp, but nowhere near bitter as the winter air he ran through from outside Hallelujah. He began to move forward without any idea where it was he should go or his relationship with this place. Wherever it was, spring preceded his arrival by several weeks. Shrubs and stubby trees covered in young, green buds twisted their way through the crooked, wooden fences lining the block. Charlie had never seen any part of Brooklyn so sparsely populated. Nonetheless, dozens of gas lanterns lined each vacant block as if to invite change into this vacuum. Neatly sewn rows of cast iron shafts sprouted from the dusty ground—fresh, black paint gleaming beneath each crystalline crown. Hundreds more lay by the roadside, bundled and stacked, waiting their turn to be planted.

Charlie drifted a few blocks more until the formal sidewalk disappeared entirely beneath a dirt path alongside the gravel roadway. It struck him he should orientate himself before he wandered any further. A row of tall, yellow, pine posts shouldered a pair of telegraph lines along what remained of the road as it continued beyond the light of the last gas lamp. Charlie stepped closer to inspect the signage affixed to the nearest intersection's pole. His heart sank as he heard his own hollow voice grumble involuntarily.

"86th Street..."

It did not take long for the mystery to untangle in his mind. Charlie had never received much formal education, but he had seen quite a few movies. Among the possible natures of his surroundings was one which did not seem much stranger than the supernatural world he was already forced to accept.

"Alright, asshole. I know you're here. Sorry I shot the TV."

When his taunt received no formal response, Charlie thought about the neighborhood. What few houses dotted the landscape all resembled the haunted houses he saw in cheesy, black and white horror flicks. They were, after all, no different than Martin Glass's ghoulish house, except his managed to survive.

The thought gave Charlie's feet a destination to focus their restlessness. He turned and continued, resigned to play whatever game he was being subject by forces that refused to confront him directly. He walked a full block to Benson Avenue without passing a single home. Acre after acre had been carved out by dirt roads. Framed within the implied network were vast fields of undergrowth approaching chin-height and splinters of neglected farmland, all lit by an army of gas lamps. Nearly an entire block more passed before Charlie found a familiar, shingled turret. It rose three stories high from the corner of the Victorian's recently completed veranda. Charlie watched the young, skinny saplings that dotted the stately lawn shiver gently in the spring breeze. He was forced to admit that, at least when the house was still new, it did not look half bad. He almost felt guilty about the rough century that would lead it to a state he found more familiar.

Charlie studied the entryway in the center of the front porch. He could almost see the outline of Martin Glass, standing there and leering out at him. Charlie stopped by the same spot he reckoned his car would be parked in another hundred years or so. A chuckle forced its way from his mouth when the view synchronized with memory. He wondered if there was a version of déjà vu which took time travel into account.

One of the gas lamps stood in the same spot as its modern-day, electric descendant. The spot on the ground shined nowhere near bright as it eventually would. The spotlight, which had fallen directly behind his Nova, brought him a pair of unwelcome visitors. The memory of the goat's bleat made Charlie shiver, but shock upon hearing the actual noise lifted his feet from the ground.

"Mah-ah-aah..."

The sound jilted Charlie enough to send a small cloud of dust into the air around his feet. His shoes scraped against the unpaved road as he searched for the beast. He looked at the halo of light circling each gas lamp, up and down the street. A donkey brayed somewhere nearby. Charlie turned to examine the yard of a much plainer shack on the opposite side of the street. Penned in behind posts and chicken wire, a pair of goats loped along, nipping at the untended weeds pushing into their enclosure. Charlie sighed, then snorted. He hocked a mouthful of spit at the ground. A tiny plume of dust spouted away from where it landed.

Something tickled his forearm as he let out the sigh of relief. Charlie looked down and saw a droplet fall from his left hand. A tiny black splotch spread along the bare earth. He raised his arm. A single, inky trail ran down from the end of his sleeve. He began to roll up his sweatshirt until interrupted again, this time from the porch of Glass's future home. A shadow stepped out of the front doors and turned to secure the lock behind him. It did not take long for Charlie to retreat to cover beyond the modest reach of the gas lamps. An unattended horse-drawn cart sat on the side of the road. The wagon was piled high with preassembled wooden rafters and trusses waiting to be raised over the barren framework of one of the neighborhood's still-incomplete houses. After waiting a moment, Charlie leaned forward slowly. The man was already shuffling across the front lawn and approaching the street. He was swift and silent. Familiar. Although his hair was greased back in a noticeably different fashion, the high cheekbones and nearly-albino fairness were unmistakable. The man who exited the front yard, turned right and walked along the side of the road was identical to Doctor Glass. As Martin's likeness crossed the front of the property, he passed a mailbox. Charlie read the name printed along its side:

A. Gauss

Without waiting to consider the man's place in Martin's lineage, Charlie began his pursuit. It was late at night, he reckoned. The world was quiet—at least, he assumed that this was considered quiet in a world still lit by flame and drawn by horse. Charlie had no idea how people who lacked UHF stations and midnight movie marathons dealt with sleepless nights. He mirrored the man's urgent pace, even as it threatened to break into a sprint.

It did not take long for the familiar stranger to reach the end of the block and cross over what Charlie recognized as Bath Avenue. Charlie quickened his own hustle to keep from losing the trail. The area they approached was far more thoroughly lit and appeared to have had its own development begun a few years earlier than 86th Street and the residential blocks between. Mechanical noises rattled in the distance and grew into a steady, clattering procession. A beacon crawled eastward down Bath and a head of steam hissed overheard. Brakes squealed. Dust shook away from the road to reveal a pair of silvery rails. The train tracks glowed as the lantern fixed to the front of the steam engine neared. Far more luminous than the gas flames, the beacon on the engine lit the block even brighter. The man skipped over the tracks when a scene Charlie knew only from Westerns entered his path. A set of two massive wheels turned under a long piston as the engine rolled directly in front of him. No subway train Charlie had ever seen loomed as high. The wonderment was brief. Panic nipped at his heels when he heard the repeat cry of the train's brakes. He remained cut off from his target who, presumably, was not standing around, waiting for the three cars tethered to the engine to roll out of the way. Beneath darkened windows, each car was branded with the same name: *Brooklyn, Bath & West End R.R.* A block-and-a-half ahead of the procession, where Charlie expected to see the bus stop for the B64, stood a building he knew had not survived to his time. It resembled a miniature version of the ornate Victorians dotting the landscape. In the light of the approaching train, the ornate, gilded lettering on the sign hung from the station's eaves sparkled: *Bensonhurst-by-the-Sea.* Charlie bobbed up and down as the windows on the passenger cars crawled by him. He ducked to check the view below the undercarriage, then rose on the tips of his toes to look through empty windows and across rows of deserted seats. On the other side of the avenue, he saw the man once more.

The brakes squealed again. The train slowed further. Charlie forced himself to accept that this world sympathized with his existence no more than the one he would eventually be born into. Just as the quaint, ornate train station would disappear along with the name on its sign and the rails dividing Bath Avenue, so too would the moment he involuntarily defied time to witness.

When the second of the three passenger cars passed, Charlie grabbed hold of the metal railing and pulled himself up the stairs of its open vestibule. A similar set of stairs lead back down on the platform's opposite side, and beneath it the other side of the dirt road crept by. It did not appear to be moving too fast. He gripped the train's railing, bent his knees, and hopped forward. His feet were on the ground for less than a second. The rest of his body was unprepared for the shift in momentum. He tumbled, rolled, and managed to plant his feet back beneath him. Charlie bounced upright, unable to completely shake the spin he carried with him off the ground. His pace unraveled for a few more steps until he found another gaslamp to catch his weight.

Swatting himself clean, claps of dust joined the cloud that followed Charlie's dismount. His hands identified no catastrophic bodily damage, though they were thoroughly caked in dirt when he brought them back up for examination. His left hand was especially soiled. Where the dirt ended, multiple trails of the black liquid wound around its fingers. Charlie's other hand rolled back the sleeve of his sweatshirt. More of the thick, dark substance had been pooling within and spilled out. He followed it up the length of his forearm until he reached the inside of his elbow. Charlie could not bring himself to look. He remembered that time was still ticking. His target still roamed free. He bunched up the slack material of his sleeve around his elbow into a makeshift tourniquet and pushed himself away from the lamp post.

Another block south, the road came to an unexpectedly premature end at Cropsey Avenue. Charlie had lost a great deal of ground, but he was able to spot the shadow making a left turn. He picked up his pace. Gas light faded as the cast iron posts thinned and suddenly shadows were not as easy to follow. The mechanical sounds of the train were long gone. Silence filled the vacuum, then receded under the waves rolling ashore not far away. The only thing which Charlie could identify with any certainty was also the largest building he had seen since stepping out of Ultimo's. Although the structure only rose two or stories over its wraparound porch, it stretched away from Cropsey Avenue over a seemingly endless distance toward the sound of the breaking tide. Above the sign for *The Bath Beach Hotel*, a flickering light illuminated a single room. A rotund silhouette lingered within the window frame, then slipped away. Charlie did not like being watched, especially not in this place, at this time. He slipped forward without looking back.

A rock tumbled off the corner of Charlie's sneaker and skipped down the road. The waves were getting noisier as he ambled, which meant the shore lie nearer to Cropsey than he was accustomed—or that Gravesend Bay was more violent. Perhaps both. Charlie lost count of the blocks when he found himself at the edge of a much wider street. A sign affixed to another young pinewood pole declared that his path intersected 22nd Avenue. He scoffed.

"Wonder how long it took 'em to rename it…"

A lone seagull cried but failed to explain when the signs would be changed to reach *Bay* Parkway. Charlie squinted toward the direction of the bird's call. Despite the poor lighting conditions, he became aware very quickly that this predecessor of the roadway he knew dropped off far more abruptly. No Belt Parkway or Ceasar's Bay Bazaar—just darkness and the calling waves. With few other obvious clues to guide his journey, Charlie answered their calls and followed the street along a surprising descent. Tightly packed cobblestones gave way to widening gaps, drifted loose and sporadic, then disappeared altogether as the formal constitution of the road tumbled downward. After a couple dozen steps, Charlie could see the waves breaking over a rough, rocky shore. Clear skies left the full moon to shimmer brightly off the crests of short, steady waves. As his view loomed over more of the hidden beach, it was apparent that moonlight revealed a great deal more of the landscape than legions of gas lamps had further inland. The increasing clarity also made it apparent that the water's edge lie rolled ashore much closer than Charlie originally suspected. The beach was narrow—a few rocky yards with a great deal of loose timber and other bulky refuse strewn across or poking upward from deep within. Dense spiderwebs of frayed rope and seaweed filled many of the gaps between the debris. As each wave surged ashore, moonlit saltwater swelled between the refuse and rocks. The avenue which delivered him to the world's end had been flattened into a mostly consistent ramp, widening out as it reached the coast, then disappearing beneath the water like a broad boat launch.

A second source of light crawled across the beach. Charlie leaned forward to watch the flickering rays. A tunnel opened on the side of the ledge not far from where the road melted into the shore. He did not realize how soothing the calm breeze had been until the wind shifted. Shortly thereafter, a stronger torrent of waves started to lash the shore. Charlie watched the reflections of the moon tracing bright, long lines along the sweeping water. The distorted moon light met the land in a diagonal pattern. Charlie followed the waves further out onto the bay. A circular pattern was beginning to emerge closer to the horizon and directly beneath the looming satellite. The spiraling tide refused to release his attention until a tumbling rock broke the trance. Charlie looked by his feet. A piece of earth skidded down the incline and splashed into the water. A wave of dust and the handful of tumbling pebbles concealed within followed in its wake. When this was followed by a half dozen cobblestone pavers, Charlie began to back away. The earth was humming, he realized. The crack of a snapping strap rose over the groaning waves. A neat cube of stacked bricks rattled loose from atop a pallet and spilled onto the beach. The landslide of building materials flattened and slowed to a rest by the illuminated tunnel. The light escaping from within strengthened. A moment later, synchronized with the vibrating ground, words joined.

"...reborn," the tunnel howled.

Charlie reexamined the motion of the waves. Moonlight concentrated and glared from the center of a sinking vortex. Gravesend Bay was being sucked downward.

"Come again into this world, my dark mentor..."

The air rumbled and morphed to mimic human vocal cords. A gust travelled over the water. It soared up onto the land as a chorus of voices rose behind it.

"Be reborn!"

A loud crash made Charlie jump. The trunk of an old tree heaved out of the waves, spun through the air, and slammed into the side of the cliff. The bay was ejecting its own depths, churning up debris and long-forgotten remains, and assaulting the shore with abandon. Charlie hesitated until he saw a skeletal shadow pierce the top of the water. It lingered over the tops of the waves, then tilted and lurched back down to the earth. He turned and scrambled back up the hill. Charlie's hands clawed at the ground as his sneakers struggled to climb the disintegrating earth. A loud, wet explosion rocked his heels. When he did not find himself flattened, he fought for a few more yards before slowing to examine the source of the noise. The ground upon which Charlie stood no more than three seconds earlier had been impaled. Although a few feet lower and still angled toward the body which planted it there, the weight of the wreckage would have been visually obvious even if Charlie had not personally experienced the force of its impact. The light flowing from the full moon, joined by the growing beacon near the sinking center of the swirling bay, was more than enough to provide a detailed outline. Despite their bitter, wet centuries together, corroded sheets of metal peeled away from the thirty-or-so feet of wooden hull to which they were long ago bolted. Streams of water dribbled onto the ground over which the broken ship's skeletal remains now towered.

Charlie decided to improve upon his retreat, uneager to find himself better acquainted with whatever else Gravesend Bay no longer wished to hide. When he was a few yards higher on firm cobblestones, he bent down and spun to face the water. The light from the tunnel flared brighter, its own beam slowly extending out over the water toward the center of the vortex. At the same time, the artificially illuminated world to which Charlie made his retreat appeared to be getting darker. He looked over his shoulder. Gas lamps had yet to march past the intersection with Cropsey, and those operating thereabouts flickered noticeably weaker within their glass boxes. The ground shook and the chanting grew louder. The gas-fed flames withered, and the bay raked the shoreline more viciously. Strong as the wind might blow, the stench coming off the water only grew stronger—fouler than the most rank low tide Charlie could remember. He pulled his knees up in front of him to give his elbows a place to rest. When he looked down, he saw the black trail following the steps that brought him to his resting place. The splotches continued over the paved roadway to the ground directly beneath his left hand. His skin was mottled and caked. With his clean hand, he rolled his shirt tighter around his elbow.

"Come into this world again," the voice continued. "Flame in the night! Light of truth! Aodhan Draynor, last chosen speaker to He Who Knows! Most fearsome and fearless Captain of the Buckriders!"

Charlie swayed, then caught himself. His head felt light. The ground beneath him surged and rattled with every word erupting from deep within the earth.

"Master Draynor! We bring your last surviving mortal remains to behold the brilliance of your ancient conduit, realized by our devoted and enlightened labors!"

The bay roared. Lightning crackled from the cloudless sky overhead, flaring and splintering as it completed a circuit to the center of the deepening maelstrom.

"By my dagger and the infernal authority impressed upon it, reunite with your mortal remains! Transcend the universal covenant and walk once more by His word! *Hail, mighty King Belial!*"

Cries of animal despair pierced the rumbling cacophony which poured from the tunnel's archway. It was faint, but distinct. When it subsided, a less subtle sound began to emerge. Charlie heard rattling behind him and turned around. Further inland, in the center of the nearest intersection, a manhole cover was vibrating and spinning. Beams of light shot through the holes perforating its metal surface. Their intensity grew rapidly, until the cover itself launched into the sky atop a mushrooming column of light and flames.   Along the sides of the Avenue, a hundred glass boxes shattered as the cast iron stalks of the streetlamps erupted. Towers of flames erupted twenty feet into the air as lamp after lamp succumbed to a cascading wave of combustion expanding deeper into Brooklyn. The final burst came from the tunnel entrance itself. A great, fiery tongue lashed across the waves assaulting the shore of Gravesend Bay

Noise and fury reigned for what felt to Charlie like an eternity before it was smothered beneath darkness and silence.   He discovered his hands clamped tight over his ears when he finally opened his eyes. Across the landscape, hundreds of gas lamps sputtered their remaining fuel supply into the air. Many others appeared to have been obliterated beyond the capability for such malfunction. Something heavy pushed aside the air as it fell from the sky. It clanged against the wreckage ejected from the bottom of the bay that had almost flattened Charlie. He watched the flaming remains of the manhole cover ricochet into the water. It skipped twice before hissing and disappearing beneath the recomposed image of the moon undulating on the water's uneasily still surface.

Someone coughed near the shore. Charlie scanned the dark rocks. A new blanket of debris and wreckage covered the already rough surface of the beach. When his eyes reached the crumbling, smoldering entrance to the tunnel, he saw a black shape crawling toward the water's edge. It was impossible at such a distance, even with the unobstructed, full moon, to discern the features of the survivor clawing from the wreckage. Charlie did not need to see a face to know who it was. From the corner of his vision, he saw a morphing, slithering shape glide over the now placid bay toward the shore. The moon now hung in the sky without a matching reflection on the water's surface. Its mirror image swayed and loped closer to where the exhausted man lie. When it was no more than a few yards away, the white, glowing shape began to elongate—not across the gentle ripples, but upward, breaching the surface of the water. An ellipsoidal dome bulged upward, followed by a pair of shoulders underneath. Two arms and legs. Though the wind had disappeared with the violent waves and the explosion of light, the glowing white cloth draped across the visitor thrashed and twisted violently into the sky. The familiar figure of Belial towered over the beach, raised the asp in his right hand, and spoke.

"You seek knowledge."

"Oh, lord Belial, y-yes! To… to be enlightened and to serve," the man coughed in response.

Although he had never heard the voice so excited or loud, Charlie knew it belonged to no ancestor or lookalike. Martin Glass pulled himself up from the ground. He staggered onto his knees and extended his hands over his head.

"Then you will remember it is *you* who serve, mortal. Those extinguished souls, who have received our ultimate grace by their own free will, are no mortal's to bind."

"Then teach me to walk as a shadow, dark lord."

Glass sounded hysterical.

"That gift is not yours to know. Nor are those gifted souls yours to control. This is the natural law of the universe and its shadow— the promise made by a faded creator and the final gift to the earliest among his creations. Your lives are yours. Your souls are ours."

"I beseech thee, my lord, with all respect and honor—if my life is mine and the fate of my soul is sealed, grant me life eternal to serve in whatever modest way you desire without end."

"Then life you shall have. Be true to my requests and this plane is yours to walk for as long as you wish. The waves of the abyss will lap at your feet ever more, lest you forget your duties. To keep your head above to the water, you need only speak my name. But when you speak my name, you must be ready to deliver that which is owed. Only souls will ebb the rising tide, though rise again it must, forever. Do you understand?"

"Absolutely, my lord. Praise be!"

Glass laid his hands upon the ground, head bowed.

"You will never again attempt to undermine the essential order. For as long as that covenant is universal truth, those sworn to my everlasting service and all the mortal souls in my dominion are mine solely to command. Mine solely to lend."

The demon's voice seemed to project across the earth without strain. Glass, on the other hand, was howling. But even underneath his maniacal shouts, Charlie could hear a new sound rising over the horizon. Rings and clangs echoed from the land's interior.

"Do you understand?"

"Yes, oh great and powerful King Belial," Glass responded, head held high again. "I understand completely."

Charlie heard shouts. A chorus of human voices rounded a corner not far behind him. He turned and saw a pair of wagons bouncing along the pavement—one black and white, the other red and piled high with brassy machinery. The teams of horses pulling the two vehicles were braced on either side by a couple dozen men in heavy black jackets. Charlie looked back to the beach. The spirit conversing with Glass had disappeared. The moon's reflection returned to the middle of the bay.

"Damnit," someone yelled. "That blasted lunatic's only gone and blown the damn gas mains!"

Charlie scurried. A brushy mess of untamed hedges and squat trees clung to the top of the cliff. He pushed some branches aside and ducked down within. Regardless of the century, he was in no mood to attract any unnecessary police attention.

Hooves clopped up to the start of the avenue's decline and slowed to a halt. Steam squealed out of the top of the red wagon's well-polished engine. The men who ran alongside began fastening hoses to a valve on its side. From out of the black and white carriage marked for the *Town of New Utrecht Police* hopped a pair of men in dark blue uniforms, followed by another gentleman in a suit. Tall and imposing, he also wielded a gut that strained against the suspenders running down his gray and brown, tweed vest. A similarly gray and brown push-broom of a moustache hung below his nose and the tiny pair of spectacles pinched atop its bridge. Approaching the beach in profile, the figure reminded Charlie of the silhouette in the Hotel's window. The man's belly shook as he shouted.

"Come out here, Gauss! This madness is all over!"

The crowd grew silent as they listened for any sign of life.

"Horseshit," the large man cursed. "I knew I saw that bastard headed this way. We might be too late."

Over the silence, Charlie heard someone sputter hoarsely. The voice rippled and swelled into a haunting cackle, then mocking laughter.

"Oh, is that you, dear Mr. Furgueson?"

Glass—or as he had been addressed, Gauss—limped up the hill.

"Glad to see that you finally took up my invitation, though I am not too sure I can accommodate the whole lot of your friends."

"My *friends* are here to haul you away! Albert Gauss, you are to be charged not only with the gross misappropriation of public funds as a part of your sewer construction sham, but arson as well for attempting to blow up the evidence of your fraud."

Charlie repeated the name in his head. Albert Gauss. Martin Glass.

"Ha!"

Martin wheezed as he laughed. He cleared his throat and spat on the ground a few inches from Furgueson's wingtip.

"I have to admit, I sold you short, Cornelius. The way I have watched you pick the pockets of every taxpayer in the county, I presumed you a fairly simple fellow to figure out. Maybe not the most ordinary of petty crooks, but crooked as the day is long. Now our self-appointed President of the Board of Improvements, Police Commissioner, Treasurer of the Inebriates' Home, and Chairman of the very same Sewers Project he slanders knows when the only correct time to let the buck pass elsewhere. No, no—you might be quite the sophisticated crook, indeed!"

Martin Glass began to laugh again. Cornelius quaked with rage. His right fist shook as it hardened into a ball. When it dug into Martin's jaw, the crack echoed across the waterfront. Martin would have landed flat on the ground had the pair of officers accompanying Furgueson not been ready to seize an arm apiece.

"The only thing of which I am guilty is giving a rat bastard lunatic like you a job," Cornelius growled as one chubby palm massaged the knuckles of the other. "Get him out of here!"

The two officers lifted Martin off his feet. Charlie felt a sympathetic twinge as he watched them toss him into the back of the paddy wagon with little extraneous effort.

"And telegraph the Daily Eagle," Furgueson continued. "Instruct them to let the people of Brooklyn know the scourge of public corruption has been ended once and for all!"

The horses pulled the black and white wagon into a tight U-turn and clopped away. Charlie watched the fire brigade continue to struggle against the uncontrolled flames still pouring out of the gas lamps. The fire by the entrance to the sewers had subsided. A fireman stumbled out and clapped the soot from his jacket.

"Hey boss," he yelled up to the top of the hill. "Tell the sheriff he can add graverobbing to the charges!"

The man cradled a round, pallid object in his arm. Charlie could not point to many encounters with bare human skulls over the course of his life. Normally he would not be able to differentiate one from another. He recognized this one from the moment it was held high. It was the same one he carried over several miles. When he closed his eyes, he could see it staring through the darkness at him. *Into* him.

Charlie did not open his eyes again until his back hit the ground. Every muscle and joint felt exhausted. Something wet and thick spilled onto his upper lip and rolled down to his mouth. He reached up to wipe it away and felt a heavy smear spread across the back of his right hand. He held the hand in front of him and examined the liquid. His left hand rose to join it, already caked in dried splotches of the same crud with a few fresh, shiny streams running down around his knuckles to the webs of his fingers. Now both hands were stained the same dark color. Not blood. There was no hint of color to the tacky substance. The fountain dribbling from his nose continued after Charlie wiped the first drop away. He felt the stream thicken, curling down the corner of his mouth and landing on his chest. The stream from his nose was joined by heavy, sticky tears weeping from the corners of his eyes. He blinked and the substance mixed with his tears, clouding his vision. He blinked again and when he opened his eyes saw only darkness.

A bright light passed over Charlie's eyes. Nerves begged his limbs to recoil. The muscles refused to obey. Once more, the beam pierced the dark, viscous tide—too bright for a world lit by gas lamps. He recognized the beam of modern incandescence that only came from the end of a handheld, battery-operated flashlight.

"Christ, call for a bus!"

The voice's accent was more familiar, too.

"We got two DOA's in here, Arnold!"

Rubber soles squeaked over a cluttered tile floor. A metal door creaked on its hinge. A bell jingled.

Charlie's heart fluttered. His chest heaved. Something sticky and dense caked the insides of his mouth and throat. The pressure from his contracted diaphragm forced the airways open. With a gasp, fresh air inflated every crease and fold in his withered lungs. Another electric surge crackled down from his brain. His muscles listened this time and brought his hands up to his face. Charlie's eyes felt dry as the tops of his fists massaged his tear ducts into action. It took more coaxing than he anticipated, but he was finally able to pry his eyelids apart. They fluttered spastically and revealed a world nearly dark and blurry as the one his hands rubbed away. The slightest hint of red traced the edges of the delicatessen and its contents. His eyes would take whatever time they required to adjust, Charlie decided. He stretched instead, informed by his limbs that they required extra attention of their own. From fingers to spine and neck to elbows, every joint popped when flexed. The stiffness, he realized, might be due in some part to his poor choice of a place to pass out. Charlie's ass was numb from the hard tile floor. In fact, every muscle below his waist felt like it had fallen asleep. He winced when pins and needles jabbed at his wiggling toes. As a distraction from the discomfort, he turned his neck toward the store's lower shelves. Saint Michael and Pope John Paul II stared back knowingly from the row of devotional candles. Lungs flowing more normally, Charlie let out a sigh. He inspected his hands and found them free of any black splotches. His sleeves, saturation now absent, rolled loosely past dry forearms and over his elbow. Comfort disconcerted. The black spots were gone—as were any other traces of track marks or bruising from years of casual, recreational injection.

Loud static and radio chatter murmured through the shop's windows. The sight of the cops' outlines returned Franco to Charlie's attention. Heart racing, he decided he could no longer easily pass for a stiff easily as the shop's proprietor. Doing his best with a pair of unsteady legs, Charlie shot off the ground with minimal commotion. The boots were coming closer, joined by an additional pair. The bell over the door rang again.

"Yeah, I checked for pulses, smartass. I'm not an idiot—they're both stone-cold goners, man!"

The store glowed bright as ever when the cop's flashlight shined over the front counter.

"Fuck, Fred. You weren't kiddin'. Musta put four… maybe five rounds in 'em. Hours ago, too, looks like."

"The other one's by the freezer, check 'im out."

Charlie did not have time to spare Fred or Arnold checking out anything at all. He crouched low. With his head ducked below the tops of the aisles, he backed toward the red light of the emergency exit. He rounded the corner away from the freezer section just as Arnold swept a spotlight across the floor.

"Where'd you say he was?"

"Whaddya mean?"

A second flashlight bounced from the front of the store to join the search.

"Where…? *Fuck me*… ya gotta believe me, there was another one right there not two goddamned minutes ago."

Charlie froze. Ultimo's was no larger than any other corner store in Brooklyn, which left it with little concealment to evade two cops for very long. The emergency exit was only a few steps away. He prayed Franco was sloppy enough to keep it unlocked.

"Listen to me, man," one of the cops whispered urgently. "Keep your voice down. Call an 85, radio for backup. We got a dead body and a missing perp with a gun if you're right 'bout what you saw."

Holsters snapped open. The pair of flashlights branched apart and moved to opposite ends of the store. Despite any earlier stiffness, Charlie's legs moved more agilely than at any time in memory. A flashlight swept the corner. Charlie pulled himself between two spinning racks of sunglasses and bagged trail mix. The beam of light passed along the floor, then turned away. Charlie held his breath and prepared to step forward. Looking out, he realized his hiding spot sat perpendicular to a crossroads of two aisles. The other cop stepped into the clearing and turned. The beam of his flashlight fell onto the two racks. Charlie felt himself moving. Air rushed past his ears in a way that felt foreign. New. Nevertheless, the room remained silent. When Charlie stopped, he found himself looming over the back of the same cop. He watched over the man's shoulder as his flashlight probed the place Charlie had just stood. The motion, the route—neither made sense. Charlie had not begun his departure from the location he now viewed more than a split second earlier, yet now he stood on the opposite end of the store.

"Check behind the register, Freddy," the other officer whispered from the next aisle.

Charlie recognized the store's counter now lie just behind him. He held his breath once more. The cop he dodged once had already begun to swivel. Charlie glided in retrograde, staying to the officer's back. Not a single wrapped fruit pie or auto magazine ruffled as he flew through thin air. He moved silently, quickly, and for the second time in nearly as many heartbeats, he found himself without explanation for his continued evasion.

Charlie felt as though he was floating through the store, carried by some swift, immaterial breeze through Ultimo's unstirring air. No matter how far he needed to go or how quickly, he passed without resistance or ruckus through the darkness. The confusion, the rapid change in perspective—even in light of everything Charlie experienced before returning to the deli—overwhelmed him. The shifting orientation made his head spin. In a journey to every corner of the store in the span of no more than fifteen seconds he found himself back where he started, a few feet from the rack of sunglasses, against the wall with the rental tapes. Graceful as he might have been, when Charlie forced himself still once more, the rush made his head swoon. He slammed a hand onto the wall to stay upright. His fingers latched onto the edge of a shelf full of video cassettes. The force jumbled one of the black-boxed tapes loose and the plastic case rattled onto the ground.

"Fuck was that?"

Without thinking, Charlie was on the move again. The tape, which had come to rest by his feet, was now about ten feet away. One of the cops hustled over and searched, flashlight frantic and gun sweeping wildly through the air. Charlie held his breath, waited. He saw the glowing red exit sign. If he knew what he was doing, he only needed one more.

He leaned forward.

The sole of his sneaker landed with a slap on the tile floor.

"Oh, come on..."

Charlie grabbed his mouth to stifle the involuntary complaint. He blamed himself for not understanding his own luck as panic rose in his stomach. He looked up at the sunglass rack. A dozen black or mirrored plastic lenses filled with two dozen shocked eyes stared at Charlie. He saw the face of the officer he wished he could still run circles around. Pairs of wide, horrified eyes reflected back at him from every pair of discount spectacles.

Many centuries of wisdom have taught me that it does not hurt to have a few extra reflective surfaces available to discern mortal associates from infernal ones.

The cop's baffled, frozen expression stayed locked on Charlie as his conversation with Martin came back to him. Whatever he had managed to get away with earlier was gone now. For a second, Charlie stood frozen.

Hurry.

The thought wasn't his own, but it filled his mind.

The dark tide rises ever, and ever hungry.

The toes of Charlie's shoes dug into the ground. He charged forward, barreling into the man's chest.

"Oof!"

The officer wheezed and twisted, tumbling to the ground. Charlie leaned into a full sprint, feet carrying him to the back of the store in a more conventional method. Then, without warning, the sensation returned. Before the cop could get back to his feet, Charlie glided through the darkness once more.

"Mother *fucker*," the cop yelled.

"Freddy! You good?"

Charlie stopped. The red beacon of the store's back exit sign glowed overhead. Slowly and quietly, he pushed the door to the stock room open. It swung back from the frame, then shuddered to a stop as it caught on something. The two cops regrouped by the middle of the store.

"Yeah, yeah. Fucker was behind me, just… *starin'*. Knocked the wind right outta me!"

Charlie gazed longingly at the sliver of darkness teasing him from the other side of the doorway. His escape was so close. The door had swung backward no more than an inch before finding blockage. He slid his fingers into the narrow gap.

"Central! This is Six Four Adam, we need additional over to Bay Parkway and Eight Six Street!"

Charlie's hand slid past the door. Then his arm. In a moment, he was standing in the store's cramped stock room, staring back through the crevice at two police officers frantically repeating their search of Ultimo's aisles. The stack of boxes wedged against the back of the door never budged more than an inch.

A rusty creak echoed across the deli. A cold breeze blew across the officers from somewhere near the freezer section. Charlie swung open the door connecting the store's stock room to the back alley.

"What the hell was that?"

Their voices grew distant, then disappeared entirely. The door slammed shut behind Charlie as he entered the unilluminated alley.

Much like the long-gone world which introduced him to Albert Gauss, this one still appeared deprived of electric light. Shadows drifted over every surface, free to stretch across the world as they pleased until the sun broke the horizon. Charlie could not say how soon that might be. If the sun was nigh on the horizon, any warm tones it might add to the sky just before it broke remained obscured by some interference.

Though Charlie was half a mile inland, he could hear waves breaking much closer. The gentle rumble of each crash felt no more than a few feet away. Urgency of a strange and unknown nature flooded his mind. Charlie rode on the night sky, silent and breathless, driven by a new and innate weariness of permitting the tide to rise any nearer.

Twelve

"The screen's dark and the first thing y'see is the date and time: *In the Future, 1996*. Big, bold, white letters. Nearly blinds ya, the way it hits your eyes when it lights up the theater. And man, when you see it, the future looks like shit. The New Angeles police have totally lost control. Turns out, no matter how many times this guy is defeated—sequel after sequel—the evil doctor's got the whole city by the balls all over again. Nick Riddle, the detective, is back again. You'd think after four or five times he's put the jerk away, just to have 'im escape and come back worse than ever, the guy'd just give up an' retire already. You guys know what I mean. That's what it's all about, right? Give 'em yer best twenty years an' then collect your pension. Maybe get yourself a trailer downin Boca? Well, maybe not the two 'a youse—but *some'a* youse. No disrespect! You two seem alright but some'a your friends can be a real buncha assholes. Guys like Riddle, though? Nah. Couldn't even finish his vacation in peace in the second one. He'll be in these *Death Spiral* flicks 'til he's the only eighty-year-old cop in the department. Shit! He'll still be fightin' Doctor Mephistopheles when they're both wearin' Depends in some nursin' home. This one didn't even have the same guy playin' Riddle. No replacin' Russle McCormack if y'ask me. This new one, Brandon Pierce? Ain't even an American. You can hear it when he speaks—dude's some kinda *Canadian*. Plays one tough sonuvabitch in the movie, though. Gotta give 'im that. Gotta be tough to play Nick Riddle. Green beret. A vet. Like me. I mean, I was Corps, not Army. '67 an' '68. We were tough, too, I 'spose. Just like my man, Nick. But this *fucker* Doc M? He just don't know when to quit. Ain't too far in the future but the world's gas is runnin' out an' this bastard's perched up top 'a the world's last oil rig. Thinks he can hold the whole planet hostage if he can make himself king of this one last fountain of black gold. Yeah, yeah. I know. It's a stretch. We're talkin' 'bout a guy who weren't nothin' but a small-time creep in the first one. Blew up a whole city block tryina' raise his own Frankenstein monster. But, of course, before they could toss 'im in the can, his little minions appeared outta nowhere an' sprung 'im from the back 'a the paddy wagon. In the next one though—man, was he a real *ghoul*. Things'd barely cooled down from his last scheme an' now he's kidnappin' all these pretty little tourist girls who've come to Chicago. Gets himself a hotel, fills it full of trap doors and torture chambers. His real character starts to show—a pure, unrestrained, hate machine. But I gotta tell ya, this is when these flicks really started goin' off the rails a little. Bad guy slips away, but he's gotta keep one-uppin' himself, right? Otherwise, why come back at all? By the time they get to the third one—Mephistopheles's lurchin' 'round the backwoods somewhere up in the northwest. Washington state or whatever. You think he's up to his old tricks again. Kidnappin' more pretty girls to work in this cathouse on the Canadian border. Or killin' em for fun. But then it turns out he's plannin' to blow up this electric dam they're buildin' on the river outside town. Wants to plunge the whole valley into darkness before he drowns 'em all. But, y'know, ol' Nick wakes up an' thwarts evil plans at the last minute for breakfast. At least in the fourth one—or maybe it was *part five?*—later on in the series, the doctor gets this one poor bastard real good. Really fucks 'im over. Y'see, this guy's ridin' round California on this *cherry* hog, tryina' forget some 'a the shit he's seen—things he can't get outta his head for nothin'. It's all this stuff he saw in the jungle. It all followed 'im back. An' under all this pain, all this sufferin'—in spite of it, because of it, who knows— there's so much truth. Pure, uncut *knowing.* Everybody's got shit inside 'em they can't turn into words. They can't talk to all the eight billion other people who got the same problems. The same feelings. No, sir. Nick Riddle don't do that. Tough guys don't do that. Can't. Don't know how. But this guy, he just rides his motorcycle. He rides with these other guys sometimes, too. Lotsa vets. They make good drinkin' buddies. Sometimes they drink too much. They go wild. Stomp some folk. He might be a good guy, but a *nice* guy? Maybe not so much. All that doesn't mean he can't be the *right* guy. Some 'a the time, at least. It's been a while since he's been right at all. Along comes that five-time loser, Doctor M. He needs to find something. Always in this real *hurry,* like, too. Like time's runnin' out for 'im. An' all this stuff the good guy's got up in his head—the secrets the Doc needs—they're up there, too. *'Trust me,'* he tells 'im. *'I am a doctor!'* So he let's 'im play 'round in his head. Experimental shit. But he pushes too far an' it backfires. The Doc was right, though—there was a whole lotta truth up in our hero's head. And the truth was that the good doctor was no good at all. He tried to fight back, but it was too late. Mephistopheles had his number. Knew his brain too well. Had a damn clever card hidin' up his sleeve just in case anybody got wise. Puts a curse on 'im. Ghosts. Demons. Suddenly it's not just our hero up inside his own head no more. Every room he walks into starts to looks like Grand Central at rush hour. No… *worse*—like the crowd lurchin' off the Staten Island Ferry into Saint George at four in the A.M. on a Sunday mornin'. Loud. Strung out. Pushy. Now he can't even be *alone* with his shitty memories. He's got lotsa different hands, always tryin' to wrestle the steerin' wheel away from 'im. Finally, the doctor pulls the trigger. A trap door opens under the poor fool's feet. He lands in this dungeon. Every time the trap door opens, another victim of the doctor lands someone new right next to 'im. It kills 'im, watchin' this place fill up. Hobos, alcoholics. Burnouts an' misfits. Little old grandpas and grandmas, too. Nobody's safe. The doctor keeps 'em alive, just knocked out. Meanwhile, time is only ever marchin' on… y'know?"

The back tires of the Chevy shuddered over a pothole. Apollo's head hit the roof. His knees ached as they rubbed against the steel partition confining him to the rear seat of the patrol car. There was one small mercy, he realized—it was the first time he rode in the back of any police vehicle without handcuffs or pending charges. They rode in silence until the officer in the passenger seat leaned to his partner and whispered.

"Which of the *Death Spiral* movies is he talkin' about? Which one of 'em was set in Chicago? Or Washington?"

"Washington… *First Blood*, maybe?"

"You're thinkin'a Stallone, not McCormack."

"I'm not sure he knows the difference," the driver responded, indifferent to Apollo's presence.   "Russle McCormack ain't American either, anyway.   He's from Britain or England or somethin'."

"Man, keep it down! Don't tell *him* that. Guy's finally calmed down from when we picked him up at that movie theater. You wanna set off a dude his size again? Elysian's only a few blocks away, anyway."

"An' that's when the power went out," Apollo remembered. "I didn't get to see how it all ends. Fuckers wouldn't even give me back the four bucks I paid for the ticket."

The cop in the passenger seat sighed.

"It's alright, buddy. We're gonna get you back to the home in a minute. Once they figure out the situation with the power grid, you can see all the movies you want."

"Just steer clear of that particular theater," the cop's partner added. "Next time, they might wanna press charges."

"Don't worry 'bout it," Apollo said softly. "I've seen enough movies. I can play 'em out in my head. End of the day, there's no defeatin' someone like Doctor Mephistopheles. Not forever, I mean. He's always there. Waiting. He can't do nothin' but cause pain and chaos on account'a everything he's done, all the stuff he's shed along the way. The deals he's made. All guys like Detective Riddle can do is put 'im back to the hole for a little while. There's no end. Ain't never any end to nothin'. Y'just get to rest every once in a while."

"So, Mister…"

The cop in the passenger seat paused to flip through the paperwork on his lap. He hesitated.

"Katabasis," the driver said. "Katabasis, Kowaliga. Don't worry. This ain't gonna be the last you've seen of 'im."

Something fizzled near the back of Apollo's brain. Warm smoke filled his head.

"Right. Mr. Katabasis, how do you *think* the movie ends?"

"Frankie," the other cop hissed. "Don't get him worked up."

"Ah, c'mon. He's chill. And you know you wanna hear how far out this can get."

"Fine. But don't come cryin' to me when he freaks and kicks out the back window."

"I ain't gonna cause the two 'a youse no trouble…"

The sizzling sensation grew. It was not unpleasant, nor was it especially comfortable.

"And Apollo's fine. Can't say nobody every called me Mr. Katabasis before. An' I never meant to give nobody back there no trouble, anyhow. But, the way I saw the movie goin', the doctor keeps burnin' people. They're just—what did the rat bastard like to call it?—*'just a means to an end.'* Eventually the Doc finds the one he's lookin' for. A sad girl. She's hurt. Her heart's broke. Worst of all, the doctor remembers her dad. He'd almost gotten what he needed from inside her old man's head thirteen years earlier, 'til Pops used a bullet to keep the door to his mind shut for good. Thirteen years pass an' Mephistopheles sees her in the hospital. Destiny. Coincidence. Who would know, but him? *'Trust me.'* Hospital lets 'im drag her to his lair an' he dives in. Doesn't take no time at all to get what he wanted. Down the trap door she goes. Another victim. Another pair of glass eyes in the basement. Chalk another one for the bad guy. He's got his minions out in force. More than ever—runnin' an' gunnin'. That goddamned skull. It's all he thinks about. One of 'em finally nabs it, just as the sun's about to come up. He's walkin' right through the front door with it *right now*. I… can see it. Dear God, I tried. *Fuck me*—I really did. After all the shit an' all the pain. It can't be for nothin'—*it can't*. Why'd you make it all for *nothin'* ya rat bastard? Step in an' put an end to it already. No, *stop!* You don't understand… don't hand it over! *Don't let it get into his hands—"*

The smoke parted. A dry, warm wheeze blew over Apollo's lips. He heard the back end of a long breath whistle through his throat. The solitary sound danced through the center of his mind. No voices. No screaming. Alone with the sound of breath, a transmission shifting into park, and echoes of residual terror. Apollo blinked. He tried to summon the last image in memory. There were two faces. One, Martin Glass. A charred other rested within Glass's hands. Those eye sockets—desiccated, empty portals for a calling abyss. The image stretched inside the vacated, silent space inside Apollo's mind. When he opened his eyes again, the morning's first slender beam of light pierced the horizon to lay a strip of light over the Chevy's backseat.

"Holy shit, dude. I'm on the edge of my seat here. Don't stop now."

"No. No, no, no," his partner warned. "Listen to him, man. He's about to blow. We're here. We're *done*. Put us 84 and help me get him inside before he snaps. Missing returned. 91. Tour over."

Apollo cradled his head within his hands. His feet executed an automatic—if not always steady—shuffle down the stairs to the Elysian Field's basement cafeteria. For the first time, the oft-repeated routine felt alien. Lost in his disorientation, eyes hidden beneath massaging fists, Apollo's head smacked against the basement's lowered ceiling.

"Shit..."

His forehead ached, though not from the impact. The room reeked of stale tobacco and the awful stench made Apollo's mouth water. His hands flexed, then sought joints to crack. It was shortly before breakfast time and several of the facility's residents gathered in anticipation. He scanned the room hopeful to catch someone in the midst of a pre-meal burn. His heart sank when he was greeted by an unclouded horizon filled only with the odor of old ashes radiating invisibly out of unchanged trays. The two dozen souls who occupied the room sat idle, too far gone to entertain the mechanics of addiction. Many of them—older, frailer—shared this space with him for over a decade. A slender strip of daylight slipped through the basement windows to begin a sundial creep over the patchy, yellow-green-blue plaid carpeting. The same faces, every day. The same uniform, anti-skid, red tube socks. They reflected somehow differently in this fresh light. Apollo felt young. Young and cheated. He usually did when he sat with his neighbors, but the thought had never been allowed to dwell long as it did now, on its own without a band of angry phantoms to nip and claw at his ego. The chatter, the surreal visitors, and verbal diarrhea. Those were the symptoms that made him such an untimely inductee, drafted into the building's faction of post-traumatic tragedies. The widowed and the forgotten left him vastly outnumbered. Apollo had known many who passed with their names, while dimes and pennies and legacies went to be inherited by the crumbling foundation of the Elysian Fields Adult Rehabilitation Center. But if he waited—him and all his broken peers—time would close that gap.

Apollo never considered as much before. Untimeliness was fleeting. Untimeliness, he realized as he searched the faces around him, would find new representatives. He had not seen *her* face before. At least, not in this place. She was still young—too young and too premature for even Apollo's untimeliness. An orderly guided her to a table. The front tires of her wheelchair swiveled over the gap of the basement's elevator door. Apollo had already closed half the distance to her when he became aware of his own movement. His mind unwound, flooded with memories he did not remember having.

The light had hit another spring morning in a similar way, many years prior. The Volkswagen's engine shuddered. When the cherry singed the back of the filter, Apollo flicked the butt out of the window and cranked it closed. Until the sun reached a certain angle, it would stay chilly.

"Marybeth," the crossing guard called out. "Whadya got for lunch today, sweetheart?"

Dozens of feet marched along the crosswalk. Tiny sneakers and shorter strides struggled to keep up with those of their parents. The preschool's parking lot lie across the street from the building itself.

"Mama made me a fluffernutter!"

The little girl held up her tin lunch box to share the celebration. From its side the sun glinted off an illustration of Henry Winkler sitting side-saddle atop a motorcycle, giving everything he saw two thumbs of approval.

The school itself was set back from the road by a wide lawn. Apollo watched parents send their children off while a teacher waited to receive them by a set of metal double doors. Most of the kids screamed in optimistic anticipation of the day's waiting activities and disappeared within. One father offered consolations to his daughter, loudly distraught and clinging to his leg. Apollo adjusted the rag, making sure it concealed the camera's telephoto lens as he angled it over the top of the faded, yellow Beetle's door. The lens rested flush against the closed window. The shudder clicked.

"Da-addy…"

Apollo scowled. He could not stand to listen to the child's blubbering. He cursed his luck for having to tail a jerk with such an annoying brat. He thought about Glass's instructions and continued taking pictures.

"Alice, oh dear," the man chuckled nervously. "We do this every day. What's wrong, my silly girl?"

"Not silly!"

The girl stopped crying long enough to unleash a primal screech. At its peak, her howl stretched the entire length of the suburban street.

"Daddy, please! Please don't leave me!"

The child stayed firmly latched to her father's leg. He sighed, then loped forward, dragging his leg to the school's door.

"Mind if I come in for a bit? She'll settle down if I sit in the room with her for a minute or two."

The teacher guided them inside. Apollo waited patiently. The other parents made their return trip back to the parking lot as the lawn gradually depopulated. After far longer than a minute or two, the man reemerged. Apollo snapped a few more pictures, tracking the man's movements from the school back to his car. Careful not to raise the camera too high, he pivoted, taking his final shot. He always captured the license plate—his signature cherry-on-top.

From inside his car, the man stared back at the school. After a minute, his shoulders slumped. The car backed out of its parking spot. In his own car, Apollo broke down his camera and returned it to its case. He was fastidious with his equipment. Rifles, cameras. It might not have broken the self-destructive young man within him, but three years in the Marine Corps had not left Apollo with a molecule of sloppiness. Two clasps secured the case's lid. A manilla envelope sat next to it on the passenger seat. There was no return address and no postage, just the intended recipients name—Jerry Weber. Apollo held the roll of film he extracted from the camera in his right hand.

Doctor Glass had Apollo follow Jerry for weeks, taking pictures and noting the man's schedule. Glass explained to his loyal deputy that the land surveyor from Westchester County owed him money for some digging project. Jerry had been a patient, too. They crossed paths once, as Jerry left a dream therapy session at the Doctor's strip mall practice in Yonkers. Not long after, he abruptly cut communications with the Oneirological Process Mission altogether. It did not take long for Apollo to memorize the man's routine. The Webers kept a nice house. They seemed happy. Couple of kids. Apollo watched them at night. He knew when each member of the family went to bed. Precautions were taken along the way. Apollo varied up the car on a day-to-day basis. One day the Galaxy. Today the VW bug. Despite his care, it was becoming clear that his presence might not have passed completely unnoticed. Glass made the decision to send a powerful message. It would be a more merciful message than any which Apollo would have employed on his own—which meant any at all. Apollo did not give warnings. He did not have the patience for them.

Apollo stared. The basement stagnated. He gripped the back of a chair at the table Alice had been pushed to and pulled it back. His knees buckled when he tried to lower himself, and he collapsed into the seat.

"Apollo," the orderly warned. "You watch yourself 'round Miss Alice here."

Apollo tried to respond. Since his returned to the Fields not an hour before, he rediscovered a lot of things in his head that he had not realized were lost. His voice remained elusive, for once. What was more, his mind was clear now and it chose to torture him worse than any departed demon. He muttered, surprised at the sound, and forced his mouth to shape words.

"What, uhh. What happened to her—to Alice, ma'am?"

"It's so sad," the orderly sighed. "Streets are full 'a kids shootin' each other nowadays. This poor one here survived a bullet to the brain. They tried sendin' her to Doctor Glass's center on 86th Street, but she's barely come outta her coma. She'll be joinin' us now, so I need you to be on your best behavior with her."

Jerry Weber had seen something in his therapy with Martin Glass. He chose to end his life to protect the world from that vision. To protect his world. As Apollo pulled Jerry to those depths, he saw something, too. When Martin found out, Apollo quickly knew the same despair. But Jerry's daughter had no choice. Apollo watched her. Her eyes stayed pointed in only the direction her unflinching head could set them. If it was possible to be a victim of so many things and voices, all at the same time, this was the look it left when the pressure displaced every drop of life from the living.

"Ain't any bullet that did this to you."

Apollo closed his eyes. In the darkness, he left the basement.

"When he lifted you up from outta the darkness, you were burstin' an' cryin'. The whole building heard you come back alive. An' then he calmed you down, told you everything would be alright. Got someone to finally tell him where Aodhan Draynor was tucked away. But nobody's gonna fool Martin for a third time."

Chipped fingernails dug into Apollo's palms. His heart raced. He bit the inside of his cheek when his eyes began to sting. It was not enough to keep him together.

"What did he lock in there with you?"

Apollo's voice cracked. Strength was returning to his lungs and he could barely contain the volume. Alice remained motionless—slouched at the head of the table and regarding Apollo no differently than she regarded the rest of her new world. A pair of attendants distributed trays to the assembled diners. Alice had an intravenous drip doing its best to nourish her. Nevertheless, as they did for the rows upon rows of others, the orderlies unraveled place settings of her very own.

Departmental Commendation Granted to the Sixty Fourth Precinct; Friday, March 30, 1990:

The Police Commissioner

of the City of New York

is honored to present this

Special Commendation to

the Sixty Fourth Precinct,
the Special Emergency Task Force,
and Detective 1st Grade Samuel Vernon

for services set forth in the following citation:

Through the combined efforts of the Sixty Fourth Precinct and the Special Emergency Task Force led by Detective Samuel Vernon, the Police Department of the City of New York successfully brought closure to the families of five victims tragically slain on February 11th, 1990. Although unable to apprehend the perpetrator of the heinous attack before she caused her own demise, their professionalism, determination, and resourcefulness brought an end to a period of terror and darkness which beleaguered our community. Their success in this endeavor proved an invaluable contribution to the lives and safety of the citizens of the City of New York, in keeping with the highest and most noble traditions of our police service and deserves our most profound gratitude and respect.

Excerpt from the *New York Morning Tribune*, Lifestyles Section; Saturday, April 7, 1990:

Hallelujah, Cold and Broken

By MITCHELL SINCLAIR

BROOKLYN — You don't really care for music, do ya? As of this past Thursday, the final chord has been played for south Brooklyn's worst-kept secret. Hallelujah (stylized *HALLELUJAH!* because, of course they did), the *'hidden'* gem of the wasteland which lies beyond bridges and tunnels, met its end on April 5th at the hands of Judge Calvin Doxsey. Following countless injunctions, over one hundred unresolved civil citations, and untold scores of investigations by seemingly every city, state, and federal agency with jurisdiction over Kings County, the doors to the historic church-turned-nightclub stand bound behind chain and padlock.

It is more meaningful to measure the lifespan of Hallelujah in months as opposed to the three years since the club's initial conception in 1987. After purchasing the property, the club's operators spent most of the intervening years battling with the Landmarks Preservation Commission to implement their renovations to the abandoned Reformed Church of the New Netherlands in the New Utrecht section of Brooklyn. As a result, it did not take long for legal fees to surpass the project's already lush construction budget. When the physical and litigious work was resolved with barely a minute to spare for a Memorial

Day weekend opening in 1989, the self-proclaimed *'new holy land of House and Rave culture'* wasted no time to let its true colors show. By the Fourth of July, Hallelujah seemed almost proud of its reputation as a sanctuary for cheap, easy recreational narcotics for teenagers sufficiently motivated to cross borough lines. Club kids by the thousands seemed little-bothered by the repetitious rotation of mediocre DJs spinning second- and third-run tracks already faded from the memories of more cachet discotheques from Manhattan to Manchester. Nor did they appear deterred by the incompetent-to-nonexistent security. Over the following weeks and months, incidents of robberies and assaults within the club itself often went unreported by patrons too doped up on overpriced, excessively adulterated party candy to remember they had even been victimized. At the same time, rumors of unpaid vendors and financial struggles joined the choir—as well as near-weekly court filings to shift ever-greater portions of the enterprise's ownership to a growing roster of silent partners.

The impossible-to-overstate final nail was driven into Hallelujah's coffin on Saturday, March 10th. An early morning altercation in front of the establishment with security personnel drew local authorities into the fatal pursuit of the now-infamous Bethany Ward, which ended with her demise in a vehicular collision on Fourth Avenue in Sunset Park. According to detectives from the Sixty Fourth Precinct of the New York City Police Department, the wreck brought an end to Brooklyn's posthumously-coronated *'satanic murderess'* and the serial, ritualistic slayings which plagued the borough for much of the latter half of this past winter. Allegedly inspired by the Son of Sam's reign of terror thirteen years earlier, Ward's crime spree inspired dozens of copycat acts of devilish vandalism, including at the church of Saint Anthony the Great in nearby Bath Beach.

As the sun rose over a city paralyzed by a power outage, a result of the same horrific crash, investigators returned to the flashpoint of the entire calamity. They discovered the bodies of Hallelujah's founder and original owner, Mervin Zero, and club manager, Erasmus Klein, dead by apparent execution in the club's basement. Police were quick to dismiss any direct connection with Ms. Ward, whom they believe lurked around the club's entrance that night to scout for her next victims among the former chapel's congregating twenty-somethings. Instead, authorities tied the executions of Mr. Zero and Mr. Klein to an unrelated dispute between the club's management and clashing narcotics dealers who operated everywhere from the dance floor to the men's room. Investigators arrested and charged Eugene Crawford with two counts of murder as well as a litany of offenses related to the trafficking and distribution of narcotics, and weapons possession in one of the club's restrooms, where a Glock semi-automatic handgun was recovered matching the caliber of bullets and shell casings at the nearby scene of Mr. Zero's and Mr. Klein's deaths.

With Mr. Crawford in custody for his alleged role in these crimes and awaiting trial on Riker's Island, officials from the state's liquor authority moved to axe the business once and for all. Judge Doxsey of the Kings County Supreme Court ruled in favor the state's argument that Hallelujah presented an imminent and unique threat to public safety if it continued to operate. Representatives of the club's surviving operators are in the process of appealing the decision, though parallel filings in municipal courts seem to indicate they are more interested in pursuing liquidation. Meanwhile, the doors to Hallelujah remain padlocked less than one year after they first opened.

Funeral services have yet to be announced.

Entry posted to the Kingsboro Institute of Technology's Online Bulletin Board System; Wednesday, January 10, 1990:

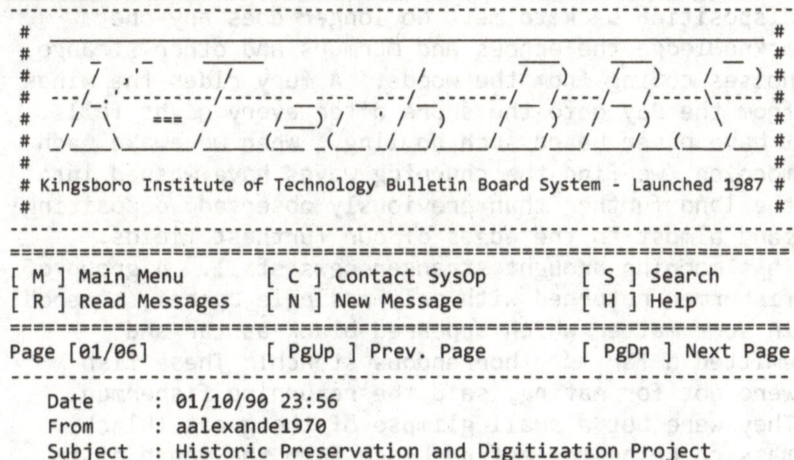

```
# ________________________________________________________________ #
# _  _   ___                       __   __   __   __              #
# / ,'  /  /                   /   / )  / )  / )  / )           #
---/_.'-----------/-------_----___---/_------/_ /----/_ /-----\-----#
# / \    ===  /     / _)/ ' / )    /  )  /  )   \         #
# _/___\______/____(___(___/__/____/___/___/___(___/__          #
#                                                                  #
# Kingsboro Institute of Technology Bulletin Board System - Launched 1987 #
#                                                                  #
-------------------------------------------------------------------

===================================================================
[ M ] Main Menu        [ C ] Contact SysOp      [ S ] Search
[ R ] Read Messages    [ N ] New Message        [ H ] Help
===================================================================
Page [01/06]           [ PgUp ] Prev. Page      [ PgDn ] Next Page
-------------------------------------------------------------------
     Date     : 01/10/90 23:56
     From     : aalexande1970
     Subject  : Historic Preservation and Digitization Project
-------------------------------------------------------------------
```

NOTE: Sorry for the delay in continuing this series.
The condition of the pages in Mr. Hutchin's diary are
growing a lot more worn as they go on, and include a
lot of non-ASCII-friendly symbols from some
engravings he observed which are a little difficult
to reproduce here. The man might have been suffering
from some degenerative mental problems, too. Indeed,
there isn't much historical information available
about his later life, except that he abruptly
resigned from his official post not long after these
entries and became involved in some risky expeditions
to map the continent's still vaguely understood
interior. It's frequently speculated that he met his
death sometime between 1649 and 1650, along with one
such expedition wherein all of its members failed to
return. -A.A.

   13th of January, 1647
This season is cruel to us. The needs of the
settlement are greater than usual, and the other
councilors and I are experiencing quite a lot of
difficultie. I find myself distracted, and the faces
===

```
===========================================================================
Page [02/06]              [ PgUp ] Prev. Page        [ PgDn ] Next Page
---------------------------------------------------------------------------
```

of the others in the commons reflect a similar
disposition back to me. No longer does any one
acknowledge the echoes and murmurs and other strange
noises coming from the woods. A fury rides the winds
from the Bay onto the shore after every night falls.
I have never heard such howling. When we awake each
morning, we find the churning waves have washed into
the land further than previously observed, depositing
sand almost to the edges of our furthest fields.
This morning brought stranger news still. A group of
fishermen returned with only a single bushel, steeped
in some matter which appeared black as tar and
emitted a far more horrendous stench! These fish
were not for eating, said the returning fishermen.
They were but a small glimpse of the great, black
mass covering the entire beach from the mouth of the
Narrows to Conyne Island. With much anguish, they
swore no wholesome fish will be produced until the
taint clears.

   January 16th, 1647
After a meeting which nearly escaped our notice, our
New England visitors requested an audience with Mrs.
Moody, the other councilors, and myself. It was at
this time that they chose to further divulge the
nature of their journey, though speculation around
towne had to this point left little to the
imagination. The party led by Mr. Sprague are witch
hunters commissioned by a convention of spiritual
leaders in and around the Massachusetts Bay. The
fugitives they are pursuing are accused to have
introduced blight to their lands and invoked curses
upon their people through the sacrifice of animal
stock, devilish incantations, and rhythmic ceremonial
rituals. I will confess, I have been the skeptical
sort since youthe, though this I have always kept
close and appeared at all church functions for the
sake of personal appearance and public calm. My head

```
===========================================================================
```

===
Page [03/06]   [PgUp] Prev. Page   [PgDn] Next Page
----

shook in judgment at what terror such hysterical
inquisitions visited upon the Continent. Today, I
find myself less ready to condemn.

   The people of our settlement are far less equivocal
than I, however. When the true nature of the men
from New England was revealed, the clamor to bolster
their numbers and initiate more aggressive
investigations were immediate. Mrs. Moody and I
agreed that we were powerless in the face of such
public desire. Thusly, Mr. Sprague, Parson Clemons,
and I made designs for the terms and scope of a
scouting party which is scheduled to depart tomorrow
morning for a tour to last until one hour before sun
set. I am reluctant to seek rest, dark as it is at
this moment and nearer the hour of our departure.
The wind out side echoes my restlessness. Verily, it
begs me listen. Persuasive currents, indeed.

   January 18th, 1647
Our return occurred much later than originally
designed. Terrible sights left behind and upon
return we were greeted by further catastrophe. A
second party sent out to provide our own salvation
has itself failed to reemerge. Our journey commenced
as was planned, if abruptly arranged it was. One
score and eight head crossed Hubbard's creek an hour
after sun rise and sought brief respite within the
fallow Seymour estate. We made use of those
abandoned cereals which yet displayed any evidence of
spoilage and rested. Before the grains had
compleately softened in the Seymours' rekindled
hearth, we became aware of a rising hum near the berm
bordering the edge of the north and westernmost
field. Though distant, the surrounding thicket
itself appeared to vibrate amidst the rumbling noise.
We forewent our porridge and picked up our camp and
initiated a careful pursuit. On the other side of
the wooded threshold, the disturbance began to fade.
We continued across the terrain for one half mile

===

more and the sound was gone. Mr. Clemons posited to
me, with more apprehension than I have ever observed
in the settlement's most senior vicar, that we may
have merely attuned ourselves to the disturbance, and
thereby find ourselves numbed beyond our ability to
train our senses upon it. His theory was proven
correct by that which we soon stumbled upon. When
viewed distantly, between the narrow and lean
woodland patches of this land's southern coast, it
appeared no stranger than any other encampment one
might encounter. Having seen it for himself and
without a moment's hesitation, Mr. Sprague called our
advance to a halt. He guided us forward in his own
steps and we began to understand what the man saw.
White, chalky piles surrounded the clearing. There
were hundreds and thousands of bones, stripped and
cleaned and bleached. I confess, I was without
explanation when one member of our party quite
correctly identified them as belonging to some animal
much larger than any steer or draft horse. I have
heard tales and read descriptions of mighty beasts of
burden from Africa and the far East, standing much
taller than a house. How they appeared on this
continent is also something about which I lack any
explanation. Yet they were there before us and we
were lost in that moment in manie ways.
The party became infected with a fervor then and it
was difficult to maintain cohesion. It was
impossible to stop the men from moving in some
direction, so it was understood that we should at
least move as one. It was by this time that the sun
climbed to its limited apex in the clear, winter sky
over our heads. Despite this, the forest cast
disturbing shadows all around us. We could not walk
for more than a few paces before one of the men
readied to unleash musket fire into the shifting
shadows. One man collapsed. He screamed that he had
seen a black goat fly through the dark, entangled

==
Page [05/06]   [PgUp] Prev. Page   [PgDn] Next Page
----

canopy over our heads, disappearing behind one tree
and then reappearing on the branches of another. We
told him we could not hear its bleating and I and
every other soul there thanked God when he believed
us.
The final clearing discovered us as much as our party
discovered it. Loosely charted as these acres were,
no such chasm existed on any of our maps. We felt
most unfortunate to find it. Even Mr. Sprague,
confident if cavalier thus far, seemed shaken when he
observed the expansive, unnatural quarry. I have
never seen such fine masonry, nor have I ever been
inspired to such awe by moved earth. When I was a
child, I walked every day in the shadow cast by the
spire of Saint Paul's. I have not seen stone
chiseled into such a shape since crossing the ocean
nearly ten years ago. Men could build two or three
more of those cathedrals to Saint Paul in the space
present in the cavity of that vast clearing, and
their collected spires would have barely come level
with our feet. I felt my stomach churn and my
balance flip. My eyes plummeted into the dark
expanse as I stood before it. At first, it appeared
to be a massive, black lake. The sun shined down but
none of its light reflected back at us. Only the
lines and carvings gave any indication of depth or
scale. Great pillars rose from what we could only
assume was some distant floor, a sick mockery of the
natural forest around its perimeter. There was a
pathway which lead down between the twisting,
crystalline towers. No one of us dared lead the
charge. The wind shifted and a familiar, horrible
odor entered my nose. As I recalled the fishermen
and their catch there arose a panic around me. I
knew for certain that I and the other men were being
watched by the depths of this unnatural, inverted
world. When I tore my eyes away, I saw the sun was
gone and it was the moon now staring down at our

==

Page [06/06]   [PgUp] Prev. Page   [PgDn] Next Page

heads.   At once, men were running in full retreat.
By some miracle, as manie of us departed made it
back to Gravesend. Those left waiting swore we were
gripped by madness. We explained that we lost track
of the time and therefore any explanation as to how
an entire day escaped us. They agreed that time had
indeed fled. When they told us that they had not
seen us in three days, it was their turn to be
thought mad. Alas, absent in their numbers was the
party sent out to look after us, still yet to return.
All we twenty and eight know is that we did not pass
them in our frenzied return. I am unable to conceal
my own fear and worry further that I am unable to
provide goode assistance to Mrs. Moody in my
diminished state. She and the other councilors seem
reluctant to discuss the matter any further. That is
the only blessing which I can count at this time.

PART III:
Hue & Cry

Fri. 04/13/1990, 0615 hrs.

Thirteen

"Anyway, I pick up the paper bag an' as I'm walkin' to the door this bitch has the nerve to squawk at me, *'uh, excuse me, sir. That'll be four-twenty-five.'* Four *fuckin'* dollars for roast beef wit' moozadell on a roll!"

Eddy's incredulity had only begun to peak as the souls within the walls of the Associazione Sant'Agata Fraternal Club benefitted from his reconstructed indignations. In her own place within the captive audience, Rita Maldonado stacked glass tumblers upon glass tumblers. She understood that she was not necessarily counted among the diatribe's target audience, but resigned herself to weather it, nonetheless. However many glasses of whiskey and grappa soaked from Eddy's stomach into his bloodstream, his night had yet to succumb to an excess of either. Where he persisted, his articulation grew rough—exhaustion beginning to succeed where alcohol poisoning appeared to fail for the umpteenth time.

"Yeah, fuckin', what are we… shellin' out M'hattan prices ovuh here, already?"

Francis, judging by the unsteady path his tongue traipsed around his words, fared worse.

"Shit, they jacked the normal price up to six for a whole hero now—but don't even get me started *'bout that.* This chick thinks she can knock off a buck or two for me and that I'm 'sposed to take that as a sign 'a respect? Nuh-uh. No, sir. So I goes, *'uh, yeah. Huh. 'Scuse you. You know who I am sweatheart?'* I mean, obviously she does or she woulda' charged me the full price t'begin with. But that ain't the fuckin' point, y'know?"

"The point—" Francis stopped short, swallowed hard. "Whas… uhh. Th'point?"

Rita watched the stubbly sack of dough quiver beneath Eddy's aggrieved chin. He was only a few years her senior, but appeared to be approaching the end of his twenties at double the speed. The brash, spoiled boy from the next block over was growing up fast. She remembered other girls around the neighborhood gossiping and ogling him. Now, in the dim, smoky light of the Associazione, his early onset gut ballooned against the bar. His hairline retreated toward the thinning spot on the back of his head. A few more years' worth of nights that ended after sunrise and Rita figured he would pass for one of those girls' uncles. They did not fawn as much anymore—at least not for free—and fragility and bruises were beginning to show on the overexposed ego just behind the multiplying lines climbing his forehead.

"The point… listen—this wasn't even three weeks ago, an' now who do you think I see tryina' get inside the Belladonna last Saturday night? I see that same homely mug over the shoulder 'a that new doorman, beggin'—just *beggin'*—to get through the front door."

Rita focused on the clinking glassware—on any noise other than that which spilled ceaselessly from Eddy's mouth into the indifferent haze lingering in the after-hours club. What men such as Eddy lacked in empathy and real confidence, they more than compensated for in limited imaginations and boundless degeneracy. She already knew where the story was heading. It was the usual palaver—impotence and inferiority redeemed by half-truths or outright fiction. Reliable or not, she did not need to relive it through Eddy's words. She succeeded in blocking out quite a few until the damp meat of Eddy's palm slapped down onto the bar top's laminated, wood surface. Her fingers scrambled to keep the load she ferried on her tray from jilting out of her arms.

"Y'told her to… to your—"

Rita rejoined the conversation in time to hear Francis nearly choke on the punchline she narrowly managed to drown out.

"I mean, c'mon! 'Course that's what I says to her," Eddy shouted with a deep, guttural laugh of his own. "This chick, she ain't exactly no looker, y'know what I mean? So, hey, she wants to get inside, that's what I'm gonna need for her to do. An' I tell ya, this bitch's face went *white*. Shit, I almost felt bad. Looked like she was 'bout to cry."

"So did—*whoo*. Did… she?"

Eddy's face went sour as Francis tried to reign in his own laughter.

"What… well, no."

Rita's feet skidded to a stop. Her mind flared with rage. She regretted it immediately, wishing instead that she had allowed momentum to carry her into the kitchen. Unless she could figure out how to melt into the shadows, Eddy's glassy eyes would soon swing her way.

"But get this—who do I see, huddled up among the rest 'a this ugly bitch's friends?"

Too late.

"Our very own *lovely Rita!*"

Rita turned her head over her shoulder.

"You're right, Eddy," Rita strained over a clenched jaw. "But the way I remember it, she laughed in your face. She had this great comeback about being allergic to shrimp."

"Oh yeah?" Eddy's voice cracked as the injuries compounded. "How 'bout Angelo? You tell him all 'bout it? Or maybe you never got the chance to let him know where you was. Y'think he'd find it funny, too?"

A steamy hiss sliced through the room. Rita and Eddy's heads turned toward the espresso machine at the other end of the bar. Francis's head completed its downward drift at some point during Eddy's rambling. Greasy strands of his formerly slicked-back hair now draped over his face as it pressed flat into the bar top, stirred neither by Eddy's loudly shrinking stature, nor the brewing of Emanuele Gentile's morning doppio. A delicate thumb and index finger gripped the porcelain cup by its slender handle and turned the lip sideways as Mr. Gentile sipped. Without turning to make eye contact, their mutual employer sighed, then spoke.

"'Nuff 'a you two's bullshittin'. One 'a you got my papers?"

"Of course, boss."

Though rather distant from where he now stood in his middle-sixties, nearly two decades of Sicilian upbringing lingered in Emanuele's diction. Eddy spun atop his bar stool and almost spilt onto the floor at the sound of his master's voice. He caught himself and stumbled gracelessly to the end of the counter. He snatched a folded newspaper from the top of a stack that rested on one of the bar's tables and offered it to Mr. Gentile.

"See here, boss? Got you a whole stack right off the back 'a this morning's truck!"

Mr. Gentile pulled the cup of coffee away to reveal a powerfully impassive face.

"The fuck am I 'sposed to do with more than one copy of the Post?"

For the first time that morning—possibly longer—Eddy was at a loss for words. Rita exhaled in relief. Mr. Gentile looked back and forth between them both. Whatever the wheels in Eddy's head struggled to press out, the old man was not awaiting any such reply. Instead, he tucked the newspaper under his arm and plucked his hat off the rack mounted by the bar's entrance.

"When I come back in," he began, then traced a finger across the room. "*Clean.*"

Mr. Gentile covered his freshly shaven head and stepped outside. The bar's singular, wide front window offered a panoramic view of Eighteenth Avenue. Rita watched as the old man took a seat at the picnic table pressed flush against the building's façade on the sidewalk and fluffed open his morning newspaper. He had remembered his hat, but left his wool coat hanging on the rack despite the unseasonable chill which winter refused to cede to the allegedly-nascent spring. At the window's edge, a phone booth also rested against the outside of the bar. Its door was still compacted behind blackened layers of frozen snow. Despite the sun's best efforts, ice clogged the gutters and gaps, too stubborn to fade into memory.

For once, none resorted to the weather's peculiar habits to sustain conversation. Winter's official end had passed weeks earlier, but a turbulent few weeks they had been. Rita was too far from Mr. Gentile to catch the headline of his newspaper, but she did not need more than one try to guess the lede. Not long after the lights came back on in Brooklyn, on the anniversary of the day the Triangle Shirtwaist factory burned down, the Bronx was humbled by a new and terrible blaze. Triangle took one hundred forty-six among the hundreds more who showed up to close out the sixth day of their work week. Seventy-nine years to the day later, a jilted maniac showed up at Happy Land to share his revenge fantasy. His ex-lover got out of the nightclub before the blaze overwhelmed the building. Eighty-seven others did not. The city still mourned those strangers who came together to dance away the end of their own week. The papers had yet to pass up any opportunity to commemorate the new record in bold lettering. Rita remembered a time, not too distant, when a fire in the Bronx had not been found as newsworthy. Entire city blocks were reduced to rubble and ash— in Brooklyn, too—when she was still in elementary school. Scenes out of Happy Land continued to fill the city's front pages. The images made those bygone, dark days feel less distant and the present less proven.

Eddy swayed back to the seat next to his snoring chum. He collapsed down on the stool and began to fidget with one among a matching set of pinky rings. Golden light shined over its polished band, while a row of diamonds sparkled back and forth. Despite the disproportionate chubbiness of the flesh swollen around his digits, the rings on either pinky finger seemed to fit poorly, loose enough to fall off. The rest of his body might have been falling apart, but his fingernails were better manicured than her own. Rita imagined that Eddy spent more on pinky rings and manicures than she still owed for her community college tuition. It was inconceivable to her how Mr. Gentile kept such a goon for a… goon. Agatha of Sicily's name might grace the sign nailed over the establishment's front door, but she knew Mr. Gentile was no saint. If Bensonhurst wanted for anything, it was not for saints. Feds loomed plentiful, though. K-cars idled at two or three corners over a thirty square block area at any given moment. They threw their weight around but never collared anybody on charges—none that stuck, anyway. Witnesses encountered conflicts. As it always turned, little could be proven in court, really. At the same time, everybody knew what happened in the back rooms of the delis and off-track betting parlors which lined Eighteenth Avenue. And everybody knew what it meant to have a seat reserved on a lawn chair or picnic bench in front of one of the *social clubs*. Mr. Gentile had heard the way Eddy spoke to her. If Eddy had shown disrespect to a *friend* of Mr. Gentile's in a similar way, there would be hell to pay. But for a woman—at least a woman yet claimed as wife or mistress or whatever fell into a shorter term than that—she received little protection. Eddy was an idiot, but he was just bright enough to keep his head. Big as his talk may have been, he watched his hands. Mere *verbal* assault, on the other hand, remained fair game. Rita was surprised Mr. Gentile interrupted their simmering argument at all. She wondered if it had been a knowing attempt to shield her. It was also possible that the old man just wanted his morning paper.

The jukebox in the corner cycled to its next song and suddenly only Frankie Valli had anything to say. Rita's mind was left to dirty dishes and The Four Seasons. She thought about Angelo. Eddy may have been a blowhard, but Rita found his threat difficult to shrug off. To say that her fiancé's baseline moodiness would not have been improved by the knowledge she and her girlfriends went out to dance clubs on Saturday nights was an understatement. He knew what happened when a group of girlfriends went to the club. Heck, that was where Angelo picked her up the previous summer— outside the bathroom of Hallelujah, queueing to score ecstasy. He did not treat her to many nights out after she accepted his ring. If Angelo found out she was hitting the town without him, he would flip. Not out of jealousy—that kind of insecurity was not the issue. Rita still thought Angelo was one of the nicest guys she ever met. But he was always on her about money. Without any revenue stream of his own or promising prospects on the horizon, he survived on a portion of the meager amount Rita took home cleaning up for the local wiseguys and wannabes who arrived at Mr. Gentile's doorstep after more reputable establishments announced last call. And Rita's weekend outings were not the only matters about which Angelo had been kept in the dark. She snatched the acceptance letter from the mailbox the previous afternoon and smuggled it out of the apartment in her purse. There it remained, hidden in the Associazione's kitchen. A full ride was not on the table, but it qualified Rita for more manageable student loans than those funds Emanuele Gentile provided for her associate's degree. Each Friday, the old man always made sure to subtract his cut before she could get her wages out the door. With the rates Mr. Gentile charged, her repayments appeared unlikely to make a dent in the principal anytime soon. Stacks of soiled glassware towered toward the ceiling atop the flimsy plastic tray. They had already begun to wobble before Rita reached the door to the kitchen.

A few cars and a garbage collector rumbled down the road outside. Rita looked through the window. The world was getting brighter, but it would take a few minutes more before Mr. the sun rise over the two- and three-story buildings. A thin trail of steam still rose from Mr. Gentile's tiny cup. He let the newspaper lie flat against the top of the picnic table and lifted his head up. No one could pass down the sidewalk without getting his attention. No one would enter the front door unless he gave his blessing. They would be lucky to cross back over the threshold without the same permission. The bar, dank and dim, suspended in stogie smoke that refused to clear, was becoming more of a home to Rita than the one she shared with Angelo. The door to the outside world was thick, windowless. A narrow glow crept in from the bottom. When it opened and closed, the pressure shifted and a wave rippled through the smoky haze. But it never vanished completely. When Rita stepped outside for a handful of hours before her next shift, no matter where she went in the neighborhood, she still felt those eyes. The letter was not far from her. She wondered if North Carolina would be far enough from Emanuele Gentile.

Steadier traffic gradually built along Eighteenth Avenue to herald the start of the day's business. A gray sedan backed into an open parking spot on the shoulder of the avenue not far from where Mr. Gentile sat. Rita saw two men in the front seats. The driver was a young man whom she did not recognize. Next to him was a face she had seen before. Too odd to forget, and dissimilar to Mr. Gentile's kind of social callers. But even if she had not seen the man inside the social club before, how could she not recognize the most famous—most ubiquitous—face to recently grace the bar's late-night television view? From midnight to six o'clock, Doctor Martin Glass graced no fewer than four ad breaks per hour. If the station lacked for other commercials, they ran the *Chthonics* advert back-to-back.

The car's headlights died, and the pair executed a synchronized exit. Mr. Gentile's attention narrowed. He folded his hands atop the folded newspaper. The last trail of steam from his coffee trickled up to the sky and disappeared on a gentle breeze.

The younger man accompanying Doctor Glass never made it to the sidewalk. He leaned back and planted himself against the hood of the car. Over crossed arms, he watched his passenger glide toward the picnic table. Doctor Glass was not an unusually tall man, but his narrow build accentuated his stature. Emanuele's eyes rose to meet the man looming over the other side of the table. Both wore matching, not-unpleasant expressions on their faces and waited for the other to make the first move. Neither seemed eager to break the tension. It was only a matter of time, Rita figured. The club would soon have new guests to be entertained. Any menial chore was preferable to being stuck waiting on Martin Glass and whatever goons followed in his shadow. Just as her feet pivoted toward the tray of soiled plates and glasses, she saw a surprisingly animated sigh escape from a thin smile on Martin's mouth. While his voice was muffled by the window, there was a condescending tone in his eyes. Rita watched him extend two open hands in greeting. Those eyes, she thought. Those hands. She wondered where he hid his knife.

Rita did not linger to find out. Mr. Gentile paid minimal return on his visitor's words. Nonetheless, the old man rose from his seat to go through the usual steps of such proceedings. Before they could reach the Associazione's imposing entrance, Rita shouldered the teetering tray past the pair of swinging doors and into the safety of the kitchen. The platter landed on the kitchen's brushed metal countertop with a much louder smack than she intended. She heard the heavy wooden door in the main room creak open. Through the narrow, pane-less service window that separated the kitchen from the bar, a brief glow made evident those morning rays stretching over the entryway's threshold. They did little to diminish the far more dominant gloom that filled the front room. After a moment, the light dwindled again as the door sealed firmly within its frame.

"Jesus," Eddy's struggling voice emerged from where he still leaned on the bar. "S'too early for the circus to be in town."

Eddy's remark, designed for his now thoroughly unconscious companion a foot away, had been spoken with sufficient volume to be picked up by Rita's ears a room away. From the man who now stood directly behind him, the comment received no acknowledgement.

"Make yourself comfortable," Mr. Gentile rasped.

Rita leaned against the kitchen counter and avoided making any noise which would prevent her eavesdropping.

"And you friend, he gonna stay outside?"

"Dexter? Do not worry yourself. The man has a lot on his mind at the moment. I assure you, this will not occupy too much of your time."

"Suit youself. But I thought we two understood. Here you are, anyway."

Rita realized what kind of conversation they were going to have. Neither Mr. Gentile nor Martin were going to be particularly direct. The only obvious takeaway was the evident lack of trust between them.

She yawned. It had been a long shift. Rita looked at the dishes and glassware and reluctantly accepted that they were not about to sprout limbs and wash themselves. Her arm reached out to twist the nob next to the deep sink's faucet. Her purse sat on the counter a few feet away. As she stared, her hand hung in the air. Rita tried to estimate how many more sleepless nights she had in her—how many mornings spent cleaning up after the men at work just to go home and perform the same chores until the routine reset. If she summoned her X-ray vision, she could see the acceptance letter sitting within the leather purse. The sink seemed less important in that moment.

"I *am* happy, Emanuele. My man recovered exactly what we needed. I am sorry to say, I have heard you do not share my satisfaction."

Bits of the conversation continued to wriggle their way into the back room.

"Satisfaction? *Your man?*"

Mr. Gentile's rising annoyance was similarly uncharacteristic.

"*That boy* made a spectacle. A liability. And what about you *girl*, huh? A month goes by and still police keep their locks on the front doors. Bullet holes take a long time to patch in the nightclub business. Car chases and blackouts, much longer."

"Cheer up, Emanuele."

Rita bristled as Martin spoke. When Mr. Gentile was in a foul mood, repeatedly addressing him by his first name did not tend to spark improvement.

"You are now the sole proprietor of the most popular dance hall on this side of the East River."

The conversation was becoming more direct as well. Both men were close to abandoning innuendo entirely. Still, Rita's attention lie elsewhere. She walked over to her purse and unzipped the top. Trifolded and crisp, she reached in and flattened the letter out:

"*After reviewing your application, it is with great pleasure that we extend to you an offer of admission into our undergraduate program.*"

The language felt foreign. The life it promised, completely alien. Not least of which was. a degree she could put toward a better life and legitimate student loans to pursue it. When she had been handed her associate's, Rita felt the shackles of her debt to Mr. Gentile chafing at her ankle. But a real education, from a real university? Sallie Mae might eventually resort to debt collectors. Rita doubted they regularly severed debtors' fingers.

There was a wide world outside the little Associazione—beyond Eighteenth Avenue and Mr. Gentile's feudal hold. Rita dared to dream and now she had to make a decision. She would have to disappear. The thought of abandoning Angelo made her heart ache. The risk of defaulting to Emanuele Gentile summoned more painful anxieties.

Rita loved Angelo. He was a dreamer. In the face of complete opposition, in open and direct contradiction with the limits of reality, he always had another idea. Another scheme on the horizon. Another scam. And she was certain of his love. Without her support, he would spiral. Angelo was pathetic—*helpless*. Rita's hand slid down the front of her dress, down to her stomach. There had been false alarms before. Angelo always talked about having a son. Angelo, Junior. Rita could never get him to budge on the name. She would roll her eyes. Angelo was already the fourth of his name, all the way to his great-grandfather. She could never stop him talking about *junior*, though. He would remind her it was only a matter of time. She always caved and gave Angelo what he wanted. Rita turned to prop herself against the counter. Angelo nagged her about money as much as he spoke about the future. That which remained after Mr. Gentile garnished her wages could not keep up with the needs of two fully-grown adults. Another mouth would strain them further.

On the other end of the kitchen stood a heavier door than the one which secured the club's entrance. Opposite its sturdy, wrought iron hinges, four separate deadbolts ran down the door to its metal handle. Mr. Gentile had been in operation for decades, lining the shelves behind that door with an accumulation of riches Rita struggled to comprehend and happily kept blind. Angelo, on the other hand, broached the topic of the safe's contents on more than a few occasions. He asked Rita a lot of questions about it. Dimensions, manufacturers' names, model numbers. The presence of Mr. Gentile's assets were a poorly kept secret. He never seemed worried. The imposing door was for show, more of a status symbol than a physical necessity. He knew that only a complete idiot would try to rob him. But Angelo dreamed—out loud. And Rita knew him well. His unemployment was only partially attributable to a lack of drive. He had a good heart, but Rita would not have trusted him to do his own taxes if he ever managed to draw a consistent income.

It was only a matter of time. Angelo always got what he wanted. He might get a bullet to the back of his head for it, too. Rita's fingers spread out over her stomach. Maybe several bullets. Mr. Gentile was not known for kindness. Generosity, in his own way. Protection, of course. Reliability, undeniable. Rita knew she could rely on his ruthlessness.

A thud rattled across the floorboards from the front of the club. Rita reasoned that Gentile must have ordered Eddy to carry the incapacitated sack of dead weight seated next to him back home. It sounded more like Francis's body had instead sprawled flat onto the ground.

Rita had to bite her lip to keep from screaming. Frustrated and trapped, a tide of rage rose within her mind. Miserable, hateful thoughts drowned out the unrelenting nuisances the club promised to parade around her for whatever days lie ahead of her. God damn useless, pig-faced Eddy and his jerk-off stories, she thought. God damn Angelo and his endless needs. And God damn Emanuele Gentile and all his blood money and all the lifelessness and inhumanity it never seemed to clear from his face. Rita continued to curse in her mind until the anger ebbed. She forced it out of her head and down to the tips of the fingers she dug into the cold, metal edges of the countertop.

Before she let go, she cursed herself. She knew what she had to do. She was no out-of-towner, desperate and stupid to the way the neighborhood worked. She grew up knowing exactly who Emanuele Gentile and the hundred other petty tyrants like him were. He was the last resort, a big fish content to feed on the desperate ocean's floor. The villains of the world seldom stood around, waiting to get toppled at the last minute—reveling in their own hubris to give the hero just enough time to squeeze in a victory. In reality, all Rita saw were joyless old men, lounging on picnic benches outside hordes of plundered cash they would never spend or share. They could not be bothered to sit down with a morning paper unless they knew some poor bastard got ripped off over it.

Rita's eyes stung. Her hands tugged up the edges of the black trash bag and twisted them to form two ends. They knotted together and the fluorescent light that gleamed from the kitchen's ceiling began to fade from the surface of the garbage piled within. Through glassy eyes, she watched a tear fall and smear over the letter's black, congratulatory text. Her hands yanked hard. The knot tightened. She did not have to look at the letter anymore. It was getting late and Rita was short on time to dream.

A scream echoed throughout the bar and rattled the air around Rita. Fright lifted her feet off the ground. Her hands dropped the bag, which tipped and spilt garbage across the kitchen floor. Rita forced herself still, mind scanning, breath carefully metered. She remembered, back in the bad old days, when just such an operation could find itself the target of retribution. Grudges and vendettas still flared up every now and then. But she did not remember hearing any gunfire before or after the terrific cry. When feeling returned to her legs, Rita stooped and slid against the wall. Between the pounds of heartbeats filling her head, she struggled to listen for any other noise reaching through the window that separated the kitchen from the bar. With a sudden twitch, her lungs shuddered. Hungry for air, her mouth released an involuntary squeak. A moment late, Rita's head dove into her hands to stifle any further spontaneous utterances before she could reassert rhythm for her breaths. Her ears failed to detect any activity in the next room. The door was only a few feet away. Rita stayed low and crept. Her hand stretched out across the wall and inched closer to the door frame. Something heavy crashed into the wall not far from the other side of the door and crumpled to the ground. Rita reeled backward. Her hands clamped tight over her mouth to stop any new yelps. Whatever happened in the bar, the kitchen's swinging door lurched toward her. The narrow gap that opened faced away from where Rita crouched. She could see only the back of the door and the shadow of the sprawled mass that came to a violent rest on its other side. Her balance shifted forward as her palms flattened on the kitchen tiles. Alternating hands and knees, Rita pulled herself forward. Her neck craned to the side and angled for a view through the opening. Her hand landed in something wet. Fingers recoiled at the sticky warmth that clung as they jumped away from the ground. Rita's eyes shot down. She flipped her shaking hand. Breath whistled between her lips as she watched a red trail dribble down to her wrist.

Nostrils flared. Her throat convulsed. Fighting the smell of blood and urine, Rita pressed the back of her other wrist against her septum. Her vision drowned as anxious tears spilled over the edges of her eyelids. Rita held her breath. She clamped her eyes shut until the tears and shivers ceased. The sound of her heart pumping blood between her eardrums still diminished her senses. She forced her eyes back open. Her hand shuddered back down to the ground, then continued to pull her forward. The pooling blood parted and slid as the task demanded. Nearer still and the angle of her view shifted. The gap between the door and its frame widened. A sport coat's shoulder emerged, seen narrowly but unmistakably. Rita's eyes followed the slight outline down the jacket's sleeve to the cuff where she found pink skin and several meaty, limp fingers crooked against the ground. The dim light of the bar provided Rita with little to identify the incapacitated body resting against the door. On an especially sunny day, natural light struggled to breech the bar's broad, yet grimy front window. A solitary ray stretched out to Rita—extended a gilded flare onto the rim of a pinky ring. The facets of its inset stones projected some extravagant, colorful geometry as the bar's front door groaned open. When it closed, quickly and firmly, the gems on Eddy's ring danced no more.

"Shit. Guess I don't gotta ask how Gentile's little *sit down* went?"

"Delay not. Speak no more until you have secured the locks on that door behind you."

Rita identified the owner of the second voice immediately. Whatever happened, Doctor Glass survived. The goon who waited outside performed as he bid. Rita heard the front door's deadbolt click and engage. She might have been able to watch if she had not been too stunned to move, eyes fixed to Eddy where they would have been instantly repulsed in any previous moment.

"Our business is concluded with these… men," Glass continued softly, "but our work to undo the sins of your brother continues."

"But… but I got that skull for you. Gentile and his goombah crew ain't gonna give us any trouble no more. What's there left for us to do?"

Daggers stabbed at Rita's tearducts. Her mind raced. Eddy, Francis—Mr. Gentile, too. She entered the kitchen to clean up their mess and curse their names minutes earlier. That world was reduced to a glimmer in the rear view, seeming years apart from the fresh terror of the present.

"For a start, you have much, *much* more to do. You have served me well. Well enough that I extended my trust to your brother. This, as we have witnessed, proved a costly. For myself… and Bethany as well."

"I'm sorry. She sped off so fast. Too fast to catch up. Too fast to…"

"You miss her. I miss her as well. She was devoted and reliable. She understood the risks and sacrificed herself to serve the Mission and our Lord in waiting. Now we are left to continue without her."

"It's not fair."

"No. The universe never pretends to be. For our current troubles—the inconveniences, the pain that you feel in your heart—we cannot blame anyone other than your brother."

"Charlie… I was so blind. He was goin' into withdrawals right outside the club, like he never quit. The signs were there and I couldn't see it… didn't *want* to see it…"

"It was he who stuck the needle into his own arm. It was he who chose to conceal the truth. It was he who sealed Bethany's fate. For your part—for mine as well—we are guilty of a serious error in judgement."

Rita heard the younger man start to speak. All he could produce was a heavy sigh. Doctor Glass continued.

"I will make amends on my own. For your part, after you are done, you will find your wayward brother."

"Doctor, I've tried. Me, my pops. It's been a few weeks an' nobody's seen 'im. We're startin' to think he might've... you know—"

"He has not. Despite his clearly demonstrated desire to self-immolate, his presence still haunts these streets. You will deliver him to me, and then he will be purged by your hand."

Both parties left the words to waft through the air, waiting to see where their horrible stench settled. The sound of footsteps came first. Rita began to rediscover her own motor functions and her eyes bid final farewell to the former customer slumped on the ground. She watched as Glass approached the younger man, then lifted a hand to his shoulder.

"Bethany gave herself to the abyss. She joins our lords in darkness in honored, eternal service. Inaction would only make mockery of her sacrifice and convey irredeemable insult to those she now serves in eternity. You will prove your love to her. You *must* prove your devotion to the universe and its masters, to the Mission for which we have all bled. You will present Charles Valerie to me."

The younger man's head drooped, then shuddered back up into a feeble nod. His eyes never returned to Doctor Glass.

"I have exhausted myself here," Glass continued. "You must return me to the Mission. There is much work to be done before Sunday."

"You want I should clean this up?"

"No. We have not the time, nor the need for such an effort. Empty the register, then tear apart the back. Appearances are important. This was a robbery, after all. You do not need to get into the old greaseball's safe, just make it look like a noble effort."

A bolt of shock pierced Rita's body. She screamed at her limbs and swore at her mind for staying frozen, eavesdropping on two maniacs instead of evading the death toll. The sound of footsteps bounced from the bar's parquet floor. Doctor Glass faded as he neared the front door, then disappeared among the swelling commotion of traffic outside. After the front door closed, Rita heard a tumbler clatter down onto the bar in the next room. A moment later, a bottle was set down next to it. Rita kept time with the noise to pick herself up off the floor. Whatever small fraction of her mind left unoccupied by flight had no memory of leaving any clean glasses behind when she retreated to the kitchen. It did not stop Glass's associate enjoying a long drink. Not yet entirely upright, Rita's toe caught beneath the hefty bag of garbage still lying on its side on the kitchen floor. She tumbled down next to the black, plastic mass and watched its contents spill further. The glass tumbler clacked down onto the bar top in sudden abandon.

"*...it is with great pleasure that we extend to you an offer...*"

The letter was inches away from her nose. Shoes pounded just outside the kitchen's entrance. Rita's fingers latched onto the letter and clutched it for dear life as she jumped back to her feet. The kitchen was not big. It had its own door exiting into the alley behind the bar. Rita had no time to consider that the room was dimmer than usual. Muscle memory informed her precisely where the door stood, obscure as it was in the shadows beyond the reach of the kitchen's lighting. Tears streamed down the sides of her face as she sprinted.

Tears of terror. Tears of hope.

Rita locked eyes with the shadows and the unkempt, greasy, blond hair and rictus lips emerging from nothingness. She tried to stop. The closer momentum carried her, the further she felt herself plummet. Those two pupils became a pair of bleak, abyssal tunnels. Webbed in a sickening mesh of brown capillaries, the yellowed whites of its eyes encircled the black holes completely. Rita's legs crumpled. She skidded onto her knees. Wind exploded from her lungs as a freight train collided with her back. Her throat convulsed to make way for a scream but found no air to make good on the impulse. Before Rita could find her breath, a hand slammed over her mouth. Another wrapped around her waist and lifted her off the ground. Whiskey fumes wafted from the mouth that appeared next to her.

"Almost gave me another fuck up to explain, didn'ya?"

The man's tone was soft, though his words sounded like he had to force them over a clenched jaw. Rita's eyes fluttered as her shoulders twisted and jostled in search of a weakness in the man's grasp. Abruptly as the ghoul materialized before Rita, it sank back into the darkness. If Doctor Glass's lacky had seen the same face in the shadows, it did nothing to loosen his grip. The tighter his hand sealed over Rita's mouth and nostrils, the more the rest of the world's definition faded along with the man in the shadows.

"There, there, miss. You might'a just helped me turn this problem into a blessing."

Rita's heart raced. While her right arm was pinned behind her back, her free hand clawed to remove the palm covering her mouth. The man's voice drifted further. His apologies, genuine or mollifying, became distorted, metallic reverberations.

"Real sorry… but you gotta believe me…"

Rita's eyes rolled on their own into unknown, dark recesses. Something crashed against the back of her head. She lost her grip and her hand tumbled limply to her side. There was a sensation of falling and words that were almost too strange to comprehend—the vocal cords forming them strained and inhuman.

"I ain't… ain't no monster."

Fourteen

"A reading from the book of the Prophet Isaiah."

Father Norman's voice filled the cavernous marble chamber of the church of Saint Anthony the Great without the assistance of electronic amplification.

"Behold, my servant shall prosper," the priest continued. *"He shall be raised high and greatly exalted."*

A prayer book rested in the rack attached to the back of the next pew. Lucy dragged her thumb over the top. She watched the book's pages, thin as onion skin, ripple between its faux-leather covers as her digit passed back and forth. Despite thirteen years spent in Catholic girls' schools, she maintained a steep drop-off in attendance ever since. At some point, she had arrived at the conclusion that church demanded too much far too early in the day. She considered herself a seasonal Catholic. Midnight mass on Christmas Eve. Weddings and funerals, more out of obligation to the betrothed or departed. This was the first Good Friday to pull her into a church in nearly a decade. To top it off, it was the first mass of the day. The morning sun's reverent cheerfulness mocked her spiritual inertia. Scattered wavelengths exploded through panes of stained glass and painted the stone walls playful shades of red, green, and blue. Lucy responded with a yawn. An internal clock recalibrated by many months spent living between the sun's set and rise did little to stir her already fatigued spirituality.

Father Norman and the altar surrounding him appeared in much better states than the last time Lucy enjoyed the presence of either. She had not set foot in this place—nor anywhere else within the confines of the Sixty Fourth Precinct—since the night her suspension commenced. In suspense she remained. Her only plan this morning, as was the case on most mornings, had been to sleep through it entirely and not leave bed before noon. The same plan had not sat as well with Lucy's aunt, now seated beside her.

"Even as many were amazed at him—so marred were his features beyond that of mortals, his appearance beyond that of human beings. So shall he startle many nations..."

"Hey! Cuz..."

The whisper from Lucy's cousin tiptoed gracelessly under Father Norman's reading.

"You musta' seen some sick shit bein' a cop, right?"

Philip, seated on her other side, sounded equally disinterested in the proceedings. Unlike Lucy, he still possessed enough energy to revisit her brief career. She clenched her teeth. The throbbing returned to her hand. Fingers uncurled and Lucy's palm turned up to look at her. The red line across her right index finger had faded as weeks passed, but its ghost brought her mind's eye back to Charlie Valerie. The scene replayed for another among countless encores. Charlie's fist slipped out of his pocket. It had not been a weapon in his hand that almost caused her to pull the trigger flush with her gun's grip. The phantom mark stung. Lucy's mind drifted back to the altar, searching for the crucifix. A new head had been attached to the figure nailed onto the cross. It lacked the horns and disfigurations impressed upon its predecessor.

"He was despised and rejected by others—a man of suffering and acquainted with infirmity—and as one from whom others hide their faces, he was despised, and we held him of no account. Surely, he has borne our infirmities and carried our diseases, yet we accounted him stricken, struck down by God, and afflicted."

Lucy had seen an overabundance of *'sick shit.'* Her toes dangled over the point of no return for making *'sick shit'* happen. And now, for all her sins, she waited in a personal purgatory prepared for her by Lieutenant Cordell.

"Sure," she replied, pulling herself up from the depths.

Lucy hated coming up with tall tales about *the job*. As it slipped beyond her control, she welcomed the distraction from darker preoccupations.

"Alright," Phillip replied eagerly. "So, what's the craziest shit you ever seen?"

Lucy felt her aunt bristle at the incessant curses her son uttered in the presence of more divine language. For her own part, Lucy tensed as she was asked to relive and regurgitate the more disturbing parts of her memory for the entertainment of a bored relative.

"Where to begin…"

It was always difficult to weave together a story of satisfying intrigue, spared the absurdly perverse terror of oversharing. Lucy turned enough to appraise her aunt's body language, gauging how much more of the woman's attention she risked pulling from Father Norman's readings.

"Alright," Lucy whispered as she leaned toward her cousin. "Y'wanna hear a ghost story?"

"Kings shall shut their mouths because of him—for that which had not been told them they shall see, and that which they had not heard they shall contemplate."

"What? I wanna' hear about gangsters and killers, not some kiddy bullshit."

An impatient sigh puffed from her aunt's nose.

"Phillip," she whispered. "I swear to God…"

"You said you wanted *'sick shit.'* Well, I've seen 'em. Every cop has," Lucy continued. "I chased after one once. Hell, I saw two of 'em on video, walking right into this church."

Lucy looked up at the altar. The tags, the messages—the paint had been power washed. A malignant, invisible stain lingered.

"C'mon, you know what I'm talkin' about. You ever shoot anybody?"

The truth intruded upon her mind every other second of the day and caught her off guard each time.

"No, but. Almost…"

"Phillip."

Lucy's aunt growled a very final-sounding warning. Confronted by a familiar line in the sand, Phillip leaned back in the pew. Lucy tried to enjoy being let off the hook, but the mental replay was primed and rolling forward on a full head of steam. She saw herself exiting the Lieutenant's patrol car and climbing the stairs back into the Sixty Fourth Precinct. His investigation—its foregone conclusion resulting in her predetermined suspension—stretched out and consumed the early morning hours. At last, when she was permitted to depart in shame, the sun was minutes away from sinking below Gravesend Bay.

"All we like sheep have gone astray. We have all turned to our own way and the Lord has laid on him the iniquity of us all."

In the days and weeks that followed, the news heaped insult upon injury. According to the Department—to Sam Vernon, the task force's lead investigator—every ritualistic killing and act of demonic vandalism that plagued southern Brooklyn had been the solitary work of the woman Lucy and Tabby chased to a premature demise. The campaign of terror masterminded by Bethany Ward, the lone killer, ended while fleeing police. Case closed. Just like that, Charlie Valerie escaped for a second time.

"Yet it was the will of the Lord to crush him with pain. When you make his life an offering for sin, he shall see his offspring and shall prolong his days. Through him the will of the Lord shall prosper. Out of his anguish he shall see light—he shall find satisfaction through his knowledge. The righteous one, my servant, shall make many righteous, and he shall bear their iniquities."

When the guilt of nearly executing him for what she mistook to be a gun would cyclically fade, other anxieties flooded the vacuum. The uncertainty of her future—spared no uncertain terms by the reports the lieutenant filed in the case against her—tugged at her heart. Banished before she could complete her probationary period as a police officer, the only prediction Lucy felt confident making was that Phillip would be left wanting for any new, exciting war stories on her part.

Lucy had come to accept the worst possible outcome, though this provided little immediate comfort. As one uncomfortable thought diminished, another filled its place. Something bigger than Lucy and her professional struggles hung over Brooklyn. Whatever the true scope and nature of the horrific circumstances she glimpsed, the hurried, official investigation left ignored—worse, little diminished. Lucy thought about the late Bethany Ward and the truth she took with her to the grave. She wondered about the cryptic messages erased from the church's walls and those which surrounded the bodies of the students massacred on 63rd Street. Lucy watched a pair of shadows pass by the church's security camera, their identities obscured in one among an consistent trend of timely blackouts. Later, another pair stalked outside Hallelujah. The official conclusion felt dangerously insufficient—it took far greater mental gymnastics to attribute the crimes which Ward was summarily tried and found posthumously guilty to any lone wolf. That there appeared, if all the incidents were related, to be at least three parties to the conspiracy and therefore no fewer than two outstanding made goosebumps ripple across Lucy's forearms.

"Therefore, I will allot him a portion with the great and he shall divide the spoil with the strong—because he poured out himself to death and was numbered with the transgressors—yet, he bore the sin of many, and made intercession for the transgressors."

Father Norman paused. His eyes swept across his congregation.

"The Word of the Lord."

"Thanks be to God," the stone walls replied.

The sun beamed into the church through a clear sky. Kaleidoscopic colors scattered from the windows onto a procession of congregants waiting patiently for their turn to taste the metaphysical phenomenon of Christ manifested the form of a wafer. Solitary heir to an empty pew, saliva drained from Lucy's mouth when she remembered the sacrament's more literal context. She had not come to miss the starchy discs during her lapse. Her aunt and cousin neared one of Father Norman's lay assistants. Lucy lost track of the priest after he granted his blessings and consecrated body and blood. The man had vanished and left two altar servers behind to feed the teaming masses. When she reached the front, her aunt's jaw lowered to accept the eucharist upon her tongue. The woman performed a sidestep and genuflected. Her right hand crossed her torso from head to heart and shoulder to shoulder, while her mouth whispered to the ceramic martyr suspended overhead.

Lucy's head hunched lower as she shuffled into the aisle. Her aunt and cousin would be back in a moment and her opportunity to leave without protest would vanish. She moved silently as possible—footsteps muffled by the organ player's subdued, meandering arpeggiations. The remorse of ditching her very observant aunt during a ceremony of much personal importance compounded with the guilt of being a disgraced, ex-police officer and would-be accidental executioner. Clouds rolled over the church's windows and the mottled stone beneath her feet was no longer as brilliant. Lucy kept her head sunk down toward the graying floor until a pair of brown loafers appeared in her path.

"Oh, Officer Madrigal," the voice greeted her with hushed cheer. "I was wondering when I'd run into you or your partner again."

The grateful, sympathetic smile on Father Norman's face only brought Lucy lower.

"Father... good to see you, too. I was just—how are you?"

"Better now, thank you. It took us weeks to get this place cleaned up. But to see you here, bearing witness to the fruits of our labor, makes it all the more worthwhile."

It took all of Lucy's strength to prevent her face betraying the sting in her tear ducts. She prayed the priest could not hear her voice cracking as she replied.

"Well... I'm glad to hear that."

"I made good on another thing, too. Fresh from the back office."

The priest's right hand stretched out toward Lucy. In his absence from the altar, the priest had withdrawn to his office to retrieve a video cassette. Lucy looked at the tape. Her heart, her head, her limbs—the weights that bound them began to dissolve. Fluttering rays of colored light dazzled her eyes. The sun on the other side of the tall windows broke through waves of clouds and painted the church once more.

"From that night," Lucy began. "This is a copy of the security cameras?"

"Yes, my apologies for the delay. I'm no technician myself and my assistants' charitable time was occupied more with restoring this place. I hope the detectives or someone at the precinct can still find use for this."

Lucy's eyes went wide.

"Or someone," she whispered. "So, you're saying they hadn't gotten a copy yet. The detective squad hasn't seen the perps in the video…"

"I suppose not. I'm not too late, am I?"

Norman, she ascertained, had yet to hear of the news: the case was officially closed without his additional evidence. The murders, the destruction, and all the infernal affectations—either through profound unawareness or an audacious lack of nerve on the part of the task force assigned to the investigation—had been accomplished by one especially talented, wannabe satanic witch. In the priest's own words, he had been preoccupied to the point of distraction— too busy to trace those same connections which haunted Lucy in her overabundance of spare time. Similarly, the evening news watchers and tabloid readers contented themselves with the Police Department's conclusion. Similar to Norman, they had not benefitted from that which Lucy had seen.

Blustery streams scattered the clouds and chased the debris past the sun. Mid-day ticked closer and the sun arced noticeably higher in the sky despite all others signs that spring's thaw was still a few weeks overdue. When the clouds parted, Lucy soaked in the momentary relief from the cold snap still nipping at the city's heels. After the cumulous tide rolled back in, she shivered. Lucy knew where to go to get warm. Just as she had done time and time again, she charted a course up Bay Parkway. This visit would be during more traditional hours, though—rather than the middle of the night, it was now closer to noon. And hiding was no longer her goal. Lucy's grip tightened on the cardboard sleeve holding Father Norman's video cassette as she ferried it to the first nearby VCR that sprang to her mind.

"Haven't seen you 'round here in a minute."

The weathered plexiglass door of the Elysian Fields Adult Rehabilitation Center shuddered and stumbled as it automatically slid shut behind Lucy. The receptionist greeted her mildly when she passed by the front desk.

"You workin' days now?"

"No," Lucy replied quickly. She tried to conjure an appropriately convincing smile. "Just here to see an old friend. A social call."

It did not take Lucy long to realize little more than the most minimal attempts at a cover story had been required, if any at all. Before she could finish her sentence, the receptionist's chair swiveled. She welcomed Lucy with a permissive nod and her eyes drifted back below the frames of the reading glasses balanced on the edge of her nose. With a flick of her wrist, the newspaper and the partially completed crossword puzzle imprinted upon it angled upward and consumed what remained of her attention.

Lucy rediscovered familiar faces as the staircase guided her to the basement. What she found jarring was the volume of them. She had seen them, one or maybe two at a time, in the nights and months she spent passing in and out of the place. But to see them altogether and accompanied by so many new, yet similarly sedate, distant expressions made her rethink her plan to hijack the building's solitary television. The TV itself was switched on, volume blaring outward from its usual corner. A red-faced Judge Wapner struggled to speak over a pair of men engaging in a passionate, profane dispute over the distribution of their grandfather's estate. It appeared the censor's bleep would be the only voice which managed to dominate. As Lucy's feet reached the landing, none of the dozens in attendance seemed especially invested in the verdict.

An older man sat in a wheelchair a few feet away from the program. His face came from somewhere in Lucy's memory, but it was out of character. The hair on his head was still thin, but mussed and greasy, begging to be visited by the teeth of a comb. The strands appeared slightly yellower and the way they wilted down his wrinkled forehead obscured the underlying fortitude of his undiminished hairline. Slight frame narrower still, drooping skin sagging lower with less flesh beneath it, and as she came closer, Lucy noticed lips moving—exhaling a silent prayer. The words were familiar as the face.

"My heart shall not be afraid."

A fissure yawned in the pit of Lucy's gut. She lurched backward but her widening eyes would not leave the speaker.

"I flee not from your cuts."

Lucy remembered the words, repeated ad nauseum, from the dimly lit living room in the lonely house Giuseppe Tomasi's shared with his night terrors. Giuseppe's unceasing prayers poured forth, past the boundaries of Lucy's memory and into the depths of the Fields. Lucy took a step forward and found her own voice.

"Mr. Tomasi… Giuseppe. Do you remember me?"

The quivering lips hesitated, then turned with the rest of his face to let a pair of silver, clouded irises flutter over Lucy.

"M'scusi… Giuseppe? Chi sei?"

His voice was weak. The confusion, though placid, was plain even if Lucy recognized not a single word of what she presumed to be Italian. It did not take long for Giuseppe's attention to fade. Already fatigued by their mutual incomprehension, the old man turned away from Lucy and the television set altogether. One shaky, fresh red tube sock jabbed at the ground. A shuddering series of pushes from the anti-skid stocking pivoted his wheelchair toward the wall.

"Non sono qui… m'scusi…"

If he resumed his prayer, Lucy would not have been able to hear it. She could barely detect any movement of the man's lips across the few feet of beaten, bleached, low-pile carpet separating them. Lucy disappeared from Giuseppe's world as the more vibrant Giuseppe she remembered had from her own.

Whatever the judgement, Joseph Wapner had the last word. Doug Llewelyn ushered Lucy and the rest of the television gallery out of the courtroom and into a musical advertisement for New York Telephone. The warm voice of NYNEX reassured her that everyone was connected. Lucy's eyes stung. She thought about her suspension, about Giuseppina, about Tabby. Her hand reached out to the television set and gripped the tuner. The knob clunked to the left. Promises of telecommunicative reunion and reconciliation, forgiveness and low long distance fees were swept off the screen in a sudden snowstorm. The dial twisted until it came to rest on channel three. Activating its power button, Lucy listened to the Magnavox VCR warm up. She clicked the eject button. The top-loading carriage glided up from the roof of the machine. The priest's cassette slid in between the guiderails, then descended into the player as Lucy pushed down. When the mechanism locked into place with a click, Lucy pressed play. The VCR hummed. The staticky squall blasting from the television's screen jumped and flashed black.

The Church of Saint Anthony the Great and the narrow street running in front of it were fuzzier than she remembered. The original footage's timestamp had been lost in the transfer and left Lucy's vision floating in timelessness. The sidewalks were too full. She found the fast forward switch and the VCR's hum reeled into a sharper pitch as the reels within spun faster. Crowds on the sidewalks waned until they disappeared altogether. Lucy shivered. She found herself holding her breath when she watched the lights begin to fade. Her finger left the fast forward button and pressed play. The video player returned to a more subdued hum. After a moment, a car entered the one-way lane and ambled to a stop by the sidewalk. The passengers inside the vehicle sat and waited. Lucy waited, too. She studied the vehicle. However expansive her vehicular wisdom, Lucy knew that chunky, boxy grille had not rolled off any assembly line in at least ten years. At the very least, she could damn well tell it was no IROC.

Doors swung open and a pair of shadows exited. Lucy made the driver immediately. A mere glance at the blurry shape floating across the sidewalk cast Lucy back into the black ocean that swallowed her beneath the Gowanus Expressway—mere feet from the ghost of the woman with the long, thin, silvery strands of hair whipping and twisting over her petite face. Lucy's eyes darted away only to find another jolt for her brain where they landed. Bethany Ward's accomplice walked around from the car's passenger side and stepped onto the curb. The night outside Hallelujah reappeared in Lucy's mind. She was jealous of her memories of that past self, specifically that self which found one of the Valerie brothers hiding in the darkness. There was so much less weight on her mind and heart at that time. Now she thought of Charlie constantly. While he haunted her conscience, she had forgotten about the other Valerie brother entirely until he appeared on the Elysian Fields's television set, walking side-by-side with Bethany Ward toward the back of the church and out of the frame. A moment passed, but the view stayed fixed. Lucy prayed Father Norman transferred the footage from the other camera after the copy of this first one concluded. She reached forward. The play button clicked back up when she pressed rewind. Spools spun until the duo reemerged on the screen and performed a backward walk-run into their vehicle. Lucy pressed down again on rewind, but the reels in the cassette kept spinning in an intensified reverse. The doors slammed shut and the car reversed down the block to exit the frame. Lucy's panicking finger found the pause button. Just as the streetlights on the television returned to normal luminescence, the reverse button popped back up with a click. Lucy looked at the fast forward button, then sighed. Caution urged her opt for the play button and for patience.

This playback felt different. The footage she had just watched somehow transformed. As light faded from the world, Lucy watched her own reflection emerge within the black screen. Confusion transfigured the face staring back at her as her eyes darted around her own image. The outline of something much larger formed a halo around her frame, something massive enough to obscure the Fields's already limited light—darkness with broad shoulders, rising out of the mirrored basement behind her.

"Do you even know what it is you're lookin' at?"

The deep voice landed on the back of Lucy's head. A startled turn brought her gazing up at another familiar face—one belonging to the rehabilitation center's largest, most peculiar resident.

"Apollo?"

From what little Lucy knew of the man after one rambling, paranoid interaction, she found it unusual that he could have lingered in silence for very long. Giuseppe was not the only resident who seemed changed. Apollo's head still grazed the basement's yellowed drop-ceiling. Late onset paunchiness continued to soften an otherwise well-defined frame. Unlike his elderly neighbor, there was no physical difference. It was his energy which Lucy found altered. Quieter eyes. Quieter mind.

A shriek made Lucy jump. She turned back to the television. The scene outside the church defused and spliced, teleporting portions of the image left and right simultaneously while bars of light and darkness and static flickered across the screen. The tape player howled as Lucy jammed her finger into the stop button.

"Shit!" she yelled.

Another button clicked and the cassette carriage jerked upward, seizing half-way.

"No! Please, don't eat this fuckin' tape."

"There's a reason nobody uses that stupid thing, no more."

Lucy ignored Apollo's emotionless remark and incautiously wedged the tips of her fingers into the top of the player. She pried the carriage high enough to extract the cassette without straining the jumbled magnetic tape lingering amid its depths any tenser than necessary.

"You used to hang out here in the middle'a the night. Hidin' out," Apollo continued softly, indifferent to Lucy's struggle to gently respool the damaged video tape. "You a cop?"

"Yeah," she replied automatically, then put aside her manual rewind. "Kinda."

Lucy gingerly pulled the last of the dislodged tape from the VCR's internal mechanisms. She laid the cassette out on a nearby dining table and began to pick at the reels with her fingernails, slowly winding the tape back inside. Apollo lumbered over to Giuseppe. Too weak to affect any further, real retreat, the old man's gnarled foot had helplessly shoved his wheelchair a few feet nearer to the wall. Beneath the holes of a threadbare blanket, frail arms knotted themselves against his sides, bracing him from waves of relentless chills. For what appeared to Lucy to be a ritualistic task, Apollo completed the chair's revolution. He turned Giuseppe to face the wall where a sliver of sunlight worked its way down from a narrow slit of a window. Apollo untangled the old man from the straining quilt, readjusted it, then tucked in the edges. Giuseppe did not stir, though the tremors persisted in a somewhat diminished degree. Apollo landed in a dining chair not far from Lucy. Following a mild slap, a red and white pack of cigarettes skidded across the Formica tabletop into the side of a waiting, mostly empty ash tray.

"What did you mean before, about whether I *'even knew what I was looking at?'* How long were you watching?"

"Long enough."

The man previously volunteered any and all thoughts without solicitation. If any holes appeared—and they frequently had—he was quick to fill them with anything at all. Now Lucy had tease each thought as if she were pulling teeth. She interrupted her manual task, picked up the cassette and tried again.

"What do you know about this?" she asked, flashing the tape.

"It's trouble."

Lucy struggled to keep her hand from returning the tape to the table with too much force.

"Why don't you tell me what *kinda* trouble, then?"

She sighed. Being short would get her nowhere. Before Apollo could respond with anything approaching her own hostility, Lucy pulled back and tried again.

"I need help here. If you know something about *this*—whatever this shit is—you need to tell me. I mean… please."

Apollo's fresh cigarette blazed at the end of its first, full drag.

"That depends," he said as he exhaled. "You a cop… or *kinda* one?"

The words left his mouth in clouds and spouts of smoke. Lucy knew she was right. Apollo was different. This was not the benefit of a good night's sleep or a new regiment of medications. He was sharper.

"Please," she repeated. "I've got nothing. I need all the help I can get."

The man's eyes trace the room, suddenly avoiding contact with her own.

"Nah. You ain't no cop."

"You're right," Lucy admitted. "I got in trouble. Did something stupid. Because of *this*."

Lucy's hands waggled the half-unwound video cassette.

"Now, I don't know."

"No," Apollo interjected. "I mean you 'been playin' dress-up. Puttin' on a costume an' showin' up for work. '*Yes sir, no sir.*' One lil' slap and you came hidin' in here. Night after night. Month after month. In all that time you never faced what you was hidin' from. Now here you are again, like an old habit. So, before you come askin' me questions, why don't you finally say what it is you're afraid of."

Lucy had not expected the dam to break so suddenly, nor for it to come crashing down onto her.

"That's none of your goddamned business."

Her hands returned to their task, frantically prodding the reels to jostle the last of the magnetic tape back inside.

"Because it's nothin' worth hidin' from," Apollo concluded smuggly.

Lucy nudged the last of the tape's innards back into the cassette and let the spring-loaded panel snap closed. She wanted to scream. With her mechanical distraction gone, it was becoming harder to suppress the urge. Her bottom row of teeth ground against the top. Forcing it to stop made her jaw clench tighter.

"Nothing I can't take care of."

"We all got demons. 'Specially down here."

His tone softened. Lucy realized how wound up she had become. She forced her shoulders to relax.

"Room fulla ghosts. Heads fulla ghosts, too. Now I see you comin' into this place, bringin' more ghosts wit'youse."

Apollo's voiced dipped and Lucy could feel his newfound vigor drift away. He spoke until his chin fell and forced the inaudible spasms of a mumbling mouth into his own chest. With a flick, he popped his head back up to allow a pair of bulging eyes to stare at the cigarette cradled in his hand. He squeezed the end of the filter between tightly pursed lips. A long drag was followed by a gruff exhale. The man exorcised his lungs and another dense fogbank melted into the ceiling.

"I'm sorry," he said. "I got a lotta shit goin' on right now. Sounds like you know what I mean."

"All the same, it seems like you're doing better."

"Yeah. Lucky me, I guess."

"No, I'm serious. Listen, I don't need any more reminders right now that my job is fucked. And God knows I spent enough time here to know how fucked *this* place can get. I came here because I need to do something. And sure—maybe I don't have the slightest clue about anything. What I *do* know is that I need help."

Apollo leaned back in his chair. Finally, he permitted his eyes to meet with Lucy's.

"This place is pretty fucked, huh?"

Lucy copied Apollo's lean. She considered the room until she returned to Giuseppe. Apollo continued to speak while she watched the sliver of sunlight climb the old man's wheelchair.

"I've been trapped down here, in this place, for a long time. Trapped up inside my own head, too. Since '77. Been thirteen years now. Don't get out much. Went out to try to catch a movie the other night, when the whole damn city went dark. By the way everything looked up there, could've told me I hadn't been gone more than a day."

"Just tell me what you know," Lucy said, eager to redirect him.

"I don't trust cops."

Apollo flexed his forearm and a faded, bluing tattoo of a winged skull flapped across a sky full of outlaw biker symbols.

"Well," Lucy sighed, "I'm probably not gonna go back to being one anytime soon if it makes you feel better."

A small burst of air rattled across the room. The cracks and lines on Apollo's face danced. Lucy had never heard such a booming laugh.

"Alright," he hummed. "You're good."

Apollo reached across the table and scooped the cassette into his hand.

"What did you see when you watched this tape?"

"Not enough. It gets too dark to make out any faces."

"No, that's not what I meant. Start from the beginning. Walk me through everything you saw."

Lucy huffed. She tilted the stiff cafeteria chair to balance on its back legs and guided her eyes through the maze imprinted on the underside of one of the drop-ceiling's panels.

"It's outside of this church, not too far from here. Late at night. You can see the street become emptier and emptier. And darker."

Lucy paused to gauge Apollo's interest. He remained quiet, still staring at the VHS tape. Lucy shrugged, then allowed the recollection to continue trickling out.

"Too dark. It's not until the street's completely clear and it couldn't have taken more than a couple minutes for all the lights to burn out."

"Burn out…"

Apollo parroted her words and let them sit. Unsure whether they were meant as a question or an agreement, Lucy decided to continue.

"These two pull up in a car. Can't tell what kinda car. Can't tell their faces, neither."

"Good for them. Impressive."

Lucy hesitated. Apollo's abrupt commentary was inscrutable as the thought processes provoking it.

"Yeah, I guess," she started again. "They walk right past this camera, and you can't make still can't tell much on account of all the lights are completely gone by then."

The ceiling tiles over Lucy's head bore a mix of deliberate and incidental splotches. The edges closest the latticework of vinyl frames, formed a dramatic, topographic landscape of tar stains from the cigarettes of Apollo and others. Before those blemishes were absorbed, a blackish-brownish labyrinth had been mechanically pocked onto the white surface of the panels during their manufacturing process. Each square's distended, sagging center drooped toward the ground. Lucy continued to weave through wobbly trails, over the landscape's sloping dips and ridges. She began to suspect that a pair of eyes could wander forever in this place—in circles or whatever shape their trail favored—without arriving at either any true dead end or escape.

"But I know who one of 'em is at least. She's the one who killed herself in that wreck on Fourth Avenue. Bethany Ward. It was the thing with the lights. I saw her do it again after the wreck."

Though she was still focused on the ceiling, Lucy felt Apollo's eyes leave the cassette tape.

"The thing with the lights. *After* the wreck."

There was no confusion in his voice. Apollo heard—*repeated*—the very obvious existential contradictions that still gave Lucy pause. But there was something else. Not doubt, Lucy decided. Anxiety.

"What'd she look like—the *last* time you saw her?"

Lucy closed her eyes.

'No longer our fathers' wayward ones.'

Black pocked blots morphed on the panels over Lucy's head. They writhed with every word and echoed the voice of the silhouetted dead woman beneath the Gowanus Expressway.

'We are the Devil's favorite sons.'

The silhouette flared and turned to pure light.

"Bright. Not just because all the lights had blown out, like *blindingly* white. I could see it through closed eyelids. And there was this wind. I couldn't tell which way it blew, but her hair was whipping—twisting and billowing up into the sky, like there was something up there trying to swallow her up. And then she was gone."

"There's another one with her on the video," Apollo continued. "Saw that much over your shoulder."

"Maybe more than that. There's this other young one. A man—a boy really. He's the younger brother of the one on the video. Ward spoke with him that night, before we took off after her."

"Damnit," Apollo whispered to himself. "The sonuvabitch… damn him."

"I don't know. Charlie's in over his head more than anything. I don't think he's into whatever shit the rest of 'em are, even if I saw him drop that… thing."

"No, I'm talkin' 'bout someone else," Apollo sighed. "Drop what *'thing'*?"

"I think it looked like… no, it *had* to have been. We saw him come outta this old church they turned into a nightclub. He had it wrapped up in cloth or something, tucked into his arm. One of the club's bouncers, well, *bounced* the kid and he dropped it onto the sidewalk anyway. The realest lookin' skull I've ever seen."

Lucy felt alone. The front two legs of her chair clicked back onto the ground. She saw Apollo, still seated in front of her. A long tower of ash replaced the cigarette nestled between his index and middle fingers. His expression was blank as the neglected cherry burned past the end of the filter to scorch the flesh of his hand. With a twitch, Apollo returned to earth.

"Hot, damn," he hissed.

Apollo snapped his wrist and flicked the cigarette into a nearby ashtray. His other hand held up the tape.

"So, you got this thing workin' yet?"

"I dunno," Lucy replied, slightly jarred by the man's shifting energy. "I wound the reels back up. Only one way to find out.

The two rose from their chairs and leaned in close to the TV. Apollo stared at the VCR, then back at the tape. His shoulders slumped, then turned to Lucy.

"Here," he said. "It's all you."

Lucy reluctantly took the tape. She carefully loaded it into the machine beneath the television set. Her palm rested atop the carriage. She took a deep breath, pushed it down, and let it click. The play button sank beneath her index finger.

White lines. Black lines. Strips of static. There was a click, and the screen went black. Lucy jabbed at the stop button, a snap judgment against an encore of the screeching malfunction.

"Nope," she said sharply as she pressed eject. "I dunno if it's the tape or this old TV, but I'm not taking that chance again."

Lucy removed the cassette and turned it over in her hands. She accepted it as a small mercy that the tape remained within the case this time.

"There's only one person I know who's a certified genius with this kinda stuff. But I dunno if she's ready to forgive me."

"Better start workin' on your apologies, then."

Not without some regret, Lucy agreed. She stood up and allowed the room and the moment within to imprint in her memory.

"How did it come to this?" she wondered aloud as she soaked in the basement and its many miserable aspects. "How did this all get so run down? Second-hand, busted equipment. Crumbling walls. Who runs this place, anyway?"

"Oh. Just this guy. Real pillar of the community."

Apollo chuckled. His fingers pulled another cigarette from the pack.

"I'm sure you've seen 'im before. Does a lot of commercials."

Fifteen

"Is there anybody I didn't call?"

Somewhere beneath Tabby's feet, in one of the many dank corners of the precinct's basement, an ancient oil heater smoldered. Streams of radiant heat burbled and circulated throughout the building. Packed into the center of the muster room, warmth built beneath her uniform.

"In other words, if you aren't here, raise your hand," Sergeant Darling added.

Tabby felt a bead of sweat materialize between her shoulder blades. It was bad enough, she lamented, to bundle up for another frigid day stuck on the same foot post—for those doubled layers of clothing to be wet from perspiration before she even made it out the front door was an invitation to catch a cold.

Sergeant Darling pushed his elbows away from the podium. The third platoon supervisor's chin extracted itself from the heel of his palm. No absent parties managed to defy the laws of physics and respond to his question. As the sergeant had throughout the course of his distracted, mumbled roll call, he fidgeted with the volume knob on the radio hooked to his gun belt. The greater share of his attention was tuned to those airwaves which, between their assigned hours of four-to-midnight, could explode at any second in between. Tabby knew from experience that once that genie escaped the bottle the sustained bedlam could prevent the radio dying down until early Saturday morning. When she was younger, she loved working the last tour to close out the day—that was where the action was. The more chaotic the shift, the faster the hands spun around the clock. In the weeks since Tabby had been unceremoniously bounced from the midnights, she realized exactly how severe a toll her years on the graveyard shift exacted. Central's unending readouts used to make her head spin in a challenging way. Now, when she found herself pacing beneath the elevated tracks on 86th Street, the ceaseless shouting contest between the dispatcher and responding units would produce a migraine long before the trains which clattered over her post.

"The Shop's still pretending we don't exist," Darling continued. "That means we're running short on cars that haven't been wrecked. Let's try not to put anything else out of service, fellas."

Tabby felt the ache in her forehead where it had come to an abrupt stop against the steering wheel a month earlier. After giving the spot an involuntary rub, she brought her eyes back to the front of the room where they met the sergeant's. Darling had addressed the *'fellas.'* Tabby did not see him share his glare with anyone else in her vicinity.

"Speaking of which, Sector Charlie'll be dropping off our favorite, blue flower pot at—*surprise, surprise*—Bay Parkway and 86."

As a parting gift with her expulsion, Tabby also received a special assignment at the request of her former supervisor, Lieutenant Cordell. She could not deny the man's tenacity. The lieutenant had a creative streak when it came to punishments. But when it came to exerting his influence beyond his own platoon, he was truly gifted.

"So, Williams," Darling sighed, his eyes underscoring a genuinely pathetic plea. "If you'd kindly refrain from so much as *looking* at the driver's seat on your way to post, I'd be eternally grateful."

Tabby's gaze shrank away. Her eyes drifted down to the memobook in her hands into which she spent the past five minutes pretending to take notes. The sergeant's voice softened as he continued.

"In return, I'd appreciate it if each of you could stop by her post every once in a while to give her a break."

Cordell's fingerprints were all over the other tours' assignment sheets. Being on notice meant being a blip on a less-than-desirable radar, and a punishment post was still a punishment post. Mercifully, his voice could not be in every other supervisors' ears all the time.

"But If Cordell catches you, I didn't say that. Hell, I'll deny I ever met you."

By the time Tabby turned back toward the front of the room to offer a shrug of gratitude, Sergeant Darling returned to shuffling and puzzling through his stack of heavily-edited printouts.

"On a final and not entirely unrelated note, straight from the borough, tonight's training memo: *'In the event of another large-scale blackout, all units are reminded to contact their respective Desk Officers without delay and standby for redeployment instructions. Special attention is to be extended to'*—there it is—*'electronics merchants and high-end boutiques. In the event of power losses which start earlier in the evening or those which ConEd are unable to remedy by the following night, all members are to remain vigilant for signs of erupting large-scale unrest.'"*

"Man…" a voice behind Tabby moaned. "What the fuck's all that 'sposed t'mean?"

"It means they know the whole damn city's goin' to Hell," someone on the other side of the room replied. "An' the next time the lights go out, we might not be so lucky that all the freaks've already scurried away for the night. City doesn't want us gettin' caught with our pants down if the whole damn grid goes out right at the peak of the *witchin' hour*."

The sergeant cleared his throat. His grip on the room was slipping.

"Right," Darling added. "But just in case all Hell does break loose, remember the most important thing: you're the last line of defense for our *electronics merchants and high-end boutiques*."

Scoffs and gripes continued to echo from the muster room Tabby as she slipped out to beat the rush. She approached the rows of portable radios sitting next to the Sixty Fourth Precinct's imposing, wooden main desk. She grabbed one, twisted the volume knob, and confirmed that it held a charge. The serial number etched into a plate on the side was barely visible through its accumulated scuffs. Seated next to the array of radios, within the lines and columns of a heavily bound, yet prematurely worn logbook, she placed the tip of her ballpoint pen.

4/13/90, 15:27, #64-119, PO Williams, Shield 3834

One of phones atop the tall desk rang. Tabby pushed herself onto the tips of her toes and leaned forward. A lone sergeant from the soon-to-conclude day tour sat on the other side. While the line rang out, he appeared more interested in testing the limits of his rolling chair, seeing how far the shoes he propped atop the desk would allow him to recline before he tumbled backward onto the floor. Tabby found the task bewildering. She never took seriously the idea of studying for a promotional exam. Suddenly, the competition seemed less intimidating.

The phone continued to ring and the boss behind the desk continued to explore his position's ergonomic limits. Sergeant Darling rushed out of the muster room and sprinted up next to his preoccupied colleague.

"Darling, how can I help you—"

He stuttered into the handset when he heard his own regrettable phrasing.

"Good. Yeah, yeah. I'll send someone to pick you up."

"The way you sweet talk 'im like that, he better pick up a coupla' pies from Lenny's on the way back," the other sergeant grumbled.

"Not sure he's got the stomach right now. Lorenzo says he's done with that shitshow over on Eighteenth Avenue. M.E.'s office picked up the bodies and the squad's releasing the crime scene."

"How'd they manage t'get all the ballistics wrapped up that quick?"

"Nah, no ballistics—three down without a single shot fired. Nothing other than knife wounds."

Sergeant Darling dragged an index finger beneath his chin.

"Deep slashes right across the neck."

"Shit," the desk officer yawned as he managed to recline further. "Guess that's three less goombas."

"*Fewer*," Tabby chimed in.

"Fewer what?" the man replied, squeaking as he swiveled in Tabby's direction.

"Three *fewer* goombas," Darling added, nodding in agreement.

"Fewer. Less. What-the-fuck ever."

The phone jingled again and interrupted their post-mortem grammar lesson. Another officer seated nearby at a more traditional desk shouted in their direction.

"Sarge, we got another one callin' in," the cop shouted, hand cupping the receiver. "Says she just saw some mugger lunge at her from the shadows, then disappear completely."

"Don't look at me."

The sergeant examined his watch. A moment later, his seatback sprang up behind him with a relieved squeal.

"But Darling here—the four-to-twelve supervisor—*he'll* be more than happy to reassure any concerned citizens that the precinct's boogeyman problem is nothin' more than an infestation of especially aggressive squeegee men."

Tabby watched Sergeant Darling's shoulders slump. She turned toward the precinct's entryway. The vaulted room buzzed with commotion. The incoming platoon of officers traded inside jokes and concussive backslaps with the fresh-faced replacements marching out of the building. One figure amidst the raucous change-over stayed motionless, a slender twig caught amidst the rush of two opposing streams. Tabby knew Lydia Dunwell. She knew the old woman looked lost. Mrs. Dunwell searched the rolling wave of faces, squinting momentarily until any potential familiarity washed away with the crowd. Her strained expression quivered and swiveled, then melted. She lit up when she discovered Tabby's eyes approach.

"I've been trying to reach Detective Vernon every day," Lydia explained. "The papers have been calling me, day and night. They say the story I gave you and the detective doesn't add up. I'm still not sure how they got my name and number."

As she spoke, Mrs. Dunwell unfolded a newspaper from under her arm and jabbed at it with her index finger.

"Doesn't add up," Tabby repeated. "What do you mean?"

"Look, dear…"

She thrust the broadsheet under Tabby's nose.

"Right here, in the Morning Tribune."

Dunwell's firm grasp had left several deep creases imprinted in the margins of the newspaper. Tabby's palm ironed them out as she began to read from the article Lydia circled in blue ink:

Calls for Reexamination Increase Following Transit Authority Report

By BERNARD SEVILLE

BROOKLYN — A report released this past Wednesday by the Metropolitan Transportation Authority indicated that a vehicular collision which occurred last month in Bay Ridge cannot solely be blamed for the multi-borough blackout which afflicted parts of Brooklyn, Staten Island, and Manhattan for nearly 24 hours. Not long after the ill-fated police pursuit of Bethany Ward arrived at a fatal conclusion in the early hours of Saturday, March 10, it was purported by City Hall and the New York Police Department that the power outage had been the result of a collision between Ms. Ward's Chevrolet Camaro and above-ground electrical equipment connecting a subway station at the location with the power grid. Further investigation of the outage by the

MTA and ConEd now indicates that the true epicenter of the blackout was located a short distance away and did not begin until nearly ten minutes after the time of the fatal collision. Authorities now indicate the blackout rolled outward from Third Avenue and Fifty-Second Street as indicated by a radius of crippled electronics and lighting equipment which expanded outward three hundred feet from that intersection.

This development comes as official conclusions concerning Ms. Ward's involvement in several high-profile slayings come under renewed scrutiny. During a City Council hearing on Monday, Councilman Russell Patrick requested clarification from One Police Plaza in the wake of a series of editorials published by the Morning Tribune. Mr. Patrick specifically inquired as to the timeline of investigations into the murders of four teenagers in Bensonhurst on February 11 of this year and apparent inconsistencies in evidence and witness testimonies collected prior to the fatal collision on March 10. The Office of the NYPD's Deputy Commissioner of Public Information has yet to provide a public response to Mr. Patrick or to questions submitted by this publication.

There was no direct mention of Dunwell, nor any of Vernon or the official account he extracted from her. It appeared to Tabby that the *'apparent inconsistencies in evidence and witness testimonies,'* included Mrs. Dunwell's statements. If the media smelt blood and Lydia was getting calls from reporters, Tabby could understand her anxiety.

"They're calling about what you told us that night, I assume," Tabby said, looking up from the print.

"All the time. And I don't know what to say to them, because… well, they're not wrong."

Mrs. Dunwell's finger returned to the article. She pointed to a pair of photographs printed alongside. One was the late Bethany Ward, looking younger than Tabby remembered. Next to it, the remains of the Camaro, twisted sideways along the ground, surrounded by ambulances and police floodlamps. The gas generators rumbled in Tabby's memory, feeding the emergency lights and reawakening sore spots on her forehead and lower back. Her hand unconsciously reached up to her head again, thumb rubbing at the ache she wished time would allow her to forget.

"Do you remember what I told you that day?" Lydia continued. "I'm sixty-three years old. My memory isn't gone yet. Not completely, at least."

"Better than mine, probably. You said you saw a car, someone in it."

"A car, certainly. But not this one. I might not know as much as my Anthony did about cars, but I'm not foolish enough to mistake the car I saw outside my house for some… *hot rod* like this one. And certainly not with such flashy silver paint. I saw an ordinary car. A normal, boring one."

"The kind you'd never take a second look at," Tabby added.

"Why, no. I suppose not."

"And her," Tabby said, looking at the picture of Ward. "Not the type you'd forget either."

"That girl's hair is white and straight as ironed bedlinen," Lydia added, her pitch getting higher as Tabby echoed her thoughts. "The person I saw sitting in that car had hair on the lighter side, but only a shade shy of brown. More volume, too, in a tangled and knotty way."

"Have you mentioned any of this to the reporters, when they call you?"

"I might have," Mrs. Dunwell sighed reluctantly. "But that don't seem to be the only thing they find so objectionable."

Lydia Dunwell's energetic tone became subdued. Tabby was worried—first by the old woman's change in demeanor, then by the realization that she was missing some greater point.

"When I spoke to you that night," Mrs. Dunwell whispered, "I told you I heard a commotion outside my house. When I looked through my front window, all I saw was the car and the person sitting inside. Not *this* car, and *not* this person. After I left the window, I heard car doors slamming. *Two* doors, one right after the other. In a real hurry, like. And then the car drove away."

"The reporters," Tabby added. "They're asking about *how many* people might've been outside your house, aren't they?"

"I don't know what else to tell them, dear. I don't want to go against what was in the detectives' reports or get anybody into trouble. But I know what I saw that night. And I *know* I heard more than one car door closing."

"Mrs. Dunwell, don't worry about getting anyone in trouble."

"—And I think those other people are still out there. Other people who know what happened that night, too. It might not take them long to figure out…"

Lydia paused. The pain in Tabby's forehead shifted to the back of her skull and showed no sign of subsiding. When no answers or words of comfort came to her, she grabbed at the next best thing.

"I'll speak with Detective Vernon myself. He's not in right now, but I'll make sure he hears about the *difficult situation* this whole mess has put you in."

"It's no mess of your making, officer. But thank you for hearing out an old widow. I don't even know how long I've been talking your ear off…"

Mrs. Dunwell squinted over Tabby's shoulder. Tabby turned and glanced over at the clock hanging from the wall.

"Four in the afternoon," she read aloud.

"Oh, Mollases!" Mrs. Dunwell squawked. "If I don't get home to feed that dog, she'll be cross with me for the rest of the night."

Tabby was surprised by the vigor in Mrs. Dunwell's step as she turned toward the precinct's front door.

"And when you see Detective Vernon, make sure he knows he's not free of me yet!"

The patrol car shuddered as an alternating series of potholes took turns battering the vehicle's tires. When they crossed the final dip, the Crown Victoria's aging suspension system launched Tabby's head into its cloth roof. Being able to hitch a ride to her foot post blunted the punishment somewhat, though it did require her to squeeze behind a prisoner partition. No longer airborne, she glared into the rearview mirror. From the other side of the partition, Officer Schiller winced.

"Sorry, Tabby."

"Even from one of my *so-called* friends on the midnights, I get punished."

"Aww c'mon," his partner Antonio cooed from the passenger seat. "Go easy on us! They got us here workin' a double on account of all the *staffing shortages* the precinct seems to be runnin' into lately."

Tabby laughed, only slightly ashamed at being the source of their frustration.

"Don't think you can lie to me. As soon as I left, Cordell pulled you all into a circle and told you I was dead to him."

"Nah, you know that guy," Schilling said, waving his hand. "A week after you left, he was already bored. Then, like clockwork, someone else gave him a reason to land on 'em with both feet. I bet he doesn't even remember who you were no more."

"I'm sure Lucy'd be thrilled to hear it."

Both partners in the front of the car shared a silent glance.

"Well," Antonio murmured, "now that you mention it, *certain people* might linger on in memory."

Barely a minute past five and the sun already hung low in the sky. Spring may have pushed the hour hand forward, but changing the clocks did little to make the days any less dim. The mood inside Antonio and Schilling' car dipped to match the dull sky outside. It was only a short ride to her foot post and, as the Crown Vic turned, the elevated train tracks over 86th Street came into sight. A long line of subway cars rattled into of the Bay Parkway stop. What few metal bits of their exteriors evaded defacement or corrosion caught the sinking sun to bloom sparse, angular rays. Most of the graffiti tags were mundane and repetitive—if they could be deciphered at all. Tabby noticed one repeated on each car as it passed: *Black Goat*.

Antonio offered a wave and Sector Charlie's taillights disappeared into the dense, crowded rush hour traffic. Tabby leaned back against one of the elevated track's support beams and pulled Mrs. Dunwell's copy of the Morning Tribune from within of her jacket. It had taken her a minute inside the stationhouse to realize she failed to return the newspaper. By then, the woman had already vanished. She wrote a mental IOU and turned to the Metro pages.

There was another article accompanying the one which Mrs. Dunwell highlighted. Statistics appeared to indicate that New York City, despite a very public conclusion to one particularly sinister crime spree, had yet to correct its ongoing descent into another year of record-setting brutality. The editorials and on-street interviews with people still seeing ghosts vastly outnumbered those statistics and left Tabby with the impression that the papers were doing their best to hang onto the satanic hype all the same. Beneath the Morning Tribune's trademark death tally in the top right corner— nearing four figures citywide with summer barely visible on the horizon—were much larger letters drawing attention to the nefarious panic still popular in the public's imagination: *The*

Nineties' New Predators. Tabby scoffed as she read the subheading: *'Will the last decade of the millennium usher in the Season of the Witch?'*

"Don't turn your back on a shadow durin' the daytime!"

A shrill voice rose over a gaggle of screams. Whatever the commotion, it tumbled across the intersection toward Tabby. She lifted her head from the tabloid and watched a swarm of preteens jostling and elbowing one another. From the cover of roadside bus stops and comfortable perches atop overturned milkcrates, pedestrians shared their gall as the noisy group intruded on the traditional, mechanical cacophony echoing beneath the elevated train station.

"The goat man's gonna come an' getcha!"

"No!" an impossibly sharper voice wailed. "Leave me alone you guys, that ain't funny!"

A small boy wobbled forward onto the sidewalk a few feet away from Tabby. The remaining children, a mix of boys and a couple of girls, lobbed taunts in his wake. Without any perceptible cue, a few of the kids began to chatter and bleat until words were forfeit entirely to a chorus of animal cries and grunts. Amidst a rising torrent of nonsensical braying, the smaller boy's visible desperation devolved to bare terror. A shiver ran down Tabby's arms and jumpstarted her feet.

"Step too close and he'll nab ya!"

"Yeah, he's got you marked, Francesco!"

"Alright, that's enough," Tabby shouted.

She pushed herself away from the support column and into the middle of the flock. The group buzzed with adolescent cussing.

"*Ohhh!* Oh shit."

"Cops gonna getcha too, Emmanuel!"

"Watchu' want lady?" one of the girls crowed.

Their collective attention swayed from the younger boy. He did not waste the opportunity to shrink away from the crowd.

"What I want is for you little rodents to knock off the nonsense and go terrorize somebody else's corner," Tabby growled. "Otherwise, I can have your parents pick each of you up from the precinct."

"We was just playin' 'round is all," a taller girl whined. "Ain'cha never heard 'a the goat man?"

"Yeah," another boy chimed in. "He's the one who's been walkin' through the shadows, grabbin' people when they ain't payin' attention."

"I told you to stop it with this foolishness," Tabby warned. "Run along. Hit the bricks before I have to repeat myself."

"Geez! Don't gotta blow your stack, already."

Their voices bristled with complaints, but the noise faded as the group splintered.

"Stupid Francesco, bringin' the heat on us again."

"Yeah! Shit, man. We *own* this block."

"We'll terrorize *whoever we want!*"

Electric motors charged up and began to squeal over Tabby's head. The bluster and softly grumbled threats disappeared as train cars rolled down the West End Line toward Coney Island. Not far behind her, Tabby found Francesco. The boy's face and quivering chin were dwarfed by a pair of glassy eyes that threatened to burst with tears.

"That means you too, little one. Run along home."

Her voice was stern, but softer.

"Yes, ma'am," he replied shakily. "Sorry, ma'am."

The boy's feet pivoted, then shuddered to an abrupt stop. From where it lingered in the afternoon sky, the sun spared expanding portions of the landscape any direct light. Broad strips of darkness sliced sharp angles across deeply set doorways. Cold, cement voids stretched on the sidewalk beneath the dense, steely staircases that lead up to the Bay Parkway station. The white tips of the boy's sneakers toed the line of just such a swath. Tabby watched as he shook his head, took a deep breath, and then plowed forward, arms flailing by his sides. His pace never slowed. The boy ran to the next block and rounded the corner.

Tabby returned to her post. She planted the sole of her left foot flat against her favorite train column's concrete base. After a few minutes, another train entered the station. Its brakes screamed. When they came to a halt, Tabby detected a slight lurch in the post behind her back. The world stood still for only a brief moment. A new rumble emerged. A slow, orderly stampede descended to each corner of the intersection. Each of the station's four, wide staircases unleashed a flood of straphangers onto the sidewalks. Another work week reached its conclusion, at least for people with schedules more routine than Tabby. They jockeyed through the morass, spurred by the promise of a holiday weekend. As it was, Tabby was set to work through their weekend before her own days off began on Tuesday. She did not complain, nor did she see the point. It was not the first holiday she would work through and she knew it would not be the last. Not for the *foreseeable* future, at the least. Tabby thought about Lucy. Cordell did not forgive. If he also did not forget, Tabby realized she might not be too far removed from a calendar similarly wide-open.

The crowd tapered off as its more impatient constituents marched into the distance. At the tail end, among the cautious elders and carefree meanderers, an erratic force bristled with impatience. The ball of energy clambered down the stairs and loped over the edge of Tabby's field of vision. Descending to the street, the woman's head swiveled and scanned. Her dark, shoulder-length hair spun as her eyes bounced from one side of the intersection to the other.

"Oh. Shit."

Tabby blinked hard. Her first instinct was to stay hidden behind her eyelids for as long as possible. She knew that the longer she indulged in the seclusion of the moment, the closer she would find the familiar face when she reopened them. Before she could face the music, she cursed herself. She should have known what tended to happen when you spoke of the devil.

"Tabby!"

Lucy Madrigal weaved through waves of pedestrians to the corner where Tabby stood. Though not quite reaching a run, there was an obviously nervous hustle to her pace.

"Lucy… how've you been?"

The warmth of her own tone surprised Tabby. She had not seen her most recent partner—her most recently *dismissed* partner—in weeks. The memories of that night and the end of that particular partnership left little room for nostalgia.

"It's good to see you," Tabby continued.

"Yeah—*hey*—you too," Lucy panted. "I've been tryin' to call you all afternoon from pay phones, but all I got was the answering machine. I ran outta quarters, so I went over to the stationhouse. They said Cordell got your tour changed an' stuck you out here."

Somewhere in the wind tunnel that blew past Tabby's ears, an opening emerged for her to get in a word of her own.

"Ok, alright," Tabby said when a gasp for beath presented the opportunity. "You good? Where's the fire?"

"The church, Saint Anthony's. You remember, right? The break-in!"

"What? Another one?"

"No, no."

Lucy pivoted her shoulder. The handbag hung thereon whipped forward into her hands.

"Here! Norman gave it to me."

"Who? Gave what?"

"Norman, the priest. His tape!"

As Tabby listened to her former coworker alternate between breathless streams to clipped nonsense, she became aware of a rising tension near her inner ear. She was also beginning to hear her own heart pound over the clamor of rush hour traffic. With each beat, the tightness behind her eardrums more closely resembled the onset of a migraine. Reluctant to allow the progression to continue, her hand reached out and landed on Lucy's shoulder.

"Breathe, girl. Dial it back and start again."

"No, no time!"

Lucy rummaged through the canvas bag like a madwoman until she froze. A second later, she ripped her hand out and thrust a thin, black rectangle into Tabby's face.

"He put it on tape! But they never got it!"

Tabby took a step back and raised her hands to shield herself against the mania. Incidentally, she soon found one of her protective hands filled with a VHS casette. She turned the tape over to examine it while Lucy continued to ramble without pause.

"There's *others*. There were *always* others. But they closed the whole thing out anyway!"

"Hold on, just—"

Tabby's voice began to rise again as she tried to find another break in the rush. Instead, she found herself back in Father Norman's office. She had prodded and fussed with the priest's security setup. Eventually, she honed the reels to the burglary. To the two figures.

"We asked him for a copy for the report," Tabby recalled.

"Yes!" Lucy shouted as she grabbed Tabby by the elbows. "And he's had it this whole time—just collecting dust in his office 'til he handed it to me today."

"So, Vernon…" Tabby mumbled. "All of them in the task force—"

"Never even looked at it."

"Never looked *for* it."

A vision of Probationary Police Officer Vernon entered Tabby's memory. For as long as she knew him, his M.O. remained consistent. When they shared the same academy class, Samuel Vernon had been quiet, nearly invisible. She hardly recognized him when he rematerialized two years in the Six Four's vestibule, newly transferred from another precinct in Manhattan. Sam's voice echoed throughout the historic building's tall ceilings as he made introductions, a boisterous compliment to the new glint in his eyes. He reintroduced himself to Tabby, then walked straight up to her previous lieutenant. A more permissive man than Cordell and a few months shy of retirement, the aging supervisor was often blinded by the light at the quickly approaching end of the tunnel. So, when Vernon made the bold proposal of teaming up with his former classmate, it was endorsed with a shrug of approval. Tabby had not been consulted. She chose to mirror the shrug and roll with it.

In her own two years since graduation, Tabby had yet to secure any steady partner. Typically, her nights were preoccupied escorting juveniles at Spofford or guarding the bedsides of sick prisoners at Gravesend General. Working with Vernon everyday freed her from babysitting duties and afforded the opportunity to tally an impressive list of arrests in a short time. When the time came for Tabby to cap off her accomplishments with a career-making collar, she found herself nursing a busted back minutes after subduing and handcuffing Brooklyn's very own white whale of auto larceny. Her enthusiastic partner did not hesitate to get medical assistance rolling, nor did he have any reservations when it came to poach her catch.

Six months passed before Tabby was cleared by a department surgeon. On her first night back in the Six Four, the platoon mustered for roll call. Vernon was nowhere to be seen and, once again, she found herself coaxing disgruntled delinquents into the back of a transport wagon. Before she could close the doors, she caught a familiar grin in her periphery. Tabby met Detective Vernon, fresh from his promotion ceremony at One Police Plaza.

Sam exhibited no shame. Tabby had never been especially religious, but she had spent enough time in policing to make her rigidly observant of a vast canon of superstitions. She placed her faith in karma. Sam had his new title, but he would never have the talent. Tabby prayed to whatever cosmic force would listen that, sooner or later, he would poach from the wrong coworker or burn the wrong boss. Unfortunately, her prayers continued to echo through the ether unanswered, while Sam Vernon had a new plaque announcing an unheard of jump from third- to first-grade detective. Not for any lack of attempts on Tabby's part, she discovered it was no longer possible to pass through the front doors of the Six Four without benefitting from the conspicuous token of the City's gratitude for his services. It traditionally took most of the department's investigators decades to achieve the same, and all but a few reached retirement long before actually earning the distinction. Vernon had little to boast, save the good fortune of showing up in the wrong place at the right time twice in Tabby's presence.

A sharp chill rode the breeze and pulled Tabby back to her foot post. A bus belched diesel fuel as it tumbled over the choppy asphalt of Bay Parkway. The fumes added to the bad taste in her mouth.

"Yeah, that sounds like Vernon. If he can't get someone else to do his job for him, he'll always settle for something else quick and easy."

"Makes sense," Lucy said. "I saw him and the rest of the task force that night, by the wreck. They couldn't wait to shout *'case closed'* and pat each other on the back."

"Whichever way the case rests now, Vernon's doin' just fine while I'm freezin' my ass off."

"Could be worse… at least you're getting paid to sit around with nothing to do."

"If I had as much time off as you, you could bet I'd look a lot better rested. I definitely wouldn't be out here shivering for free."

"Don't be so sure. From what I've heard, it sounds like the old Tabby didn't let things like warmth or rest stand in the way of making a case."

"There is no case!"

Tabby was surprised by the sudden rise in her voice. Annoyance outweighed sense and harsh words tumbled free.

"It's over. We blew it. At this point—*if we're lucky*—the paper's will catch on and somebody else might actually notice how bad Vernon blew it, too. 'Til then, enough is enough. Whatever you're digging into isn't gonna do you any favors if you actually care to get your job back. I'm doing what I can to hold onto mine."

"This isn't what I wanted, it's not the only reason I came out here. I didn't think—"

"Oh," Tabby scoffed, "I know you *didn't think*."

"It's because I never got to say I'm sorry."

Tabby let her head lurch back and smack against the cold, steel column. She stared at the underside of the train tracks. A line of pigeons roosted on the bottom lip of an I-beam. Their heads tucked deep within their feathers, while their eyes swiveled for any slight morsel to swoop down upon.

"You wouldn't know they were cold," Tabby grumbled. "No way in hell they aren't, but they barely let it show."

She looked back down and found her former co-worker thoroughly confounded. It was Lucy's turn to look like she shared the company of a crazy person.

"I know you're sorry," Tabby continued. "I'm sorry, too. For unloading like that. You've got more than enough to worry about, even though you seem dead set on adding to those worries. So, tell me: how may I be of service?"

"This tape. There's gotta be someone we can get it to. Like, someone at the Post or the Morning Tribune. You said it yourself— they're asking a lotta the same questions lately."

Tabby lowered her head. She crossed her arms and shook the tape in Lucy's direction.

"*This*, if memory serves, is a video of a couple blurry shadows breakin' into a church."

"A pretty beat up one, too."

"What? How? You said you just picked it up."

"Shit," Lucy said, rolling her eyes. "We don't all have fancy science degrees from KIT."

Tabby peeked into the cassette. The tape felt loose as her thumbnail played with reels.

"Also, as soon as we started watching it, the machine ate it."

Disgusted with the condition of the tape and distracted by the expanding conspiracy in its orbit, Tabby abandoned its physical appraisal.

"What do you mean *we*?"

"Well," Lucy said, voice climbing an octave as the word stretched. "Y'know. Me and a patient. A nursing home patient."

"Why are you screening video tapes of burglaries at a nursing home?"

"Because other than the one in the church's back office, the Fields was the only place nearby I knew had a VCR."

"Oh, ok," Tabby replied sarcastically. "Of course. Who doesn't enjoy movie night at the local nut house?"

"What can I say—can't talk me out of a good time. Anyway, how do you think I spent most of my career? And get this: there's this guy there, he catches me watchin' this tape—turns out he knows all about this spooky stuff."

"One of the patients at the Fields?"

"Yeah, so what?"

"Stop me if I'm missing anything: you've hunted me down and brought me a tape that shows the perp from the crime spree burglarizing a church—"

"Burglarizing the church *with an accomplice* the night before the shooting outside Hallelujah and the car crash."

"And now you and a mental patient wanna recruit me to help you *very publicly* blow up the official conclusion to the biggest crime story in the city in over a decade?"

"Right!"

"Lucy," Tabby sighed, "do you even know who the other person is on this tape? Have you looked into who you might be lumping into this? Vernon pinned the whole thing on a dead woman. Accused rightly or wrongly, dead women don't hold grudges."

"Not under normal circumstances, no."

"Unidentified, at-large murderers might be a different story. You're talking about rippin' the bandage off to bring some mystery men back into the mix?"

"When you put it that way, I guess you're right. Taking this directly to the news might be a bad idea."

Tabby handled the agreement with skepticism. Experience informed her the younger officer was unready to give up so easily.

"No," Lucy started again. "You're onto something. We need to track this other guy down ourselves first, figure out who we're dealin' with. Catch 'em doing the deed with our own eyes."

"That's not what I meant—"

"Well, how do we know it's *just* this guy? Remember when we saw Dexter Valerie?"

"Unfortunately, yes."

"And then who popped up a minute later a few feet away? His brother, Charlie. The kid I almost... the kid we saw get tossed from Hallelujah. And then, before we could even talk to him, that Ward chick comes peeling outta nowhere."

When Tabby had caught up to Lucy, she saw her partner and the assembled club kids, silently glaring at the same thing: Charlie Valerie. And the human skull by his feet. Tabby remembered the explosion, then the Camaro and the woman inside. Bethany Ward lead them on a chase across Brooklyn—lead them away from Charlie and Dexter. The same woman shouted something to the younger Valerie brother. It took a second of hesitation before his unkempt, long hair was fluttering in the breeze while he booked it down New Utrecht Avenue. Whether it was all the unwashed grease or the contrast of the pail flesh filling the boy's face, the color of his hair was almost too dark to be called blond. *'Mousy'* was the word Mrs. Dunwell used to describe the person she saw parked in front of her house.

"Lucy, I want to help you. I really do. But look where we are."

Her former partner responded with a literal check of her surroundings.

"What I meant was *in trouble*," she continued.

Lucy scoffed, fighting a grin away from one corner of her mouth.

"What's so funny about that?" Tabby howled.

"It's just... you never struck me as the type of person who let a punishment get under her skin. A hairbag, maybe..."

Tabby gnashed her teeth. She was losing patience again.

"But a *shakebox*, too? You're stuck on this post because some assholes planted you here without even hearing you out first, and you're still worried about what they might think. I know from experience: you don't get understanding by suffering in silence."

"Maybe I'm not interested in letting you get us *both* fired," Tabby snapped.

The evening grew late, but the sidewalk was still crowded. A few heads turned, intrigued by the police officer engaged in a long shouting match with the woman in plain clothes. Tabby's cheeks burned over her chafing collar and betrayed her embarrassment, or worse—her regret over the choice of words.

"Keep the tape," Lucy replied, exhaling heavily. "If you don't wanna sit down and watch it, that's your decision. I'll still do whatever I gotta do and you can tell anyone who asks that you had nothing to do with any of it. All I need from you is to take a good look at the cassette. Maybe try to fix the reels or whatever to keep it from jamming up again. It's evidence, right? Technically?"

"Technically, sure."

"So, it needs to be preserved. Other than that, we never spoke of it as far as I'm concerned. I won't get you burned. Again. And, I'm sorry. *Again*."

The sting returned to Tabby's eyes, and she was more determined than ever to keep it from showing. Her hand attempted another discrete brush, but it arrived too late. A damp trail tumbled down along the side of her nose.

"It's alright," Tabby mumbled as she ran the back of her thumb along the teardrop's path. "Yeah, I've got a dual deck at home. I can try to transfer it or something."

"Thank you."

"No problem."

The longer the conversation lingered, the harder Tabby had to bite the inside of her cheek.

"Listen, I'll get outta your hair now. You're busy with—" Lucy's voice dropped off. "You're busy."

Not awaiting a response, Lucy turned back toward the station's entrance. Tabby wanted to shout. She wanted to be able to apologize effortlessly—or effectively—as her younger peer had. She was afraid of the cracks that threatened to pierce the edges of her voice. Lucy saved her the effort and turned her head over her shoulder after a few steps.

"You should really try and find a place to warm up. Trust me. When the sun's gone for good, you'll need some kinda cover. If I'd had all these delis and grocery stores on my post, I wouldn't have had to make friends with so many mental patients. That was the second rule, right? Like you said: *'a good cop doesn't get cold.'*"

Alone again but for the storm raging in her mind, Tabby fought to keep order over a disparate abundance of thoughts. The guilt, still pressing down, did little to ease the mood. She cursed Lucy for refusing to let it all go. She cursed the poorly chosen words she could not take back. She cursed herself for failing. Tabby remembered Lucy running off after the collision. Her own injuries were not yet so severe to follow—at least, the surge of adrenaline would have prevented her holding back on account of them. Lucy survived whatever it was she thought she saw. If she was only chasing after things that were not really there, she faced little risk to her own safety. The knowledge their crazed gunner was safely DOA only a few feet from where Tabby stood mitigated much of the guilt of letting her partner off the leash. She chose not to follow. Instead, she raised her radio to her mouth. Lieutenant Cordell acknowledged. He followed the directions she transmitted and was able to track down Lucy before anything bad could happen. In retrospect, she was no longer confident in any of those presumptions. Not least among her regrets, Lucy absorbed so much of the lieutenant's ire when he did find her that it was difficult to still describe the way he came down on her as *nothing bad*. Yet, what Tabby found far more dire was that her ideas about the shadows and that which lurked within were no longer as certain. She saw the remains of Bethany Ward with her own eyes. She also witnessed a great deal of movement from the top of the wreckage which she could not explain. Rather than backpaddle, Lucy was planning to double down. She might be losing her marbles, but she shared none of Tabby's uncertainty.

Tabby did not need long to wonder what the present would have looked like if the shoe had been on the other foot. She was confident they would both be in search of a new line of work if Cordell had scooped them up, side-by-side and taking shots at ghosts beneath the Gowanus Expressway. All the same, Lucy would have been there. For better or worse, she would not have suffered a moment's hesitation to back her partner up, nor be left looking back for reasons to justify any.

Tabby felt it in her teeth. Pulsing, percussive chimes spilled around the corner of the next block. The noise reverberated down the street until it pulsated through her fillings. Jolted from troubling thoughts, her ears struggled to decode the distraction. Tabby's mind returned fully to her physical surroundings and the sound became obvious. Though it could be nothing other than an alarm bell, its tone was out of place. Out of time. A dozen curious footsteps later, Tabby caught herself. She strayed from her assigned post without any conscious effort. She sighed and grumbled aloud.

"Now who's leaping before they look?"

She pivoted to turn back toward the intersection behind her. 86th Street. Bay Parkway. Southwest corner. Only. The instructions had been made too simple to allow misinterpretation—willful or otherwise. Tabby reached for the radio on her belt. Her hand twisted the volume knob. She listened. Minutes passed and the dispatcher stayed silent. The antiquated call of the alarm rang with stubborn tenacity while the rest of the world refused to acknowledge. Tabby tried to block it out, let time wash the irritation away. She locked herself in a staring contest with the traffic signal suspended from the underside of the train tracks.

Green. Amber. Red.

City busses lumbered along while smaller vehicles jockeyed and shuffled into the slightest openings between them. Disinterested clusters of pedestrians passed Tabby. None of the customarily concerned citizenry approached her with any questions or cause to investigate further. The world around Tabby affected a seemingly universal deafness which she failed to enjoy.

Green. Amber. Red.

Tabby blinked. She sneered at the traffic signal. Whatever was happening around the corner behind her refused to subside on its own while it still failed to earn a call to emergency services. She sucked her teeth. Her hand swiveled the radio out of its holster, then paused. If she announced her response to the alarm job over as a spontaneous pick-up, the grave into which Cordell pushed her would be dug by her own hand.

Amber. Red. Amber.

Immediately before the crash and until they disappeared altogether, Tabby remembered the erratic lights along the entire length Fourth Avenue. The groaning wreckage of the silver Camaro shimmered and morphed, further twisted by the arrhythmic flickering.

Red. Amber. Red.

The shapes of the world stretched and cast long, exaggerated shadows past Tabby's feet. She exhaled. Her frustration hung in front of her in a cloud of steam.

Red. Amber. Green.

The steam from her mouth shimmered, traffic signal beams refracting as they passed through. When the escaped breath cooled and faded, a shiver trembled down her spine. Her rookie listened—*'a good cop doesn't get cold'*. Tabby wished she had been as good a partner. She wished she could think of a good reason to keep her feet glued to the sidewalk beneath her for the five hours remaining in her tour.

Red. Red. Red.

"Ah, fuck this."

The ringing refused to subside. Instead, it grew steadily. Block after block, Tabby homed in on its source. When she reached Bay 26th Street, the siren's pitched rattle jumped in volume. Tabby turned the corner and continued to follow the sound. She could not image a more typical block in this part of Brooklyn. Attached two-families. Lonesome, narrow shotguns. Four-story, brick tenements.

Over the course of hundreds of nights on patrol in the neighborhood, Tabby knew she must have passed down this one-way street countless times. When the aged Victorian rose in front of her, she stopped. If not fresh in condition, it appeared new to her memory. It was a foreign object, clearly predating all the neighbors Tabby recognized more firmly. It stood—or was it leaning?—into one corner of an unusually wide parcel of land, immune from development and division as it endured from some primordial era in the city's evolution. This building, apparently spared any of Tabby's second thoughts over the years, seemed to her ears to be the source of the chiming blast. The alarm continued to pour from a partially open entryway, even as its thunderous volume threatened to tear the decayed door frame apart. Unkempt inches of wilted, frozen, brown grass lie toppled and tangled, concealing a brick walkway beneath. At the edge of the lawn stood a sign, starkly newer than the wrought iron fence to which it was bound:

Future Site of Another
ONEIROLOGICAL COMMUNITY-REINTRODUCTION HOME
of Brooklyn, LLC.

With the alarm's blare monopolizing her sense of hearing, Tabby could only feel the crunch of neglected, overgrown grass beneath her boots as she approached the house's unlatched doorway. The sound itself warped with each step. Waves of noise flowed around Tabby—*through* her. They collided with the wall of houses across the street, then rebounded on a return trip through the sharp aches reawakening in her back. Every warble and trill spurred a spasm in her muscles while an invisible undertow drew her forward. Alternating steps carried Tabby across the yard and finer, infinitely recursive deterioration expressed in any surface she considered. Yellow and brown sheets of sun-parched, water-stained newspaper clung tight against the insides of windowpanes. Where no panes remained, inquiring eyes stumbled into dark, empty, rectangular voids. Thick, jagged peels of paint curled away from moldy clapboard siding. Tabby squinted. A gentle flutter swept back and forth over the front of the house. The loose curls of paint beckoned delicately. As her right foot planted itself atop the first step up to the porch, Tabby forced herself to stop and assess the landscape. She could not feel any breeze to attribute the wafting gyrations wafting across the house. Yet, in the still, cold air, and the fading daylight informing her eyes, they stirred endlessly. Tabby's hand rose to her face, index finger and thumb rubbing the sight away. With another sense temporarily diminished, the rumbling within her amplified. The tempo felt slower. The alarm shed its tinny, metallic ring and replaced it with the resonant jabs of a gigantic woodpecker. When Tabby reopened her eyes, the sickly mansion reemerged from behind fading, spinning black circles. The whole structure shivered and danced, stubborn as ever and announced to the world it had every intention to finally deconstruct itself on top of her—until all she could hear was the alarm's last ring washed away by a wall of silence. Tabby's body shuddered as the tremoring racket was torn away without warning and the massive house froze, stagnant and motionless, bound firmly to the earth.

Tabby stretched her jaw and forced air into her sinuses. Her ear drums popped, and her jaw clicked. From the base of the porch's stairs, she surveyed the area around the front door. Its already impressive scale from the street paled in comparison to its true stature. Beneath decades of accumulated grime, the double-doorway towered several feet over Tabby's head. It was wider than most modern entryways, but the height of each of its twin doors was excessive and gave the opening an illusion of being far narrower from a distance. Evidence of elegant plate glasswork still lined the matching doors. Mounted to the left-hand door was a profoundly tarnished, yet lush and leafy brass handle. Tabby took a step closer, climbing higher on the stairs. It appeared that the matching handle on the right side, on the door that sagged backward into the house's dim interior, had been removed with indelicate force. The empty screw holes dotting the unpainted silhouette of the missing fixture stared back at her. As the imprints left by the alarm gradually faded from Tabby's eardrums, she listened for any signs of activity on the other side. A moment before, she expected the house to come tumbling down from the commotion within. Continuing her careful climb and mounting the porch, the house betrayed naught but emptiness. Tabby reached out to the opened side of the doorway and applied pressure. Where the partially opened door rested, it exhibited no desire to budge any further. Tabby unhooked the flashlight from her belt and clicked it on. Before the beam breached the gap between the twin doors, she caught herself holding her breath. Tabby huffed at her apprehension, then continued. Light swiveled across the shrouded interior. The environment that shined back was expansive and barren. Sweeping the light back and forth, Tabby was forced to accept that the opening in the doors was too narrow to provide much of a view. The shadows within the house proved too deep for the distant Maglite and the search came to a halt. No objects, clutter, or unexpected movements came to light in Tabby's eyes, nor did any sounds of life to her ears. It was her nose that gave her pause. As Tabby had leaned forward, desperate for evidence of anything at all within the vacuous house, she braced herself for an odor of stale, protracted decay to match the overwhelming disrepair of the house's exterior. She expected the usual residue of human life and lifestyles, stale and forgotten. What flowed into her nostrils on a gentle breeze wafting out of the doorway, were sweet, fine particles of sawdust. A sneeze stabbed at the depths of Tabby's sinuses. She brought her hand to her septum to stifle it, but not quickly enough. Her attempt to block the sneeze instead amplified the noise. Tabby ducked and shuffled to the side of the doorway. She clamped her nostrils shut to fight off any accompanying, consecutive sneezes. It might not be enough, she realized—if whoever broke into the house remained therein, they were as free of the deafening alarm as she. They may already be closing in on the sound at their doorstep.

The gap between the tall, stubborn doors refused to provide easy passage for the surplus width added by Tabby's gun belt. Her flashlight bobbed in her right hand as she braced against the stuck door with her left. Slowly, carefully, she wiggled up and down. Squeezing forward, Tabby pushed herself past the threshold while keeping the handheld light pointed toward the uncharted space of the empty entryway hall on the other side. With one final twist and a contraction of her lungs, Tabby stumbled inside. Another wafting current greeted her as it made a departure through the opening. The air was a mix of mellow, older wood, underscored by the slightly different odor of freshly sawn lumber. As these subsided, there were deeper notes that landed on the back of Tabby's tongue and throat. Almond and vanilla aromas reminded her of the stacks of books fermenting in her college's library, while the accompanying odors of the receding, nighttime tide were a peculiar paring.

Tabby waited by the doorway, orientating herself as she continued to listen for company. All she heard was a draft passing between empty chambers. Nearest to satisfaction as Tabby expected she would arrive, her flashlight continued to probe the house's depths. The floor was completely cleared of furniture, as it also was of any other evidence of human habitation. A slight sheen still covered the wooden floors. Particles of dust drifted past her, though they did not appear to accumulate on any visible surface. Tabby moved forward and examined the walls. Every inch was clad in ornate wooden panels which rose to come flush with similarly trimmed ceilings. It was clear the edges and joints of the panels had warped some over the past century, though they remained almost entirely unblemished. In places, sharper rectangles and squares contrasted with the rest of the surface to imply the more recent removal of long-hung wall decorations. Holes and perforations were evidence of spots previously fit for gas lights and electrical fixtures. Archways on either side of the hall opened into empty sitting rooms, dining rooms, and other chambers whose original utility were erased with little obvious intent toward redesignation. Vacant as the house seemed in the light which led Tabby deeper, there were no signs of neglect or abandonment shared with the exterior. The only non-structural object she could find still hung to one of the walls—a great, wide, metallic frame covered beneath a thin, white sheet. Tabby stepped closer and picked at a corner of the covering. Her thumb and index finger rose to reveal a large mirror centered in a faintly tarnished silver frame. She let the cloth drift back down and turned. Opposite the hanging mirror was another opening in the hallway, and beyond that a vast, empty room. When the beam of Tabby's flashlight proceeded along the floorboards and through the archway, it was swallowed by an abrupt abyss replacing most of the room's floor. She traced a path around the edges of the room. Clean and freshly cut, the portal looked down onto the basement level below. A narrow walkway of aged, gray floorboards and support beams trimmed the room, enduring as a balcony to encircle the perimeter. It occurred to Tabby that this room once served as the manor's kitchen. Imprints of cupboards and counters, antiquated cooking appliances and food pantries pocked the walls. Unlike the rest of the house, this room did not lack for clutter. Tabby moved closer to the floor's edge and searched the unfinished, earthen ground level below. A breeze blew up and across her face, damper and more mineral in odor than before. That which smelled fresh and oceanic earlier was quickly becoming stagnant and marshy. She felt a few, larger bits of dust kick up at her until the long, steady gust faded and passed by. Gas and Diesel-powered machinery occupied much of the basement floor. A large storm generator was strung to clusters of power cables, and the entire assembly was ringed by portable floodlamps. Tabby's eyes reached the center of the room just as a much stronger gust entered. It carried another strong wave of maritime odors, followed by a faint, breathy groan. Not as large as the hole carved into the kitchen's floor, a second, circular opening in the ground lie at the focal point of the construction equipment below. The wind continued to billow from the pit, growing heavier and less patient. After a brief lull, another wave of air emerged from the ground.

The edge of the opening was formed by a circle of dull, stone bricks from which a tight ring of spiraling steps descended into darkness. Over the few feet Tabby's flashlight would show her, the masonry's style became more elaborate as it descended. Asymmetrical carvings caught the light, contrasting and eventually replacing altogether the neater, more traditional lines. The sight grew more chaotic every inch it sank, until any semblance of manmade masonry was lost—all form and shape coagulated seamlessly into the bedrock itself.

The wind blew in uninterrupted waves, pressing against Tabby and causing her to rock. Lost in the ebbing, flowing howl, she was startled by a creak beneath her feet. Tabby pulled her flashlight away from the exhaling pit. The tips of her boots hung nearly half an inch over the edge of the severed floorboards, though she had no memory of any conscious effort on her part to bring them there. Remarkably well-preserved as she had found the house, the floorboards were not originally designed for such dramatic alterations. Another creak escaped the boards. Tabby felt her center of gravity shift. She tried to overcompensate, making circular motions with one arm and then the other to swing herself back over the edge. As she lurched backward, the flashlight spun up and out of her right hand. She kicked up one of her feet, then twisted ninety degrees. The flashlight came spinning back down just as her left hand passed by. She pulled both hands toward her body and gripped the Maglite tight to her chest. Both of her feet came back down onto firm ground. Relieved to have not been swallowed up by the earth itself, she took a deep breath. Louder and from somewhere deeper, a redoubled blast of frozen air roared out of the ground. Tabby's nose and lungs filled with acrid, chemical exhaust. She found her mind overtaken by a conglomerated stench—still wells poisoned by sulfur and saline, the bloat of decaying organic life, and uncontrolled chemical fires. The balance she fought to regain fled on the wind as it needled through every exposed pore on her skin. Despite reasserting control on the flashlight, the world went black. Tabby's eyes rolled backward. All that remained was the sound of the bellowing, respirating pit. A nasal cry joined the atonal, earthen pipe organ as Tabby struggled to relocate herself. From the depths, riding the wind to the surface, came the bleat of a goat. Tabby grabbed her chest. She felt herself begin to fall. As both the soles of her boots clapped down onto the wooden floorboards, her flashlight came loose from her hand once more. She was unable to react as quickly this time. Her eyes cleared to reveal a Maglite suspended in the air, spinning end-over-end in an arc toward the center of the room. When its spin slowed, its plummet accelerated. The circular walls of the tunnel flashed briefly as it inhaled the wobbling ball of light. Tabby watched a face emerge on the surface of every ornate brick. They exchanged glances with one another, then turned to laugh and jeer at her misfortune. When the Maglite's faded completely, darkness filled the room. Tabby stifled a gasp. She listened for any report to indicate the flashlight reached the bottom of the broad well. Long as she waited, there was no sound aside her own irregular breaths.

Tabby lost track of time until she noticed her own shadow stretching out in front of her. A glow was building in the hallway she passed to enter the kitchen. Her heart sank as she became conscious of her exposure. Tabby spun to catch a glimpse of whomever approached. On the wall of the hallway, opposite the kitchen and beneath the cloth draped protectively over its frame, the mirror caught the glare of some pure, white light. The air continuing to billow out of the ground tugged at the edges of the sheet. Ripples danced higher through the white sheet until the entire covering was lifted over the top of the frame. Tabby watched pure terror fill the face of her own reflection. She saw the glow form a halo around her figure, then reduce it to a thin silhouette. Behind her, the earth groaned louder than ever. The goat cried again. A turbulent, chaotic symphony of shifting, cyclonic notes battered the room. The light in the mirror eclipsed her entirely and a new figure lurched forward. Its face stared down at her—a bald man, with piercing, black eyes, covered in sheer cloth bright enough to have been sewn from strands of light itself. It spun around him in a white blaze, twisting high over his head and then arcing down toward the pit in the ground. Tabby's throat burned. Her lungs ached from screaming.

By the time Tabby regained any semblance of linear thought, her feet stumbled to a stop at the edge of Bath Avenue. She turned the corner and collapsed, taking cover against the wall of a shuttered pharmacy.

"Shit."

It was the first word her numbed vocal cords managed to articulate. She let her diaphragm stretch and then relax. A sliver of sunlight peeked at her over a rooftop to the west. She held up her wrist and pulled the sleeve of her jacket back to reveal her wristwatch: *7:15 P.M.*

"You've gotta be kiddin' me. Four hours left…"

Sergeant Darling cradled a phone against his face. He appeared more beleaguered than usual. Behind the precinct's main desk, the tip of his pen hovered over a piece of notepaper. He looked up from the desk to include Tabby in his puzzlement.

"I'm taking lost time," Tabby announced.

"Uh," Darling stuttered into the receiver. "Sorry, boss. I'll be with you, one sec."

The sergeant pulled the phone away from his face and held a hand over the receiver.

"Wait, you good? Aren't you supposed to be on that foot post?"

"Fuck that noise. I'm leaving early."

Tabby continued toward her locker room without slowing her stride.

"But, what about—"

Darling was lost. After a moment, he looked back at the phone and shrugged.

"Alright then. No, no. It was nothing. Back up for me, just a little bit. This waitress—you're saying you think we've got a missing person on top of that whole mess over on Eighteenth Avenue?"

Sixteen

"And that is why, my brothers and sisters, when you say that you are lost, remember that you need only look to one place. In dreams, the truth of your innermost desires stands naked, while the soul communicates in total honesty with the universe. Without shame, without guilt. But you will not get there counting sheep, as many little, lost sheep as there are to be counted. No, only the unreserved trust and vulnerability of your own essence, face-to-face and starborne amidst the glorious, infinite cosmic ocean. As the first Awoken memorialized:

"There are truths which bring men comfort,
and truths which rend soul from mind.
Planes of ashen cities top the rising depths
to where the lost are drawn,
Where dreams fill opened eyes
when no escape their souls can find.
Awakened, walking, dreaming—
it tears away thy temper,
And raises the Kingdom 'neath the Midnight Dawn.

"As you know, the practice of *Chthonics* does not exclude any other faith or creed. Many of you will spend this coming Sunday celebrating the resurrection of Christ. While you do, I ask that you keep your own spiritual resurrections in mind—by which I mean the resurrections *of* your minds. In my own dreams, I have witnessed the approach of that very Midnight Dawn. A great awakening, foretold as I have read, will bear to you its first glimpse at the height of darkness before the sun rises on Easter morning. Thus, I must implore you, do not lay your heads down to rest Saturday night lest you imperil your own awakening. Instead, at the precise minute of the night's zenith, at 12:55 A.M., fix your gaze toward the sky. Lend your eyes to the world over our own. Bare your soul to the watching universe. Open your mind and receive its ancient knowledge."

Waves of heat radiated from the lighting array. Dexter stood behind the camera, reflective umbrellas angled to photographic lights on either side. Even shrouded in the darkness beyond their respective beams, he felt their warmth searing the sides of his face. Copious, soft light diffused from the pair of lamps and splashed a uniform luminescence over Doctor Martin Glass and the theatrical approximation of an office behind him. The rest of the Oneirological Process Mission's garage remained, like Dexter, steeped largely in darkness.

"I pray you will join me, my brothers and sisters, whether you are right here in Brooklyn or among our growing number of communities across the globe. We are humbled by your expanding outreach efforts and ever-generous contributions—so much, in fact, that you will find a copy of the second and newest edition of *Chthonics* accompanying this video tape."

Dexter watched Glass lean forward, rising slightly in the monitor's frame. He shifted his weight away from the stately, mahogany desk against which he rested to converse with his audience waiting on the other end of the supply chain. Without breaking eye contact, he moved around to the back of the desk and approached the shelves full of books which lined the backdrop.

It was a fairly simple job, Dexter reflected. Keep the camera in focus. Follow the Doctor's movements. It beat licking stamps. He rubbed the tip of his tongue against the roof of his mouth, probing for friction burns. Glass assured him the new copies of *Chthonics* would not overnight themselves. Lately, he eschewed regular sleep for emptying batches of second editions, fresh from the printer. Dexter divided the books, then repacked them for individual trips to every corner of the country. Since the predawn trip he shared with Doctor Glass to Eighteenth Avenue, he had yet to find enough time to sneak in a nap. The lens remained centered on Glass as he gestured to the neat rows of spines.

"Each of these cassettes and the included books will also ship with expanded ministerial instructions, allowing you to spread our blessed, glorious wisdom with those disillusioned souls, so urgently in need of salvation."

Something rustled in the darkness behind the backdrop. Dexter looked over the viewfinder and squinted. In the back of the Mission's dim garage, a pair of shadows struggled with a wheel bin. Stacks of manila envelopes, sealed and post-office-bound, rattled atop the container's brim. Dexter shook his head at their efforts to pull the container up the loading dock's ramp. There were a lot of strange faces around Glass's repurposed theater these days. Demand for his vision of universal wisdom and existential serenity peaked with the sensational wave of panic dominating the public's consciousness. A greater share of Dexter's time was devoted to logistical mundanity, and it did not help that Dexter was left to shoulder the work without Bethany. Once again, as in countless times throughout the day, he found his mind stuck on her. The frayed wires connecting his brain's receptors and the channels forged by chemical dependence could not remember how to function without either alcohol or Bethany. Her absence was everywhere, including in Glass's increasing demands and increasingly expressed disappointment.

"Until next time, as you stand strong against cruelty and decadence, you must ask yourselves: where will the voice of cosmos find your mind when it calls for you? As always, I bid you good night, my brothers and sist—"

One of the nameless shadows made an untimely dash toward the spotlight fixed on Doctor Glass, but it was the overladen bin which reached the set first. Glass jumped a moment before the modular office wall and its ersatz bookshelves tumbled. The many neat rows of *Chthonics* spines didn't budge. Dexter had hot-glued the fake book spines to the set's shelves himself. His handiwork was sturdy, and it remained sturdy as it cracked straight through the broad desk aside which Glass perched his elbows atop seconds earleir. The likeness of mahogany split apart. A thin layer of dark, spiral grains printed onto cheap laminate ripped and tore to expose the bright tan particle board within. Wood chips, sawdust, and the resin once binding them into the shape of a desk scattered across the garage's floor. Glass pulled himself up and surveyed the damage. His attention turned next to the pair who lost control of the careening bin. The doctor said nothing. After a moment, the two began scurrying to reload the dozen or so packages which had flown loose upon impact.

"Please do not tell me that you are still using up my film to record this, Mr. Valerie."

Dexter stared for a moment, then jumped. He reached for the camera and jabbed at the controls to stop the recording.

"I'm sorry, Martin. Doctor. I can see if the backdrop held up after the—," Dexter stammered as he slowly approached the wreckage. "Well, I guess we can try another take for that last line if I keep it up real close and tight—"

"You have run out of time for that."

Dexter stopped immediately. Glass seldom let impatience show.

"You will perform tonight's duties and then you will edit away this… interruption… without me when you are done. It is vital to our next ritual that the transfer from Elysian Fields succeed without any further disappointments. You *can* bring a bus to a filling station without causing a disaster, can you not? Or did you require the guidance of Ms. Ward for as simple a task as that?"

The name took the wind out of Dexter's lungs. He had been momentarily distracted, but Martin Glass resurrected her in his mind.

"Yes, sir," Dexter croaked. "I'll get it done."

"It has been a very disappointing day, Mr. Valerie. I certainly hope that the remainder of the day improves for both of us."

Dexter's fingernails dug into the palms of his hands. He felt the shakes begin. Glass stared at him. Appraised him. When Dexter willed the shaking to subside, his hands relaxed.

"We all have our trials, Mr. Valerie," Glass continued, his voice returning to its baseline, aloof calmness. "Mine appears to be that I am left to unshackle the universe and usher in its rebirth with a sentimental child for an assistant. You mourn Ms. Ward, as does the entire Mission. You are not alone in feeling at a loss right now."

"I'm sorry, Doctor Glass. I can do better. I *will* do better."

"I trust that you will," Glass said, laying a hand on Dexter's shoulder. "And I trust that you can prove to me that the liability I have come to associate with your family is limited only to your brother."

Dexter had not seen Charlie in weeks. Other senses, however, made him question how estranged the two had really become.

"His carelessness, his abuse of my generosity and trust, may have cost you a lover, but it cost me a valuable protégé—a pupil in whom I invested years of tutelage. If you wish to prove your worth to me—your worth to *yourself*—I need not spell out what must be done. As the Midnight Dawn rises, as it erases the resurrection of the dead God from living memory, countless, tortured souls will find themselves filing the swelling currents of the arriving maelstrom. For you to include him in this sacrifice will be your ultimate act of redemption, and your most fraternal demonstration of mercy."

"I will… I will do as you command."

Dexter wheezed. His voice choked, treading a flood of emotions and an irrepressible compulsion toward devotion. The words, rote and repeated, over and over, came flooding out routinely as a breath.

"May you and the coming darkness forgive my weakness."

"All worlds must sink," Glass whispered.

"And raise the Kingdom beneath the Midnight Dawn," Dexter affirmed.

"It took me thirteen years to fix the mistakes of those I last entrusted. Thirteen years to arrange all of this. I will not be subject to any repeat embarrassment, nor will I be merciful as I have in the past to those who embarrassed me."

"Did you really see it, Doctor?"

Dexter was desperate to change the subject. He was more desperate not to consider the clear threat made against his own mortality or the impending burden of fratricide. A rare look of surprise emerged on Glass's face and made Dexter forget either.

"See what, Mr. Valerie?"

"The Midnight Dawn. The universe told you it's really gonna happen?"

Martin Glass looked like he was about to laugh, though the amusement quickly disappeared with a roll of his eyes.

"Rapture is the consequence of creation, my dear boy, but the universe is meandering as it is timeless. If you want your dreams to come true, take such things upon yourself lest old age take you first."

Martin walked past Dexter and continued to speak.

"In turning my dreams into reality, I must trust you to be my right hand, Dexter. But more fool the man unwilling to sever his right hand to secure victory for the rest of him."

As a consequence of its seniority at the intersection of Bay Parkway and 86th Street, decades of operation had been unkind to Ultimo Delicatessen. Dexter approached its lowered roll-down gate, angular and lopsided beneath a few remaining strips of crime scene tape flailing on the breeze. Despite the weeks which passed since he last saw Charlie next to the store's deceased cashier, the business appeared reluctant to attempt a comeback. A few yards away, a beat cop braced her foot against the side of one of the columns holding up the elevated train stop. She looked familiar to Dexter, but decades of run-ins left too many interactions into which she could be singled. The brass numbers on her jacket's collar betrayed her to the Six Four. If there was a single cop assigned to the command who had not visited his father's house over the years, they probably had not been around for too long. With the potential for identification in mind, Dexter wondered if she had been briefed on the faces of any persons of interest. For the moment, her newspaper appeared more interesting. Dexter had yet to receive any official inquiries concerning either his brother's whereabouts after visiting Ultimo's or his own presence at the scene of the murder within. All the same, he had not sought to invite any such inquiries, nor had he made himself available at the mailing address he previously shared with Bethany. Even if the apartment did not torment him with her memory, obligations to Doctor Glass precluded him leaving the Mission for long enough to reach its front door.

Despite himself, Dexter supposed his troubled, younger brother might have finally figured out how to maintain a low profile.

Disappearing altogether would have been the wisest decision. There was another possibility altogether to explain why Charlie had yet to resurface. It was one Dexter regretfully placed more weight behind based on his brother's history and the hunger in his eyes when they last parted ways. The bountiful cache of narcotics stashed inside Ultimo's—and liberated from its late proprietor— may have already accomplished that which the doctor charged Dexter. If a body had turned up, Dexter had yet to hear. New York City was home to more John Does than any other place in America. By the time they finally reached the potter's field on Hart Island, the story of the journey which had brought them there was lost with their names.

In either event, unless the vacant store itself woke up and started rattling off clues, Dexter would receive no new information from the last space the two brothers shared. Tired echoes of locomotive brake pads bounced off the canopied roadway as a train overhead came screeching into a brief stop on its way to Coney Island. The cop flicked at her newspaper, then lifted her head to scan huddled passengers pressing impatiently down worn steel steps. His feet never risked the chance of the rest of him being spotted among the crowd's other faces. Instead, they carried him westward, further down 86th Street. Other kin, with whom Dexter found himself even more reluctant to invite confrontation, were his only bet. If anyone had come looking for Charlie, or to deliver news of an untimely death, they would have the same destination in mind. Dexter wondered if the old man who lived there was enjoying his solitude. He wondered if Adam Valerie discovered any peace in the abandonment he finally succeeded in beating out of his family.

Dexter let the steady flow of marching commuters carry him down the block until he peeled away onto the side street. None joined to jostle beside him, but he maintained their hurried pace. The many-numbered Bay streets bore through Bath Beach toward southern ends and an artificial shoreline formed from the dredged bay floor and other forgotten refuse turned landfill. As Dexter neared his father's solitary, ground-level tenancy, the road guided him past the statelier address of Martin Glass. In actuality, the structure had not served as a residence for Glass in over a decade. Passed down through his family for generations, back to the first builders of the resort neighborhood along Bath Beach, the plot was little more than a vestigial limb clinging to the greater body of the Mission's functions. Now, as the stark, new sign secured to the estate's warped wrought iron fence announced, it had been nominally rebranded as a new kind of rehabilitation facility. Dexter was still unsure what differentiated the newly re-registered

Oneirological Community Reintroduction Home from the rest of the city's decentralized network of halfway homes. If nothing else, he was certain those others did not serve as one-way entrances to a literal oblivion.

Dexter reminded himself of the fullness of his own schedule. He was no closer to tracking down Charlie and Glass still demanded he oversee the transfer of additional patients from a nearby facility to this house over the course of the approaching night. The structure's lifeless, deceptive exterior stared back at him. It gave away little of the picture within—or below. The remaining chunk of Dexter's life yet to be monopolized by Martin Glass had been consumed by the operation taking place within the bowels of the mansion. The doctor preached that there were unseen channels winding their way through the universe, conduits for the tremendous power of timeless forces. Outer space and Brooklyn had quite a bit in common. A little less dirt and a great deal of perspiration rejoined the house on Bay 26th to another network. Maps and mapmakers were quick to erase the many discreet pinpoints plotted throughout the tumult of what was once an emergent, churning landscape. Deep, material arteries lie buried beneath the conscious world, mirroring the cosmic architecture above. Dexter stopped. He closed his eyes. The ground breathed once more. It was humbling. When he lost himself to drinking—nearly forever—he had been blind to the immensity of all things hidden beneath the surface. Doctor Glass had brought Dexter a clearer vision not long after he opened his eyes to the glaring fluorescence of Gravesend General's emergency wing.

A gust wrapped itself around Dexter, not for lack of any effort to slice straight through him. The odor it carried made him reopen his eyes. The breeze faded, but the smell lingered. It came not as a gale travelling down the canyon of the city street. Dexter had walked in through the front door of Glass's house earlier that day, after the clean-up on Eighteenth Avenue. He dropped off a guest, but he did not make the same return trip. After tying up that particular loose end in the house's expanding depths, he made use of the tunnels winding throughout the neighborhood to reemerge in the basement of the Mission itself without returning topside. Now, existential dread bore into Dexter's own depths and rivalled the ferocity of his first sober glimpse at the true spirit of the world. The house's entryway was missing a doorknob.

Three strides brought a muffled shoe atop the first crumbled, concrete step. Another singular leap raised Dexter fully onto the porch.

"I locked the fucker," Dexter mumbled to himself. "Yeah. Bolted it tight before I brought her down."

He stared at the entrance. The set of double doors stood firmly closed within their frame. There were no signs of distress around the edges. His attention stayed locked to the pair of empty, round boreholes in the rightmost door. Formerly occupied by the deadbolt which Dexter used to secure the premises not two hours before, they now whistled as icy drafts streamed outward. Dexter held his breath and listened. The door was still shut tight. If the girl busted out, she would not waste time closing it behind her. Still, the higher air pressure within might have closed it for her as she booked it. Dexter thought about the cop, foot kicked back as she read the newspaper. He thought about the Six Four. The precinct's stationhouse was only a few blocks away, no more than a minute's jog. Dexter allowed himself to exhale. He did not hear any sirens.

If the girl had escaped, the consequences would be dire—and swift. Dexter's worry over the possibility subsided, but his mind soon found new paranoias to entertain. It might have been a squatter or punk kids looking to devote an afternoon to vandalism, if any of either remained unrecruited by Glass. Maybe a nosey member of the press was investigating the entire Oneirology organization. No matter the reason someone might have forced entry into Glass's false front, it would be problematic to let such a breach go uninvestigated. Dexter turned, pleading with his muscles to execute the steady motions his mind ordered. There were no signs of movement along the street. No cops. No unmarked cars waiting to pinch him. His lungs returned to normal operation, if somewhat subdued. A few cautious steps closer to the house, eyes still scanning the roadway. Dexter's hand found the door. A finger wriggled into the hole formerly filled by an ancient brass doorknob. Not even a little heartbroken, Dexter gave up on any reunions with Adam Valerie. Only the lingering task of locating Charlie nagged at his mind.

The door always stuck. As intended, ingress and egress were not meant to be easy. A view of a dim interior hallway widened before him. The air within the house was damp and desperate to escape. It made the most of the gap between the doors as he slid past the edge of the vacuum. He gave his eyes time to adjust. He knew the layout of the three story, twenty-room house as well as any among the succession of one-to-two bedroom apartments he had been lugged to and fro throughout his childhood. Not until the first time Dexter stepped inside Martin Glass's house did he understand how much stillness and quietude such a cavernous abode could afford.

The nearest functional lights were concentrated in the depths beneath the former kitchen, surrounded by the rest of the heavy equipment and generators. Dexter did not need his full vision to navigate the house, but as his eyes adjusted, a particularly foreign newcomer fluttered in the limited light. Glass removed nearly all the unnecessary furniture throughout the building. One exception was an abundance of mirrors. Every wall featured one, bare of obstructions and polished clean. Glass always wanted to be able to see over his own shoulder.

"When you are trafficking with ghouls," Dexter remembered him saying, *"you must provide yourself every advantage."*

One of the most imposing mirrors rested on the wall opposite the room formerly housing the kitchen. Most of the floor within had been carved out to form a provisional mezzanine for the excavations taking place on the basement floor. There was much to fear emerging from that pit. As such, Glass installed the broadest reflective measure to monitor the opening. Dexter approached cautiously. The ornate, tarnished silver frame still boasted its etched, floral pattern through the white sheet of cloth surreptitiously draped over the mirror's entire length. A protective gesture in any other context, in this place the tarp was an obstruction neither he nor Glass would have introduced. They knew the risks of blocking the mirror's view. So too did whomever covered it.

Amidst compounding anxieties, Dexter nearly forgot the dangerous realities of either an escape or intrusion into the place by mortal forces. His hand rose and grabbed at the sheet. As Dexter's shoulders twisted to rip it down, one hand grabbed his chest. The next grabbed his stomach. He looked down. In the limited light of the broad hallway, he could not see where the shadow's claws ended and its dark limbs began. Dexter's fingers slipped away from the edge of the sheet before they could yank it free. The bottoms of his shoes flew out in front of him as the arms lifted him in a death grip. For a moment, Dexter was a foot above the floorboards and hurtling backwards into the kitchen. His stomach soon turned as he watched his view sink lower, down past the edges of sawn kitchen floorboards and into the impossibly darker basement below. His fingernails tore at the arms binding his torso until they sprang outward to release him mid-flight. Dexter's back slammed into the exposed, earthen floor. A cloud of soot kicked up around him. Free again, his diaphragm quivered and expanded, filling his lungs with dusty, moldy air. He hacked and wheezed. Tears streamed from the sides of his eyes, vision muddied by the settling century-old detritus. Stilted, panicked thoughts filled his head with orders.

The lights. The generator.

Dexter stumbled. The circular, stone hole in the ground yawned. His thoughts were straight enough to be weary of accidentally tripping over its edge on his own. Something, whatever it was, had already succeeded in flinging him across the room once. Coughing and floundering as he was, his disoriented state would not make a toss into the pit too difficult.

Dexter's left shin slammed into the side of the diesel generator. He gritted his teeth through the added pain, grabbed for the primer, and yanked. A pathetic mechanical stutter echoed across the cavernous room. As the generator's pistons turned over into a low rumble, electricity spread out to the floodlights positioned in the room's corners. The sudden glare mixed with the sediment still caking Dexter's tears. His fingernails clawed at his own face, wiping dirt away and massaging the muscles of his eyelids to relax. Everything in the room glowed, save the black pit groaning in its center. The dull, ebony stones lining the opening refused to give any luster under any circumstances . Adrift in a haze of dust and disoriented terror, Dexter frantically surveyed the periphery. The industrial lighting revealed no attacker. He coughed again, gathering dirt and saliva, and cleared his nostrils. Dexter's spit splattered onto the ground. He walked backward and slowly guided his back closer to the nearest wall. When the heels of his shoes tapped against the edge of the wall, he leaned back. A rusty utility panel jabbed his shoulder. Dexter turned to look at the metal box to orientate himself. It was the house's old alarm box. The round bell in the middle could have benefitted from polishing, Dexter realized. When he turned back to the center of the room, he traced the edges of the flood lights' beams. Two beams from opposing light rigs passed a few feet in front of him, but did not completely illuminate the corner in which he rested. Beyond that, there was no evidence he was anything other than alone.

The joints in Dexter's hands ached. His fingernails clawed deeply to get whatever seized him to release its grip. He stretched his fingers to loosen their joints, then pulled them up to his face for inspection. A crack split the nail on his index finger. Each of the others looked to Dexter as though he dipped them in a puddle of oil or black paint. He looked over at the spot where he landed after being pulled down from the upper level. Specks of dust still settled to the ground. There were no obvious pools of spilt liquids to be seen. Dexter looked back at his hands. The crevices beneath and alongside the beds of his fingernails were stained. He raised his hands to his nose. It felt dry as he brushed beneath his nostrils. Dexter stretched his arm toward the light. His hand entered the beam and confirmed there not a single spot of blood on his hands. Beyond the edge of his glowing skin, less than a foot in front of him, the shadows stirred. Dexter's hand shot back to brace his chest as a column of darkness rose. The silhouette of a head and shoulders blotted out the light. There was a face in front of Dexter. He squinted.

"Charlie?"

The generator choked and sputtered. Beams of light retreated into their respective metal lamps and invited darkness to blanket the room once more. Dexter's lungs nagged at the bottom of his throat. No air came to fill them. He grabbed the first thing his hand could find, but the rusty alarm's switch could not hold him for long. The clattering bell rang out and his feet were off the ground again. Cold, damp air screamed past his ears. The sensation in the pit of his stomach told him he was losing altitude. The alarm's cry faded overhead, while the sounds of waves crashing against rocks echoed up from the bottom of the long, vertical pipe below. There was no light to fade from Dexter's vision. He was only briefly aware of the approach of unconsciousness when he felt the gasps fill his lungs with water.

Seventeen

It dried with the blood under the nail and soaked deep into Apollo's cuticles. Digging and digging until the sun rose turned the stains black as ink. As it tended, the dirt got everywhere else, too—in his mouth, up his nose—but the stains on his hands were always the meanest to wash out. Apollo growled and cursed every bastard who ever went and left their blood there.

The knife traced the nailbed of his ring finger and discovered the rare nerve yet to callous over. Fresh blood welled up and overran the grime he had been picking at. He turned the blade over and dug into the thick, dark arc embedded beneath the nail's tip. Apollo watched the knife's edge on the underside. Clean steel pushed aside the caked filth. He never trimmed them. They seldom extended too far on their own, instead worn to flat, blunt ends over the course of Apollo's daily routine. Bits of the gory mixture that dried on his hands drifted down to the floorboards. Before joining the pile between Apollo's leather boots, the black flecks fluttered through the thin bands of sunlight that squeezed through his studio apartment's window blinds. High noon. On the last Saturday of July, the Marlboro Houses baked and the stagnant, humid air outside refused to clear the haze clogging the skyline. Apollo kept it dark as possible. He did not care for electric fans or air conditioners that could be pushed in by unwelcomed guests. The apartment's total of three windows remained locked tight all year round. Dust undulated in lethargic ribbons through the natural beams of light, joined by the speckled evidence of a violent, early grave that emitted a rustier luster as it flaked through.

Apollo's pupils ran away from him. He forced his eyelids wider. Sleep was inevitable, if never desirably restful. Glass was running them all dry, more demanding than ever. Their cool and collected guru had also become unexpectedly explicit with his policy toward the land surveyor from Scarsdale. Money was short. Time was short. The excavations in the old aqueduct in Yonkers never moved quickly as the Doctor wished. When Martin learned that the man was planning to pack up his happy little family and run, the coffin earned its last nail.

Intimidation had not worked. Apollo knew it would not. He glanced at the telephoto lens pointing toward him from atop his dresser. In a warped, black reflection, a pair of lifeless eyes stared back beneath a scalp pulled back into a greasy ponytail of bundled black hair. Apollo offered his efforts a critique.

"I got too close. Too soft."

Lately, every meeting at Glass's house served as an introduction to an expanding circle of sycophants. New faces—faces which reminded Apollo he was not getting any younger. The same passage of time seemed to elude Martin Glass, who looked fresh as ever, if more distracted and impatient. Thusly, the instructions were imparted without any pause for input from Martin's closest and earliest follower. Worse, he found himself volunteered to the task with unrequested assistance. Another local freak appearing out of nowhere with a suspiciously chummy attitude toward Glass, hair buzzed into a mohawk and an upper lip framed by brown peach fuzz to simulate a moustache. The type of punk Apollo used to get drunk and stomp back west just for fun. Martin handed down the orders and then abruptly turned away before Apollo could protest. Mr. Weber had been declared delinquent, already made part of a promise—a dark and intimate covenant—payable toward Glass's own debts. After the meeting, Apollo wondered if the man from Scarsdale was the only person about whom Martin experienced a change of heart. Now, as he picked the blood from his nails, he knew it did not matter anymore. The job did not go as Martin wished, and there would be no mystery where either man stood.

"The whole bunch of 'em," the kid in the passenger seat crowed. "Glass wants 'em to choke on their own blood after the last light turns out."

By the time they reached Scarsdale, Apollo's jaw ached from being clenched tight throughout the evening drive. Every bouncing fidget, every sneer and boast that left his understudy's acne-ringed mouth drove a jagged spike into Apollo's brain. The car idled by the side of the road, a few houses down and at the peripheral edge of the oblivious Webers. The sun was getting lower. Night approached. The unwitting premium of Martin's latest deal pulled into the driveway. He stopped on his way up the house's front steps to check the mailbox. Along with a couple of letters, he withdrew a thick manilla envelope. Apollo sighed. He visited the home earlier without the company of Glass's loyal, little helper, and shuffled the envelope in among the regular Friday mail. In addition to a year's worth of reconnaissance photos, Apollo included a letter addressed to Mr. Weber. Apollo did not rely on a clever command of written words to motivate people. He was confident any spelling errors or grammatical lapses contained therein would not prevent a simple message coming across. The man hesitated. He turned over the yellow package with no return address or postmark. Apollo read his mind, knew he wanted to check the world over his shoulder. Weber resisted. With shoulders angled a little lower, he walked up the stairs. The man opened the door and greeted his family like the loving father he still was.

When the sun crossed the horizon, Glass's prize geek was running mercifully low on hot air. An hour passed since Apollo last offered so much as a grunt to acknowledge the younger man's idle idiocy. A full moon emerged. The world's geometry shifted. The hazy glow of liminal space mixed into the summer sky, washing away the last red, horizontal bands. Apollo counted the windows on the side of the Weber's house. Some were dark. Others beamed. One flashed. The report echoed out from the top floor and interrupted the chirps of crickets and cicada.

"What the fuck… didya' see that? Something's goin' on in there."

The stooge was apoplectic. Apollo did not flinch.

"No more waitin'! We gotta wipe the rest of 'em out, an' hope Glass doesn't—"

Apollo did not have to listen to any more of the nasally adolescent's words. The glovebox reported a wet thump a moment later to confirm as much. Smoke drifted into the dark vacuum that followed the intense flash of light within the car. Apollo's ears rang. Wisps of smoke flattened and soaked into the car's drooping cloth ceiling. A damp, sticky vapor settled as a thin dew across the remaining surfaces of the car and its occupants. The solitary light of the radio glowed at the corner of Apollo's vision. Its noise began to leak back into his ears. So too did the rips appearing around the edges of suburban serenity. The clamor transcended and expanded, pleading for the chords which a desperate pair of mortal lungs could never fully oblige. The walls of the Webers' home trembled amidst the pressures of freshly discovered trauma within. Apollo's car lurched. The body next to him skidded toward the door. Hands and arms performed a precise, mechanical U-turn. Another set of shattered souls disappeared in the rearview mirror.

The tip of Apollo's knife buried itself in the floorboard against which it was flung. His back unrolled onto the mattress behind him. He had dug two graves over the course of the night—one for Martin's flunky and an only partly metaphorical one he might soon come to occupy. Another long night loomed ahead of him, and even if it was executed perfectly, he found himself at a loss for how he would redeem himself in the Weber matter. The same twerp who stained Apollo's hands was scheduled to take part as well. His absence would not go unnoticed. For not the first time, Apollo considered that it might be for the better if he were found absent, as well.

The city was tearing itself apart, jumping at the thought of another blackout whenever a lightbulb flickered. Every morning newspaper was unfolded hesitantly, with each *Dear Reader* loathe to bring another reprinted letter signed by the maniac son of death and chaos unto their breakfast table. Apollo had not helped write any of those himself. Not a man of letters, nor wishing to be identified as one by authorities, he was vocally skeptical of the tactic. The doctor permitted his other goons to produce and disseminate those rambling, goofy notes. Martin assured Apollo that *"all press is good press."*

The publicity made Apollo feel paranoid. Floundering as they were, the cops and the FBI had hundreds of detectives and investigators monitoring every bridge and tunnel. Glass was becoming obsessed with the attention—how to gain it, how to direct it. Or misdirect it. Whether or not he realized—if he even cared— it made his unending list of demands that much more difficult for Apollo.

The mattress and the springs it jabbed into Apollo's backside did little to bring him ease. He hated sleeping during the daytime. He hated sleeping at any hour. In the decade since he first met Martin, Apollo had not always been a trusted co-conspirator. He began as a patient. Too many memories from too many extended deployments overseas. Too much crank clogging too many neurons after years riding with successive outlaw motorcycle outfits.

A self-proclaimed doctor in San Francisco and his clever little experiments marrying spiritualism and LSD changed that. Martin Glass divorced himself from MacLean and deGrimston, but affected the role of both teacher and oracle nonetheless. Elaborate and ceremonious, it reminded Apollo of the church masses he shirked in his youth. Those Sunday mornings never penetrated his defenses the way Glass's ceremonies did. It was like confession. Intimate. When he slept, he dreamed—but, he would never find himself alone again. In their sessions, it felt like Glass was inside his head. Others, too. Eventually, those forces revealed themselves to Apollo. As powerful as they were ancient, a forgotten hierarchy of kings and dukes each with their own courts and knaves made themselves known. They joined him in his slumber and expressed their eternal, unsatisfiable hungers. Apollo got his dreams and his memories and more, but the unblinking, black depths of the ocean over his world gained a new servant.

"Serve the meal. Or be the meal."

Weber's life was taken by his own hand, before it could be spilled in ceremony. His family survived, albeit mentally shattered. This was a state very contradictory to that which had been promised. Apollo thought about all the new faces waiting in the wings of Doctor Glass's sinister operation. He thought about what he himself had done to people Martin deemed enemies. His worries coalesced where his head rest on the bed. The light seeping through the blinds faded entirely.

Apollo's knee jerked. Vestigial impulses kicked his leg skyward, warning away any encroaching slumber. In the intervening time since he lay down, the window blinds ran out of sunlight to filter. If the stale air in Apollo's apartment still stirred with any dust, he was blind to it now. Shock brought the rest of Apollo's limbs away from the bed in one single, dreadful instant.

"Damn me," he swore to himself. "Musta passed out."

Calloused fingertips and palms scratched up the wall to the compact apartment's singular light switch. When the switch finally snagged between the joints of Apollo's index and middle fingers, they flicked upward. In darkness he and his apartment remained. The switch clicked down, then up again. Nothing. A burst of furious waggling flicked the switch repeatedly, bringing nothing other than disgust from Apollo's mouth.

"Fuckin' ConEd."

Apollo's mind returned to the citywide blackout a couple of weeks earlier. If the same chaos was a declaration of a second round, he could not hear as much turmoil on the streets outside his apartment. No shouting, no car horns blaring. It appeared quite the opposite—from his darkened window came a degree of tranquility uncommon to Avenue X. For a moment, Apollo thought about Glass. He wondered if the Doctor managed to pull the city's plug twice in under a month. It did not track with the plan he laid out for the night—another big hit for the Sam sequence. The prey they sought needed to have their guard down.

The air around Apollo felt thin. It shifted over the sweat building on his forearms as he felt his weight shift downward. He caught himself and braced against the wall to stop himself tipping sideways. He realized he was still in the dark with no idea what time it was. He might have missed the gig already. If it had not gone down already, Glass would already be there himself. Apollo and the dead stooge would be noticed MIA, leaving Martin and the one of the less-green kids from Yonkers to eventually plow forward without them. Bath Beach Park on Shore Parkway was only a couple miles from Apollo's doorstep. He did not hear any sirens. Not yet, at least.

Blind feet probed through the darkness, then wiggled into a pair of motorcycle boots. Apollo inched closer until he found the door. He twisted the doorknob and pressed. When he found nothing there to resist his weight, his muscles shifted backward. From somewhere in the studio apartment behind him, a blast of cold wind countered his attempt to set himself right. There was no door—no solid matter at all to prevent his fall. The courtyard of the Marlboro Projects was not rushing up toward Apollo, but the dune that met his face knocked the air from his lungs and left his tongue and gums clogged with sand. Gritty mucous flooded the cavities deep within his nose before draining into his mouth and crunching between his molars. Apollo's neck ached. His chin carved a trough across the beach as he dragged it in an arc to survey his surroundings. The ridges running along the sand glistened. He pushed himself onto his back. A full moon beamed down from the center of a twinkling sky, brilliant and unhindered by the urban interference which normally drowned out his own Brooklyn.

"Alright," Apollo sighed. "Let's get on wit' it. Youse got me. You fuckers've got my undivided attention."

Apollo snorted in through his nostrils. A mixture of phlegm and dirt gathered into a ball near the back of his throat. He pulled himself up and arced his head. The wad rocketed out of his mouth and melted into history a few feet away with a soft *plop*. After the first year or two of Doctor Glass's sessions, he developed a keen selfawareness of his circumstances within the confines of his own dreams. If he was perpetually a rat stuck in a maze, at least he was a rat *aware* of the maze. Initially, he tried to intervene, tried to fight his way out. The universe was adamant. Apollo learned to oblige.

A voice nearer the shoreline wafted across the beach. The call was echoed by a similar response from a second voice. A pair of slick, grinding sounds ended with an abrupt halt. Within the vast spotlight of the moon, silhouettes rose over the lapping waves. Heads and shoulders jostled to the edges of broad row boats. The faces on the shadows remained obscure beneath abundant hoods. Heavy, woolen robes billowed as feet swung over bows and planted boots to trod the shallow tide. While every step sank into the wet sand, the metal fixtures and buckles strapped to their ankles and insteps glowed. Not traditional sailors' footwear, Apollo noticed— though these men dismounted the waves, they wore riding boots. He watched them line the boats' sides. They cried in unison, heaving the wooden vessels higher ashore. Another figure rose over the bow of one of the boats. Unlike the others, his head was circled by a wide brim. The generous edges of the hat flapped when his feet landed on the beach. His back straightened and his figure towered over the men still laboring aside the boats. Impressive as the unfolding scene was to Apollo, the figure's profile in silhouette reminded him of the face staring out from the side of an oatmeal tin.

As was the case with his hooded minions, the man's identity remained obscure beneath the shade of his headgear and the shadows hanging past more angular facial features. Nonetheless, Apollo lost his eyes within the space the man's face would have most naturally occupied. Such was the dream's will. There was something he needed to find in it. Behind it. Resigned as he was to oblige the vision, Apollo felt his anger rising. Fear, too. He cursed the dream. He cursed Martin. As he always did, he cursed himself for what he had done to invite this punishment—to earn more than the universe's attention, but its inscrutable *interest*. The shadows over the man's face cut deeper. Wherever his eyes were in that abyss, Apollo knew the stare was intended for him alone. Anger ebbed. Terror multiplied. It was all a dream. It was a promise, too—only less actionable than reality by a degree trivial as it was amenable.

The man's head angled nearer the moon and the shadows began to recede—or was it the moon that sank? A tide of light washed over the man's face, but never enough to fill the sockets over his bony cheeks. There were teeth without lips, nostrils without cartilage. Apollo felt himself being pulled into the vacuous eyes of the naked skull. The land between himself and the figure shrank. The oarsmen faded with their ancient beach and hope died. Another dazzling display of power loomed over him and always would, every time. In dreams, the dark masses of space spoke to Apollo in a grand and magnificent language designed singularly for him—tailored to render impossible any potential misunderstanding. In ten years, not once had they lied or deceived. Apollo's eyes stung. He begged for the nightmare's end. At once he pined for and dreaded the crushing weight of truth and vulnerability that awaited when he finally woke.

Apollo felt the air around him thinning. Gravity grew disinterested. When it all tilted into freefall, the hands appeared. They wrapped around the edges of the now disembodied skull, grasping at its sides. A phalanx of new fingers appeared, each cuticle and crevice stained dark red, crawling over the first set. They grappled and scraped until overtaken from behind. New waves of desperate hands clutched and swiped at the last like a fresh row of teeth cutting up through a shark's gums. Each was redder, bloodier— more disfigured and scarred. The struggle disappeared beneath the mighty clap of one pair of massive hands, glistening and dripping. Black, bloody smears coated every pale inch of the skull. The shockwave issued by the final grip filled the universe in which Apollo and the rest of creation hung. It reverberated back and forth until no corner of space was left untouched. His own hands shot up to his ears in a failed attempt to block the warping thunder. A bomb exploded behind him. Mortars and rockets burst louder than those he ducked in younger, conscripted years. Apollo turned the scream he did not remember willing his mouth to release toward the sky. A thunderous rip like the buckling of metal and bursting of rock tore through the night. Fabric seams appeared between constellations, straining until they ripped toward the horizon. Vast, inverse chasms of light gazed downward from beyond the multiplying edges of a splintering cosmos.

The skull floated at the center of inevitability. Pointed ends emerged along its boney surface. Spikes pressed outward and pierced the final, surviving pair of hands without resistance. They extended until the circular ridge of a crown formed over the skull's brow. Where the grip of the mighty hands had been lanced, brilliant cracks spread. White hot veins erupted through decaying, mortal flesh. They wound and weaved their way through subdermal channels until they extended upward to reveal the frame of a man. Arms and shoulders. A neck and a torso. A face. Webs of light thickened until every gap filled and a full figure formed. A dishearteningly familiar gaze outshone the skull and space beyond. Apollo recognized the face of Doctor Martin Glass, but the name no longer fit. He strained his eyes and tried to refocus. The man at the center of his vision was warping, radiant as it was distorted. Around the figure's edges, the world bent inward. The last remaining stitch in the fabric of the universe buckled and split. Everything which lie beyond streamed forth. Narrow tendrils of light twisted down to the Earth, tracing grand, cyclonic arcs through the heavens as they neared. Meandering and elaborate as their paths might have appeared, they left no doubts where they would soon touch down. From a smirk to a sneer, the man's lips curled back over two impeccable rows of ivory as the columns of light intersected around him. An impulse clawed its way through the back of Apollo's mind. It begged him to turn away. Unheeding eyes fixed themselves, arrested to witness the world's end.

Finally, the man spoke. Lips articulated and flexed. Words were formed and departed to wander the void. At the other end of the expanse, they entered Apollo's ears. The ambient bars and tones of universal destruction evaporated, and silence pressed down. Apollo stood on the edge of darkness, alone with his own quivering breath. There was no more Martin Glass with whom he could share this space. Falling light coalesced around the figure whose name he used to know, gyrating and undulating into a pure, white ball of energy. It grew larger and stronger, to magnitudes far beyond that which Apollo could endure. The flesh of his own closed eyelids became inadequate, too transparent to block the glare. He tucked his head down, bracing his chest and face. The swelling light spun into a beacon and bulged to fill the vacuum. Apollo looked at one of the arms he had wrapped around himself. The back of his hand flaked away. He expected the shift in pressure, but not the undertow drawing him toward the light's nucleus. Apollo watched greater and greater pieces of his remaining self shake loose, then drift away to the center of the storm. The light continued to expand as gravity pulled inward. Apollo's consciousness and that which was left to constitute his body turned away from the vicious pull of the undertow. He looked to the shadows, desperately searching for what he hoped lie beyond the ravenous expanse. Something in the darkness stirred. The light of the force ripping him apart shuddered with realization. In the moment before Apollo crossed the horizon of complete material and spiritual consumption, he heard the shadows' reply.

* * *

The sun rose over the Elysian Fields Adult Rehabilitation Center. Apollo felt his throat convulsing and burning—lungs left without a single, whimpering molecule of fear to expel through his mouth. When the last, faded echoes of his screams bounced off the shared bedroom's drooping, stained ceiling tiles, he felt his spine jerk back down to the mattress. Apollo stifled his gasps as his diaphragm tried desperately to regain control. If his roommate stirred, the steady, mechanical rhythm of the respirator between their beds gave no indication. Apollo's shoulder ached as he reached over to the nightstand. He propped himself up slightly to avoid reawakening an old injury to his rotator cuff. A picture frame stood not far past his knuckles while his hand probed for his pack of smokes. The search paused. Thirteen years had long begun to fade that which remained of the father and his young daughter from Kodachrome nearer to monochrome. Thirteen years adrift in the fog with waking nightmares and spiritual arrest. Apollo traced their faces with his eyes. If the color was no longer as sharp, their place among the shambles of Apollo's mind was vivid as ever. The fog was lifting now as Apollo pulled himself out of bed.

Alice's younger eyes looked past the edge of the picture frame—far beyond her tears and the kindergarten building that loomed in the background—to her father's impending separation and the approaching subterranean world beneath the Elysian Fields.

Apollo watched her as he pulled a chair back and lowered himself to the table. His thumbnail caught the corner of the pack and flipped the top open. Three bent smokes rustled around inside. Five urgent pulls made two. Apollo thought about the fog. His grasp of what caused it to suddenly lift was limited, but he was ready to entertain some theories.

"If the fog can lift for me…"

An attendant rolled a stack of food trays out of the kitchen by the stairs. Its four tiny wheels squeaked and wobbled as they struggled to traverse the threadbare and tattered ridges of industrial carpeting. The navigator let the tall cart drift for a few inches on its own momentum, then reached down to extract a tray in each hand. Apollo counted no more than a dozen plastic, teal domes. His experienced nose informed him that the squares of toasted white bread concealed within were already hard at work wicking moisture out of unflavored grits. His eyes informed him that no more than ten residents would even receive the disappointing meal. Apollo counted himself and Alice among a suddenly dwindling population. When the orderly bent down to slide a pair of trays for his table, Apollo added a familiar face to the tally, plus a new one beside it. He recognized the younger cop, even without her uniform. The one next to her appeared in plainclothes as well. It might not be pinned to her chest as she approached, but most cops could never hide the shield tucked inside their pocket from the right sort of eyes.

"Y'ever find yourself walkin' into the front door'a your house, an' you can't remember how you even got yourself there?"

Lucy nodded.

"Sure."

A pair of surplus dining trays cooled before each of the two off-duty cops. The one who had been introduced to him as Officer Williams—then reintroduced by herself as Tabby—let a plume of steam escape when she lifted the tray's round, insulated lid. The dissipating steam and momentary composure did little to obscure her repulsion. The lid came back down and Tabby slid the tray down the table. For her part, Lucy did not seem aware of the tray in front of her at all.

"Used to be I'd come in-an'-outta dreams all day long. Real nightmares, with no warning."

Apollo grumbled as he spoke, vocal cords still hoarse from an unpleasant awakening. He gesticulated with a piece of toast while making no attempt to bring it to his mouth.

"Now it just feels like someone else is playin' with the fast forward button, clickin' it on and then off again and there I am."

"Better than seein' ghosts and demons all the time," Lucy added.

Her friend sitting next to her bristled, then continued studying any patients besides Apollo.

"True," Apollo permitted. "Now I only gotta worry about my demons when I actually manage to find some sleep."

"Looks like nobody's got any shortage of demons around here," Tabby said.

"There's more than you could imagine."

"It's always nightmares?" Lucy asked. "Never anything good? Or just nothin' at all?"

"Not lately, no. Plenty a'old stuff. Warnings. Shit that I didn't listen to good enough the first time. Otherwise, I woulda never landed in here with the resta his broken toys."

"They all knew Martin Glass?"

Lucy did not miss a beat and Apollo felt her eyes lock on him. Tabby finished her own visual laps around the room and her curious glare came to rest in the same place.

"Jimmy's *'middle-of-the-night, new age fruitloop'* from the cheap commercials?" Tabby asked.

Apollo sputtered as he exhaled a fresh cloud of tobacco smoke. The smoke wafted into his eyes. His head felt light as he tried to stifle a wheezy, involuntary laugh.

"Nah," he coughed. "They didn't all *know* 'im, not exactly. But they got tossed in here with me for more or less the same reasons."

As he trailed off, Apollo felt another laugh brewing. The smoke cleared, but a familiar fog was lowering around him.

"'*Fruitloop,*' she says. Wish I'da told 'im off when I had the chance. That fruitloop—that *fuckin' prick*—is a pretty good actor, though. A real hustler."

A small part of Apollo's conscious mind cursed his babbling mouth. It took years to regain clarity. He clenched his jaw and pulled his giddy tongue back.

"Well yeah," Tabby said. "Anybody who can rub two braincells together can see it's nothing but a scam."

"Not exactly," Apollo whispered, tightening his grip on the reins.

"Of course it is. It's stage magic and hypnotists' tricks. *'Open your mind, dig deep into your subconscious. Deeper into your pocket, though.'*"

"You're half-right. Wouldn't call 'em *'tricks,'* though."

Apollo leaned back in his seat. When he was sure he was in control again, he reached back through time. When he found what he was looking for he opened his eyes, found his visitors, and spoke:

"Darker and tenacious, drawn higher
is that murk upon which slouches,
The sleepin' infernal pantheon's kingdom
of grotesque, wicked Houses,
And pulses the fanatical rhapsody
from their groanin' stone halls,
From the ashes of dying stars,
faithful warriors to answer their calls."

Apollo noticed that his voice was becoming choked, panic building as the lines reentered his life. He paused to refill his lungs. While Tabby's eyebrows froze at exaggerated latitudes, agony and impatience filled Lucy's face.

"The Darkest Star's sinister hand lends power
while the other beckons gore,
And to thy many legion bidding servants
a taste from those patrons they swore.
By offerins' and forfeiture
they may suffocate light by their own hands,
To hurry life into death, turn they humanity to terror
o'er blood drowned, ruined lands."

Apollo punctuated the poem with a cough, then pulled hard on what remained of his cigarette. The smoke numbed his lungs and the nicotine did its best with the fear.

"Were those lines from one of Glass's books?" Lucy asked.

"Didn't sound too *new*-agey," Tabby added.

"No. Much older. Passed down from person to person, from some as a warning and from others as a pitch. They're words of history. Words of power. They can be very powerful things, comin' from the right mouth—or maybe the *wrong* mouth. There's ears at every corner of the universe. Very distant ears. Resentful, restless ears. All that blackness you see when you look up at the sky at night, all that space between the twinklin' stars. It's easy to let the light dazzle you. Easy when you can't see. But it's really an ocean. Lotsa mean critters beneath the waves, stranger and more alien the deeper you go."

It did not take Apollo as long to summon the words. They rose from the depths fast as he could rattle them off.

"Terrific names like Astaroth and Bathym, Paimon and Bune,
He hails Caym and Marbas and Vine and mighty King Belial, too."

Lucy went pale. His suspicions confirmed, Apollo continued.

"A false monarchy of demons
bestowed a mockery of crowns,
From Creation's Hand the net slipped
and, still bound by His Will, they are drowned."

"That's the name *she* said. Bethany. Under the highway. She said that name: *Belial.*"

"Just, *stop*," Tabby snapped. "Bethany died where we found her. Inside the car."

"Not her body," Lucy insisted. "Something else. Whatever was there was whipped up in this cyclone of light. Twisted, pulled into the sky."

Where the concern on Tabby's face melted, fear grew. Apollo found himself pitying them, watching their expressions begin to match each other.

"That haunted-house-looking joint off Bath Avenue," Tabby spoke more slowly. "The one they're turning into a new halfway house."

Apollo knew the place by even the most limited description. That Tabby described it as a new halfway house in the making gave him pause.

"I was on foot last night," she continued. "I heard an alarm goin' off. Went stickin' my nose where it didn't belong."

Somewhere beneath the gloom, a smirk etched its way across Lucy's face.

"Don't know what I was thinkin'. Don't know what made me go in there. But there was this man—huge and wrapped in this billowing white light. Came at me outta nowhere. No, not nowhere. He came outta this giant, goddamn mirror."

Apollo snorted.

"What the hell did you two squares get yourselves into," he huffed.

"Oh, excuse me. You find something funny about all this?"

Tabby growled as her palm slapped down onto the table. Lucy jumped.

"Relax," Apollo said, struggling to suppress a laugh. "I'm sorry. Just thought all youse cops was supposed to be hardasses, is all. Never thought I'd see a coupla *the boys* spooked by the same ghouls I've been fightin' off for too many years to count."

"Alright, guy. If you're so slick, why don't you tell us what's really goin' on."

Apollo leaned in.

"Alright."

The table groaned and tilted as his elbows straddled his own untouched breakfast tray. He jabbed his index finger in Tabby's direction.

"You seen one'a the king demons himself. Belial. One'a the biggest fish in that big, black ocean hangin' over us."

He shifted. His finger swung to Lucy.

"An' you. You seen what happens when one of his devoted fans comes up short on their end of the bargain."

"Bargain?" Lucy repeated slowly. "What kinda bargain?"

"A deal. Y'know, your run-a-the-mill black covenant."

Apollo soaked in the silence infecting the pair. They demanded and he intended to deliver. After a moment, he continued.

"You say the right words to the right one. You spill a little blood. You get a little novelty magic trick of your own. But you gotta keep the cycle goin'. Gotta keep your head above the risin' tide. That's the biggest catch with the whole deal. Sure, it's nice to terrorize people. Rob 'em after you've sucked the light from the air around them. Melt into the shadows an' leave no trace that you was ever there. But the interest is always compounding. If you wanna even make a dent in the principal on that debt, you need to pull of something *real big*. Otherwise, the waves pull you under before you're ever close. Next thing you know, your soul is just another little fish in a very big, very dark, and very vicious sea."

"So, all of this," Tabby said, "the murders, the ghouls, and the panic—it's all because some hack televangelist has to pay off some loan?"

The question tweaked a nerve somewhere deep within Apollo's own doubts.

"I don't think so. I used to, I mean. When I first really got into the whole thing. This guy, Glass—it was obvious from the get-go he was only in it for the power."

"How long was he your teacher?" Lucy asked.

"Nah, he's no teacher. A pusher. A pimp. When I first ran into 'im in the sixties, out west, I was about to knock his block off. Jerk thought he could lean against my bike. But I knew he ran with a buncha other freaks driftin' 'round that part of the world in those days. I'd heard 'bout the Process Church. Organized Satanists. Misfits and contrarians. Mosta the people runnin' the show were only in it for the philosophy or the sex. Or both. But Glass knew there was something real in it all, something bigger than Satan and Lucifer and Christ himself. Problem was, he mighta had the book smarts, but the powers that be out in universe never trusted 'im."

"Too sketchy for the spooks?" Tabby asked.

"Maybe," Apollo grunted. "Temptation, manipulation—those are mortal impurities. Motivations based on weakness. True power doesn't need to deceive. There ain't a single Leviathan or Behemoth lurking in those vast, empty, black patches in the sky that ever came down to Earth uninvited. There's always been someone willin' to throw the door open to let 'em cross the threshold. Someone harboring slights against their pride. Someone who understood how the world really spun, but couldn't make it spin *for them*. Someone desperate, back against the wall."

"And followers to take cover behind," Lucy added.

"Martin roped people into *meditation sessions*. Handed out free dope. He got into our heads while we was asleep. If it was too costly to talk to Belial himself, he'd just tap the phonelines instead. If the powers that be didn't like it, Martin made sure he wasn't the one to get burned—but they wrote the rules. It was still *their* game. They didn't care for someone with greater reverence for the loopholes than the law. It was clear in the way he was actin'—it was clear in what they were tryin' to tell me—that come Hell or high water, Martin was gonna do whatever it took to get all the power for himself. Even if it meant tearing up the rulebook itself."

"It can't be that easy, can it? If we're really talking about things *that* powerful, how can some poseur bring it all down?"

"Other men have tried. One almost did. Now *that* guy—he was the real deal. Way more powerful than Glass. More powerful than anyone before or after. Didn't keep 'im from losin' his head, though. Took an entire village to finally wake up to what was happenin' and stop him. But people are quick to forget. There's lotsa stuff people don't remember anymore even though it's buried all 'round us. A couple centuries later, another guy comes along, thinks he's smarter than that. Maybe he is."

"How'd you go from his right hand to… this place. Why the change of heart?" Tabby asked.

"Huh. Not sure many people've ever accused me of havin' a heart to begin with. All I can say is, when the darkness grabs you by the neck to warn you about someone, they ain't foolin' around."

Apollo paused to light another cigarette. Alice, impassive in her chair, reappeared behind his lighter's extinguished flame.

"It was all over that point, anyway," he continued. "I made a decision. Chose to preserve what life I could instead of always taking, taking, *taking*. I failed. Nobody was saved. I paid the price. Lotsa other people payin' for it, too. If I threw a wrench in his plans for a little bit, it only delayed the inevitable. Glass disappeared while someone else took the fall. Before he ducked out, he stuck me in this place. Thirteen years later, I'm still here and Martin's got himself back on track and found what he was lookin' for."

"How far does it go?" Tabby asked. "The mail-order ministry, obviously. What about all the stuff he isn't parading around on local TV? How much is there he wants to keep discrete?"

"I've been doing some digging," Lucy said. "Martin Glass and the whole Oneirology thing are pretty big. They've got outreach programs across the country. They've spent the last couple years buying up real estate and opening therapy centers across the city. Rehab centers, too."

Apollo leaned back in his chair. The Elysian Fields Adult Rehabilitation Center had never known the same owner or operator for more than twelve months in a row. No matter how many new deeds were drafted and executed, neglect lingered in the stagnant air and clung to the walls between beads of recondensed nicotine vapor.

"That's his M.O. Dredging the gutters and clinics. Gathering up the desperate and the loners—people he could dazzle and influence without families or obligations to get in the way. People who wouldn't be missed after their usefulness ran out. There's free chairs openin' up all the time."

"We've gotta stop him," Lucy urged, rising from her own chair. "We can bring you to the precinct."

"Nope."

"But… you just said yourself, it's happened before—"

"Not happenin'. S'too late, kid," Apollo interrupted her. "After all these years, he's finally found the last thing he needed to pull off whatever it is he's plannin'."

"*Bull. Shit*," Tabby said. "Tell it like it is. You'd watch the world burn before you cooperated with the police.

"*Cooperation?* I'm a loser, sure. But I ain't an idiot. *Cooperation* got me an' a whole buncha' other punks shipped to boot camp instead of prison. I seen the world burn plenty since then. Not once was I stupid enough to think workin' for the man was gonna put out any fire unless it was us that was bein' used to smother it. Besides, while your friends with the shiny, gold badges are busy braggin' to everyone how they saved the day, Glass is pushin' ahead strong as ever."

"It's not too late—"

"We were all pulled into his endgame weeks ago. 'Bout the same time I got my marbles back. Sorry, ladies. Not much an old burn out and two ex-cops can do against the operation he's built up."

"Two?" It was Tabby's turn to jump out of her seat. "I still got my job."

"Not for too much longer if you're spendin' your free time snoopin' 'round the properties of an upstanding and very visible member of the city's spiritual community. Without a warrant."

Apollo watched Tabby's face trade offense for loathing before he could finish his sentence.

"And just to show I'm not entirely ignorant of the reality of my circumstances, it wouldn't help that your only witness is a violent, repeat felon involuntarily committed to a less-than-respected rehabilitation facility for forms of schizophrenia and mania that continue to defy more than a decade's worth of medical treatment."

"Well," Tabby countered through clenched teeth, "I don't know if you've noticed, but the sun still rose this morning. You say this asshole's got everything he needs, but here we are. You know everything—tell us how all Hell hasn't broke loose yet."

Apollo considered the question. He looked at his cigarette. The cherry burned its way toward his knuckles and a steady wisp of smoke rose to further taint the ceiling. He knew the cops were waiting. He pursed his lips and took another drag.

"That's what I thought—you don't know shit," Tabby said as she stood and turned away from the table. "Sit here for another thirteen years then. Or until the rapture. Whichever comes first."

"Fine by me. I'm ready. Hope you can say the same."

"No," Lucy shouted.

She grabbed the back of Tabby's arm.

"If Glass hasn't made his move, it means is we still have time. But not enough to waste on petty bickering."

"Maybe," Apollo said. "Maybe not. Maybe we'll all be seein' Belial again real soon. Or the good doctor—whoever wins *that* fight. When we're all trapped in the shadows, nothin'll be clear to see except who gets to count themselves among the real losers."

"So, what?" Tabby said as she pulled her arm away from Lucy. "You're just gonna spend the rest of the time talkin' in riddles? Maybe you've still got enough time to let your dreams bring you back to everyone you ever hurt. Might be you'll even figure out if you feel worse for them or yourself."

Apollo's incisors bit through the cigarette's filter. Despite the local commotion, the living things beyond his table—at least, the closest the Fields had to offer—carried on without pause. The same attendant who distributed meals now picked at one of the weathered wood paneled walls with a straight razor. His fingernails peeled the tattered remnants of lingering Valentine's Day decorations and scotch tape residue off the wall, then let them drop into a box by his feet. Once each one was removed, he picked up a new, flat, cardboard decoration to tape to the wall. A bunny holding a bright purple basket. A yellow baby chick followed. Finally, a colorfully decorated egg, artfully placed to conceal a splintering section of the panel.

"Or maybe you wanna actually do something and tell us where these creeps might hang out? Cops, not cops—whatever reasons you wanna think up to spite us, at least give us that much. If you're right, you'll get to stay just as satisfied with yourself. You'll also have to spend all eternity never knowing whether you could've made the difference."

"Have it your way. It's your funeral," Apollo warned.

"If you were still one of his goons, where would you and him be right now?"

"If I were unlucky enough to find myself in that prick's shoes, I'd probably be droolin' over the skull of the last guy who nearly pulled it all off. In some dank, underground shit hole not too far from this one.

"That's a start," Lucy said.

She turned to Tabby.

"That actually worked. Good job."

Tabby smiled.

"Voluntary compliance," she said.

"Rule number one," Lucy added. "Beats doing things the hard way."

"Hmph," Apollo grunted. "Nothin' ever beats the hard way."

Eighteen

Droplets streamed down the driver's side window. Condensation fogged Lucy's view of the sidewalk. The engine of her Corolla idled between frame-rattling quivers. Her hand reach for the dashboard and swiveled an air vent away from her, redirecting its fans to the diminishing view. She checked the time again: *4:12 P.M.* The faux-Colonial steeple of Chemical Bank rose toward the low, gray ceiling of rain clouds slouching inland. Two synchronized sets of black clock hands, mirrored on the southern and eastern faces of the steeple, managed to stand out in the gloom. Their bold, dark lines made clear indications of hours and minutes, dense as the weather conditions were. Despite the historical affectations in its design, its even and well-pointed red bricks appeared decades younger than the fourth- and fifth-floor, pre-war apartments looking down on the bank's ornamental clock tower. Lucy wondered if any of the tenancies within those apartments predated the bank.

It was immediately clear that the shape shuffling in-between puddles on the sidewalk toward the car did not belong to the person Lucy awaited. Before she could decline the service, his squeegee slopped down between the rivulets running down the windshield. The Toyota's own wipers, already active, thumped and shuddered around the sponge at the end of the man's handle.

"That won't be necessary—no, really," Lucy stammered through the closed window, replicating her words into the appropriate universal gesticulations. "You don't gotta—"

The man continued. His own gaze bounced with the drizzle off the windshield's convex surface. Lucy felt the Corolla list. A hand lurched out of the car's back row and landed next to her shoulder. The back of her own seat groaned as it tilted back. Apollo pulled his head forward over the center console. The window cleaner's rubber wick squeaked to a halt. The squeegee man on the other end did not flinch when the car's wipers brushed his hand aside. His eyes had been yanked back down to earth to land squarely in the broad scowl spanning Apollo's face.

"No, Apollo," she whispered. "You don't gotta threaten the guy."

"Threaten?" The corner of Apollo's mouth curled upward.

"I didn't say shit."

Lucy watched the disheveled man's face. Rain dribbled down between locks of dense, tangled hair and into the corners of petrified eyes.

"I mean, don't set him off. We're supposed to just lie low here and wait for Tabby to get to her post."

"Your man here's smacked outta his skull," Apollo chuckled.

"*My* man? You're the one staring him down!"

"What did I do? I ain't even said nothin' an' he looks like he's about t'freak out. That ain't got nothin' to do with me—that's the look of a bad trip."

Lips parted to reveal crooked teeth and black voids where teeth might have otherwise plugged his gumline. Words began to take shape.

"Black goats!" the man hissed as he backed away. "Hear their dark hymns!"

"Oh, no," Lucy muttered. "Not *now*."

"On a plane of ashen cities, amidst the risin' depths, lost generations are drawn!"

Flecks of spit mixed with precipitation. If the clouds brought no bolts of lightning, the man's voice provided thunder to spare.

"Awakened! Walkin'! *Fuckin'* dreamin'!—to raise and to depose that Kingdom 'neath the *goddamned* Midnight Dawn!"

His feet shuffled confidently backward until his heel was interrupted by the base of a fire hydrant. He tumbled and rolled, then sprang back up.

"Sounds like our squeegee man here's been takin' advantage of some familiar literature. Wonder where he picked it up?"

"It's the same poetry?" Lucy asked. "The stuff you were sayin' before?"

"I guess you don't gotta wonder *too* hard, then. The story, the words—they're much older than Martin and those thirty-dollar paperweights he peddles on TV. He's one hell of a plagiarist. He's an even better salesman."

Upright again, the feverish howling continued.

"The sky that looks down on Paradise and Now is inevitable and bleak! Hastens with its pace, the forgotten maelstrom arrives to be deposed! The *fuckin'* black goat and the *fuckin'* rider and their *goddamn* shadow will be exposed!"

Lucy found herself transfixed. When she managed to pry her eyes away from the ongoing spectacle, Apollo appeared absorbed as well. For their part, the scattered crowds milling along Bay Parkway seemed equally content to feign indifference to the bothersome spring weather as they did the mad man screaming archaic verses and timeless obscenities. Not until his flailing limbs knocked the umbrella from one woman's hand did public opinion turn. A nearby man, braving the conditions without the advantages of shirtsleeves, bellowed. The woman scrambled to snatch her umbrella from the sidewalk. She brushed rainwater off the plastic bag she employed as a hairnet, then turned her ire toward the unabated disturbance. A sopping *thwack* glanced off the squeegee man's temple. The trance broke and his prophecies sputtered. The curses spilling from his mouth now focused largely on more contemporary, vulgar profanities and blasphemies.

"What the hell," someone moaned from the sidewalk.

As she watched the squeegee man's public reputation suffer, Lucy realized she had forgotten the reason she and Apollo waited by the corner. She failed to notice the police officer leaning herself up against the side of the car until she spoke.

"The both of you show up on *my* corner while I'm clockin' in at the precinct, just to work the local natives into a frenzy before I can thumb my way out here?"

Tabby pulled the passenger's side door open.

"The guys droppin' me off took one look at that mess on two legs and wished me luck as they sped off."

Lucy surveyed the roadway as the car door opened. She could see the fading taillights of the patrol car a few blocks away, but the man screaming at her moments earlier had already vanished.

"You sure they aren't gonna swing back around anytime soon?"

"They've barely checked in on me all week," Tabby said as she landed in the seat next to Lucy. "Now crank the heat. I only walked a half block and I'm already soaked."

"This *is* cranked," Lucy replied. "And I thought you said good cops didn't get wet. Or was it cold?"

"Neither. Ain't neither of us been great cops lately anyway, so what do I know?"

Tabby pulled the eight-pointed cap off her head and smacked it against her hand. Droplets bounced into the air.

"So," she continued. "What kinda plots have you two hatched while I was away?"

"I told him about the Valerie brothers. We already know Dexter was snooping around the periphery outside Hallelujah. A few minutes later, Charlie flew out the front door with that skull."

When Lucy mentioned the skull, she saw Apollo wince in the rearview mirror. He reclined into the center of the back seat. The car's suspension sighed and adjusted the vehicle's tilt accordingly.

"We ran the tape from St. Antony's again, too." Lucy continued. "Dark as it looks, the profiles match Dexter and Bethany."

"Mmm, sounds right," Tabby said. "From what I heard on 63rd Street, I'm thinking those two were the ones who broke down the front door. No way there was just the one party crasher in that apartment. Somewhere between entrance and exit, our sole witness peeped the littlest Valerie keeping the car warm."

"Glass ain't doin' this alone—*can't*," Apollo added. "He's clever. He's book smart. Dangerous, too. Individually, he's always come up short on raw talent."

"He puts on a good show on those informercials," Tabby replied.

"He's gotta. Can't just hire that kinda help. He needs *believers*."

"So, what makes a guy like Charlie trustworthy to someone like Glass?" Lucy asked. "What makes him a believer?"

"I wouldn't *trust* that kid to be up before ten thirty if he *believed* McMuffins came with a deck on the side," Tabby said. "With help from a burnout like that, it's a wonder Martin Glass's whole house of cards hasn't collapsed on its own."

"He's young," Lucy said. "A younger brother at that, and with no real father figure to speak of. He's only got one other person in his life to follow. Could be that Dexter's the true believer, while Charlie just tagged along for the ride."

"Burnout brothers?" Apollo asked. "Lemme guess—broken home, lotsa cops rollin' past?"

"Charlie? Sure," Tabby agreed. "When we weren't prying his neck out from between his old man's claws, we usually had to yank him outta the cars he'd broken into scrounging dope money. Dexter's a different story. I haven't run into him much since he sobered up a year ago. Used to be a regular customer on the midnights, like the younger one. Last time anyone called 911 on account of him, he'd nearly drank himself to death. After that, I heard he found God or something."

"Or something," Apollo echoed.

"Hmm," Tabby added.

Lucy pulled the shifter down into first gear. She sighed.

"Guess it's time to drop in on the Valerie homestead."

A fine coat of mist filled the spaces between the raindrops trickling down the windshield. The air had grown denser as they approached the coast. The cloudy ceiling came lower to the ground, lost definition. A spot was found, inconspicuous enough along Shore Parkway to idle and wait. On the other side of the chain link fence which separated the local road from the parallel Belt— through rare gaps which untamed brush and vines chose not to fill in the lattice of rusted diamonds—the horizon beyond the highway loomed gray and swollen. Waves of salt water, lethargic as they were heavy and relentless, hissed and groaned against the manmade breakwater. Lucy looked at the dashboard. The orange, electronic digits on her radio read *6:08 P.M.* Already severely limited by cloud cover, the obscure sun acquiesced and accelerated nightfall. Glowing orbs of color bled back into the world where streetlamps and occupied apartments acknowledged the time. For over an hour, Lucy, Tabby, and Apollo surveilled only one window. While its neighbors joined in the spreading glow, the Valerie home fostered a vacuum.

"One of these assholes has gotta come home eventually."

Tabby slumped down as she grumbled. Her hand slid down over her face to cover her eyes. Windshield wipers trembled and squeaked across the Toyota's windshield. Lucy leaned on the steering wheel and examined the streaks and trails left in their wake. As the wind whistled, it routed sheets of salty dew off the bay's surface and draped them onto her car. With every trip across the windshield, the wipers packed more and more salt residue into the dull, brown border ringing the window. Far beyond the front bumper, the vast, hazy sky and the body of water below grated against one another. The steady drone of the swelling tide washed over the landscape. Like static on a warming television screen, a monochromatic surge of black water and white foam rode up the side of the seawall and surged into the sky. Lucy's eyes followed the successive crests until they spouted higher than the streetlamps illuminating the seawall's walkway. Mistier remnants of the airborne mass wafted inland, and another sheet of brine blanketed the Corolla. Lucy watched the rest of the fragmented wave mix in with the falling rain and splatter down onto the earth. The heavy splash barely registered over the sound of the sea battering the engineered coastline. A more solid thud crashed down onto her car's trunk and broke through the white noise.

"*Shit,*" Lucy and Tabby agreed.

Tabby corrected her slouch and shot upright in her seat. Lucy's eyes darted up to the rearview mirror and found that it made a perfect frame for the image of fury staring back at her from behind the Toyota's trunk. Dark, stringy tendrils of hair flicked across a pale, thinning scalp—rising into the sky and then falling back to down as the wind flared.

"What the fuck d'youse cocksuckas want now?" Adam Valerie shouted from behind. "Yeah—I seen the whole buncha youse! I see that fuckin' blue uniform, *missy!*"

Lucy saw Tabby's nostrils flare. The uniform patches on her shoulder bristled as her teeth bit down on her lip.

"Fuckin' cops! Fuckin' *muthafuckas!* I know it's my place youse all're watchin'."

Tabby reached down. The window cranked a half inch lower, smoothly as her tensing muscles would allow.

"Ain't here for you," Tabby growled, watching him walk closer in the side mirror. "Not right now, at least."

"So what-es'actly-the-fuck is it youse all want, then?"

"Dexter. Charlie. Your boys."

"Hah!"

Even in the rain, Lucy could see the distinct line of spittle ejected as the man laughed.

"Those two ungrateful sonsabitches? They're all yours—*take 'em*. For all I care, I wish I'da left 'em both as stains on the mattress."

"Ugh," Lucy groaned. "What time are you expecting them home? Just got a few questions for them is all."

"Youse all new at this shit?"

Adam Valerie's voice cracked as he backed away from the car.

"I dunno if youse're blind or what, but 'dose two little shits ain't been 'round here for weeks. Damn near a month."

"Alright," Lucy continued, "then where have they been staying?"

"Don't know. Don't fuckin' care, neither."

Lucy felt desperate. If Adam maintained his usual, baseline hostility, she did not sense he was being dishonest.

"Maybe they're somewhere else around the neighborhood? Maybe you can think of some friends they're staying with?"

"*Maybe* rippin' off somebody else for dope money for a change," Adam grunted. "Or *maybe* they finally fuckin' went an' got themselves killed. Go ahead—ask me if I give a fuck?"

An audible click made it clear Tabby had unclenched her jaw.

"Well," she said, "you inflicted them on the world. How about you try giving a fuck where your two sons are for a change?"

"Hell no. Not even for a *second*. But if it's me that's gotta do all the detective work for youse, I'd bet my left nut the little one's floatin' face down in some gutter somewhere with a needle still stuck in his *goddamn* arm. An' that slick brother'a his? That church for new age fruitloops is his new home now. 'Prolly callin' that prick Doctor Glass his *'Pops'* by now."

"Just go, already," Apollo's voice rumbled in the back seat. "Pointless wasting our time on a fuckin' fool like this."

"I heard that, asshole!"

Rainwater bounced off Adam Valerie's saturated shoulders as he stooped down to the rear window.

"Why don't youse step out'n say that to my fa—"

The senior Valerie's nose and right cheekbone could do little to stop the Corolla's back door opening. He lost his balance for a moment and landed on his knee. The thick lenses of his glasses gathered rainwater as they dangled below his chin. Apollo's feet swung out of the car and onto the asphalt. Adam Valerie's exposed eyes climbed to the sky, struggling to focus on the man's face above him. When he picked himself up from the ground, his balding head rose soared to meet Apollo's. Lucy watched the each man do his best to stare the other down. Tall as Apollo was, Adam's own head still rose a few inches over him. He was outclassed in weight, though. What pounds Adam Valerie carried had collected almost exclusively around his gut. Apollo was not without his own paunch, but he was undoubtedly ready and capable of snapping Adam in half. Glasses or not, Adam saw as much. He lifted the spectacles up from his chin and brought them back onto the bridge of his nose. When he finally broke his stare with Apollo, he turned his head, sucked air into his nose, and spit.

"You fuckin' *pigs* better stay away from my house. I don't care what youse're lookin' for. Those two ain't here. I ain't got nothin'!"

He backed away, then turned and walked toward the courtyard of his building.

"An' if you see either of 'em, let 'em know their old man says there ain't a snowball's chance in Hell they're comin' back here, neither."

Waves of raindrops and ejected sea water trampled the roof of the Corolla as Lucy gently eased the gas pedal. The one-way lane was a tunnel of vacant automobiles lining either shoulder beneath a rustling, patchy canopy of barren oak and London plane branches. Airborne water drifted in restless stops and starts over the increasingly lamplit street. The multiplying cones of light did what they could to illuminate the roadway, but largely featured the dazzling, angular, twisted curtains of rain.

"God. *Damn*," Apollo's voice muttered behind Lucy. "Buzzin' bastards. Everywhere—*no*."

Hairs stood one-by-one along Lucy's neck. She could hear his breaths grow erratic, unformed anxieties buckshot-scattered among wandering thoughts.

"All those *fuckin'* lasers."

"Sounds like our best bet is the theater," Lucy said, eager to inject some form of focus into their mission. "86th Street. The Oneirology Mission. That's his main base, right?"

"It's his main *front*," Apollo added in a clearer tone. "Everything else—everything we need to worry about—is underground."

"Clearly. I wasn't about to suggest we start looking for any signs advertising the '*murderous, demonic, doomsday cult.*'"

"No. Underground. *Under the ground.* There's hundreds'a years' worth of old hidin' spots beneath us. Caves and tunnels for everybody that never fit in. Sewers and cisterns built by a possessed maniac, wiped from the city's maps."

"He's right," Tabby said, exhaling with a huff. "That house, a few blocks over on Bay 26. The one that looks like it's about to fall in on itself. From the outside at least…"

A grunt of agreement drifted up from the back seat.

"But yesterday," she continued. "Yesterday I was over there. The alarm'd gone off. I could hear it from a half-mile away. So, I poked my head inside. There's some kinda diggin' goin' on in the basement. The whole thing is this dilapidated shell covering a modern excavation project. And there was this hole, down in the ground. These… black stones. Never seen anything like that. That was when I saw…"

Tabby drifted off just as Lucy felt Apollo lurch forward.

"That's his house," he said. "Glass. That house an' his operation in the old Loew's Oriental are both connected to the same old sewer network. It was abandoned and never finished, but there's still a few places 'round the neighborhood where you can get down there. Those tunnels go down—*deep*. All the way down to the natural caverns and water channels."

"How do we get inside?" Lucy asked. "If Glass is hiding the mouth to Hell right under our feet, that's where we gotta go."

"Hell, *no*," Tabby cried. "I ain't about to set foot back in that house. *Fuck that place*."

"Well, we can't just walk right up to his faithful flock over at the Mission, neither."

"*Stop*," Apollo commanded. "Stop right here."

The car's tires screeched to a halt as the ground rumbled beneath them. Another wall of seafoam and black water breached the seawall, stronger than any previous wave. Before Lucy could turn around, the backseat was already empty. Cold, wet air billowed in through the back row's open door.

"Don't built 'em like they used to," she heard Apollo mumble.

He emerged on the side of the car and marched forward through its headlights.

"You can't hear em," his voice began to trail off. "Don't need to. You *feel* 'em—"

"Fuck it," Tabby said. "Looks like we ain't stayin' dry today. Breakin' all the rules…"

"There," Apollo shouted, pointing ahead as he marched.

Lucy's eyes followed the line from his fingertip down the remaining stretch of pavement. The road turned at a right angle where it departed its parallel path alongside the Belt Parkway and the coast to make way for an offramp. Just beyond the turn, beneath the highway offramp and a cluster of towering trees, the lawn dipped and became increasingly dominated by neglected plant life and roadside debris. Apollo trudged forward, indifferent to the sky cascading down upon him. Lucy flipped up her rain jacket's hood and jumped out to follow. Raindrops rode on gusts of wind, falling down often as they flew upward and across—chaotic and untethered to gravity's traditional tendencies. Without waiting for an invitation, Tabby did the same. After a few seconds, her flashlight's beam joined the procession. The light sprinted ahead of Apollo and landed in the bushes. Gray paint and red bricks shined back at them through the mess of branches and shrubs. Tabby's flashlight traced the edges of the brick shack and the twin lightning bolts etched into the trim of its flat roof. Apollo's feet crossed from the roadway and *sploshed* down between tufts of long, sopping blades of grass.

"There y'go," he said. "That's one of 'em, right there."

"Whatever it's *one of*," Tabby said, "it doesn't look like anybody's used it for much of anything in a long time."

"Exactly. Before he bought that theater and turned it into his own, personal Vatican—before he dug halfway to Hell beneath his house—this is what him and goons like me used to use when we needed to get real invisible, real quick. The hatches inside these old access shacks go deep, just like the ones under his house or the Loew's. Not as direct, but deep enough."

"Are they safe?" Lucy asked.

"No. Not at all."

"Then what are we supposed to do?"

"*We* ain't doin' shit," Apollo said as he began to move again. "*You two* are stayin' up here. I'm goin' in."

"What? You can't do this alone. I thought we said we were in this together."

"*Can* you actually do this alone?" Tabby added. "Not sure if you're aware, but you've been talking to yourself for the past hour—"

"I've got a lot on mind!" Apollo snapped. "Lotsa shit goin' on right now… I'm sure you've noticed."

"I'm sorry," Tabby replied with feigned sincerity. "I didn't mean to disrespect the *diagnosed mental patient* who wants to wander off alone into the city sewer system during a rainstorm."

"I'm pretty fucked, yeah. But I've been fucked for a long time now. *I* know how to deal with *me* better than anyone. What's thirteen years in halfway homes gotten me?"

"You don't wanna be there?" Lucy interrupted. "You don't wanna go back? That's fine. We can deal with that later. But Tabby's right—we need you too much right now to risk you getting distracted or… lost. We need you to calm down and work on staying focused."

"I ain't some eighty-year-old cripple, shittin' in a diaper, can't answer what year it is or who's the president."

Apollo approached them slowly, his voice lower but no less powerful.

"All this shit—the shit you two think I'm tryin' to hide? That's a *fraction* of how much those people down *there* are ready to fuck you up. You don't gotta have one foot already in the grave before they suck the soul outta your body. True sufferin', true *despair*. Powerlessness in your own body. All the safest places in your mind and happiest memories invaded by every hateful spirit circlin' the void while doctors and hacks play fast an' loose with pills. Every second you're dyin', there's always somebody who feels the need to remind you to just '*calm down*' and ' *stay focused.*' That's how you stretch a human lifetime into an eternity in Hell…"

A dog barked as Apollo's words faded in between the raindrops. Cars raced up and down the Belt Parkway, tire tracks noisily slicing through growing pools of water heaved inland by the churning bay.

"And I don't wanna' hafta' see it happen to anyone else," Apollo's voice cracked. "I don't wanna' bring a single other person down with me. You just gotta trust me."

"Do we have a choice?" Tabby asked, consciously throttling any frustration from her voice.

"No. I know my way down there better than either of you. Can't have you two trippin' all over each other—and *me*. I'll go in there first. Scout it out. If it turns out the *stupid jerk* ain't even down there, we won't have wasted too much time. If he *is*, well… we can worry about crossin' that bridge when we come to it."

"And what exactly are we supposed to do in the meantime?"

"Back your car down the block. Keep the lights off. Listen to the radio, get dry, and keep yourselves from fadin' out. I thought the two'a youse was cops. Shouldn't hafta' tell youse how to do a damn stakeout."

Tabby clicked her flashlight off and flipped it over in her hand.

"Take it. Brand new."

She held the butt of the flashlight out towards Apollo. He waved it away.

"Nah," he said softly. "Don't need it. My head's pretty fucked up, but some things you don't forget. I've spent a lotta time down there. I know the shadows pretty well."

"You might," Tabby added, "but after all that time and all that misery, what if they know you better?"

Apollo stood silent, contemplating. His arm reached forward. He tucked the stubby Maglite into his back pocket, then turned and continued his march into the darkness.

"If you don't come back in an hour, we're comin' in after you," Lucy said.

"If I ain't back in an hour, it 'prolly means we're all fucked anyway."

Apollo's palm gripped the side of one of the shack's doors and pulled. The metallic whine harmonized with the howls of the wind. When the back of Apollo's head was overtaken by the darkness, Lucy and Tabby turned back toward her car. Lucy pulled the gear shifter and the car began to reverse. From their new point of view, the headlights barely penetrated the undergrowth surrounding the brick structure. The door had not swung closed behind Apollo, and a sliver of the light managed to beam inside. Behind an indistinct pile of refuse and invasive vines, white paint peeled and flaked. Lucy reached for the dashboard and turned the headlights off. Everything inside the shack went dark.

Nineteen

Nearly every other metal slat among the dozen which ran the length of the louvered metal door either slouched onto the next beneath it or bent inward with the expressed intent to peel free entirely. Prominent, rectangular gaps signaled some already had. Apollo reached forward. He braced his hand against the cold, aluminum frame. The patches where the door boasted its most recent touch-ups of lead paint felt slick and dewy. The filmy surface formed little more than a thin barrier to conceal the bubbles of metallic corrosion rising beneath. Closer to the door's worn edges, Apollo's fingers felt the exposed, oxidizing iron as he pushed. Although it protested sharply the entire way, the door scraped inward. As Apollo turned sideways, he sucked in the paunch which time and inertia graciously visited upon him. The doorway leading into the squat, brick shed was slender and purely utilitarian. It had not been designed to welcome many into its seemingly cramped quarters. Apollo's feet crossed the threshold. His gut relaxed. He took a deep breath.

Within the thick walls, the sound of falling rain and the turbulent bay breaking on the other side of the highway were muffled. Apollo listened to the rhythm of his own breath while his eyes scanned the floor. Light from the front end of Lucy's car filtered through the still partially opened doorway and the multitude of lesser gaps featured thereon. The years had been fruitful for the already extensive collection of junk and debris strewn across the floors and lurching up into the room's four corners. Just as Apollo did now, the abundant and infrequently tamed flora outside probed every gap in the shed's interior. Through an abundance of opportunity and structural deficiencies, webs of wandering, brown roots traced the brickwork.

The tip of Apollo's boot ran along the edge of a stack of splintered plywood sheets. He grabbed the handle to an old manual push mower beneath. Its bladed wheel had rusted over, stuck completely and uninterested in spinning out of Apollo's way. As he shimmied and shoved at the machine, he could see the edge of the hatch. The mower's blades finally gave and the remaining debris followed it aside. Apollo grunted as he stooped. The hatch itself rose without any physical or audible objection, swung aside, and permitted the dark world below to gaze upward without obstruction. As Apollo leaned over the opening, the headlights outside died. Like a geyser, the darkness surged to fill the room. He felt the butt of the flashlight tucked into his back pocket. It was increasingly clear to Apollo, reacquainted with clarity to fluctuating degrees over a short period of time, that Martin had not left him with the same faculties or memories. He resisted his move for the flashlight and recommitted himself to exploring the depths with only his memory.

What little noise of the raindrops and the sea penetrated the brick shack above, none survived as the murky tunnel climbed over Apollo rung-by-rung. His hands came to a rest on the ladder. The opposite wall of the slender shaft was near enough to lean back without fully extending his arms. Apollo tilted the back of his head against the cold, stone wall. It was impossible to avoid the disorientation—that much he remembered. The world stretching above looked blank as the abyss into which he descended. He chose to embrace the dizziness and his hands and feet agreed to lower him. An expanding vacuum of time and space surrounded Apollo until a moment of hesitation spread from his stomach to his brain, then out to his fingers and toes. A memory. His right foot carefully probed the black pit below. The ground reached up in confirmation.

Apollo dismounted the rungs and brought himself tight against the wall. The corridors and hallways at the bottom of the ladder stretched the length of the waterfront. He needed to remember which turns he would need to take, which to avoid—which were dead ends and which, without the aid of light, would send him tumbling to an end of his own. Long-dormant memories and the spaces between leaked out of his mind to project across the void. Cold neurons and synapses reawakened. Strange chemicals seeped into Apollo's veins and mixed with his blood stream, complimenting the acrid, caustic aromas billowing into his nose. Stranger thoughts and thoughts of strangers followed, begging for attention amidst a tempest involuntarily summoned inside his head. Walls and turns and corners, metrics measured in footsteps filled the darkness. So did emotions and people. Apollo yelled at himself to get a grip. He could taste blood on his tongue.

"Focus you *goddamned burnout*," he growled as his molars dug into the inside of his cheek.

Apollo felt the hallway in his memory fluctuate. Though the space in which he found himself stood still, his shifting recollection of its layout made his stomach churn. The sound of his own voice chided him.

"You're fucked.   This time, you definitely fucked yourself good. Darkness ain't emptiness. Shoulda' known better."

Apollo crumpled down. When he found himself on his knees, his fingers spread onto the hallway's dirt-covered cement floor. The cold earth leeched up into his palms.

"You're gonna stumble 'round in circles. You're gonna lose your mind, screamin' like a maniac. Take a step into a pit, break your leg. Scream. Bleed out. Maybe they'll find you an' slit your throat before you black out. Or maybe they'll just sit in the shadows and watch you die on your own."

The voice bounced off the walls without ever leaving the inside of Apollo's head. Insults and promises of failure rambled down the hallway, then sprinted back full speed to barrel into him. Fresh mockery called before the last could fade.

"No better than them—"

"Doesn't change a thing—"

"The whole bunch of 'em—"

"Gettin' what you deserve—"

"Better off dead—"

Apollo's voice cracked. Fluids filled every cavity of his sinuses. His diaphragm seized and his esophagus erupted.   Hot bile splattered across his fingers. When his mouth was empty, he gasped. Impatient lungs pleaded for more air of higher quality than the stale, moldy vapors he struggled to pull in past his paralyzed throat.   Eyes bulging and vision vibrating, Apollo strained and begged to hide his pupils from the limitless black ocean around him. With no other option, he scoured the darkness between the waves of static that crept into the corners of his vision until they coalesced, rushing over his eyes in an explosion of light. In the fleeting blast, he saw the silhouette of a second story windowpane.

"You'll never get away—"

"Choke on their own blood—"

"There's no light at the end of the tunnel—"

"But they don't gotta suffer, too—"

"Gotta wipe the rest of 'em out—"

"The only way to keep 'em safe—"

"Do yourself in first—"

Apollo's right hand twitched. His fingers remembered every word. His heart remembered everything else. Smoking barrels and dripping knives. Rattling lungs and rictus faces.   Fathers and mothers and sons and daughters and dozens and dozens more. Another warm torrent dribbled down between the webbing of his fingers and soaked with the decades' detritus in a pool beneath his palms. His mind circled a spinning tide of faces. He felt himself sinking as the voices weakened his grasp between retching volleys.

They loomed and drifted away until one remained—anguish in the face of loss in the photograph, despair in the face of imprisonment in the basement of Elysian Fields. Apollo focused on her pain. It had carried him to the doorway. If he did not continue, even in vain, he would secure that agony for all eternity. Her face faded and the fog that filled the darkness began to part. One face, which he did not recognize, remained. As soon as they passed through a corner of his vision, the features of a young man quickly faded on the tail end of the madness and Apollo found himself alone in the quiet, pitch black tunnel.

"Get a—huh," he wheezed, wrestling back control of his voice. "Get a *grip*…"

Apollo rested on knees and elbows. His forehead rolled side-to-side on the soiled backs of his hands. The air, thick and stirred by panic, coated his burning throat in a chalky film. The particles accompanied the air into his nose and filled his thoughts with simpler moments and familiar odors. Cloying chemical sweetness. Wispy, sulfuric fumes. Ballistic residue. Chalky, mineral rings marked the peaks of long forgotten pools of stagnant, saline water, then dissolving back into the returning tide. Apollo grunted. He pulled himself off the ground. His knees wobbled. Apollo reached for his back pocket and sighed. The button on the side of the flashlight clicked, and a dull, dusty hallway appeared between the fingers shielding his eyes. Apollo leaned down again and removed his left boot. He pulled down the sides of one of the red, anti-skid hospital socks. The boot slid back over his naked foot and the flashlight slid down into the thick tube sock. The light which came out of the lamp was a little duller—a little redder. It was more than his own eyes required. His hand kept the beam low, illuminating the ground only a few inches ahead of his shuffling toes, while his ears kept alert. His thumb hovered over the Maglite's switch. With any luck, Apollo prayed he would be quicker than whoever he might hear approach.

Every step found a new patch of dull, sooty cement for Apollo's boots to grind over. Inches and yards became inscrutable as seconds and minutes. The sunken world around Apollo was indifferent to time or space—to any dimension other than its own hermitic twilight. It knew dark, cold, and damp, despite what the calendars above indicated. Anything else had no future in such a place. Any*one* else might not share in what the darkness and Apollo understood mutually. He would periodically come to a stop and raise a fluent hand to his side. This time, his palm did not return to him covered in the ashen grime which progressively tallied streaky hashmarks of incorrect doorways swiped across his shirt.

Calloused, dusty fingers softened and relaxed as the dew on the doorframe flooded the ridges and pores of Apollo's hand. He flipped his palm and ran the back of his knuckles along the rusted metal arch. Cold as it was around him, the back of his neck bristled when his skin confirmed the frigid wetness. This water had not condensed out of the passing air. It trickled in from another place. Apollo turned and entered.

The muffled, ruddy light seeping through the fabric of his removed sock confirmed an abrupt break with conventional architecture and materials. The rift grew more evident as he continued. The initial transition from the Twentieth to the Nineteenth Century was stark in every perceivable sense. The height and width of the individual bricks shrank inversely to the route's overall breadth and peak. Apollo's back ached from stooping for so long, though he remained successful in avoiding any unnecessary collisions between his skull and the many low-hanging pipes or other irregular, provisional features strapped ad hoc along the previous tunnel. He stood fully upright now and the more senior masonry formed a fanciful arch over his head. Alternating patterns of glazed enamels shined back down at him from a vaulted ceiling designed purely for the aesthetic pride of its designers and theoretical enjoyment of the small handful of technicians and maintenance workers who would ever wander through. Closer to the littered earth, patterns and drawings scratched into the bricks indicated more recent guests, though no less anticipated by the system's chief architect. Apollo counted himself among them, even if he never shared their artistic flares. He read their graffiti again for the first time in over a decade. Crude, satanic imagery. Names and years gone by. Poorly reproduced magic triangles and summoning circles. Misspelled demonic seals. Incorrectly oriented pentagrams. Empty bottles of booze, candles, and used condoms gathered dust along the edges of the walls.

The ground developed a growing slope as Apollo continued. With no visible horizon or end ahead of him, it was difficult to pinpoint exactly where the initial change in grade occurred. Ever thicker splotches of black mold burrowed deep into the mortar between the bricks, and any downturn in the masonry was indistinct. When Apollo's borrowed light next returned to the walls, the grime progressively spilled over to infect their collective mosaic and render each brick a dull, blackened mass. The corruption continued until the raw bedrock itself swallowed the tapering brickwork. Carved from stone itself, the walls broadened further. Gravity and subtle declination pulled Apollo forward along a path grown wider and taller, with irregular, imperfect clefts and incisions along the way. The path was older and grander than the vaults which marked the turn of the previous century, predated by centuries turning ever earlier.   His foot slapped the ground, unexpectedly level once more, and he wobbled. Apollo came to a stop and listened. The noise of his misstep echoed on ahead. He waited, wary of anyone else betraying their own presence. Nothing returned through the passage to indicate such.

Apollo slowly removed his palm from where it throttled the top of the flashlight's lamp. It crept along the ground just ahead of his feet. After a few yards, it swung to explore the wider world once more. The ground remained smooth as it unfolded before him, while the walls and sky ebbed and flowed in igneous seamlessness. If the cavity had been forged by natural or human efforts, the intervening time left either origin indiscernible, and any question of such nature soon became irrelevant. Just as the earlier designs of an industrious era twisted and disappeared into the descending earth, now too did organic logic become disfigured.   Reconfigured. Rearranged and reconstructed into something brutal—vulgar as it was bafflingly refined and alien as it was innately and disturbingly relatable.   The universe's perfect, black geometry loomed over Apollo. Polygonal planes of hexagons and squares, octagons and triangles with neither identifiable gaps nor comforting patterns emerged from the rock. As they had in the past, they still reminded Apollo of the insides of geodes—but these ebony tiles had not crystalized by the Earth's desire or schedule. They were shaped by devotion and erected by zealots—constructed over hundreds of years by generations united in purpose but never in place. Apollo returned to their cathedral, head bowed as ever. Though the slabs of obsidian grew more massive and polished, when the beam of his light occasionally reached them, little light escaped their facets. What returned to Apollo was only a latticed glare where stone rested upon stone—scattered photons suggesting grids of constellation-like outlines making up a framework of some greater whole.

There was, however, a more conventional brand of craftsmanship and artistry featured prominently along the base of a pair of columns. Most of the stones surrounding Apollo's path remained unblemished blocks of relentless blackness. Into a few arching over the pathway were carved ornate mandalas and tributes, articulated by more enlightened and authoritative artisans than the amateurish graffiti now far behind and above. Rarer others depicted forceful busts and impressive tributes to powerful figures. In some scenes they towered over reverent choirs and fearful, huddled crowds. The images were hollowed out as counter-reliefs, with inverse sneers and pupils that followed Apollo as he passed. Stone ribs bulged and gradually splintered from the walls into separate columns, thicker and more numerous until the tunnel's walls disappeared behind a polylithic thicket of black, light-devouring pillars. A cavernous clearing opened before Apollo. An array of dark stumps and plinths and megaliths surrounded the vast, sloping room. Some towered overhead without ever connecting to the ceiling. The floor slumped like a deforested crater until the columns, complete or otherwise, thinned to extinction. Apollo gazed down upon the heart of the massive chamber, at its broad plateau and the simple altar, for the first time in years.

Strange shapes—strange to Apollo and strange to the room's sublime decoration—assembled together near the center of the expanse. There were modern things and unfantastic devices designed for less-lofty utilities. Gas-powered tools and generators. Dormant construction lamps. Cages and chains. Under a pile of disheveled clothing lie a man, prostrate and nearly motionless, not far from the altar. Apollo squinted. Beneath the clothes, smeared and dirty, the man's chest rose and shuddered as it exhaled. Apollo extinguished his flashlight and listened to the distant, laboring breaths. They came from multiple, struggling mouths, he realized.

Above them all, the ceiling peaked around a narrow aperture. This singular portal to the world above permitted the subterranean world's only source of natural radiance. Apollo's eyes adjusted and eventually the room and everything around it emerged in simple, monochromatic outlines. The floor rippled in wide, cyclical circles as it descended and levelled out into the center of the chamber. Apollo held his breath as he became aware of motion. Not a carving or optical illusion—nothing he had ever observed in this place in the past. With every rotation around the room's perimeter, every subsequent wave of shadows grew thicker. Oscillating between more liquid and more gaseous tendencies, the shadows collected around the edges of the clearing, swirling and rising to obscure the already modest light. The tide lapped at the edges of the platform, reaching further atop the edge as it circled. Riding one decisive crest, the shadows lapped at the fallen man's feet. Another excited wave spread the darkness under one hand and the next over it. A choking noise bounced across the room. The man jerked upright and wobbled onto his elbows, sputtering and coughing. He grabbed at his nose and wiped, then flipped himself over. The spinning floor suddenly seized and retreated.

"What," the man croaked. "What the fu-uck..."

The shadows climbed higher as they receded, then lurched forward to hover over the man. Gathering his bearings continued to present a challenge. He stumbled as he tried to climb atop his own feet. With a wince, he collapsed back down and hugged an ankle.

"Charlie. I... I know."

His teeth clenched tightly as he gasped. The room responded with silence and the darkness continued to close in. As he heard the name called, Apollo remembered the oaf with whom he came toe-to-toe. His imagination recalled the slurred speech, subtracted a couple of decades and added a year of sobriety. Strong similarities emerged. If that identified the injured man as Dexter—the older brother, the oldest son—it validated Apollo's intuition. This was the place, he realized. He thought about the girls. They would wait, but only for so long. Apollo's mind wavered. While his frame shifted on indecisive feet, Dexter continued to wail at the swirling shadows.

"I know you're here."

He grunted and pushed his own weight back onto his stronger foot. What balance he maintained was visibly tenuous.

"Face me, damn it! Come out and show me your *fucking* face!"

A glint shimmered over the forest of black glass. The unexpected sheen elicited simultaneous flinches from both Apollo and Dexter. A younger man, lesser in stature, stepped casually out of the looming void. Apollo examined the man's feet more closely. Not stepping, he realized. There was nothing to tether him to the solid ground. The figure's feet floated with the rest of the billowing darkness and drifted closer.

"Charlie," Dexter barked at the apparition again. "It didn't have to be like this."

Tears choked the senior Valerie brother's voice. His words wilted to an uncontrollable mess of rambling murmurs.

"It didn't have to... I'm sorry..."

Dexter collapsed again. If it was an exhaustion of physical strength or emotional composition that grounded him beneath the impassive figure, Apollo would never tell the difference. Mixed cries of pain and despair overtook his tearful pleas. Apollo detected no further serious attempts by Dexter to rise. His throat whistled and his breathing became labored without any obvious attempts to reassemble himself. Charlie slowed and stopped. But for his stagnant approach, the younger brother remained motionless until a slight jerk travelled down his shoulder to his left hand. Fingers twitched.

"Dext..."

Charlie's hand rose and reached forward.

"Run," he hissed.

Pressure shifted in the room. The breeze sent a chill over the backs of Apollo's arms. The last impulses to retreat dissolved amid a rapidly growing sense of terror and dire exigency. Apollo knew they would follow after him. Thirty minutes or an hour may have already passed. For all he knew, they may have started after him already, blindly retracing his steps when he failed to reappear. One look at the black sacrament advancing before his eyes was more than he needed to assure him any such precautions or interceptions on his own part would come far too late.

"No," Dexter sobbed. "We can both get out of here. Away. From… *him*."

"Never."

A vacuum was emerging somewhere directly below the apertured ceiling of the chamber. Gusts and gales pulled the air, lifting Charlie's greasy, knotted locks into the sky, higher and higher until the young man's hair twisted and turned. A new, radiant glow emerged from within the billowing, black fog in bursts and sparks. It smoldered amidst gloom and electricity and assembled a towering thunderhead. The vaporous pillar grew brighter and taller—looming behind Charlie, twisting until it fractured. One tendril and then another spun out from the mass, extending into fingers. In one of the materializing hands dangled the form of a black snake. It writhed and hissed, fangs snapping and dripping with black venom. The other hand expanded into a claw, then lunged forward. When it landed on Charlie's shoulder, the air shook violently. Beams of light bled from the boy's eyes and mouth, then spread across his body. Apollo's jaw hung low until he forced it shut, while his eyes rose over the brilliant torch Charlie had become. Another head, bald and pierced by a plethora of black spikes, floated over Charlie's.

Apollo had never laid eyes upon Belial outside the confines of his dreams. He hated those dreams. They made him fear what awaited him in his sleep. When Martin Glass cursed him to suffer a life of waking nightmares, one small mercy was the sudden and unbroken absence of the head of the infernal pantheon. Although Belial was made no part of that covenant, Apollo was sure three was nothing to make those circumstances worse. Regretfully, the events unfolding before him indicated otherwise.

Charlie reached down. His hands clamped onto the sides of one of the loose obsidian slabs scattered irregularly upon the chamber's central mesa. Without effort, the stone rose into the air. From its size, Apollo estimated it must have weighed twenty or thirty times the young man lifting it. As the beams of light continued to pour from Charlie's face, his features lost definition. Black blood dripped down a stark mouth among the remaining, characterless orifices. The sight became unbearable, and Apollo watched his view shrink behind one of the room's many pillars. His eyelids slammed down, trying desperately to wipe the stubborn, pernicious images away.

None of this could prevent him hearing Dexter's mouth string together a few desperate, exhausted sounds.

"Why'd ya 'follow me?'"

A sharp, wet *crack* reported around the vast, stone forest. After a silent moment, something clattered loudly against the ground. The last whisper of wind hissed over Apollo's head, swept away with the rest of the noise into the hole in the cave's roof. Apollo rose slowly, prying his eyes open and peering toward the platform. Dexter's body lie parallel with the floor once more. By his head—still mostly *over* his head—rest the massive stone slab. Another dark shadow spread from beneath it, thicker and more sluggish than the foggy substance which fled the room with the wind, the demon, and the vision of the fratricidal younger sibling.

Apollo's hand trembled as he braced against the nearest stone plinth. He grabbed it with his other hand to steady himself. Both hands trembled together. The despair and guilt Apollo brought down with him were absent. That weight, gone from his shoulders, shifted to somewhere between his heart and stomach. Apollo was still returning to sanity when his remaining senses recognized the approaching footsteps. Reflexes pulled him aside the path of more urgent strides clopping down the hard, stony ground. The newcomer's feet accelerated into a hasty sprint. Apollo kept himself still and low, but near enough to feel the breeze that filled the wake of the rushing figure. It was a man. His feet reeled to a stop as he surveyed the scene.

Apollo watched Doctor Martin Glass approach the crumpled, bloody heap. His hands began to rub together involuntarily, one over the other, as he glared at Martin. The flesh on his palms felt rough, cracked. They grated over the skin covering the backs of his hands, sagging loosely between old scars and the emerging ulcers of a life spent over-exposed to the sun's radiation. None of the same decay stained this black chamber or the man standing at its center.

Anger pumped into Apollo's muscles. It all felt so much longer than thirteen years for him—it looked no more than a day for Martin. His motor functions were beginning to drift. From a fidget to a shuffle, Apollo became aware of the movements threatening to betray his presence. As alternating heels lifted, his calves seized them, forcing them slowly and gently flat against the ground. His foot shifted again and found something soft blocking it. The darkness squealed and Apollo jumped.

"Ah!" the voice rasped. "H-help… where…"

Apollo scoured the shadows, desperate to separate himself from the sudden commotion and find new cover. Too late—Martin's face and shoulders, relaxed and motionless, faced Apollo before he could realize the man had turned. The shadows began to ripple and writhe around him. Another face looked up from within. The young woman's hand trembled as it reached up. The shackles bound to her wrist jangled, slithering through the darkness with serpentine sheen to extend a plea. A mass of corroded, metal snakes joined her, all connected to rows of disheveled hospital gowns and the withering, shivering humanity which barely filled them. Fitful red socks squirmed at the bottoms of soiled sweatpants. More familiar faces emerged among them. Giuseppe's wheelchair was nowhere in sight. Instead, the man slouched along the frozen earth, chained together alongisde the rest of his fellow patients. Cold air flooded Apollo's veins. He watched the black, stone forest soar as his own perspective came closer to where Giuseppe lie, curled and shivering amidst the stirring desperation. For a moment, they were beneath the Fields, watching the sunlight slide across the floor through the basement's thin windows. When the flash cleared from his vision, he counted the rest of the fields—dragged unknown fathoms to bristle under chains and darkness. Mouths gasped and begged for air—lips and tongues struggled to form cries for help. Only one face remained steadfast, singularly motionless among the other prisoners. Apollo lifted himself slowly and followed Alice's catatonic stare back to the center of the room.

"Kowaliga. Apollo. An old friend, by any name."

"Monster," Apollo replied.

"Me?" Glass replied, feigning indignity. "It seems as though you are the one with blood on your hands, old friend. And that of yet another one of my devout, loyal pupils, nonetheless. Another victim of a weak man and his petty jealousy."

"You're a *fuckin' monster*. Martin. Albert. Whatever-the-fuck you wanna call yourself."

"Very insightful, for once, whether or not you fully realize it. I agree—what *is* in a name? None to which I have previously answered will matter soon. Many have called the Gods monsters now and again. If ever it was intended for disrespect—the last drops of venom from wounded beasts—perhaps it was never untrue. Maybe that is for the better."

Martin raised his hands and stretched them forward in a welcoming gesture. He embraced the air before him and took a step toward Apollo.

"In truth, in respect, I always yearned to be half the monster you are. At the very least *were*… in your prime. Whenever we took in some new riff raff off the streets, you were the shining example I would use to inspire them. You were the prototype. However, I also wish you could have been half as loyal—half as *dutiful*—as those very same people you repeatedly insist on taking away from me."

"Hah!"

Apollo tried to pack the laugh with venom, but the result was not nearly as intimidating as he had hoped.

"You've got bigger problems than me, *'old friend.'* You always did, however many centuries you wanna keep this crap going."

"Oh, dear," Martin continued to mock him. "I apologize if I ever gave you the impression that I considered you a problem. Quite to the contrary, no one has given me more enjoyment over the past… oh, tell me. How long has it been?—"

"Don't fuck with me, asshole! You know damn well how long. You enjoyed every goddamned second of what you put me through."

"You are right. How rude of me. I am ever so sorry, dear Kowaliga, but you know what they say about time: it just flies by when you are having fun."

Apollo had no memory of crossing the dark expanse, nor of stepping onto the platform. Nonetheless, he found himself a few feet away from Martin and towering six inches over the man's head in a heartbeat. The doctor did not move an inch as Apollo's body quaked and twitched with rage.

"I'm gonna rip that smug fuckin' face a'yours offa' your goddamn shoulders."

Warmth wrapped around Apollo. His fist disappeared into the darkness and the punch it carried dissolved. Memories of rituals and bloody mist filled his nose. The air was getting thicker and more resistant to Apollo's movement.

"No. Not much of a problem at all," Glass continued.

Apollo tried to throw his hands in Martin's direction once more, but the man sidestepped the attempted grapple without effort or doubt.

"But we must cheer up! How tremendous is fortune which delivered you to enjoy the company of your closest friends and neighbors in this hallowed place, at this most transcendent moment?"

"No idea," Apollo hissed through locked teeth.

"No? Of what?"

"No idea… of what's goin' on. In the dark… *as usual.*"

"That is difficult criticism for me to appraise, given how limited your view of the bigger picture has always been."

"You and your… *bullshit.* It's gonna kill us all… kill *you* too…"

Martin's feet stopped pacing and wheeled him around to face Apollo once more.

"You have come to me in a moment of spirited generosity. With a little reluctance, I must agree. You may be right."

The persistent joviality in Martin's voice made Apollo's blood boil. His arms strained, but remained frozen in place.

"Yes, my friend. You will die tonight. They will die, too. And, whether I succeed or fail, *Doctor Martin Glass* will most certainly die along with the rest of you."

"Not if… you die first…"

Foam and spittle gathered in the corners of Apollo's mouth. Pain racked his body as he tried to combat Martin's spell. Veins bulged through his skin as his blood pressure soared, either through his own frustrations or as a result of the mystical poison filling his body. Apollo's vision grew narrower. His mind separated further from his body and its place on the conscious plane. Shadows crept into the edges of his eyes. Martin's words became distorted and scratchy as Apollo continued to fade. Dozens of feet shuffled around them.

"Relax. I do not need you to be that warrior any longer. I need only your dreams, as ever, without end."

Twenty

"In a press release issued this week the H.J. Heinz Company, owner of the Star-Kist brand of canned tuna fish, announced that it would no longer process and distribute tuna captured in the style of nets known to also ensnare dolphins. The statement from Heinz was joined shortly thereafter by similar commitments from Bumble Bee Seafoods, Inc. and the Van Camp Seafood Company, producer of the Chicken of the Sea brand. The three companies, owners of the nation's most popular and widely distributed brands of canned tuna, account for nearly 70% of domestic sales. Reports by several environmental and wildlife protection agencies earlier this year estimated nearly 100,000 dolphins are killed each year among the millions of yellowfin tuna captured in the circular nets as they trawl the oceans' depths. Once the marine mammals become trapped among the schools of tuna, they become unable to resurface for air and drown before the nets are hauled."

Tabby checked the radio's display. It was getting close to ten o'clock and WNWS 990 had repeated the day's top headlines, traffic, and weather reports nearly a dozen times since she and Lucy last saw Apollo. Before he was out of earshot, whether he could hear it or cared, Lucy promised to follow if he did not return after an hour. That deadline passed more than thirty minutes earlier, and neither she nor Tabby had chosen to broach the subject. Instead, they sat in suspense with the white noise of AM radio.

"In an effort to persuade increasingly concerned consumers, a spokesman for Heinz stated that the company plans for all of its Star-Kist cans to boast new 'dolphin-safe' labels within the next three months."

A tempest blossomed in the darkness over Gravesend Bay. Wind blew sheets of rain and ejected seawater ashore, rocking Lucy's Toyota Corolla on its suspension. From stratosphere to treetops the storm was violent as it was murky, and what it chose to withhold from vision was made plain to every other sense. Tabby's eyes could only track the storm's advance by the strobes of lightning that burst to animate erratic frames of expanding, bubbling clouds. Every silent flare illustrated the lifecycle of fresh thunderheads descending from the swirling, black nebula. Violent arms thrashed and glowed, then collapsed in upon themselves and melted away. The Corolla's radio antenna whipped back and forth.

Static rolled across the repetitive broadcasts, buzzing as each wave battered the shoreline.

"Prominent environmental and wildlife activists applauded these decisions, but some remained skeptical:

"They don't fully realize what's going on beneath the surface," a new voice chimed in a recorded commentary, *"but they drop their nets and scrape the oceans' floors anyway. Earth's oceans cannot be treated like vast wells to be drawn upon for unending food or fuel or profit. They do not belong to any individual. They cannot sympathize with the goals of men or the boundaries of civilization. The world below the waves is more than some abstract, arbitrary, or alien ecosystem—it persists as the ancient wellspring of all known life, a singularly exceptional place in an otherwise indifferent universe. You cannot simply reconfigure the usual tools, paint some fresh slogans on the practice, set sail, and expect it to produce anything other than the same, old death and discord before you have finally realized your own fate."*

"Now, to sports," the newsreader returned. *"Speaking to reporters after a three-nothing win over the Texas Rangers, Bucky Dent anticipates a bright future for the Bronx Bombers despite the season's delayed start..."*

Though Tabby endured the same segue several times already, the tonal shift grew unbearable—however, it was Lucy's hand which reached the volume knob first.

"Enough," she said. "What're we gonna do?"

"He's a big boy," Tabby replied. "Then again, there's always bigger..."

"I know you're just as worried as I am. We told him and he heard us. One hour, just to scope it out. It's been nearly *two*."

"I'm not even supposed to be here right now."

"I wouldn't worry about that. Cordell won't be around to break anybody's balls until he comes in to do his midnight around eleven. Anyone else drives by, all they're gonna see is an empty corner with the skies opened up overhead. They'll just assume you're in the coffee shop, dry and well caffeinated."

Punitive or trivial as it might be, it was not the fear of being discovered in dereliction of her assignment which forced Tabby to lean forward onto the edge of the passenger seat. The portable radio on her belt was freshly charged. Though the call volume on the tour was picking up, as was custom when afternoon matured to evening, there had been no indication of any inquiries as to her whereabouts. Following Apollo's footsteps underground would render her police radio little more than an inert, plastic brick. She turned the radio on its swivel and unlocked it from her belt. It was heavy and unevenly balanced toward the bottom as it turned, end-over-end, from hand to hand. If nothing else, Tabby realized, it could make an effective bludgeon if the shadows decided to leap out at her.

Tabby twisted the knob on the top of her radio. The central dispatcher broadcast calls faster than the responding units could offer dispositions.

"At this time in the Six Four, receiving a call for a 10-54 EDP," Central droned rhythmically. *"Third party caller states there's an unknown woman screaming from the rooftop of his building, shouting nonsense about something in the sky."*

"That's called the weather channel, Central," someone responded. *"Mark it ninety-yellow—"*

"Standby, units. We've got two more calls coming in from the same location, possibly one-in-the-same," Central continued without acknowledging the sarcastic transmission. *"Reports of multiple suspicious persons, possibly a disorderly group, heading southbound on Kings Highway toward McDonald Avenue from within the confines of the Six Five Precinct. The description is…"*

Tabby's stomach flipped. There was something in the voice as it faded away—the effect of some message unravelling on the dispatcher's terminal incongruous enough to reconfigure skepticism into hesitation.

"Not a good sign when someone paid to talk for a living finds themselves at a loss words," she murmured as Central stammered their way back from nonfluency.

"Be advised, that description… approximately twenty-to-thirty individuals in all black clothing—does that say 'too dark to make out clothes or features?'—disrupting traffic and marching down the center of Kings Highway, knocking out streetlights along the way. Multiple Six Five units en route. Six Five patrol supervisor now requesting all available cars from the Six Four converge at the Precinct boundaries to intercept their path."

Lucy's hand shot toward Tabby's radio. She dug her thumb against the transmitter button.

"Read that description again, Central," she asked. "The clothing, the perps. What did you say they looked like?"

"Uh, well," Central began. *"This is just what the 911 operator typed in, but both… no, now three callers… they all say the same thing. All black clothing… robes? Six Four Adam, Six Four Charlie, I'm gonna need to redirect you over to—"*

"This is Six Four Adam, Central—negative," the unit responded. *"You'll need to raise up another sector. Be advised, we're still out on these seventy missings over here at the Fields."*

The world shimmered outside Lucy's car. A ripple spread from one streetlamp to the next. The dark flourish wove its way across the neighborhood, then washed away and returned life to each light. Tabby watched a house across the way disappear, illuminated windows and front door momentarily dampened behind a billowing curtain of rain and far-flung sea water. When a delicate glow returned, the light wavered, imperfectly restored to life.

"*Six Four Adam,*" Central came back quickly. "*I'm gonna need you to redirect, regardless. At this time, that Kings Highway job is being upgraded to a 10-33 of an explosion, unknown in nature. I show FD and the Six Five rolling. Details still coming through, standby. Receiving another job now, on Cropsey Avenue—*"

The same electrostatic torrent rolling over the land overloaded the capacity of the radio's already strained VHF band. Disheartened voices and distorted electronic chirps dissolved beneath a swell of static buzzing.

"It's starting," Tabby's voice added over the frenzied chorus. "Apollo was right."

"Then, are we too late?" Lucy asked.

"I dunno. Probably. All the more likely the longer we sit here considering the possibility."

Tabby leaned forward, straining as she twisted to the left. The discs in her spine issued a satisfying series of pops as they realigned. She flexed to the right to mirror the exercise. She stretched to her limit, then beyond. No matching release materialized. Disappointed and unwilling to insert a cramp between her ribs, she pulled at her door's handle.

"Guess that means it's time to get this over with," she heard Lucy mutter as her own door handle clicked.

A gale of icy, wet needles rode the currents. Tabby wiped the raindrops away as they gathered around her eyes. Lingering warmth on the back of her hand slid across her cheek, though numbness had already begun to seep into both. Her feet crossed over the curb, from asphalt to the unkempt, patchy lawn sloping down to the squat utility shack. Rivulets cascaded around Tabby's boots as they trampled over the drooping muck. Another burst of lightning framed the storm overhead. Seconds later, the dull roar of thunder followed. The noise withered to a distant grumble and a red light flared to life on Tabby's radio.

"*Six Four sergeant, Central,*" the radio crackled once more. "*Show me rollin' eighty-four. Be advised, the street's clear. Storm's knockin' out the lights is all—*"

"*No—the walls. Look up on the walls!*" a voice in the background of the transmission urged. "*The shadows, they're movin'! How many is that?*"

Tabby could not remember when her feet broke into a full sprint, but she found herself breathless by the time she was within an arm's length of the shack's louvered, metal door. Without waiting for her hand, a gust of wind swung the door wide. Her stomach flashed unease at the sight. The fury of the weather and the telegraphed reports of Hell clawing its way onto the streets and emergency radio bands of Brooklyn carried her feet over the threshold. Lucy joined her within a fraction of a second, any misgivings similarly abandoned outside with the frigid rain. Tabby turned and pressed her forearm against the edge of the door. After a brief struggle to seal the entrance, she welcomed the stillness. While rain still pounded against the roof above them, the wind was reduced to a draft.

"A part of me wishes you hadn't given him your flashlight," Lucy admitted somewhere in the nearby darkness.

"Tell me about it. Second one I've lost this week. That shit adds up."

Tabby gave her eyes a moment to adjust. Windows had not been considered in the shack's design. The dented, warped slats on the doors might have permitted some ambient light within. As it was, the light without was too scarce to make a difference. Thusly, when a dim glow began to crawl toward Tabby's boots, her eyes followed it to the source. A few feet away, through a trough carved into the junk and debris littering the room, rectangular seams emerged along the ground. She recognized the rim of a partially opened hatch and crouched lower. Faint glimmers poked through rusty fissures in the corroded metal plate. Tabby and Lucy held their breath, fixated on the portal. It began to whisper.

"—and that's the last of 'em," a distant voice spoke. "That's why Glass said to sweep all the entrances. We can't have any loose ends—can't afford no more fuck-ups."

Tabby slouched down from the tips of her boots and onto her belly. She reached down to her belt and twisted the volume knob on her radio until it clicked off. Dust scraped against her jacket as she squirmed closer to the hatch. She squinted, closing one eye and directing the other over the edge and into the shaft. The distant, bouncing light exposed a faint, dull series of crusty ladder rungs. Beyond that lie a murky concrete floor—slick and slightly damp in the path of an approaching party.

"What do you see?" Lucy whispered.

Tabby shrugged. She saw a thirty-foot drop and little else. Whoever approached the path below, carrying a flashlight of their own, was not someone whose attention she wished to earn. The floor at the other end of the shaft disappeared. A head of black hair stepped into its place and turned. Tabby jerked herself back from the edge of the hatch a moment before the full beam of the flashlight rose upward. The rays drifted back and forth across the underside of the metal plate, scattering light throughout the shack. Tabby turned. She saw the outline of Lucy's head, low to the ground between a push mower and massive a spool of ancient, frayed electrical cable. The light wagged upward, then retreated back into the earth.

"Alright, enough 'a this," another voice rose up from the tunnel. "We've wasted enough time. Let's get this bitch goin' already!"

Tabby allowed a few heartbeats and the group below to pass. The light grew dimmer and the commentary of the muttering goons below them faded.

"Won't need a flashlight if we got *them*," Tabby said.

"You wanna follow them?" Lucy whispered back. "How do we know they won't see us?"

"What other choice is there? You heard 'em—they're headin' straight to whatever-the-hell's goin' on down there. Better if *we're* tailing *them*. Last thing we need is to be left stumbling around in the dark and they get the jump on us. Or they get the jump on Apollo—"

A loud thud travelled up from the tunnel and interrupted Tabby. A hoot followed.

"Oh, wudda' jerk!"

"Shut up, asshole. That pipe nearly knocked my head off!"

"Quit yer cryin' an' keep your eyes forward, dipshits."

Lucy let out a thoughtful hum. They were young. Morons, too. Going by their accents, any one of them could have been selected from among the usual rotation of local, teenage delinquents. She knew what it was like, watching them like hawks before they stumbled into all the most easily foreseeable legal missteps. If Doctor Glass was keeping this bunch in line, Tabby realized she owed the man credit. There was also the very real possibility that the trio of braying jackasses below represented the best he could do.

"Fair enough," she whispered to Tabby. "All the demons and black magic and in the universe can't fix that kind of stupid."

"Right," Tabby agreed, prying up an edge of the hatch. "We'll hang back, just far enough."

Tabby squinted, attempting to gauge the length of the tunnel which stretched out in front of her. She heard Lucy descend the last of the hatch's rungs and softly flatten the bottoms of her shoes onto the ground. The group—three males, white, late teens or early twenties, she reckoned—pressed on. The ambient light from their flashlight faded to little more than a meager flicker as they charted their own stumbling path through the heavy darkness. What few rays returned to Tabby and Lucy provided only minimal hints to their immediate surroundings. Tabby was more than happy to watch them concuss themselves on every low-hanging pipe snaking across the cramped tunnel's ceiling. For her part or Lucy's, she could not afford any such knocks or slips. Loud as they were, they would quickly turn on any blunder which they could not use to pin ridicule upon one another over.

The space grew tighter as the journey continued. The goons were unable to stand three-abreast, let alone walk completely upright. The third head bringing up the rear of the bunch loped along a yard or two behind the lead pair. Occasionally, irregularly, his profile turned into her view. If he was aware of his tail he offered Tabby no indication, but each time he looked over his shoulder—whenever the flashlight's ambient glow revealed another detail on his face—she suspected they would not find each other so strange.

On their own, Tabby and Lucy never attempted to stand at each other's shoulders. An abundance of precaution and physical limitations made Tabby commit to an exaggerated stoop as she scurried along. The ache in her lower back urged her to scurry faster, but she resisted. Dust and chipped concrete scratched at the bottom of her boots louder than she would have preferred. She let her palms stretch out ahead, guide her hand-over-hand, weary for unexpected protrusions. Multitude pipelines and conduits had been braided over and through one another as passing decades and functions dictated the tunnel's keepers. Every cranny her fingers brushed added a stream of pebbly detritus to the soot grinding beneath her feet and Lucy's a moment later. More than once, Tabby jerked away from smoldering, exposed pipes whose protective linings had either been gnawed away or slowly succumb to decay. For her own sake, she prayed the insulation on the tunnel's electrical lines fared better.

Finer senses of mental and temporal awareness diminished. Motor functions took over. It was difficult to gauge the duration or distance of the plunge into the underworld as Tabby's body navigated more mechanically. It was even harder to stop her mind straying along its own path through the twilight until their quarry made a sudden, sharp turn. The beam of light and the babbling, jostling heads disappeared. The only indication they were not entirely abandoned to a world of pure darkness was a faint, indirect glow escaping an opened archway on their distant left.

"My head's still poundin' like a motherfucker…"

"Thought youse said y'knew this place like the back'a y'hand."

"I'll show you the back'a my hand, already!"

The more they squabbled and delayed, the more the extraordinarily dire circumstances of Tabby's descent took on the unwelcome flavor of adult babysitting which routine policework entailed to dispiriting if reliable degrees. If they stopped to finally come to blows, she and Lucy might find themselves stranded behind the melee. On the other hand, if one of them managed to kill another, it might only result in an extended delay before the survivors picked up and continued.

With a crack, the light flashed a little brighter. It hissed and shimmered, then settled into a soft glow.

"Don't put that match out yet," the more nasally voice urged. "Old bastard'll never notice if we're a few minutes late."

It did not take long for the smoke to billow back to Tabby and Lucy. Tabby recognized the tobacco scent, but there was a sweet, acrid note in the air as it wafted in her direction. She leaned forward. As her view extended around the corner, she watched the three young men. Two passed a bottle and a clove cigarette between each other. The third man shook a rattle can in his right hand, took a step back, and admired the room's much taller, much smoother, brick wall. Between them, a tall glass jar stood upright on the ground and a modest flame burned atop the single white candle within. Tabby followed his eyes to the mark he left. The black circle he had drawn was relatively even. There was a look of deep concentration on his face. A frustrated finger pointed at the circle, desperately trying and then mentally retracing a five-pointed star. He had achieved three lines on the wall already, though the path culminated in a broad, bleeding splotch indicating some confusion as to where the rattle can's nozzle should go next to complete the pentagram. He took a breath, stepped forward, and let the stream continue.

"Alright," he assured himself once more. "Whada'youse guy think?"

"Great job, Bobby," one of them replied, sputtering and coughing as he exhaled. "'Cept'ya drew it upside-down, dickhead."

Bobby jerked back and turned. His shaggy brown hair bounced. Tabby squinted. Thin rays of light reduced his already thin moustache to little more than a light brown smear on his upper lip. The familiar voice gained a familiar face and name.

"Bobby… Robert," she whispered.

"Olivera?" Lucy added quietly.

"Yeah," Tabby nodded. "That brat."

She sealed her lips tight, though Mrs. Olivera's delinquent, baby boy had not overheard the exchange. His indignation lie far away.

"What the fuck?" he stammered. "It's a fuckin' star in a circle, ain't it?"

"Yeah… sure thing, my guy. Glass'd be *real proud*."

Their snickering died down and the cigarette burned down to the filter. Bobby's artistic spirit withered and he grabbed the bottle away from the man who had rendered the nasally critique. The three began to move once more, deeper into the much broader brick tunnel. The tunnel sloped downward in the distance and soon their heads disappeared beneath the path's curvature. The candle continued to burn in their absence and illuminated the new room's vaulted ceiling for Tabby and Lucy to inspect. Lucy approached Bobby's attempted pentagram. Tabby carefully picked up the abandoned candle and brought it closer to the wall. Despite the accumulated layers of spray paint and less-easily identifiable grime, the glazed brickwork beneath shined. There were many other pentagrams and attempted devilish renderings layered amidst the *'Hail Satan'*s and *'Shine the Bleak Abyss'*s and *'Hurry The Dread Maelstrom'*s with which Tabby found herself uncomfortably familiar. The light from the candle drifted further along the wall as each step carried her deeper. Tabby ventured ahead and the lines of the graffiti and the circular arcs of the diagrams oscillated nearer to orderliness. The ground drooped and the individual flaws and quirks in the artwork disappeared. Officious-looking seals emerged. Borders shed their irregularities and boasted clean lettering. The drawings reminded her of the electrical engineering classes at KIT. She had been introduced to the world of electrical diagrams while she still entertained a future apprenticeship with Local 3. The similarities to those schematics were striking. Symbols and relationships. Components and connections. Instructions for unorthodox pathways.

The light from the candle flickered across the bricks and filled each round sigil with a glow. Tabby read the letters clockwise from the top:

MARBAS

AMASARAC

PAIMON

BERKAIAL

She pulled herself back from the wall. The next seal in the sequence was much larger than the others. It had been imprinted on the wall with a different medium as well, which made the candlelight shiver as the light emanating from it spread over the wall:

Tabby's feet continued moving backward to facilitate her view of the great seal until an elbow landed in the middle of her back. The candle jumbled around inside its slender glass jar, nearly jumping free of the vessel's rim completely.

"Woah, hey," Lucy whispered. "Easy. Something spook you?"

Lucy reached out and braced Tabby's shoulder to stop either of them stumbling.

"Yeah, just the… everything. Think I'm startin' to lose it down here," Tabby sighed. "Fuck this place."

"Nah, pig. Fuck *you!*"

Tabby felt something heavy rush through the air next to her head. In the next second she watched a glass bottle explode against the wall. Broken, jagged splinters and whiskey droplets sparkled in the faint light and rained down onto the ground. Before she could turn, a forearm swung out of the peripheral shadows and wrapped around her face to lock with the hand waiting on the other side of her neck. The glass jar slipped from her hands and tumbled, wick popping and flickering atop the candle as it rolled across the floor.

"Looks like we've caught us a couple'a *lost piggies*, Bobby. Run and tell Doctor Glass!"

Tabby wrestled her fingers between her throat and her attacker's arm as he tried to jerk back. She planted her left foot forward and swiveled. Her weight dipped with her shoulder while her right foot kicked behind and to the left. The goon's arms flailed over the top of her head as he stumbled. He looked down to see her knuckles dig into his belly. Tabby reached for her gun belt. Her thumb pressed against the holster's retainer strap as she backed away. The shadows stirred, looming higher as the candle fizzled and spun along the base of the tunnel's wall. The goon was still there, shuffling and wheezing as he tried to reinflate his lungs. Tabby squinted, then pulled her hand away from the back of her gun. She yanked at the other side of the belt, then flicked her wrist. The metal baton's expanding segments clicked outward, then arced in front of her. A swift, metallic *crack* bounced off the bricks. The goon spun and gagged. His mouth sprayed a mixture of spit and blood and misshapen expletives into the darkness. Tabby lunged. Her hand grabbed the back of his sweatshirt. She wrenched the fabric up, then over thee back of his head until the shirt obscured his face. He did not see the second punch as it landed between his eyes. The sweatshirt remained fast over his head when he tumbled onto the ground.

Another loud thud vibrated across the floor. Tabby turned her attention to the commotion behind her. The other man's fingers yanked at Lucy's hair, pulling her head back while his other hand wrapped around her stomach.

"Quit strugglin', damnit," he growled.

Lucy's feet skated over the ground. They stirred desperately in the accumulated dust but failed to find the footing they sought blindly. Tabby swung again and the baton responded with a sickening snap as it slammed into several of his lower ribs. The same reflexes that made his jaw drop also caused his fingers to shoot open. Lucy pried her hair free. The soles of her shoes slapped flat against the concrete floor. Without hesitation, her fist rocketed below his beltline. He went rigid, began to tip. One of his hands cradled his aching side while the other shot down to offer untimely protection to his crotch. Lucy scruffed his shirt collar and pulled. His face levelled with her oncoming forehead, which proceeded to invert the soft cartilage constituting the tip of his nose deep into his own sinuses. His legs buckled and his folding frame collapsed into a fetal curl beneath the settling cloud of dust. Tabby sighed, catching her breath.

"You… you good?"

"I'll live," Lucy groaned as she massaged her scalp. "But what about—"

Tabby turned. Beyond the pair of goons still whimpering and moaning on the ground, unimpaired feet pounded ahead into the tunnel. A flashlight strobed frantically in Bobby's hands as he booked it deeper underground. Tabby stooped forward and grabbed the glass jar containing the candle off the ground. The tunnel sloped dramatically as it dipped into the earth, but its vaulted ceiling was generous enough to offer a straight shot. Tabby's shoulder stretched backward until her arm shot forward. The candle whipped and tumbled through the air. Its wick twinkled and pulsed, painting a golden ring across distant lengths of walls and ceiling until all of its light reconverged on the back of Bobby's head. The cavernous expanse reverberated with the sound of shattering glass and stumbling feet. Tabby watched the flashlight spin out of his hands as he fell forward.

They worked quickly as possible in near complete darkness. Only two sources of light remained. One of the goons kept a lighter in his pocket, though its radiance extended no more than a few feet around Tabby. The distant flashlight, which Bobby had been abruptly forced to discard, lie on the ground many yards away in depths far beyond. Still, it was not terribly difficult to locate the two nearest incapacitated thugs by their continued, helpless groans. The second of Martin Glass's still-nameless lackeys was heavier than the first. With one final heave, Tabby propped him up next to his dazed partner. Lucy reached behind them both. The links connecting the two handcuffs rattled against the back of a tall, vertical pipe running from the floor to the arched ceiling above. A few rusty chips of paint and decaying iron flaked away from the back of the pipe as she stretched the cuffs from the first man's wrist to the heavier man. Tabby heard a series of clicks, followed by one extra for good, snug measure.

"That should keep them out of our hair," Lucy said as she stood back up, still massaging her head. "For a little while, at least."

"Yeah, *them*, maybe," Tabby agreed. "I'm sure we've still got a bunch more assholes to worry about."

"Like…"

"Yeah."

Tabby looked down the corridor's long slope. Freed from his grip, Bobby's flashlight had rolled against the wall. There it remained. Its lamp projected a cone of light back in her direction but shed no light on any activity in its immediate vicinity or beyond. She held her breath and listened. Whatever noises may have lurked below the groans and grumbles of Bobby's friends, they did not rise high enough to register in Tabby's ears. She extinguished the cigarette lighter and hugged the opposite wall, avoiding contact with as much of the flashlight glare as was possible while closing the gap with slow, deliberate steps. Even with one hand held up to block the beam, her eyes were too dazzled to scan the darkness with any confidence. Her eyes quivered as she fought the urge to squint. In the moment her vision fluttered, she saw the face coming toward her. Bobby or someone similar—more worn, with a hollow look in his eyes. Her involuntary scream echoed off the walls. Her feet desperately jumped into as defensive a posture as they could find on the slanted grade beneath them. Her baton sliced through the air with a *whoosh*. The movement repeated in another full arc in front of her, never making a connection.

"Tabby," Lucy yelled. "What is it? What do you see?"

"I can't see shit," she wheezed. "Come out here, you *fucker*."

Tabby could not keep her feet still. She turned, twisted—fiercely pivoting for any angle to give her some perspective yet to materialize in the dark. She saw someone. She saw *something*.

She felt more motion behind her. Lucy launched past, landed by the flashlight, and snatched it up from the ground. The beam of light widened, travelled along the bricks, and whirled across the floor to scan the opposite wall.

"I saw—I…. I dunno."

"It's ok," Lucy said, calming herself as well. "I think Bobby's long gone."

"Bobby," Tabby replied. "Sure."

They continued to probe the shadows for a few moments. Tabby found the remnants of their candle and its shattered jar. The lighter reignited its wick, and after a hiss and a puff of smoke, it glowed once more.

"So much for keeping a low profile," Tabby sighed.

"Yeah. If he ain't still around here, he can't be far from Glass."

"Which means we've got even less time to spare than we did before. You keep the flashlight out ahead of us. Time to move with a sense of purpose."

Tabby speed walked with the lit candle in her left hand and the baton extended in her right. Lucy followed a step-and-a-half behind, flashlight digging ahead into the seemingly endless depths. No matter how quickly they pressed forward or how often they paused to size up any potential intrusions on their progress, the world continued to sink deeper and deeper. Tabby noticed the tunnel's fanciful bricks gradually recede and dwindle, melting and morphing into natural, mineral contours. Before long, all the world surrounding them and towering over their heads was damp, dark stone. If it took hundreds of hands and hundreds of years to gouge the bedrock, they left behind no evidence of blundering chisels or ugly blasting scars. The smooth walls surrounding Tabby and Lucy appeared more the product of tremendous erosion than excavation, until a pure glimmer sparkled at them from the shadows. The glassy, black bricks began to appear on the walls with greater frequency, interrupting and parting the fluid stone like rocks breaking the flow of a stream. No matter how much Tabby studied them, she could find no two blocks conforming to the same dimensions. When she looked closer, she noticed the inscriptions.

"That ain't graffiti."

"Doesn't look like any letters I've seen before, either," Lucy added.

No matter how thoroughly she examined the engravings—thorough as their pace would allow—she could make no logical sense of them. Right to left. Left to right. Top to bottom or back up again. Hundreds of languages made homes in New York City, and she estimated she encountered half of them on a daily basis. The words surrounding her were unlike any she had ever seen. The more she examined the strokes of individual letters, the more details she found lying within. Symbols formed by strings of other symbols. Tabby nearly lost her balance just as her nose bumped the obsidian slab. She straightened her back and forced her eyes to uncross.

"You good?"

The muscles behind her ears ached as she massaged her temples. Lucy had wandered some distance ahead before noticing how far behind Tabby fell.

"Yeah, yeah," Tabby said. "Just lost myself for a bit."

The blocks were among the most polished she had ever seen, despite their presumably advanced age. In the limited light, Tabby caught her own reflection as she began to move forward again. Even after she caught up with Lucy, she continued to watch the strange shapes the light made, drifting along as they moved. The image of the glowing flashlight bounced to match their steps, but Tabby could not identify a reflection matching Lucy or herself. Instead, other outlines matched their pace. The light from the flashlight was momentarily amplified by a pair of columns grown independent of the walls ahead. The flare rippled across the rest of the hallway and the images reflected within—of other bodies with faces belonging to strangers. They were all men, cloaked in black and brown. Wide brims extended from the hats on their heads. Some let burning torches guide the way. Others grasped long-barreled firearms in shifting, nervous fingers. Tabby found herself fixated on one young man's face. His cheeks were pale and smooth, too young for the regimental, wool coat he wore. White knuckles choked his rifle's wooden stock. His pupils were narrow pinholes, constricted by terror. Tabby realized she would not find her reflection among this crowd. She did not need any visual confirmation of her own fearful expression—it was there in those faces. If they shared in the same terror closely as she estimated, they certainly shared in the circumstances pulling them toward uncertain destiny.

The scene dimmed. Tabby blinked. When she regained her focus, the glossy brickwork gave only the vaguest indications of her own frame and Lucy's hunched-over shoulders. Nothing more. That terrified child soldier and all the others—marching solemnly toward something too fearsome and not distant enough—were gone.

Tabby could not remember when the ceiling lifted high enough from the path to disappear completely, nor could she have said where it was that the walls finally splintered into a forest of black columns. Haphazard, yet infinitely recursive as every other slab and stone, they soared higher than the flashlight could reach. The slope of the trail gradually softened, and the petrified trunks scattered around the edge of an emergent clearing. There was a single point of light overhead. Looking down at a world of darkness, the miniscule glow was ample enough to make every line of strange dimensions in the vast chamber glisten.

"The moon?" Lucy asked as she clicked the flashlight off.

"With that storm outside? Impossible."

"Is it? Look around you."

Lucy reached over to Tabby's candle. Her thumb and index finger pinched the wick. A wisp of smoke drifted upward. As her eyes adjusted, the room's geometry glimmered. Every corner and edge caught the light overhead. Toward the chamber's center, stubbier stacks of black stone replaced the massive trunks of the columns from which Tabby and Lucy emerged. One vast, round plinth sat at the focal point beneath the beaming dome. There were two figures at its center. One gesticulated rhythmically, flared sleeves thrashing the air beneath a wild pair of hands. The man before him rested on both knees, broad shoulders hunched forward. With every dramatic circle the first man traced in the air, a shockwave battered the second. The convulsions racked his frame, nearly picking him up from the ground. Teeth ground and gnashed against each other while black fluids sputtered out of his mouth.

"Apollo."

Tabby heard herself call the name involuntarily. Her own hand clamped down over her mouth a second late to keep it completely leaving her lips. She cursed herself and looked over at Lucy.

"Quick, we gotta move," Lucy whispered. "Keep low and get closer—"

"There they are!"

Looming forward between the many stacks of black stones, the shadows around them reared hooded heads. Tabby could not discern any features, but she knew that the faces the hoods were all directed toward Lucy and her.

"They're the fuckin' *pigs* who jumped Louie an' Mikey," Bobby wailed.

Tabby heard the rush of footsteps behind her. She turned to see a pair of robed hands grab Lucy from behind.

"A couple'a girls, Bob?" one of the figures hissed. "They're the ones that cracked you over the head?"

"Shadup," Bobby cried. "Just grab 'em."

Tabby felt the breath on her neck. Her elbow flew backward, connecting with a cheekbone and digging deep. When she looked behind her, she saw Bobby nursing a fresh wound.

"Back for round two?" she growled.

"I don't fight fair with no cops—not when I got *backup* of my own!"

The ground flew away from Tabby's feet. Damp palms locked on to her arms and wrists. They pulled her down as she fought— fingernails clawing, teeth tearing at meaty hands when they squirmed too close. She could not overcome their numbers. Tabby felt the thumb break on her holster pop open and the pistol within drawn loose by a stranger's grip. The rest of her gunbelt was torn away. When she hit the ground, her lungs struggled to reinflate. More hands dragged her by the shoulders and pulled her against the ground until her back landed against a low wall. Someone squirmed next to her as shackles clamped down around her wrists. She could see Lucy yank at her own chains, seeking any give where they bolted to the wall. Tabby turned to her other side. There were more bodies and more manacles, all linked together and sprawled along the ground.

"What's the plan," she roared. "What're you doin' to us?"

"The better question is, what will we achieve *together*, dear sister?"

The voice of a many a late-night infomercial called out from the center of the stage.

"I am so pleased that Kowaliga—your dear Apollo—brought such noble, spirited tribute with him tonight."

Martin had paused his ceremony and Apollo was left to droop rather than writhe. He shuddered slightly as he forced his head to turn toward them.

"Let him go," Lucy yelled. "You're torturing him!"

"No. No, no, no, sister. I apologize if I ever gave you any false impressions, but that is not who I am. I do not *torture* people. I trade in enlightenment. I bestow *insight* upon the unfortunate, ignorant multitudes."

"Oh, will you shut the fuck up?" Tabby snapped. "Nobody asked you a goddamned thing about yourself."

"Oof…"

One of the cloaked figures ringing the central platform quivered as he suppressed a laugh. Martin did not flinch, but Tabby saw something change in his eyes. Pupils and iris and whites disappeared. A black tide washed over them. Glass's hand extended outward toward the man.

"No, it was an accident. Please!" the man screamed, hands rising defensively. "I'm sorry—oh, God, *no!*"

The room was silent, except for the high-pitched squeal that erupted from deep within Martin's regretful follower. Slits of light appeared between clenched eyelids and the man rose off the ground. He winced and squirmed as he floated. None of his peers offered any assistance. They did not dare join him. Finally, the man broke. His eyes shot open and his jaw dropped. Tabby could not comprehend the noise which escaped from his mouth with the beam of light as anything other than inhuman. His eyelids peeled wide and two more spotlights exploded from his head while a burning web ruptured outward from the center of his chest.

Fissures formed and cracked until the flood overwhelmed what was left of him to unleash a supernova of light. It left Tabby nearly blind as it spun like a top and hovered higher overhead toward the center of the room. The image remained, burned into her eyes, even after the newborn star reached its terminal peak. It was a window, and in the moment before the mass collapsed and died, she peered into an infinity from whence things predating creation gazed down patiently. She could hear ashen remnants scatter onto the cold, hard ground, but could not shake the ghostly vision drifting about her retinas—of beings with countless eyes turning upon wheels within wheels inside that terrible orb of unnature.

"Oh, my dear," Glass hissed, "thanks to you and your fellow brothers and sisters, soon I will never have to speak my own praises again. I have spent lifetimes speaking the words of the Gods. For one hundred years, I have brought flock after flock to gaze upon the Gods' true faces. I have sacrificed much. I have sacrificed *many*— so many to bring us all to this day. To the end."

Despite the enormity of the cavernous chamber, a thick cloud was beginning to build toward its vast ceiling. The already dark underworld grew dimmer as the haze throttled its only source of clean, pure light. An array of colored powders and metallic vessels fumed, arranged in faintly glowing ceremonial circles on the platform. Martin Glass stood in the middle, still gesticulating over Apollo. Some of his followers chanted and proceeded in circles around him. Others tended the flaming instruments. Bobby stood guard over Tabby and Lucy and the rest of the captives. The top of his robe bulged over the stolen gunbelt he fastened around his own waist. The butt of her handgun poked out from the holster.

Tendrils of the noxious smoke sagged lower and lower until they began to choke Tabby and her fellow prisoners. Some appeared quite elderly. All were apparently too weak to overcome the weight of their bindings. The person bound next to Tabby hardly moved at all. Their chest shuddered occasionally as breath rattled out. Tabby gathered the slack in her shackles and reached over. It was an old man. The skin on the back of his hand was cold to the touch. She found a round, white, plastic bracelet dangling around his wrist:

Tomasi, Giuseppe; Elysian Fields A.R.C. of Brooklyn, NY.

His thin hospital gown provided little insulation. Tabby tugged at her jacket. With both hands bound, she could not remove it. When she looked at the old man again, the stinging in her eyes grew worse. Over the din of chanting and shuffling, fizzling chemicals and wheezing mouths, Tabby heard a deep laugh. Martin held a dagger in his hand as he spoke to Apollo.

"Not my first choice, of course. But then you had to go and crush the poor boy's head."

"Fuckin'… *idiot*," Apollo growled in pain. "Blind… as usual."

Martin flicked his wrist and spun his palm to face the sky. Tabby felt no draft, but some unseen wind lifted Apollo to his feet. The unseen forces constricting Apollo's body tightened around his neck. Arteries bulged beneath the skin of his throat. Fresh, black foam cascaded down the sides of his mouth. Martin turned and grabbed an object from a small, nearby altar. He held the yellowed skull between either palm and approached Apollo. Stooping down, he placed the skull at the center of an ornate white circle traced on the ground.

"Maybe this will be better in the long run. For all of us. You accomplished so much under my direction. With the right kind of bindings and an entirely different soul to fill that able frame, you may yet find yourself a little redemption. I spoke quite honestly when I told you I wished I could have been half as gifted as you. But I have arrived at a realization over the past century… that you do not need to *be* the greatest—you only need the greatest bound to do *precisely as you command them.*"

While he spoke, Martin walked slowly toward a wide, metal urn. He turned the dagger in his hands, examined it, then plunged it deep into the ashy substance smoldering within the brazier.

"History demonstrates a tendency for people to be quick to forget. Sanity, any appearance of peace in the world, is predicated upon this. If the people of New York knew what history's greatest sorcerer nearly accomplished in this same place so many centuries ago—if they knew what the *fools* who dared defy him witnessed— they would never again awaken from a restful night's sleep. Brooklyn has no stomach to serve as the opened jaws of hell, despite what your police department's statistics might indicate. Yet, if Aodhan Draynor had his way that first time, it would be from this place that every bleak and despicable speck and specter circling the void beyond—each and every petty demon bound serve to the great King Belial himself—would freely enter this plane like a God with their heads held high."

Glass yanked the dagger out of the embers. A trail of crackling sparks followed the blade. It glowed and smoked as it sliced through the air. Black clouds accumulated overhead, then began to billow and writhe.

"What's he gonna do with that…" Lucy mumbled hoarsely. "Apollo. No…"

"We were too late," Tabby groaned. "Out of time, but front and center for the end of the world."

Tabby found herself transfixed until Giuseppe coughed. It took all of her strength to tear her eyes away and turn to the old man sprawled next to her.

"My heart… shall not be… afraid," he whispered. "Never alone…"

The smoke grew harsher as it roiled and whipped. Martin paid it no mind while he continued his slow, ambling pace around the stage. His feet stopped behind Apollo.

"On this Easter's eve, we must consummate the most unholy of resurrections. What finer, more twisted mockery could be paid as tribute to our *dearest* Master Belial? Together, we shall raise the great wizard himself: *Aodhan Draynor*, who ferried the dark flame to this new world, who was cut down and burned by lesser fools, to be reborn in bonded servitude. When the maelstrom takes the seventy suffering souls before me as tribute, he will finally open the void."

Martin grabbed a handful of Apollo's hair. He yanked the man's head backward and exposed his throat.

"After much delay, Aodhan Draynor's hand will reach into the abyss and snatch King Belial's crown for his *new master*. Thusly, I call upon him once again, to return to this world. Flame in the night! Light of truth! Master Draynor, last chosen speaker to He Who Knows! Most fearsome and fearless Captain of the Buckriders! We bring your last surviving mortal remains to behold the brilliance of your ancient conduit, realized by our devoted and enlightened labors! By my dagger and the infernal authority impressed upon it, reunite with your mortal remains! Transcend the universal covenant and walk once more by my word! *Behold me and hail your new, mighty King!*"

Glass's hand jerked. The dagger traced a line across Apollo's neck. The violent, churning sea of smoke parted around the vaulted ceiling's central aperture. A beam of light pierced the darkness once more and the black clouds began to orbit around it. Down below, in the center of the spotlight, Apollo did not flinch. His knees remained steady, whether a result of the unseen forces binding him upright or through sheer willpower. His lips wriggled and parted to bear his teeth.

"You know what they say," Martin laughed, excitement growing. "What does not kill you must only make you stronger."

Within the circle on the ground next to Apollo, the skull began to glow. It rose slowly as if picked up by some invisible, yet steady hand. A hazy glow extended beneath it as it rose to the same height as Apollo. The faint shape of a man materialized and followed the skull as it drifted closer.

"Let go of that weakness. Let go of all that disappointment—all of your… *mediocrity.*"

The spectral torso's foot leeched through the instep of Apollo's boot. Hazy whisps of fingers massaged the back of Apollo's hands until they merged with his flesh. Tabby watched the ghost's frame progressively follow in between each spasmodic tendon, until a new disturbance drew her attention. The skull shuddered, then tilted with a sharp jerk. Apollo's fingers flexed and curled. Whatever returns to corporeality the ghost approximated, its outline rippled. A sharp hiss washed over the room. Tabby felt it in her core, deepening until it shook the breath from her lungs. Another roar joined the chorus. Tabby looked at Apollo. His jaw hung low as it unleashed a powerful scream of its own. His spine, previously seized upright by unseen forces, lurched forward. One of the flexing hands tore free of the spirit's wavering grip. His fist blurred as it shot toward Doctor Glass. When Apollo's fingers reappeared, they clenched Glass's dagger by the blade and squeezed. Tabby had seen plenty of blithe, aloof serenity on Martin's face—both in his commercials and, as of this evening, in person. As he watched Apollo wracked and tortured, Tabby even caught hints of pleasure. When the blade's edges sliced between the joints of Apollo's relentless grip, the emotions converging on his face now were all new. Facial muscles contorted to expose wrinkles. Glass looked furious and—more uncharacteristically—unsure. He was unpracticed in hiding doubt or fear.

"No," Martin roared. "You *will* obey me. *NOW!*"

His command of Apollo—perhaps of Aodhan Draynor's restless, powerful remains or even the universe itself—slipped. Blood trickled down Apollo's forearm and pooled on the smooth, stone floor. Pained as the expression on his face grew, his grasp on the blade burying into his palm tightened. The ground trembled when Apollo's left foot stomped down. His shoulders turned. He pivoted away and yanked the dagger free of Martin's hand. Apollo shifted his weight again and continued to spin. The dagger turned in his hands to point outward. Instinct drove Martin to lunge forward and reclaim that which had been snatched away. He failed to anticipate the momentum of Apollo's mass as the larger man's rotation continued. Overhead, the black cyclone raged. From the opening in the cave's ceiling and through the eye of the storm a narrow ray of potent light beamed. It reached the raised platform and danced across the edge of the blade as Apollo reemerged from his spin to face Martin once more. Thick, red drops dangled in the air as his hand thrust forward. The dagger never hesitated as it dug a path through the first few inches of the ornate patterns and flowing ripples of Glass's robe. Tabby lost sight of the blade's sheen as it sliced across his stomach. Exiting higher, nearer Martin's ribs, it reentered the light imbued with a fresh, ruddy luster. Apollo's graceful stroke ended with a stumble. He collapsed backward, but his unsteady weight was too much for the knee which caught him. After another wobble, he hit the ground with his lower back and rolled onto his shoulder.

Glass's lips fluttered. Tabby could not hear what noises they had made amidst the totality of the chaos. If Apollo heard his old master's words, they did nothing to discourage his continued struggle. He propped himself up on his shoulder, raised the dagger in his hand, and flicked his wrist. Point-over-pommel, the knife spun in a high arc through the air, slowed, and fell. Smoke and ash exploded. The dagger landed with a flash in the same vessel which Martin had tempered it moments before. The reversal resulted in immediate violence. The spinning, dark clouds above began to swell and disintegrate. Thick bands broke loose and lurched lower until they brushed past the tops of the chamber's forest of black pillars.

Aodhan Draynor's reanimated skull twitched and stirred. An invisible neck twisted and flexed in every direction until its empty eyes sockets found the lone figure still upright on the stage. With a long loll, it pivoted downward, tracing a path along the ground to the spot where Martin Glass clutched his deeply lacerated abdomen. Satisfied in its new prey, the skull's cracked brow never strayed from Glass. The intentions were not lost on him. He grabbed his robe and hugged the wound beneath. Fast as the man moved it was impossible to tell how dire his wound was. The growing pool of red following Martin as he tried to plant his feet firmly beneath himself was unmistakable.

Apollo's stillness stood in stark contrast with the scene unfolding before him. His movements diminished to the point where Tabby could detect only the slightest trembles when his chest struggled to rise. Her own wrists and arms ached, and she looked down. She did not remember straining and pulling against her own chains, but found her arms nearly dislocated from her shoulders as she tried to pull closer to Apollo. They refused to budge. She could only watch as he turned to her, indifferent to Glass or the ghoul drifting hungrily toward its newly christened host. Whatever was happening, he did not appear nervous. Glassy eyes flicked between Tabby and Lucy.

"Thanks," Apollo's lips shaped silently. "The botha youse. Thanks for listening."

Tabby heard someone scream next to her. She looked at Lucy, struggling against her own bondage while she yelled. When Tabby noticed the shadows creeping over Apollo, she also screamed.

Long, snaking whips of smoke spun around the room and brushed the top of the platform. Most of Glass's followers stood still, entranced and baffled by the turning tide of their ceremony. A powerful gust sent a pair of narrow, tall braziers toppling over. Sparks and ash joined the whirlwind. The ceremonial lines and diagrams traced on the ground washed away. Despite the deafening crashes and roars, Tabby swore she heard a growing chorus of animal cries. A broad tendril of black smoke landed between Glass and Apollo, dragging itself toward a group of the robed cultists. When it collided with them, Tabby heard the unmistakable bleating of a goat. The men were lifted off their feet, then knocked to the ground. For a moment, they tried to stand, but their limbs were already stretching out from beneath their heavy robes, evaporating and fuming. Hands and feet and faces melted into black smoke, carried away with the chaotic updraft and merging with the storm until only empty vestments stirred and drifted along the ground. What remained of Glass's flock scattered in horror. Those ceremonial decorations which had not yet tumbled from the wind came crashing down while robed figures tripped over them and one another. The panicked face of Bobby Olivera appeared in the corner of Tabby's vision. Another of the vortex's long, spinning arms was close behind him as he tried to run past his prisoners. His terrified expression contorted into shock. A black, twisting lance of wrathful shadows emerged from his chest. His hands turned to smoke and the hood of his robe collapsed. Tabby's gun belt spilled down onto the ground with the tattered remnants of Bobby's clothes. She pulled at her chains again. The tip of her boot probed along the floor and pressed down on one of the robe's frayed edges. Her ankle twisted and scraped until she was able to shimmy the tangled mass closer to her. She kept a spare handcuff key behind the belt's buckle. It was increasingly difficult for Tabby to imagine a place in the world for a loving God as she witnessed a kingdom of demons clawing its way out of the bowels of Brooklyn—until the cuff key turned, the shackles popped loose, and she found herself filled with eternal gratitude for whichever divine force led Glass's goons to purchase the same, standard handcuffs as the NYPD.

The buckle of Tabby's gun belt clicked tight over her waist. She rubbed the tender, swollen skin of her wrists as she passed the handcuff key into Lucy's palms. Lucy, in turn, wasted no time undoing her own bindings. Tabby weaved her way forward through the rocky, stubby pillars ringing the edge of the platform.

She tried to focus on Apollo's chest. If there was any movement from his breathing, it remained too slight to be detected even as she came closer. She pressed her palms down onto the edge of the cold, earthen plateau and hopped. Her legs swept sideways over the elevated surface and carried the rest of her weight with their momentum. As she pulled herself upright, a blast of wind repelled her progress and threatened to send her teetering back over the edge. Another of the storm's massive arms slithered in front of her. The twisting, black tendril missed the tip of her nose by no more than an inch. It wove between the collapsing remnants of Glass's ceremony, then curled onto itself like a spring before it pivoted and bolted in Apollo's direction. Tabby's feet raced toward the same point. Her hand dug under Apollo's arm and she pulled. Her own weight was a fraction of the man she struggled to pull from the path of destruction. Suddenly, he began to turn on his own. Apollo turned onto his back and let gravity squeeze the breath from his chest. He stared at Tabby.

"Run."

His massive palm pressed against her sternum. With a firm shove, Tabby was airborne. She refused to tumble any further away than she had been thrust. Her hand wrapped around the wrist that launched her and she began to pull again. Apollo's eyelids came down. The darkness washed over him. Tabby fought to maintain her grip while the wind threatened a more forceful ejection than the one Apollo had used. Fingers squeezed closer to one another until all she could feel between them was crumbling ash. Her fists throbbed as she felt the gust depart. She felt something crumple against her palm and uncurled her fingers. A few whisps of black smoke drifted away from beneath a thin, laminated hospital band.

The smoke around Tabby cleared, absorbed into the rest of the darkness as the vortex's arm rose higher and the platform before her was left barren. She rubbed her eyes. The soot refused to clear. Apollo was still gone, as were Martin Glass and the ghost which had been turned to stalk its conjurer. Beyond the platform, amidst the tall columns, another black tendril slammed down into a pack of robed goons. It scraped across the ground and when it lifted they had disappeared. One figure remained, and it scrambled between a pair of tall, reflective stone plinths. Tabby watched Martin's face reflected inside the many black mirrored surfaces that decorated the sides of the pillar. While the multitudes of his flock were reduced to a few panicked stragglers by airborne furies, the doctor's attentions lie elsewhere. Still grasping his sides and bowing lower between more frequent and violent coughing fits, he glanced desperately from mirror to mirror. Wide eyes searched desperately in the spaces behind his own reflection. With his attention split, he did not see the rising skull until it already loomed over his head.

"NO—"

Martin flinched and twisted. Aodhan Draynor's vacant sockets locked onto his terrified face as he tried to back away.

"Mah-ah-aah..."

The bleating sound echoed across the chamber. A pallid hand landed on Glass's shoulder. Tabby could not say if it was the stranger's force or Martin's own shock that made him turn to face his visitor. To the left, in one of the many mirrored stones towering over him, she saw the face emerge. Long, unkempt strands of dirty blond hair tumbled from the top of the figure's head and down to its shoulders. Cracked lips pealed back to reveal two rictus lines of yellowed teeth protruding out of receded, blackened gums. Martin screamed, physically and mentally incapable of composing himself for flight or approximating any sort of coherent response. Gradually, every facet of the pillars filled with a new face: to his right, a similar looking young man, a few years older and with darker hair; overhead, a woman with a small, round face and a furious glare framed by long, pure white locks; behind him, a man with a massive head and broad shoulders. As each of their hands clamped onto Martin Glass, their ashen complexions glowed brighter. He fidgeted and squirmed, but never shook loose from the spot they held him to meet the skull drifting nearer his face. The same luminosity which implied form on Aodhan Draynor embraced the man who summoned him. Thrashing with diminished energy, the doctor's face began to glow like the others surrounding him. Tabby looked at the sky above him. The dark ceiling had begun to descend once more. It twisted lower until it slithered along the ground. It grew thicker, then began to pull back toward the ceiling and reveal a pair of bright, white feet in its wake. The Vitruvian form emerging as the black curtain pulled away was wrapped in a thin, white veil of its own. The sheer material whipped and twisted toward the sky like a flame pulled high by a violent updraft. Tabby could make out all the normal features of a human being beneath the fine clothe, except for the jagged, ebony thorns pressing out of the gargantuan figure's bald head. The wind continued to swirl and she saw something foreign drift away. The toupee nearly struck Tabby in the face before it disappeared into the darkness behind her. Her eyes ignored its continued flight path and remained glued to Glass. Serenity erased the terrfied expression beneath Glass's freshly exposed pate. The sudden exposure combined with his ongoing merger with Draynor's hungry spirit appeared to age him by several decades in the course of a few seconds and had yet to slow. The giant's arms stretched out to either side. Tabby recognized the snake twisting in his right hand. Her legs remembered how they had run the last time she witnessed it.

Tabby turned around and found Lucy at the edge of the stage, no less bewildered than she was certain she appeared herself. The added sight of Tabby barreling toward her must have jogged her senses, and she quickly joined in the retreat.

"Come help me," Tabby shouted. "We gotta get the rest of 'em outta here."

Dozens of dazed, tired captives remained bound in the shadows. One-by-one, Tabby and Lucy unlocked their chains.

"If you can move your legs and your arms, pick up someone who can't," Tabby barked and pointed. "Then pound it back up that path like there's no tomorrow."

A column of red socks hobbled up the long slope toward the chamber's entrance. Tabby reluctantly realized that a few of the cultists—at least those who had yet to find themselves violently consumed by the nascent rapture swelling to fill the space—might have ditched their robes to blend in with the refugees. It could not be helped, nor did they have the time to address it. Tabby scanned from face to face. Most of Glass's faltering contingent of wolves did not seem bright enough to notice the distinct footwear which would give them away if they attempted to hide among the sheep. If they got wise and tried to blend in by liberating a pair of red socks amidst the panic, she needed to be ready.

Tabby noticed one particular evacuee stood very obviously apart from the crowd. Not only did she appear much more alert and healthier in nearly every other aspect, she was dressed for work. The woman wore what looked like a waitress's apron around her waist. Judging by the abrasions and cuts around her wrists, she did not appear to have been brought to the ceremony under circumstances any more voluntary than the rest of the formerly chained captives.

"Know how to use this?"

Tabby removed the baton from her belt and offered the handle to the woman. Her expression was dazed, but her hand accepted the weapon anyway.

"I suppose," she muttered. "Is there any special technique to it?"

"All you've gotta do is wind up and smack any creeps you see trying to sneak up on us while we run outta here."

"Creeps?" The woman's confusion seemed to fade as she weighed the word and the blunt object in her hand. "When you put it that way, I think I can make do."

After a minute or two, only a handful of captives remained bound in place. Tabby looked up from the daisy chain. There was no clock on the wall to gauge how dire their timetable had become. Instead, Tabby witnessed a scene too unsettling for Revelation. Kneeling before Belial's feet, Martin Glass's thin horseshoe of natural hair drifted from the sides of his head. Before the last whitened strands could be swept into the storm, the skin covering his head dried and flaked away in patches of increasing size. What was left of Martin more closely resembled the disembodied skull baring down on him until every patch of living tissue decayed, crumbled, and faded with the breeze. His mouth fell open to unleash a final shriek. Like the vanishing image of the man, his dying breath also withered to a low rattle as his jaw stretched and sagged lower. When the final, lingering memories of flesh were reduced to dust, his bare jawbone tumbled and clattered against the floor. The vigor which pulled his bare skeleton upright a moment later made Tabby jump. Seemingly animated on its own, it writhed and danced and stooped in the presence of Belial and his solemn court.

"Maah-ah-ah-aah!"

Martin's lips were long gone as his tongue. Time caught up with his mouth and everything else, save those bare bones which Belial chose to spare. In her gut, Tabby knew the source of the animal cry still echoing around her, impossible as the apparent physical limitations made it. The remains of Martin Glass cried out to the night again as an array of shiny, black spikes erupted from the top of his skull. White flecks shook loose as the horns grew wider along its surface. Every inch of bone flaked and cracked to reveal the charred, black enamel emerging from within. One last pair of horns emerged over the skull's temples. They rose over the rest of the crown, lengthened, and then twisted into a pair of ram's horns.

"Hurry," Tabby urged. *"We gotta fuckin' hurry."*

Another patient stirred in the shadows. The younger girl was trying to pull herself off the ground atop a pair of unsteady legs.

"Where?" she whimpered. "Is this… another dream?"

"Not quite. But, you're good now," Tabby said as she thrust her forearm under the girl's armpit and pulled her up. "Just hang on Ms.—" she began, then checked the girl's wristband. "Webber."

Lucy limped up next to her. Her arm was wrapped around Giuseppe, who in turn feebly grasped her shoulder.

"That's the last of them," she wheezed. "You got this?"

"Yeah," Tabby replied. "Stick close and don't stop for goddamn anything."

The ground shook. Something had come crashing down behind them. While the initial shockwave rolled out and dissipated, a consistent rumble oscillated throughout the chamber.

"Don't look back, just run."

Lucy went first, hobbling but refusing to dip below a steady pace. By contrast, Tabby immediately broke her own instructions. A mixture of ash and debris was still settling where the now universally, uniformly obsidian skeleton's feet landed. Tabby squinted. Not feet, she realized. Glass's leftover parts stood on all fours, but those *fours* no longer resembled human limbs. Supported by four massive, black hooves, the rearranged structure of the skeletal beast let out another roar. Four curled horns bucked atop its head as it swaggered and kicked at the ground with cloven paws. The monster's swaying eye sockets slowed when they came level with Tabby. A pair of might hind legs coiled, then sprung. Tabby was already running with Alice over her shoulder when the creature launched into the air. The sound of hooves clacking against stone was deafening.

Tabby's eyes never returned to the chamber's central platform. A calamitous babel filled the air around her. Sideways laps by obsidian hooves rattled the chiseled ceiling and pillars. The occasional peripheral glimpses of the raging beast's shiny, black contours as it galloped over walls and ceilings in thunderous, oblique arcs were more than she needed to remain motivated. Bursts of cries and whines and debris rained down through the rupturing air as it vaulted from wall to wall. The beast's hooves pummeled the side of one of the massive, black columns near enough to send a hail of shattered stone rattling against Tabby's face. Her legs leaned into longer strides. As her thighs burned, she watched the cracks splinter and twist along the tower's base. The entire structure pulsed. All the intricate and infinitely recursive geometry which covered the mighty, black pillar's surface slouched aside in a decisive, diagonal fissure. Lucy was a few feet ahead of Tabby. She stumbled. Giuseppe began to slip down to the ground as his grip weakened. The looming column shuddered. Pressure forced the structure to twist as its collapse accelerated. Black splinters exploded from compounding fractures. Tabby felt the air shift over her head as the tower's falling weight filled its place. Her calves screamed threats of their own collapses. When her shoulder connected with Lucy's back, it sent them flying forward. The pillar's jagged trunk slid from its base and perforated the path in their wake. Untethered, it continued to twist and roll against one of its neighbors. Tabby heaved Giuseppe back onto Lucy's shoulder while a chain reaction multiplied behind them. Towering stone dominoes leaned and toppled into one another. Not far enough overhead, four wild, bucking hooves continued to thrash the ancient stone. Shrapnel rained as it completed lap after lap around the chamber's walls and ceiling. Pairs of desperate, weary, anti-skid feet dragged and limped over the rising trail for what felt to Tabby like a mile until the commotion drifted further behind them. She could see the ceiling over their path descend back into sight. Columns merged back into narrowing walls and the crowd tightened between them. Waves of smoky air and flecks of ricocheting debris nipped at their heals and urged them forward even as they became slighter and less forceful. The underworld's explosive collapse dwindled to a persistent, steady rumble. Tabby realized she lost her mind to exhaustion and mechanical rhythm until she noticed the last of the polished, black facetted stones fade into the earth's natural bedrock. What feeling her legs could still register faded into dull throbs of pain. Alice seemed to be bearing more of her own weight, for which Tabby was silently grateful.

The tunnel levelled off and the crowd slowed. Hooting, hollering, and the rattling of chains echoed from the graffitied bricks ahead. The refugees from Elysian gathered around the two men still handcuffed around a tall pipe.

"What the fuck is this shit?" one of them cried. "Get your fuckin' hands off'a me, ya freak."

"Where's Bobby? Did that stupid jerk let youse all out?"

"Don't worry about Bobby," Lucy grumbled. "'*Youse all*' won't be seeing him *no more*."

Alice managed to keep her own pace a few feet behind Tabby. This freed her hands to periodically shove forward Glass's shackled goons when the waitress's baton failed to produce adequate motivation. Whatever discomfort they were feeling as they occasionally stopped to grouse and whine was little more than a distant concern for Tabby as her palm planted firmly between their shoulders to apply manual encouragement.

It was difficult for more than two people to walk next to each other in the tunnel system's narrower, modern passageways. The survivors' pace slowed and restlessness spread as they maneuvered through the tight environment. They wheezed and mumbled under their breath.

"Officer," Giuseppe coughed. "Not sure if I can... d'ya know how much further?"

"We're getting there," Lucy urged. "Just hold on."

"Gotta find that damn ladder," Tabby added.

The earth had long returned to stillness, due to either the chamber's ultimate collapse or the distance which the long walk put between them. Their march slowed further as the calamity subsided, and if anyone or anything remained it had yet to come upon them. In the corner of her eye, a red glow flickered. The sound of a staticky hiss filled the air. Tabby looked down at the radio hooked to the side of her belt.

"sssss-show me rollin-sss-ix-Four-Charl-sss"

Tabby gripped the volume knob and twisted.

"ss-all units-sss-tand by for-sss"

It was a sign of life, if difficult to interpret. The depth and mechanical nature of the radio's surroundings corrupted the signals its antenna struggled to relay. Voices disintegrated into staccato echoes and chirps, only to be interrupted entirely by other voices endeavoring to make simultaneous transmissions of their own.

"ss-yeah-sss-Toyota, New York plate comes back t-sss-adrigal, Lucille."

"sssss-Six Four Lieutenant. Additional confirmed collapses-ssss-Eight Six and New Utrecht, at the Loew's Oriental. The second one, residential structure-sss-Bay Two-Six street."

"sssss-vehicle appears empty at thi-sssss-I need additional over here, forthwith-sss. Now damnit—"

Tabby felt her weight lurch forward and her muscles noticeably less capable of correcting the sensation. Her legs shuddered. A wave of exhaustion spilled over her. The frantic, desperate tone of the voices coming from the radio pulled her back upright for a moment, but the feeling was almost immediately followed by doubt concerning its longevity.

"—Shore Parkway. By the utility shed. I'm goin' in."

Tabby's stomach flipped. Static still riddled the airwaves, but where white noise distorted the speaker's words distant whispers filled in the blanks. A spear of light pierced the shadows, shimmering down from the ceiling. The hatch's entry ladder emerged from the darkness as the light continued to probe. Distressed stitches struggled to bind the frayed boots to their balding, rubber soles with every rung they descended.

"Tabby," the voice called into the tunnel. "You down there, girl?"

The flashlight continued to search the cement floor as the boots alternated from rung to rung. Tabby stepped into the spotlight. She looked up and smiled as she spoke.

"All Hell musta really broken loose up there, if they had to throw your ass out on patrol."

"Excuse me," Jimmy cried with mock indignity. "Maybe if certain misfit cops didn't keep disappearin' off their posts, my night woulda gone a little differently. Cooping's one thing, but don't go tellin' anyone you learned any kinda scam like this from me."

"Nobody'd believe me if I tried." Tabby's voice broke as she forced her voice to continue. "About that and a whole bunch of other shit."

Tabby's head sank back on its own when she crossed through the utility shack's entrance. Barren tree branches sparkled red and white. Raindrops soaked into the soot covering her face, recollected, and tumbled down her chin. She turned around. Lucy emerged from the shadows of the shed. One of the Elysian Field's patients clung to her arm for support.

"That's the last of 'em," she said. "Everyone's out."

"Almost everyone. For better or for worse."

A maze of dozens of marked patrol cars filled the wide, sloping embankment that lead back up to the street. Beyond them, ambulances tended to a swarm of cold, exhausted refugees.

"We can't keep 'em here for long," Jimmy said as he stumbled toward them. "The Belt's flooded. Weather's not showin' any signs of lettin' up and the whole thing might come spillin' over the seawall."

"What the hell happened up here?" Tabby asked. "What happened while we were gone?"

"Besides the storm that snuck up an' caught every weatherman in the city with their pants down? Or the earthquake and the half-dozen sinkholes openin' up all over Bath Beach?"

"What I meant was—"

"Or maybe you meant all the sand and black slime and shit churned up from the bottom of Gravesend Bay and covering everything from Ceasar's Bay Bazaar to Coney Island."

"Alright," Tabby yelped. "I get it."

"'Course, if it hadn't been for half of Brooklyn callin' in to say an entire army a' darkness was marchin' down Bay Parkway, nobody woulda' checked in and noticed you weren't on your post."

The radio chatter was still deafening. Tabby's eyes ached. An ocean of spinning lights glared at her from every inch of asphalt.

"What about you?" Jimmy continued. "What the hell happened *down there*?"

Tabby's eyes began to wander. Her neck bent backward again. She studied the swirling clouds overhead.

"I wish I could tell you," she said. "I really do. I can't even begin to figure that out for myself."

"Just *what the fuck* were you thinking, Williams?"

Tabby bristled. The shout rose somewhere behind Jimmy.

"And you! Madrigal!"

Water gushed where Lieutenant Cordell's feet squelched into the supersaturated mud. Every muscle in his body was seized by rage and spiking blood pressure. Excess flesh trembled and jerked with each step bringing him closer to Tabby.

"Of course," Tabby grumbled. "Perfect timing."

"You hold your goddamn tongue, missy."

The pressure building in Tabby's jaw threatened to crack every molar in her mouth. Cordell's hand flew up within inches of her nose. Individual fingers sprang up from his balled fist as he proceeded to enumerate his complaints.

"Failing to respond to your radio. Abandoning your post. Conspiring with suspended—no, *dishonorably dismissed*—members of the department.

"Oh come-the-fuck-on, Lenny," Tabby groaned. "The day's been way too long a for your bullshit."

The ambient chatter of dozens of police officers and emergency responders screeched to a halt before Tabby could finish her sentence. All eyes turned in time to watch her brush past Cordell.

"*Discourtesy to a superior officer!*" Cordell's throat blared like a steam whistle. "Nothin' but dead weight! You're done, now. *The botha you!* Congratu-*fucking*-lations, Williams."

Tabby let the air building in her lungs vent through her nose. Her lips made no attempt to part. She decided there was at least one thing she could say with confidence as she let her eyes drift over Cordell's thinning hairline to the stirring sky above—that he would never be worth another moment's thought or frustration. He might, in fact, have been the smallest thing imaginable in the entire universe if she felt like paying him any further attention at all. It was no concern of hers if the man ever lived to realize the same.

"And thank you very much," he shouted. "Oh, I'm gonna enjoy this. *Boy-oh-boy*, it'll be my pleasure."

Something made Tabby swallow hard. At first, it was just the bottoms of her feet as she came to a stop. Soon she found her teeth chattering involuntarily with every continued pulse.

"Now I get to suspend one and *shitcan* the other in the very same night! I promise you, I'm just gettin' started."

Tabby watched the sneer Jimmy directed toward the back of Cordell's head fade. The rest of the crowd—either still awed by Cordell's very public dressing-down and the complete lack of a reaction elicited by its intended target, or rolling their eyes from proxied embarrassment—began to exchange looks of concern amidst the approaching rumble. They were not as intimately familiar with the pounding trot that rose high in the ground beneath their feet.

"Hell, you give me enough time and I'll *personally* find you both a pair of neighboring cells in the House of Detention!—"

The shockwave yanked the ground away from Tabby's feet. Just before the sopping lawn rushed back up at her, she saw the surprise on Cordell's face disappear within the wave of debris riding the blast. The chunk of concrete that cracked against the back of his head had a distinct lightning bold chiseled into it. Trails of rainwater ran down the hill and past Tabby's face as she buried it in the ground and braced the back of her head with her arms. When she felt the last flecks of the disintegrated shack patter down onto the Earth, she allowed a few seconds to pass before uncovering her eyes. Not a single person remained upright. Ten feet away, Cordell massaged his head.

"What the fuck was that?"

Bright red blood trickled from his nostrils as he howled. Tabby rubbed her eyes. A brilliant glow blanketed the entire lawn and everyone still pulling themselves up from it. It covered the houses in the neighborhood and every assembled emergency vehicle. Red and amber and white lights still spun atop their rooves, but not strongly enough to outshine the radiant tower rising behind Tabby. She twisted and turned over. Propped on her elbows, she watched the beam of light stretching out of the crater formerly capped by the brick utility shed. It pierced the storm clouds and tapered into a needle extending endlessly into space. Black clouds whipped and flared in concentric circles. They spun faster and parted wider as the beam swelled. Tabby could see stars where the clouds retreated—multitudes of impossible density filling the deepest, furthest corners of the night sky, more plentiful than she had ever seen. She had never seen them drift and spin, either. The stars spun into a vortex and the beam of light came to life. It twisted and rippled like a wildfire of sheer, white cloth. A face gazed down at them from within. The figure, a towering reflection of humanity, stood taller than the bare tree tops.

Tabby saw twin bursts of steam spurt from a pair of nostrils concealed in the woods beyond the fresh crater. A black hoof pawed at the ground. Barren eye sockets studied the crowd, still frozen in place by collective shock. The beast, a massive black skeleton in the shape of a ram, lurched closer to the ground. Its limbs exploded as they sprang. A gasp echoed around Tabby. Many quickly turned to cries of fear. The beast barreled forward and the ground shook with every step. It pushed off the Earth and leapt over Tabby. All four legs continued to pound at the sky, kicking and galloping as its altitude increased. It ran in a wide arc through the air, then turned back toward the beam of light. When Martin Glass's repurposed remains pierced the light surrounding Belial, the demon king's cowl lifted from his feet. It continued to unravel over him, lifted to that distant point in space around which the stars now danced. Tabby saw no human form beneath the retreating sheet as it twisted away. Her mind struggled to make sense of the immense mechanical fluctuations and twisting, grinding bands. She could not count the number of wheels, spinning and rolling within innumerable other gilded wheels. Embedded along each wheel's rim was an endless row of unblinking eyes—eyes that beheld everything in the universe at once while the wheels turned in concentric orbits around a singular, brilliant black star blazing at the mass's apparent core. Tabby's hand shot to her eyes and trembled as it cleared the tears from her vision in time to watch a pair of wings unfold behind the twisting, golden machinery, joined soon by another pair. The four wings stretched and then flapped down. Belial's unveiled form lifted away from the planet. Glass galloped beneath and ascended with his master into the sky. The vortex of stars fluttered as they twirled and opened into a chasm. Great ribbons of light wove and dipped to form an inverse valley within the vast rift. When Tabby reasserted her grip on conscious thought, she realized the sight had dazzled her vision, though she could not say for how long. Nor could she find Glass or Belial in the rapidly collapsing portal. The light dwindled to nothing. The tear in space mended itself. What clouds remained drifted and thinned as the maelstrom dissipated. Light pollution returned to overtake the sky's weaker, more distant bodies until only a handful of the usual stars were left to twinkle at the disoriented spectators.

Tabby's eardrums felt primed to pop. She stretched her jaw and tried to force a yawn, but realized there was nothing wrong with her ears. Quiet had returned in abundance. The waves no longer tore at the shoreline. Tabby's knees seemed skeptical, but she lifted herself off the ground anyway. A black mirror of perfectly still water stared back from the surface of Gravesend Bay. Over the water hung all the familiar constellations and a gibbous moon in its first waning phase.

For all the midnights she had ever worked, the sky above the horizon appeared the same as ever. She asked Jimmy for confirmation, but he was too distracted to join her looking below the horizon. He could not see the lingering reflection of the broad, celestial rift still staring back at her, framed within the tide's unnaturally calm surface. Tabby turned. She found Lucy. Silently, her eyes followed the path of Tabby's finger out to the bay. She begged for affirmation while Lucy stared. Lucy's mouth opened, then hesitated. She took a step backward and limped toward an ambulance without commenting.

Entry posted to the Kingsboro Institute of Technology's Online Bulletin Board System; Friday, February 9, 1990:

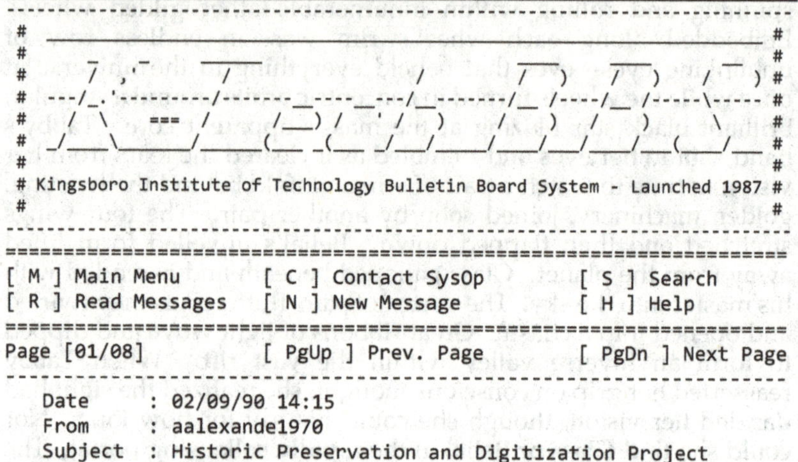

```
--------------------------------------------------------------------
 #  ________________________________________________________________  #
 #                                                                    #
 #    _/ ,'   _____          /      _)  _)    /  _)  )                 #
 #  ---/_.'--/-------/-------___/_-------/_-/----/__/-----\-----       #
 #    / \   ===     /___)/   '/  )     /  )  )  /   )      \           #
 #  _/___\____/____(__(___/__/__/__/__/__/__(___/__          #
 #                                                                    #
 # Kingsboro Institute of Technology Bulletin Board System - Launched 1987 #
 #                                                                    #
--------------------------------------------------------------------

====================================================================
[ M ] Main Menu          [ C ] Contact SysOp        [ S ] Search
[ R ] Read Messages      [ N ] New Message          [ H ] Help
====================================================================
Page [01/08]             [ PgUp ] Prev. Page        [ PgDn ] Next Page
--------------------------------------------------------------------
   Date    : 02/09/90 14:15
   From    : aalexande1970
   Subject : Historic Preservation and Digitization Project
--------------------------------------------------------------------
```

NOTE: Not without quite a bit of regret, Mr. Hutchin's journal now reaches an abrupt end. The remaining pages which follow these last two entries appear to be his own transcriptions of something far more ancient. Unfortunately, it's also far less coherent, far less linear, and contains a lot of language and symbols that will be difficult to reproduce within the limitation of ASCII. I plan to eventually attempt my own transcription, but I'm going to seek some outside help first.
   -A.A.

   January 22, 1647
The Devil himself sits in our gaol this night and there is no rest to be had for any of the towne. Mr. Sprague calls the Devil Aodhan Draynor, and he and his men keep watch over him now. I have never held in high regard those stockades and thus wish not to delay judgment any longer. Nor do I trust any persons present to keep that place or the evil festering within secure, be they servant to Mr. Sprague or of Gravesend itself. There were voices

```
====================================================================
```

===
Page [02/08]   [PgUp] Prev. Page   [PgDn] Next Page
----
echoing that black pit familiar to my ears. Voices
from our own happy square. The same hands I embraced
in my own as a gesture of peace before the altar of
Christ, I will now forever remember stained by their
neighbors' blood. I have ordered a portion of timber
from our already withering reserves to be assembled
on the edge of towne without delay and four stakes
erected amidst a great pyre.

We elected to imprison this demon among our own two
days past, when a companie of G.W.C. riders
dispatched from Fort Amsterdam arrived alongside two
score volunteers levied from among the manors and
plantations around Nieuw Amersfoort and Flatlands.
They assembled with Mr. Sprague and his men, as well
as our own volunteers lead by myself. When we once
more crossed Hubbard's Creek, we were sixty-seven
strong and armed with thirty-three guns between us.
Though we found the day's light dim upon our arrival
at the chasm's edge, it was not difficult for an
observer to differentiate the previously acquainted
men of Gravesend and those men who followed Mr.
Sprague from the rest. After a brief silence of
disbelief, there were manie a Dutch-tinted murmur.
Whether we were a man borne of the Continent or Great
Britain, the New World or the Caribbean, in that
moment we were all fluent in fear. Though the
tongues of Gravesend might have been kept silent
behind rigid, knowing jaws, there was nothing to stop
us quivering.

From our original elevation, a thin trail of smoke
reaching up to the sky indicated activity deep within
the bewildering assembly of bleak pillars. After
some bickering between the G.W.C. men and the
farmers, order was reasserted and the decision was
made to descend in as regimented an order as we were
capable. That is to say, we shuddered and shuffled
and agonized with every step between the rising
forest of black glass and stone, stopping only a
handful of times to cautiously bark a return to order

===

at those whose wavering nerves tempted them to break
formation and flee. This became the source of
tremendous fatigue and after a while the value of the
fortitude of our party in my mind was eclipsed by new
concerns. As unlike any trees these titans were to
any flora I had ever observed, so too was the odor of
the approaching fire to any fuel which I had ever
smelled. The intoxicating fumes made my eyes dance
over the surfaces of the stony pillars. Though the
open sky above us was grey and dwindling, that which
reflected back from the dark rocks and bricks were
scenes of twilight. The stars were familiar, but
fewer in their numbers and less intense. Angular
silhouettes rose up toward them, pocked and burning
in a dull, broad luster of their own. There was no
warmth in the light coming out of them but for a
single crimson ember, twinkling as it traced an arc
and steadily disappeared beyond the edge of one of
the great, black trunks.

   These visions diminished my caution and nearly cost
our concealment. The terrible woods dwindled and
opened upon a vast clearing with a raised altar at
its centre. A ceremony reached a pitch thereupon and
the cabal surrounding it took no heed of our party.
Distant as the homelands among us were, none
recognized the words leaving their mouths. Mr.
Sprague and his men appeared especially dispirited.
"We followed eight men from the Narragansett," I
heard him whisper, "but here I see more than twenty."
Indeed, I counted nearly thirty strangely decorated
persons writhing and flailing. Not all were
strangers from distant settlements. I am reluctant
to recollect in completeness here the name of each
familiar conspirator, but I will confirm that John
Seymour, the younger son of Mr. Wm. Seymour, now
occupies our gaol alongside Mr. Draynor.

   If they were aware of our presence, they offered
no indication. The chanting continued even as those
men who still remembered Mr. Sprague's instructions

made a valiant effort to storm the ceremony and
breach the discord. There was a great blast and a
wicked, white flame which escaped into the air over
their infernal bonfire. The surging tempest removed
my feet from the ground and shattered many spirits
around me. Some men fired wildly without being
ordered and with-out care to aim. As of the most
recent counting, this resulted in fourteen
casualties, six of which were inflicted against our
own party. An additional five deaths on the part of
the witches appeared to be the result of blunt
trauma. A far greater source of death for all involved is more difficult for me to explain on these
pages. Alas, I will not seek to obscure the horror
of this fatal magick, though I cannot command words
descriptive enough to explain exactly what it was I
saw. The same white flames which burst into the sky
turned back upon us all. It split and fractured,
piercing man to man, and re-ducing them to pillars of
salt as they came unto its skewer. Eleven of the
witches were taken by the horrible storm. It took
from us nineteen, all rushing evermore urgently with
each dying man, blinded by blood and clawing madly at
Draynor to bring about an end to the furor. The
withered infernal priest, wheezing and bleeding beneath the crumbling chalk remains of the battle's
dead was nearly bludgeoned to death where he lie but
for the intervention of Mr. Sprague. It was only by
the grace of God and exhaustion that anyone permitted
Draynor and the three other survivors to be manacled
and returned to stand trial here in Gravesend.
As the site of their judgment is assembled, twenty-
five new graves are being prepared in the cemetery.
I pray that what remains of this harsh winter costs
us no further.
    January 23, 1647
I count my interrogation of the towne's night
watchmen among the last of the duties of my office.
They deny any lapse in vigilance around the cooling

==

coals of the pyre as the rest of the towne departed
for the evening. They deny seeing any strange
persons approach the site or abscond afterward while
the towne slept. Now word arrives that the damned
trackers cannot recover the trail back to that black
chasm beyond the woods. My credibility is injured
and the environment continues to deteriorate rapidly.
A towne of damned gossips! I find the land to which
I returned changed, though they regard me with looks
reserved for a stranger! Twenty-five dead. Nearly a
dozen more of our own identified among the twenty-
four witches struck down in that place. But so many
more new and strange faces arrive in towne every day,
hungry and heedless to the dire horizon which
besieges every morning. The land shakes with
disharmony if the clamoring rabble would fade to
permit it heard. I must find somewhere quiet. Some
peaceful place where I can listen. Learn? Fate has
shown me it is not here, but will some God tell me
where? I can barely brace my hand to put the words
to paper, for I cannot pray these thoughts to vanish
from my own ears. They cannot find that damned,
black pit and they dare to tell me it is gone!
Disappeared, just as Aodhan Draynor's charred head
from his smoldering corpse. Unlikely! I saw the
jagged, splintered remains of his neck. If the
watchmen did not see who hacked away at that wretched
stump atop Draynor's shoulders, if they did not hear
the laborious deed as it was performed, then they too
must conspire against me and see into me and wish me
destroyed.
Parson Clemmons offers me no solace, no spiritual
comfort. In truth, our dear vicar is but a modest
man, and a man of no great insight into such abstract
matters. The only remaining evidence of anything,
aside from new graves and nightmares, is a tome he
carried out of that black valley. He claims that he
wrenched it from the wretched sorcerer's own fingers.
Upon his return to the village, Mr. Clemmons poured

```
==================================================================
Page [06/08]            [ PgUp ] Prev. Page        [ PgDn ] Next Page
------------------------------------------------------------------
```

over the book without pause. When I visited with
him, I watched him lift the book's rough, leather
cover. From over his shoulder, I watched him turn
every page. When the cover closed once more, I became aware that night had fallen. In a fit of
madness, Parson Clemmons began to roar. Nonsensical,
vile words poured from his mouth as he grabbed the
book and hurled it with monstrous and inhuman vigor
onto to the fire burning within his hearth. I did
not immediately feel my knees dig into the ground,
nor the searing pain of the burning book in my hands,
but I found myself diving into the flames to inter-
cede without premeditation. I jumped and cried and
still do not understand what forces drove me to
attempt to retrieve it, for the attempt was in vain.
I witnessed the tome's ultimate con-sumption in those
flame. I heard the embers crackling and the good
Parson jabbering. But as each page found immolation
I heard a demonic tongue recite to me each and every
word within. So many hours later and they still echo
in every corner of my mind and the home in which I
sit. I reproduce its preamble now from memory without struggle nor, though it shames me, without the
mercy of mine own self-governance:

   The Great Mockery of Crowns

O, thou weary!, watch the horizon fall under the tide,
Turned upon Fortune's wheel by wheels within wheels.
Cast down with goode times, whence horrors bide,
That power's twisting faces thou gazed, now unseals.

Fairest darkness itself,
wrapped and swaddled within stolen light—
Bleak stars borne heavy crowns
nearer to Heavens without suns,
And bearing Eternity's other vestiges
and insatiable appetite.
'Twas thy fate to reign o'er shackles
and the shackles' to be undone.

```
==================================================================
```

When to thine highest depths,
behind Heaven's glimmering coat,
With the churning, boiling madness
of Adam's children descending,
Bonded raiders with borrowed saddles
mounted upon manie a black goat,
Past barren Elysia gallop legion buckriders
o'er abyssal fingers extending.

From that ancient Ocean's floor,
grown higher is the murk upon whiche slouches,
Groaning stone halls what echo
fanatical rhapsodies in unmeasured time.
His sleeping infernal pantheon's Kingdom
of grotesque, wicked Houses,
Towering ever o'er pitch-black fields
of the gathering, rotten, fetid slime.

Rumble call of terrible, gilded machinery
spun to snarl and bend-
Ezekial's revelation shrouded 'neath veil violent,
hiding the visage of sooth,
Of manie great wheels within wheels,
grinding a continuum of eyes without end,
In their endless vigil for innocence
spilled by the hands of hopeless youthe.

Praise is sung to dark King Belial,
and until His Crown dismiss,
Hundred and one hundred more
at end of blade, and to beat of drum.
Our bloodshed flows for thee,
who shine darkly in that bleak abyss,
Dance yon feet and flourish knives
to hurry His Great, Dread Maelstrom.

==
Page [08/08]　　　　　　[PgUp] Prev. Page　　　　[PgDn] Next Page

There are truths which bring men comfort,
and truths which rend soul from mind.
Planes of ashen cities top the rising depths
to where the lost are drawn,
Where dreams fill opened eyes
when no escape their souls can find.
Awakened, walking, dreaming—it tears away thy temper,
And raises the Kingdom 'neath the Midnight Dawn.

When I ruminate upon these words, it is not mine
own voice which regurgitates them to me. There are
many among the chorus, but little harmony. They are
urgent and portentous, and I must listen closer if
only this damned towne will ever quiet itself. I
must return every verse and revelation to paper, in
spite of that damned fool Clemmons. For now,
dwindling matters of that which remains of my office
and title demand my attention. Thusly I leave to
address the towne and its fearful many and Lady Moody
herself. I must assure them, the neighbors and the
conspirators yet hidden among them, that all is well
and the terror from beyond our good towne has been
truly vanquished. But terror and fear are little
more than the reactions of the living to the
aspersions of the damned-- aspersions rained down
from tongues lately silenced, ever to echo over these
plains and fields of Broeckelen.
　　　　　　　　　　　　　-Hon. Wm. Hutchins, Esq.

Excerpt from the *New York Morning Tribune*, **Metro Section**; Thursday, August 15, 1996:

Notes from the Thunderground: Art Collective Evicted by City

By LUCY MADRIGAL

QUEENS — Protesters took to the streets of Long Island City yesterday following the eviction of approximately 25 residents from 98-50 Wolkoff Street. Most of the nominally industrial, 19th Century warehouse's floor space had been occupied by the Thunderground art collective since late 1991. The location's inhabitants asserted their legal right to continue living within the structure on the understanding that it was being utilized within city guidelines as a live-work space and protected as similar buildings by the state's Multiple Dwelling Law. The building's previous owners and City Hall appeared content with this arrangement until May 1994, when the property was sold to development firm Worsted-Atwells, LLC ('W&A'). In the same week W&A completed the transfer of ownership, the developer filed multiple, parallel evictions petitions against the Wolkoff Street tenants in Queens County Supreme Court. While most of these decisions remain either undecided or under appeal after the two years which followed, the Giuliani administration interceded on Wednesday on behalf of W&A. Just before noon, officials arrived with police escort to forcibly evict all remaining tenants on the grounds that they were illegally squatting and created a public safety hazard by obstructing city and utilities inspectors from entering. The Department of Buildings, ConEdison, NYNEX, and the Long Island Lighting Company were not observed present during or following the property's seizure and have yet to return requests for confirmation of earlier attempted visits.

Many of those present at the protest were adamant that a campaign of targeted harassment began months before the deal with W&A was complete, with the tenants' ultimate dispossession a foregone conclusion. They argued further that yesterday's actions were proof of this long enduring enmity, orchestrated as an insurmountable, extra-judicial death stroke to the Thunderground, and driven by city officials unduly sympathetic to the property's new owners and indifferent to the cultural value and economic struggles of the experimental art scene in New York City's outer boroughs.

During the five years the collective inhabited the location, it became a venue of substantial renown within the avant-garde performing arts and music communities for its unconventional exhibitions and shows. A great deal of the artwork and sculptures crafted over those years was on display during yesterday's events, carried to the curb by a carting company contracted by W&A to clear the space. Investigators from the FCC and FBI were also observed removing property from a basement entrance, including a great deal of telephonic equipment, Internet modems, and several inscrutable, complex structures composed of what appeared to be telephone and electrical cables.

Demonstrations in front of the site continued until the early morning hours. Police arrested 34 of the protesters before the crowd broke and dispersed; all but 4 were released from the nearby 117th Precinct shortly thereafter on Desk Appearance Tickets and Criminal Court Summonses. The identities and charges pending against the remaining 4 protesters have not been released by officials.

Advocates for the displaced residents of the Thunderground are expected to file additional injunctions today and tomorrow.

Years Later

There was no clear path forward, deep as Lucy journeyed in search of any. The warehouse was one of the oldest structures still standing in Queens County, and it was difficult to imagine it had ever been swept as clean in those hundred-and-thirty years. Its most recent turn as a warren for those who sought to push the boundaries of experimental art and tenants' rights laws was infamously and sometimes purposefully grungy. Lucy had been inside the building only once before, and each empty room she crossed compounded her regret that no one, herself included, would ever return to that place. She once counted herself among the bodies twisting past one another in its narrow hallways—rustling the dense, crinkling leaves of ephemera which lined every wall as they maneuvered to find some new chamber full of things. Arrangements of sound and light. Communal reactions. Negative space sparking sensory overload. The sheer abundance of negative space Lucy discovered on this visit was far more underwhelming. None who experienced a second of the Thunderground's five-year-long, irregular, avantgarde festival of noise rock and hyperrealism would ever recognize the place—might even swear it was all a dream if they toured the empty rooms Lucy backtracked. Despite the art collective's abrupt and substantial eviction, its material erasure appeared to uncover little more than four densely carved floors, tall as they were tight, all leading ultimately to dead ends and doorways sealed by exceptionally well-reinforced plywood.

Lucy returned to the basement to depart through its separate entrance. A day earlier, she watched the accumulated possessions of a few dozen displaced tenants carried unceremoniously—and incautiously—through the same before being chucked over the rims of rented dumpsters. The cellar was cooler than the upper levels and only a little damp—comforts which Lucy knew she would soon be deprived as she approached the opened hatch which led back to Wolkoff Street. Her watch band clung to her wrist as she read the time: *7:19 A.M.* The sun barely crested the neighboring factories' rooftops, but the summer night's stale warmth kept the robust, cloying bouquet of Long Island City and Newtown Creek potent for any waiting palate. Two inches of rain had fallen three nights prior, and ten million gallons of overflowing, raw sewage still ripened atop the surface of the East River's toxic tributary. In less than an hour, the nascent volume of truck traffic would approach its peak. The descending smog of diesel exhaust would contribute an entirely new dimension to the industrial neighborhood's aura.

Less than a day had passed before several of the Thunderground's survivors cut the padlocks keeping them from the place they had been ejected. The police drove them off a second time but did not reach into their own pockets to replace the locks or resecure the boards over the bulkhead which descended to the building's cellar. Lucy patted the pocket of the camera bag strapped over her shoulder. Two rolls of film bounced inside. As experience often proved to her, the most fruitful part of the structure lie underground. The photos she took in the warehouse's basement filled the entirety of one roll and nearly all the exposures in the next. Whether they would leave her any less lost after development was unclear.

Like the rest of the building, not much had been left in the basement. Art could look like anything. In the case of the Thunderground, it was especially—perhaps *deliberately*— impossible to separate utility and refuse from any other components of the much larger whole. The hands that carried the cellar's contents were another matter entirely, and their ultimate destination a bigger mystery. Lucy watched them work for hours on the day of the eviction. They could not hide the letters of their alphabet agencies, not that they appeared to have invested much effort into the illusion as they completed return trips to the backs of unmarked vans with federal government and D.C. license plates. Their attempts at plainclothes constituted unintentional uniforms— solid colored polo shirts and creased slacks. Their shaves were closer and their strides much brisker than the men with the names of carting companies printed on their T-shirts. They worked fast, and when that did not prove quick enough, they scorched the earth behind them. The feds looked hard for whatever lured them to the Thunderground, no matter how firmly they understood that which they eventually found. Based on what they left behind, they might have thrown their hands up in frustration and slashed what they no longer wished to carry home. Based on her own brief stint in civil service, Lucy was confidant it would all be reported as a job well done in the resulting paperwork, regardless.

The remaining evidence of an extensive and very deeply rooted network of telephonic and electrical wiring was still immediately obvious. Rust stained the floors and walls where heavy equipment succumbed to the basement's insular, damp climate. Indeed, many tan and gray rectangles which Lucy could only vaguely recognize as computers were delicately hauled up the day before. Black strips still adhered to the walls and on the ceiling between trusses where foam sound insulation had been torn away by. Thick bundles of wires still gathered along beams where time to slash them free ran short. It would not have been inconceivable for the building's artists to fashion a recording studio in the bowels of the warehouse. Given their history, it also would not have been too out-of-character to run heavy-duty power cables to siphon electricity from neighboring factories, nor to obscure any spikes detected on their own meter. Lucy knew it might be nothing. She also knew there might be less or nothing remaining at all if she returned when new questions arose later. Two rolls of film put her mind a little more at ease, especially when her gut told her whatever was being recorded and somehow transmitted over telephone lines from the cellar was separate and distinct from the noise being generated overhead—and earned its creators the attention of a very specific, very hurried audience from out of town.

There had been many bystanders for Lucy to interview as the operation progressed. Dozens of people mourned the death of art itself. One wandered from the topic, but the things he began to describe—of computers that talked to each other over electronic networks using a language of high-pitched chirps and squeals like a fax machine—was lost to her. Those same notes sat crumpled inside her bag, next to her film. She still could not read much into them, but she had someone in mind who might.

A breadcrumb-trail of severed wires and rusted, heavy-duty staples slithered along the rafters toward the exit and led Lucy onto the street. She looked up. The wires rose to join the telephone network, slouching overhead and converging in a tangled rats' nest halfway up a slanted pole. A few severed ends came back down and gently swayed in a breeze too thin to register on Lucy's skin. Based on rumors she overheard in the Morning Tribune's office, NYNEX had bigger problems looming on their horizon and would not be free to prune those less-than-official-looking lines anytime soon. Those wires which were left uninjured exploded outward in a dozen directions. Lucy followed one strand as she walked down the sidewalk. She was halfway across Jackson Avenue and dodging box trucks to reach the Court Square subway entrance when she realized she lost the thread. A hundred wires crisscrossed in a hundred directions. No matter where they started or where they ended, each connection looked the same.

Her editor was indifferent to such leads. They tolerated the resulting articles and, after heavy editing, occasionally found some fit to print. As long as Lucy brought home the usual bread and butter—traffic fatalities, bodega robberies, whatever the mayor ate for lunch—she would stave off starvation for another couple days. Today's duties were no different: municipal government was throwing a celebration in its own honor.

Thirty minutes made a world of atmospheric difference in many ways. Whatever colors the rising sun injected at earlier angles had bled away from the sky over Centre Street. Even obscured by a gray blanket of haze, the sun was a white disk broiling the red brick pavers that lead to One Police Plaza. A group gathered by one of the building's public entrances. Cops in dress uniforms mixed with wives and husbands, lifted children off the ground and onto their shoulders, and directed strangers on the operation of disposable cameras. Another round of promotions, no different than the last, needed to be covered. As she had on every previous occasion, Lucy inquired with her editor if it would be easier to just reprint the last version of the event's coverage. The answer would be *'no,'* but Lucy did not wait to hear her boss's response. Before she could finish scanning the Police Department's roster of promotees, she left his office without a fight. Not a single new word or fresh perspective would be shed on the topic of municipal ceremonies, but Lucy went forth knowing she might gain some insight on another story if she could single out a specific acquaintance.

Handshakes and *attaboys* clogged the auditorium's entrance. Clusters of newly minted detectives and supervisors occasionally spilt past, then jammed once more. Lucy waited, watching the jubilation. After a few minutes, she stood tall and raised a stiff, opened hand to her temple. She was surprised she could still render any such courtesy to any police supervisor, much less a lieutenant. Tabby looked even more surprised to be on the receiving end. When the shock wore off, she smiled, then smacked Lucy's hand.

"Knock that off," she sighed. "I'm surprised you can stomach being anywhere near this place."

"The Morning Tribune needs three hundred words about how great a job you're doing. You know me, I always do what my boss tells me."

"Don't we all?"

"So, this makes two promotions in what? Three, four years? At this rate you'll make Inspector before the new millennium. They might even give you the Six Four to run for yourself."

"Hell no. I'm done as of next year. Last thing I need is to see Sam Vernon's face again. Or worse, stick around too long and start falling apart 'til I turn into the next Jimmy Daley."

"I know what you mean," Lucy laughed. "The resemblance is beginning to show. All part of life's rich pageant, you know?"

"It's a rich pageant of *shit*. Is that what brought you here? Does your new beat cover our little side of that pageant, or are you looking for an *unnamed source*?"

"Nah, I ain't here to talk to no cops…"

Tabby's smile faded. Lucy was sure hers had, too. The impression of Adam Valerie had been an impulsive attempt at humor, but it left a bitter residue on her tongue.

"But if you know someone with an accredited education in electronics, that might help."

Tabby paused for a moment. Curiosity and knowing apprehension waged a war behind her eyes.

"What kind of shit are you digging up now?"

"That transparent, huh?"

"Does it have anything to do with—"

"It's got something to do with something," Lucy's shoulders rose defensively as she interjected. "I've got this feeling it leads somewhere—maybe not *there*… but *somewhere*. If you were to take a look and that's what you saw, it is what it is. Otherwise, I'm at a complete loss."

"*Regardless*, it's a complete loss. You saw everything I saw. I'm still not sure it was worth it."

"I can think of seventy-odd people who would beg to differ."

"*Odd* people, at that."

"And if they had been trapped in that place—if they had been swept away with Glass and his pack of psychos—certain interdimensional guests might have decided to stick around for more tribute. At the very least, we got everybody out."

Tabby's eyes darted to the ground.

"Not *everybody*."

Lucy bit the inside of her cheek and cursed her choice of words. Tabby showed no interest in correcting her. She reached inside her jacket and pulled out a thin wallet. Her fingers reached behind a credit card and pulled a white, laminated band from within. Its creases uncurled in the palm of her hand as she reached toward Lucy. The plastic wristband yellowed some in six years, but the black words were clear:

Katabasis, Kowaliga A.; DOB 11/01/39;
Elysian Fields A.R.C. of Brooklyn, NY

If I appear lost or disoriented, please dial 9-1-1 and wait with me.

"Whatever we did," Tabby continued, "I'd prefer not to do it again."

"You're right. I get that. I didn't mean to come here and push you into anything. But I'm not sure it really matters. Things are always happening, especially things like *that*. I guess I figured that if it was happening, it'd be nice to have a head start for a change."

Tabby's fingers closed around the wristband. When it was tucked back into her wallet, one hand returned it to her pocket while the other rubbed the bridge of her nose.

"This has been really great," she grumbled. "Just like old times."

"You still haven't said '*no*.'"

"Oh, for fuck's sake," Tabby stifled a shout, "…you damn well know I'm not gonna say '*no*.' Whatever you've got just hand it over, already. But I swear to God if you smile or look satisfied any way, I'll rip it up and toss it into the first trash can I come across."

Lucy pulled her notes out of her camera bag. Before her hand completely left the bag, Tabby snatched the folded sheets of paper.

"Easy now," Lucy warned. "Someone might mistake that aggression for enthusiasm."

"The first trash can, *I swear*."

"There's photos to go along with it too. I gotta get home and start developing them, but as soon as they come out—"

"*If* I'm on board, I'll reach out."

"I'll clear my answering machine. Just know that lunch is on me. Wouldn't want a good cop to go hungry."

"Whichever hairbag taught you that wasn't a good cop."

"Better than I ever was."

"Maybe," Tabby replied. "Maybe not. Some people show up for thirty years or longer without being good for a single day."

"Sure, but how many of them tangled with the devil and lived to tell about it?"

"Tell?" Tabby sucked her teeth. "Don't you remember? It was all carbon monoxide exposure. Sink holes, electrical explosions, burst gas mains. I don't know about you but my own personal special agent was very clear about it. Everything else—"

"—Everything else we take to our graves. Yeah, I remember. The same hairbag with the rules about being cold, wet, and hungry fed me that line, too."

"Might not've been a good cop, but that doesn't make it bad advice."

Lucy nodded, but her raised eyebrows betrayed some doubt.

"We'll see," she said.

The crowd had cleared the auditorium's entryway. One Police Plaza's split-level lobby was a decentralized, boxy, brutalist maze of red bricks. All bones. No flesh. Distant bursts of laughter echoed throughout the building's otherwise empty hallways.

Without further discussion, Lucy followed Tabby through a pair of smoke-tinted glass doors. She squinted as her eyes struggled to readjust to the light filling the building's main plaza. Where none of the ceremony's attendees remained within, only a handful lingered without. A half-dozen cops assigned to security duty paced slowly along the plaza's perimeter. Tourists emerged along the diagonal sidewalks that fed into the plaza from Centre Street and up shady stairways from Park Row.

"Excuse me. Uhh, officer?"

Tabby slowed and leaned over to a man with a fanny pack. A small girl shielded herself behind the legs of the woman next to him. Lucy could not hear his request, but the gesticulations of the camera in his hand were clear.

"Sure," Tabby replied. "I'd be happy to."

"I'm sorry," the woman laughed. "The birthday girl's a little shy today."

"That's alright. You want to take a picture with me, little one?"

The girl's eyes shot toward the ground. She shifted on her feet. If she could not disappear into thin air entirely, she tried to compress herself tight as possible behind her parents.

"Well, we'll see what we can do," Tabby said. "I'm going to take a picture with your mom and dad, but I think they might be a little scared, too. Do you think you can keep them company?"

The girl's eyes never left the ground, but her feet shifted after a moment. Tip toes brought her in front of her mother. Lucy examined the camera, took a few steps backward, and guided her four subjects into frame. The camera's shutter snapped.

"How about one more?" Tabby suggested.

The little girl on the other side of the viewfinder still refused to look at the camera, but at some point her hand had risen to clasp Tabby's. Tabby turned to the parents at her side. They nodded. When they finished inching away, only the little girl and Tabby remained in frame.

"Alright, one more time," Lucy chirped. "Smile!"

The girl's eyes rose to meet the camera's lens and brought a small grin with them. The shutter clicked again.

It was a little before noon, but Lucy's apartment was dim behind drawn blinds. Her switch in careers had not graced her with a more regular sleeping schedule. The sun had yet to rise when she left for Queens. Certain as she was that she opened them before departing, she let them stay closed.

Under cover of darkness, she pulled the two rolls of film from her camera bag and twisted them onto a pair of developing spools. Two bottles of developer and fixer warmed in the bathroom sink. When the tap water was warm enough, Lucy pulled the bottles out. She leaned over her processing cylinder, dropped in the two spooled reels of film, and drowned them in the warm fluid. Her egg timer counted down to zero and the process advanced to the next bottle's caustic fluids.

Lucy found herself short on breath as the fixer solution returned to its bottle. Not long into the process, her cramped studio apartment's proportionately tight bathroom filled with fumes. She worked faster, activity spiking as her breath grew shallow. One-by-one, strips of developed negatives draped down from clothespins hung on the shower's curtain rod. What little residual fluid remained on the strips of as they dried over her bathtub coalesced into no more than a few fully-formed droplets. She gave each strips' exposures cursory examination, eyes stinging as the subterranean scenes reemerged. Inverted light filled negative space. She squinted, and excess tears drained along the edges of her eyes. Focusing only brought more frustration and Lucy reached for her magnifier. Through its lens, the walls and their scars stood exactly where she remembered. New shapes, new patterns joined them. Something stung her hand and she dropped the magnifier. She turned the hand to face her and followed the burning sensation to the crook of her right index finger. A dull, red line pressed up through the skin of the finger's joint.

An involuntary shudder made Lucy gasp. Her head reeled as her lungs drowned in bleachy, chemical vapors. Her vision twisted with every recursive, spiraling line of inarticulable words and immortal names pressing up through the basement's dingy paint. Sixty-four 35mm portals hung over Lucy's head—windows into the Thunderground's guarded depths and the dark promises lurking just beneath every surface therein.

Lucy stumbled through the bathroom door. She threw herself toward the nearest window. Her fingers gripped the bottom of the windowpane, then stopped. The sun was gone. A black mirror image stared back. Behind her silhouette, the room's solitary, if faint, source of light was the azure glow of a nightlight plugged into an outlet next to the bathroom door. The city's ambient light pollution permitted only the brightest stars to shine in the night sky. An impossible amount of time had passed since she entered the bathroom to hang her drying film. Lucy thought about the fumes. Her hand patted over her head. If she had passed out, hit her head, she felt no pain. The plain truth of the night stared back at her, regardless.

The windowpane creaked. Even when a breeze did materialize in the summer months, they rarely billowed hard enough to compete with the howls of winter. Nevertheless, when she heard the pressure shift outside, a chill crept from Lucy's shoulders to her forearms. She found herself frozen until some distant emergency vehicle's siren squawked. A second chill stung at her gut and forced her to blink. When she saw her reflection staring back at her, her perspective had become somehow shifted. Something was different. Her silhouette filled the center of the window, framed by the twilight world beyond. The outside stared in.

Lucy staggered away. She needed to bring herself back down. She turned and let deliberate footsteps guide her through the darkness toward the nightlight, over which was mounted the kitchen's light switch. Though her finger still burned, it did not hesitate to grasp the switch and flip it. The switch rocked upward. Lucy turned and examined the lightbulb mounted in the ceiling. For however many times she reversed and repeated the motion, the filaments within refused to ignite. She did not remember blinking, but the dim world around her was consumed for a fraction of a second. When the dull blue light returned it seemed diminished. Lucy looked down at the nightlight plugged into the outlet. The tiny bulb concealed within the translucent, plastic bluebird flickered. The light shuddered three more times, returning weaker and then not at all.

Lucy had long since pried her attention away from the suffocating nightlight. The apartment door hung open in her wake, though not wide enough for her to hear the phone ring as she retreated down the building's stairwell. Her answering machine was adjusted to engage after five rings. As the fourth ring's chime echoed out, a hand lifted the receiver.

Tabby's voice went unanswered, though she swore she heard breathing. After a few seconds, she hung up. She reexamined the notepad pages full of Lucy's chicken scratch. Loathe as she was to admit, she would have no choice but to try again later.